BURDEN FALLS

KAT ELLIS

DIAL BOOKS

DIAL BOOKS
An imprint of Penguin Random House LLC, New York

First published in the United States of America by Dial Books, an imprint of Penguin Random House LLC, 2021
Copyright © 2021 by Kat Ellis

Visit us online at penguinrandomhouse.com.

Library of Congress Cataloging-in-Publication Data is available.

Printed in the United States of America

ISBN 9781984814562

10 9 8 7 6 5 4 3 2 1

SKY

Design by Mina Chung • Text set in Monticello LT Pro

For Ian, as always, but also in memory of Pilot—a most excellent cat and constant writing companion. I miss you, my boy.

—K.A.

ONE

A year after I (almost) died

The manor echoes as I walk along its hallways. It sounds like a tomb—and I would know.

I stop at every room, checking to make sure I haven't left anything behind. Not the furniture or the paintings; not the grand piano I never had the patience to learn to play. All those things are long gone, either sold or dragged out of here by the movers. No, what I'm doing is cataloging, mapping every corner of every room in the place I grew up. Fixing it all in my memory like I'm sealing it in wax. Thorn Manor, the home of my parents, and all the Thorns who came before.

Here is my parents' room, with the wallpaper covered in songbirds, and the big bay window where Mom used to spend Sundays reading because she said it had the best light.

Here is Dad's office, which was always officially off-limits, though he kept a box of my favorite candies in the top drawer of his big walnut desk for whenever I snuck in to see him. The room is an empty box now, with only faint impressions on the blue walls where Dad's nineties grunge posters used to hang.

Here is Grandpa's study, where his green wingback chair sat next to that dark oak fireplace. The scent of pipe smoke and apples still clings to this room, like he's become a part of it. Mom would've said it's his ghost, "*And there's always room for one more in Thorn Manor.*"

Uncle Ty and Carolyn's room still has a few boxes left inside — the last items they'll be bringing to the new cottage. It's almost time for the three of us to leave. We're the last in a long line of Thorns to live in this house, and after today I'll never set foot inside it again. Which sucks balls, actually.

I move on, more quickly now. There are moments when I think I hear another set of footsteps following at my heels, see a second shadow stretching out next to mine in the corner of my eye. But it's only the creaking floorboards. Only the slant of the late-afternoon light.

"*Are you sure?*" I can almost see Mom's smile, teasing but not, and shake my head. There are no ghosts here, even if I some-times wish there were.

The west wing was mostly shut up after Grandpa passed, so I don't linger there. I go down the galleried staircase and into the lounge, the sunroom, the library. The breakfast room (where nobody has ever eaten breakfast, as far as I can remember) lead-ing out to the orangery Uncle Ty uses — *used* — as his art studio. The floor still carries faint smears of paint, too long embedded to be removed by simple cleaning. Shit for the new owners to deal with, I guess.

I finish with the kitchen. I'm about to pass through and head back up to my room when my eyes land on the cellar door. I know I should go down there too, to complete my final tour of this place. It's the only room that'll still be full — the racks of Thorn's Blood Apple Sour were sold by special arrangement along with the house.

But it's the one room in the manor I hate. Always have.

I turn and head back upstairs.

There's only one box left in my room, sitting like a little lost boat in the middle of the window seat. It holds all my art supplies and sketchbooks. I go to pick it up, glancing out of the window as I do. My room looks out over the blood-apple orchard—the source of Thorn's Blood Apple Sour, and all the money it took to build this place. In the center of it stands the peaked roof of the old pavilion, and seeing it reminds me that I still have one last important task to do before I leave.

Beyond the orchard, I can see the flowing form of the river as it rushes to meet Burden Bridge, which sits right at the point where the river tumbles into a sixty-foot waterfall.

There's someone on the bridge.

Burden Bridge is on our land—ours for the next few hours, at least—so it's not some dog walker admiring the view. My skin prickles in warning like it always does when I think I see someone out there.

Is it . . . ?

My breath catches, and I lean closer to the window. But it's not who I think it is, only Uncle Ty. He's leaning against the waist-high guardrail that's attached to the low stone wall of the bridge, just staring out into the rising mist.

Propping the box on my hip, I give a stoic nod to my room, then head downstairs and outside to where Bessie waits. Bessie is my old-as-dirt Nissan, once green but now a faded color I can only call "sludge." The back seat is already packed to the ceiling, so I put this last box on the front passenger seat, then crunch my way down the gravel path to the orchard.

* * *

I stand on a stepladder in the pavilion, paint roller in hand. I've taken off my ever-present black gloves for this—hard to paint with them on—and the last throes of winter stealing in through the windows make the scars on my palms ache. I flex them out, one hand, then the other. The pink crisscross lines brighten to red as I do, but there's no chance of them tearing open now. A year is plenty long enough for a body to knit itself whole.

The wall facing me is covered in painted images, all bleeding together like a sleeve of tattoos. They are the bad memories, of the crash that changed everything, and what came after. The ones Dr. Ehrenfeld suggested I write in a journal, as if that would scratch them out of my head somehow. But I've never been much of a writer. I take after Uncle Ty that way. Art is our thing. So I painted my memories on the walls inside the pavilion, because who the hell would ever see it but me? Except now some rando has bought my home, and I don't want a stranger stumbling across this little slice of my heart-matter.

I carried a can of black paint down here yesterday, meaning to cover over the mural. But I still wasn't ready to let go. Now I have no choice.

For a second, I think I hear something. A voice? I peer through the window, even though it's pointless. The orchard is dense, dense, dense—grown wild as it raged against the disease that took hold last year. I still smell the blood apples, even though the branches are black and bare-knuckled now. The blight hit at the same time as a freak cold snap last May, leaving the trees covered in perfect ghost apples, the little icy cases showing where the fruit had once been.

A shout rings out from somewhere nearby—sharp and curse-shaped, though I can't make out the words. It's Uncle Ty. And I remember where I last saw him: leaning against the low wall of the bridge.

Shit.

My paint roller falls to the floor. I jump down from the ladder and run. The tangle of low-hanging branches claws at me as I force my way through. Finally, I clear the orchard. As I sprint for the bridge, I hear Uncle Ty again, fogging the air around him with curses.

I skid to a stop. He's fine. Drunk, I think, but fine.

One summer, when Uncle Ty was seventeen, he had some friends from school over to the manor. I remember sneaking around watching them, these teenagers who seemed so grown-up to seven-year-old me. They took a couple bottles from Grandpa's collection in the cellar and went outside to get wasted where Grandpa wouldn't see. I watched from an upstairs window for a while, too shy to go outside and be told to get lost, but I quickly got bored. They were just boys. But Uncle Ty came running in a while later, yelling that one of his friends, Jerome, had fallen from the bridge, and could Grandpa come quickly . . .

It didn't matter how quickly Grandpa came. Even then, I knew there was no way for someone to survive a fall from Burden Bridge.

The guardrail was added to the low stone wall of the bridge the next day, and Uncle Ty never brought anyone back to the manor after that. Not until Carolyn, his wife. But I do see him down here sometimes, talking to the mist, and I wonder if he's whispering his burdens so the water will take them, like the old legend says, or if he's really talking to Jerome.

I cross the bridge to where Uncle Ty still leans against the guardrail. Burden Bridge hums under my feet, rattled by the power of the waterfall beneath it.

The dark mop of Uncle Ty's hair hangs forward as he hunches into the cold. Dad used to tease him that he looked like a surly teenager when he did that, and I can kind of see it. Uncle Ty is twenty-seven — almost ten years older than me — but he looks barely out of his teens. Maybe it's because he's short and slender, like he still has some growing left to do. But everyone in our family fits that mold. People around here don't call us "Bloody" Thorns because we're brawlers. We're just not the kind of people you want to piss off. At least my parents weren't, nor Grandpa before that.

"Uncle Ty?" I say it loudly to be heard over the waterfall, but not loud enough to startle him. I don't want to be the reason he falls.

He startles anyway, but his clear eyes tell me he isn't as drunk as I thought. "Ava? Oh, I dropped my . . . dropped something over the waterfall." He gestures vaguely.

I'm pretty sure I know what that *something* is. He's been drinking a lot the last few days, even for him. And I know from personal experience that the water vapor on the bridge makes a bottle get slippery real quick.

"Hoping the water'll wash away your burdens?" I say, only half joking. He shrugs.

I doubt ditching a liquor bottle off the bridge is going to fix anything for Uncle Ty. I lean against the rail next to him.

"Remember when you brought me here and taught me how

to spit?" I demonstrate, making it arc so it doesn't get swallowed by the waterfall until it hits the basin below.

"You've been practicing." Uncle Ty sounds mildly impressed. He never could hold on to a bad mood for long. "Anyway, I was only passing on the lesson your dad gave me."

"That was right before you left for college, wasn't it?" I say, a smile inching onto my face. "The next time you came home, you had artistic sideburns and a Boston accent, and insisted everyone call you *Tyler*."

He groans. "Don't remind me."

"*Tyler* was too good to spit with his favorite niece. *Tyler* wore Oxfords. *Tyler* thought he was capable of growing a mustache."

Uncle Ty laughs. *Good.* "Dad told me he'd seen more hair on a side of bacon. He actually followed me up to the bathroom to make sure I shaved it off."

Grandpa was never shy with his opinions.

"You done staring into the abyss now?" I push away from the rail and cross my arms faux-impatiently. Uncle Ty stands up, salutes me for some goddamn reason, and turns to head back toward the manor. But as he passes me, liquor-breath trailing behind him, I spot something moving between the trees at the far side of the bridge.

"Ava? I thought you came to corral me back inside?"

"Yeah, I'm coming . . ." I scan the shadows a moment longer, but there's nothing there.

TWO

It's an hour later, the daylight already fading, when we're finally ready to drive away from the manor for the last time. Carolyn and Uncle Ty rumble away down the driveway in his sports car. Bessie waits patiently for me, stacked to the roof.

The manor's windows are all dark and hollow, its stately architecture lost in the twilight like a memory already grown hazy. It feels so wrong to be leaving like this. I'm not ready. But there's no choice—I know that. After Mom and Dad died, it turned out the family distillery was in really bad financial shape. Uncle Ty and Carolyn tried their best to save it, but we ended up having to sell the manor.

The old mill cottage Carolyn rented for us isn't far, though. If you look south from Burden Bridge, you can see the rounded wall of the mill butting up against the riverbank a half mile or so downstream.

Carolyn gives a cheerful toot of the horn as they reach the iron gates at the end of the driveway. Even without seeing her, I know she's wearing a determined smile as she steers the car out onto the lane leading up to Red Road. She won't look back. It's not her style. Uncle Ty probably won't, either, but that'll be because he can't face it.

I climb into Bessie and give the usual murmured *hail Lucifer* when she fires up on the first try. As I pass through the iron gates onto the lane, I stop. The new owners will drive through these same gates when they move in tomorrow. I try to picture it—picture *them*—but I can't.

A light blinks on and off in one of the cottages facing me across the lane. It flashes on-off again three more times in quick succession. Then I see it: Hanging from the window is a home-made banner bearing the words *BYE, BITCH!* And grinning above it is my best friend—best *guy* friend, at least—Ford. I shake my head and open the car window.

"You're an asshole!" I yell up at him. I get an elaborate bow in reply before he disappears from view. But Ford's jackassery works its magic, like always. I'm smiling as I close the car window, shutting out the cold, and follow Carolyn and Uncle Ty to our new home.

There's a sign on Red Road marking the western town limits of Burden Falls. It tells you it has a population of 9,504, and shows a dark-haired girl with her back turned, gazing at the majestic waterfall. There's no reason to think the girl is dead, but everyone here knows it. She's like the unofficial town mascot.

I turn the other way, toward the center of town. If you picture Burden Falls as a face viewed from above, the manor forms the left eye, with Red Road arcing just above it like an eyebrow. It connects onto River Road running south (the nose, if you will) and I follow it down and turn off past the gas station where I work some evenings and most weekends, and into the grin of tiny cottages beneath it. The one farthest left is the old mill cottage— now ours.

Carolyn and Uncle Ty have already gone inside by the time I park out front. I've seen the cottage before, but only from the outside. I think some part of me was still clinging to the idea that if I ignored it, the move from the manor might not happen. *La-la-la,* etc.

The cottage is vaguely square, but then there's the round tower of the old mill at the riverbank, and at some point the two buildings were joined together to create a garage in between. But the cottage is cute, with its poky little windows already blazing with warm light. I grab my box of art supplies and head inside.

The front door is rounded at the top, as if hobbits live here. "Hello?"

There's no answer, but I can hear muffled voices drifting down the narrow stairs, so I head up. Three doors lead off the landing, two of them open. One is a bathroom. The other is a large closet, I assume, because there's no bed, just a stack of boxes labeled as Carolyn's clothes.

"There you are!" I turn to find Carolyn standing behind me in the doorway of the third room. "I was starting to think you'd gotten lost," she teases.

Beyond her, Uncle Ty is making up the bed in there.

"Where should I put my stuff?" I ask, nodding at the box I'm kind of struggling with at this point.

"Here, let me show you your room." Carolyn takes the box from me easily and heads down the stairs. "I think you're going to love it!"

I follow Carolyn out of the kitchen, through that weird garage extension, and into the round building of the mill. The space has been divided into two half-moons. The first is full of boxes, but the second half is apparently my bedroom. Inside, it's cold and smells like fresh paint.

It's . . . nice. I mean, the mill's got to be well over a century old, just like the manor, which kind of makes it feel like home. And there's a tiny window, round like the porthole of a ship, which looks out over the river. It whistles faintly where a draft sneaks in through a crack in the old window frame.

The bed is already made up for me, and they've painted the walls a calm, dusty blue, just like my old bedroom at the manor. Carolyn sets the box down on my desk by the window.

"It's bigger than that dingy little room upstairs," she says, "and it has its own bathroom, so you won't have to fight with Ty over who gets to shower first in the morning. Plus, if you wanted to, say, sneak in and out late at night, you could do that without waking Ty or me." Carolyn winks and nudges me. "Do you love it?"

"Sure. It's great."

Her face falls. "Oh no, you hate it, don't you? Damn it, Ty told me I should run it by you. But I wanted it to be a surprise — a space that's all your own. I thought it'd be one nice thing at the end of a tough day." She picks up the box she just put on the desk, looking thoroughly bummed. "Sorry, I'll get you moved upstairs right away."

"No, Carolyn, honestly — this is perfect," I insist, taking the box and setting it back down. I hate that I just sounded like such an ungrateful brat after everything Carolyn has had to organize and get done today. I think shiny, happy thoughts, trying to funnel even five percent Carolyn-ness onto my face. "I'm just tired, so my brain isn't keeping up with everything."

She pauses, studying me. "Are you sure? Because we can get you set up in the little room next to ours, no problem . . ."

"I'm fine in here, really. I love it. I promise."

Uncle Ty is quiet over dinner. He glares at the fast-emptying pizza box like it's to blame for where we are. But pepperoni never did anyone dirty.

"It's weird thinking about strangers in the manor, huh?" I say, aiming for sympathetic rather than salt-in-the-woundy. Carolyn's knife and fork (because she's the only one of the three of us who eats pizza that way) clatter down onto her plate.

"Ty, seriously? You still haven't told her?"

I almost choke on a giant mouthful of pizza. "Told me what?" The half-chewed bite lodges uncertainly in my gut, waiting for bad news to land on top of it. Maybe I was too hasty with my pepperoni endorsement.

Uncle Ty takes a deep breath, cuts Carolyn a put-upon side-eye, then turns to me. "I meant to tell you this sooner, but there never seemed to be a good time, and you've already had so much to deal with this year."

Shit. This is *definitely* not going to be good news. Uncle Ty sounds like he's rehearsed this a hundred times in the mirror.

"Tell her, Ty," Carolyn urges softly. "Can't you see you're freaking her out?"

He sighs. "Madoc Miller bought the manor. He's moving his family in tomorrow."

Something wet hits my cheek, and I vaguely register that I've dropped my pizza slice onto the table, splattering tomato sauce everywhere. "You . . . sold the manor . . . to Madoc Miller?"

It's a joke—a totally sick, unfunny joke. There's no way Uncle Ty is actually telling me he sold our home to the guy who killed my parents. Who damn near killed *me*.

But he doesn't crease up into a *gotcha* grin like I expect. Uncle Ty just spreads his palms. Then, probably realizing that isn't helping—what with the fact that *my* palms are covered in scars thanks to Madoc Miller—he laces his fingers together in front of him.

"We only had one offer on the table."

"I don't believe you," I say, looking at Carolyn for backup. She just sighs and reaches out across the table like she's going to touch my hand, but then I see she's holding out a napkin for the pizza sauce. I ignore it. "There's no way you'd sell the manor to him."

Even if Uncle Ty overlooked the fact that our family and the Millers have been at each other's throats for generations, there's no way he'd take money from Madoc Miller after the crash. It's blood money.

"I didn't have a choice, okay?" Uncle Ty shoves away from the table, grabbing the last slice of pizza and his car keys. "I'm going out."

"Where are you—"

Carolyn's question is cut off by the slamming of the front door.

"I'm really sorry, Ava," she says after a long, awkward moment. "But Ty's right—he didn't have a choice. The bank would've seized everything if we hadn't sold when we did."

Somewhere in my mind, I know Carolyn must be right. There's no way Uncle Ty would've sold it to that man unless there was no other option. But I'm still reeling, imagining him and his smug wife and their two venomous offspring *in our home.*

Carolyn takes a deep breath, then grabs a glass of apple juice and one of my favorite chilled coffees from the refrigerator.

"At least *we* can toast our new home, right?" she says, raising her glass. There's a fragile note in her voice, and I know I can't take this out on her. I can't really take it out on Uncle Ty, either. This is just the kind of outrageously unfair shit that happens to us now.

"Home sweet home," I say flatly, and drink.

Despite how tired I am, I don't sleep well later that night. The river is a constant whisper outside my window. Whenever I think about it, it makes me want to pee. And I have the dream again — the memory, I guess — about the crash. I feel it: the impact, the fear. Crawling, alone, from the wreckage. Seeing Madoc Miller standing next to his barely scratched car.

At around one a.m. something shrieks upstairs in the rafters of the mill, jolting me awake. For a second, I have no idea where I am, or what the screaming was, but it slowly clicks into place.

I'm at the cottage. There's no ax murder being carried out nearby. It's just a barn owl — probably the same one I used to see around the manor grounds sometimes.

And my parents are still gone.

I let out a choked sound, trying not to let it turn into outright sobbing. Gradually, my breathing evens out. A screeching owl is as familiar to me as the creaking floorboards of my old home, or the random cold spots that seemed to spring from nowhere in the manor — those little things that might give my heart a quick jolt, but are nothing sinister, really, even if Mom would always arch a knowing eyebrow and declare the place haunted. But she'd grown up listening to the superstitious rumors about Burden Falls. I've lived in the manor my whole life, and its creaks and mutterings — and, yes, occasional screeches — are just part of its charm.

Looks like the old mill has charm too.

I drag myself out of bed and climb the rickety ladder up to the floor above mine. The light from my phone casts eerie shadows as I shine it around the loft space, but the damn bird is nowhere to be seen. Everything is silent and still.

My foot lands on something crunchy. I recoil, thinking it must be a cockroach, but it's actually an owl pellet.

Owl pellets are what the owl pukes up after it's eaten some small creature. It usually contains all the bits it has no use for — bones, fur, that kind of stuff. This pellet is old, dried to a white crust, and where it's crumbled apart under my foot I see a perfect little skull. I lean closer, shining my light on it. I think it's from a mouse at first, but then I notice the teeth. They're pointed, with elongated fangs. A weasel's skull, maybe.

It's pretty cool, though. Or it would be if finding it hadn't involved getting dried owl puke between my toes. I'll come back in the morning and see if I can clean up the bones. Might look good on my windowsill.

After dealing with the foot mess, I go back to my room. I know I won't sleep, though. I'm too on edge. Instead, I sit at my desk, doodling on a sketchpad. But my gaze keeps getting drawn back to the window, and the silvery line of the river winding north to the waterfall, and Burden Bridge, and the manor.

Home.

Except it's not home anymore. No lights shine from the manor house. It's barely a smudge against the distant landscape. For a moment, I swear I see something on Burden Bridge; it's only a speck from this far away, but I think there's someone crossing the bridge, heading toward the manor. I lean closer, my breath lightly misting the window.

Is it her?

I reach up to clear it with my sleeve, but the figure is gone.

THREE

My friend Daphne works at the Pump'N'Go with me most weekends. It's a gas station, if you were wondering, despite its name making it sound like Fuckboy HQ. Maybe that's why some of our customers act like assholes.

Daphne's dad drops her off in his squad car in the front lot, probably on his way to work. Officer Chavez gives a little *whoop* on the siren as she opens the gas station door, just like he always does, then roars with laughter when Daphne yelps in fright. She stomps inside, shaking her head. Her deep brown skin is flushed, and not just from the cold.

"He gets me every. Single. Time," she groans as she takes up her spot next to me behind the counter. I know she doesn't really mind her dad's pranks. Daphne and her dad are super close, the way I was with mine. "It's totally his fault I just stepped in that puddle. Look at the state of my favorite boots!"

I look down at the tan leather slouch boots, and yeah, they're fucked.

But, in fairness to Daphne's dad, *all* her boots are her favorites. I'm smart enough not to point this out, though.

Daphne's big on upcycling clothes she finds in thrift stores and online. She puts together mixed-retro outfits that shouldn't work, but weirdly do. Today, for example, she's wearing a 1960s orange shift dress, red Cheshire Cat wool tights, and her beloved tan boots. Her hair is in fresh two-strand twists, held back by a green silk scarf. She also makes all her own jewelry, and today has on three necklaces that I happen to know started out as parts of an egg timer, a ukulele, and a lamp.

Dressed all in black next to her, with my batwing eyeliner and chipped black nails, I know I look every inch the pasty, white goth I am.

The Pump'N'Go is pretty hectic this morning, with no fewer than three whole customers stopping by in the hour after opening. It almost justifies having two cashiers.

"How was your first night in the new house?" Daphne asks between customers. She and Carla—the third member of our little triad, and Daphne's girlfriend—already checked in with me last night on our group chat, so they know about the Millers buying the manor. They were both suitably outraged on my behalf.

"It was—" My words are cut off by the jangle of the bell above the shop door. Liam Walsh, a college student who works part-time at the public library on River Road, stomps the worst of the snow off his boots as he walks in. He's a tall, wiry white guy with too-neat hair that makes him look younger than he is. Liam nods hello when he sees me.

I've been spending a lot of time in the library lately. Specifically since we had our Wi-Fi cut off at the manor, though I've never told Liam that's the reason. I don't know him well, but I get the feeling he'd be sneery about it.

Liam picks up a candy bar and newspaper and places them on the counter.

"Heard you had to move out of the manor," he says. I feel my jaw clench. But I'm not surprised he knows. The people of

Burden Falls are probably all gossiping about my family's fall from financial grace. "That must suck."

"Yep."

"What's your new place like? It's not far from here, right?"

"It's okay," I say. I'm not trying to be frosty, but I also don't want to talk about it. "Can I get you anything else?" I ask, and throw in a smile that makes Daphne wince, so I guess it doesn't give off the friendly vibe I was going for.

When Liam leaves, I find Daphne staring after him, eyes narrowed.

"What's that look for?"

She shakes her head. "Something about that guy gives me the squicks."

We've been friends for over a year now, and this is the first time I'm hearing about "squicks." Still, it's not hard to guess what Daphne means by it. She's wearing the same look she gets whenever some sleazy straight guy learns she has a girlfriend and asks if he can "watch." As far as I'm concerned, that's a green light to throat-punch, but Daphne manages to tear most of them down with just a look. It's truly impressive. She says she inherited it from her witchy ancestor—specifically one of the Red Road Witches, a group of women who fled Massachusetts during the witch trials. Five of them made it all the way to Burden Falls and settled here, and one of them was a Black woman named Dorcas Dane—or, as Daphne refers to her, Grandma Dorcas.

Personally, I think Daphne's withering look is entirely her own. And pretty much everyone in Burden Falls says they're descended from a Red Road Witch.

"Anyway, I know what'll cheer you up. Let me give you a

reading." She whips out her tarot cards. "You haven't let me read for you in ages."

I slump onto the counter, big drama. But that just puts me eye to eye with her tarot cards.

The deck itself is really cool in my very biased opinion. I made the cards for Daphne as a gift for her birthday last November, right after she started getting interested in tarot. I hand-illustrated each one, using the jewel tones I know she loves, and the four corners of every card have evil eyes on them. An evil eye is drawn in concentric circles: the black pupil, the blue iris, the white outer, and the dark blue outline. It almost looks like a target, or a tool for hypnotizing someone.

To me, asking a deck of creepy cards for guidance always feels like shaking a wasps' nest and expecting to get honey out of it. After the first few times I drew the cards and produced spreads that could only be summarized as "DEATH DESTRUCTION EVERYWHERE YOU'RE GONNA DIE HORRIBLY," I decided to hard-pass on all future readings.

"Shuffle, and ask your question," Daphne says hopefully, ignoring my scowl. "Come *on*. You know you're not *actually* cursed."

"Tell that to every other person in this town," I grumble.

The rumors about my family run thick in Burden Falls. The curse is apparently tied to the waterfall, and the awful luck we Thorns seem to be having—especially considering what happened to my parents. I don't believe in curses, though. I'm pretty sure most of the bad turns my life has taken are because of Madoc Miller. If I looked back through my family history, I could probably pin all episodes of shittiness on one Miller or another. They have a long-standing tradition of being assholes.

"So that's a yes?" Daphne says, nudging the tarot deck toward me.

Before I can reiterate my *hell, no,* the shop door opens. Carla stands in the doorway, brushing off snow.

"Hey, villainesses."

The greeting is a new one. Last week Daphne and I were "she-devils," although I think Carla also includes herself in the names she gives us. I have a horrible feeling she's hoping one of them will catch on, and we'll be like an emo version of the Plastics.

Carla is a strong supporter of boyfriend jeans and rock-band hoodies, and she wears different colored contacts almost every day. Today's hoodie is a washed-out thrift-store find featuring the album cover of some nineties band called The Flys. Her naturally blue eyes are currently black and violet (one of each) and her hair is bleached white-blond with a buzzed undercut, which she's wearing screwed up into two high knots like a punky Minnie Mouse.

"You won't *believe* what I've had to put up with at home this morning." Carla advances toward us like it's somehow our fault, then switches gears as she leans over the counter to kiss Daphne.

"Is Corey still trying to learn to play the glockenspiel?" I ask, pretending not to see the dopey grin they share.

Carla's expression turns thunderous again. "He's switched to violin."

Her younger brother, Corey, is not as smart as his about-to-be-valedictorian sister. He's convinced he's secretly a musical prodigy—he just needs to find the right instrument. Pretty sure Corey's gone through eight or nine different ones just in the past year. It hasn't exactly made it easy for Carla to study at home, or to keep her already short-fuse temper. But her dads refuse to "stifle Corey's self-expression" or whatever. If I were them, I'd intervene before Carla resorts to stifling Corey's self-expression with a pillow over his face.

Carla glances down at the counter and sees the tarot deck. "Oh no . . ."

Daphne turns on her most winning smile. "The only way I'll get better at reading is if you two let me practice."

"That's a no from me," Carla says firmly. "Ask Corinne. She's into that shit." Corinne is Daphne's cousin, and drives both Daphne and Carla to school most mornings. And she is actually *into that shit,* as Carla so bluntly put it.

Tarot is one of the few things Carla and I actually agree about, though our reasons are different. Carla is a stone-cold skeptic about anything she can't measure or explain or . . . I don't know . . . math away somehow. I just think the cards need an attitude adjustment.

"What's got you looking like such a joy-vacuum, anyway?" Carla says, turning on me with narrowed eyes. "Are you sulking about your birthday again?"

I find "joy-vacuum" harsh, even by Carla's standards, but she's not entirely wrong about my birthday. "I'm not sulking," I say. "I'm just not having a birthday is all."

"But it's your eighteenth!" Daphne protests, like that makes a difference.

"I just had to move out of my home, I have no money, and"—*my parents are dead*—"I don't really feel like celebrating." But Daphne isn't about to let it go. I shoot Carla a killing look for bringing it up, though I suspect she did it to distract Daphne from the tarot.

"We'll arrange a *danse*," Daphne insists, and I groan. "You won't have to do anything but show up and have a good time."

Danses macabres have become a tradition in Burden Falls. Ever since Covid, when we couldn't all gather inside, kids at Burden Falls High arrange a *danse macabre* to mark big events like a death, or occasionally a birthday if the kid is popular. *Danses* are masked parties, usually held somewhere outdoors like the woods or the cemetery, where we all get dressed up like it's Halloween, only fancier. How else do you party in a mask?

"Can you please *not*?" I say, grateful when my phone pings with a message, ending the conversation. It's from Ford, who I also rage-texted last night to tell him about the Millers invading my old home. Damn, I still can't believe Uncle Ty sold it to them.

Ford: Millers are on the move. Four trucks so far.

My throat tightens. The Millers are actually moving into my home. My *old* home.

Ava: Are the twins there yet?

Dominic and Freya Miller aren't actually twins, but everyone calls them that because Freya—who is allegedly some kind of genius, though I've never seen any evidence of it—got bumped up to the same year as her brother when they moved to Burden Falls High last year, right before the crash. Unfortunately, that puts them both in my class, so I get a faceful of Miller nearly every damn day.

Daphne, Carla, and I have a certain level of notoriety at school, but the Miller twins' clique are like celebrities.

The four of them—Dominic and Freya, plus two other guys from school named Mateo Medel and Casper Jones—star in *Haunted Heartland,* a cheesy online series that's basically a *Most Haunted* rip-off. They post videos of themselves all running through abandoned buildings and screaming into wells and shutting each other inside dark rooms. It's fake as hell, yet somehow they have over a million followers across a bunch of different platforms, and get offers for acting and modeling work and all kinds of stuff because of it. Dominic and Freya's parents also run a movie-location scouting business, and the twins act like that makes them Hollywood insiders or something.

Ford's reply comes through:

Ford: Saw Freya, no Dominic yet.

Ava: Which room is she in?

I immediately want to claw the message back from the ether. I don't want to know if the viper will be sleeping in my old room. But, when Ford replies, it's to say he doesn't know. Of course he doesn't—he'd need a super-telescopic lens to see through the manor windows from his bedroom.

Ford: Mom's making me take over a cobbler. Come hang at mine later and I'll give a full report.

That's so typical of Ford's mom. Ms. Sutter would offer the Dark Lord himself a slice of pie if he showed up at her door. But I wish she'd rein in the niceness just a smidge where the Millers are concerned.

I wonder what Ford will find when he gets there with his cobbler. The place is bound to be crammed full of tacky furniture. I mean, their last house in Burden Falls was a nice red-brick Victorian, which they ruined by taking out the feature bay windows and putting in ground-to-rafter tinted glass, like an ugly gray stripe obscuring all the character of the house. That tells you everything you need to know about their taste. I got a good (virtual) tour of the place after the Miller twins threw a New Year's Eve party there and basically livestreamed the whole night.

How long have the Miller twins known they'd be moving into the manor? Before I did, that's for damn sure. I'm surprised they haven't taken the opportunity to rub it in my face at school. Although there's still plenty of time for that, I guess.

I picture Freya in my room now, overseeing some minions while they paint the walls gold. And then ice-cold dread washes through me.

Painting . . .

Shit!

I forgot to finish painting over the mural in the pavilion. My whole gory personal history is laid out on its walls. If the Millers see it, they'll think I've lost my mind. Not only that, but they'll probably do one of their gross little online ghost stories about it, and let the whole world see inside my head.

No. I can't let that happen.

I need to go back.

FOUR

Uncle Ty is watching *Jeopardy!* when I get back to the cottage after my shift. I pop my head into the living room.

"This South African city has the nickname Jacaranda City."

"What is Cape Town?" Uncle Ty says, eyes still glued to the screen, even though he must've heard me come in.

"What is Pretoria, actually."

Now he does glance up. "Oh yeah?" His smirk says he thinks I'm wrong, but it also tells me he's forgotten all about storming out after yesterday's bombshell. At least one of us has.

"What is Pretoria?" the contestant says.

"That is correct!"

I turn to go, and Uncle Ty laughs and throws a cushion at the back of my head. "Hey, are you home for dinner? I'm making risotto."

I pause. It's been quite a while since Uncle Ty bothered to cook, and he's phenomenal at it.

"How come?" I ask warily.

"To make up for last night's shitty revelation," he says. I guess he hasn't forgotten. "I'm sorry it came out that way."

I nod. I'm still mad about the situation, but it's shitty for all of us, not just me. "Sure, I'll force down some of your awful risotto. But I'll go hang out at Ford's after dinner, if that's okay?"

"I'm not your boss." Uncle Ty waves me away, his focus already recaptured by the quiz.

* * *

I tell myself it's a nice evening to be out walking, the ground crisp with frost, and the stars overhead seeming ten times brighter than normal. Truthfully, it's cold as balls, and I'd much rather be driving, but Bessie didn't want to play tonight. I probably need the walk after wolfing two helpings of Uncle Ty's risotto anyway.

The path along the river's edge is the most direct route back home — to the manor, I mean. It follows the river a half mile or so, then cuts away and joins the road uphill to the lane where Thorn Manor and Ford's house sit.

I reach an oak tree with an evil eye carved into its trunk, the carving grown shallow and faint with age. This tree marks a point where the river widens around three enormous rocks known as Copper Bell Dam. It's hard to say whether the rocks were placed there intentionally to slow the water's course or just dumped by a glacier passing through, but the dam looks like it's been here since the dawn of time. When you reach it, you feel like you've stepped into something not quite real, as if passing the carved tree takes you through some invisible barrier.

It's a shadowy place, even in summer when the sun is shining. Now, with the crackle of frost trying to settle in the trees, something about it sets my teeth on edge. Like I'm not alone, except there isn't anyone else nearby. I'm sure I'm just imagining another set of footsteps echoing mine, or maybe it's the sound bouncing from the rocks or the water, but I find my steps quickening all the same.

They say the Red Road Witches used to gather here to cast spells over the water, ringing their copper bells to keep evil at bay. Some people still hang bells from the tree branches leaning out

27

over the water and carve evil-eye symbols onto their trunks, like the one I just passed.

But there are hundreds of eyes in Burden Falls—carved into almost any markable surface. There was even one inside the manor, hidden away in a dark corner of the cellar. I have no idea how the eye-carving started, but pretty much everyone does it. You stop noticing them after a while.

I hurry on along the bank until I have to veer away from the river, then make the trek uphill to where the manor sits. I shake out my hands as I trudge the last few yards to Ford's house. The scars on my palms sing a sharp protest at the movement.

Ford's cottage sits right across the lane from the manor's east gate, and I'm glad when I reach it and see the lights shining out from the windows.

"Ava, love!" Ford's mom answers my knock at the door as if we haven't seen each other in years.

"Hi, Ms. Sutter. How's it going?"

Her eyes are tired, but her smile couldn't be warmer. Neither of these things is unusual for Ms. Sutter. Or for Ford, either, now that I think about it, although his tiredness is due to late-night gaming sessions and the occasional joint rather than long shifts at work.

"Oh, same as always, you know! Mom was having a good day today, though, so that was nice."

Ms. Sutter's a nurse. Last year she switched from working at the local hospital so she could work at the nursing home her own mom moved to, just so they'd have more time together. Ford doesn't like to talk about it, but I get the impression his grand-mother doesn't have long left.

"Ford isn't home, though, sweetie. Does he know you're coming over?"

"Yeah, but I wasn't super specific on the time." I try to hide my annoyance. It's not like Ford is a habitual flake or anything. (He absolutely is.) "Do you know where he went?"

"He's over at your place." Ms. Sutter stops, looking mortified as she corrects herself. "Sorry, I meant at the *manor*. I asked him to take over a welcome plate."

"I thought he went to do that hours ago?"

Ms. Sutter nods. "I guess he's hanging out with the Miller kids. But if he knows you're coming I'm sure he won't be much longer. Would you like to come in and wait?"

It takes me a second to formulate an answer, my brain still tripped up on the fact that Ford—*my* Ford—has seemingly spent the whole day chilling with my enemies.

No. He's probably somewhere else, and just didn't tell his mom.

"That's okay, Ms. Sutter. I'll catch up with Ford at school tomorrow."

"All right, I'll let him know you stopped by.'"

I make sure the Sutters' door is closed before I walk across the lane to the manor gate. That swirling ironwork has always looked so inviting with my family's name wrought into it. It made it seem as though we were a permanent fixture—there forever. But now the gates loom over me in the moonlight.

Get a grip, Thorn.

I only pause for a moment. The glinting lens of a camera above the right gatepost is a reminder—not that I need it—that I'm not supposed to be here. But this is probably my last chance to cover over that damned mural in the pavilion before one of the Millers finds it. I mean, it's possible they already have. But it hasn't been plastered all over their *Haunted Heartland* feed yet, so my gut says I'm not too late.

There's a tall brick wall surrounding most of the property, so I follow it around the side to where a little practiced shimmying allows me to climb over it under the cover of trees. Luckily, I know this spot isn't within camera range. At least, as long as Madoc Miller hasn't added any extra security yet.

The trees here are mostly red oak, but they only shroud my path as far as Burden Bridge. There I'll need to make a dash to the far side and into the orchard, hoping nobody happens to be looking out from the upper floor of the house at the wrong moment.

I have to keep reminding myself that I can't get caught here, sneaking around what just yesterday was still my home. But even as I near the bridge where I've spent so many hours of my life, and see the shape of the manor in the distance, I realize something feels different.

Maybe it's that I know the Millers are crawling around inside it, like the bottom feeders they are. Or maybe it's just me — maybe in the last twenty-four hours I've become Ava from the drafty old mill instead of Ava, last daughter of the Bloody Thorns.

I walk quickly to the bridge, drawn by the familiar thundering of the waterfall below it. Even though I know it's vital I'm not spotted here, I pause for a moment at the center of the bridge. This is where I thought I saw someone walking across it in the dark last night — just like I am now.

A sudden chill burrows its way into my bones. I admit it can be a little spooky here at night, where so many people claim to have had ghostly encounters. But I've always loved this spot all the same. When I was little, I used to think I could see the whole world from right here. It turned out I could — at least all the parts that mattered to me.

I glance over the edge, watching the torrent pour sixty feet straight down to the churning basin. If I stand here for a minute, I know my skin will mist, as though something cold and ghostly is breathing down my neck. I've seen more than one visitor to Thorn Manor start to shake on this bridge and have to be yanked back from the edge.

I don't linger tonight. The mist recoils from me as I continue across the bridge and steep myself in the waiting shadows of the orchard. I haven't taken more than a few steps, though, when I spot a figure walking toward me, following the perimeter of the blood-apple trees.

My mouth dries so completely, my throat clicks when I swallow.

It's . . . I mean it can't be, but I think it's actually *her*.

Then the moonlight catches on a woman's short blond bob, and I realize it's someone even worse than a ghost.

Lucille Miller — Madoc's wife. And with her is their enormous dog, Pilot.

I melt against the trunk of an apple tree. Rotten bark bites at my cheek, but I keep perfectly still. I don't think Lucille's noticed me, but then Pilot's ears twitch in my direction.

Nothing to see here, puppy. I close my eyes, like that'll help telegraph the thought. *Just keep walking.*

The dog lets out a short growl, and a bark. My eyes fly open, but he's not looking at me — he's sniffing the ground. Will he smell me? Or do I just smell like his new home? It's been so long since I had a dog of my own, I've forgotten how they work.

"Shh, Pilot. No chasing squirrels tonight, okay?" Lucille croons to him. He casts a last suspicious glance at the tree I'm hiding behind, then they carry on along the gravel path that sweeps in a circle around the manor.

I wait a couple of minutes before unpeeling myself from the tree, just to be safe. When I'm certain Lucille and Pilot are gone, I turn and have taken exactly two more steps into the orchard when I hear a voice.

Damn it, she's circled back!

But it's not Lucille this time—it's Freya. I can't see her, but I'd recognize that obnoxious tone anywhere. She seems to be muttering something. To herself? To me?

Then I spot her up ahead, leaning against one of the smaller blood-apple trees. She's holding a hand up to her ear. Of course—she's on her phone.

I wait, hoping she'll finish her call and fuck off, not necessarily in that order. She'd only have to go a little way for the sound of the waterfall to keep her from hearing any twig-snappy noises I might make as I wrestle my way through the orchard. But she doesn't do that, of course. I almost curse out loud when she circles around the trunk of the tree and stops right on the other side of the one I'm now hiding behind. She's so close I can smell the orchid-scented shampoo she uses. (Freya really must slather her whole head in it, it's so strong.)

". . . I thought you'd like that last pic . . . Yeah? I bet I know some other parts of me you'll think are pretty *lovely* too." She giggles, and I throw up in my mouth a little bit. "Uh-huh . . . I took it while I was at school, thinking about you so close by . . . Of course I was careful. But I'm tired of just sending nude pics—we *are* gonna be together soon, right? You know I'm not the kind of girl who waits around forever for a guy."

You'd probably think she was teasing just from her words, but there's a steeliness to her tone that makes me think whoever she's talking to had better take her seriously.

I do not want to be listening to this. Whatever's going on between Freya and her—sext friend?—I don't need to know about it.

"Of course I believe you. I just want us to be together for real, you know? And my parents are going out of town for work Wednesday morning, so we could have the whole afternoon . . . You mean it? Okay. I can't wait."

Freya ends the call and lets out a happy little *whoop*. It's so un-Freya-like, I know she'd be pissed to know I'm listening.

Her phone screen lights up, casting the shadow of the tree on the snow in front of me. If I move even a couple inches, I'll be lit up like a star on Broadway.

I hold my breath, waiting for her to turn and catch sight of me. But she doesn't. Instead, she pockets her phone and ducks to avoid the low hang of spindly branches as she leaves the orchard and heads back in the direction of the house. I wait where I am, watching as the glow from the windows lights her path to the manor, urging her to hurry the hell up so I can finish covering up my mural in the pavilion.

Freya lets herself in by the front door, her long hair swishing at her back. My fingers clench against the trunk of the tree I'm still hiding behind.

It's not your house!

But it *is* now, technically. I hiss as one of my fingernails bends back painfully against the trunk. My eyes tear up, and I have to blink several times before they clear. When they do, I notice something in one of the upstairs windows of the manor. Inside my old room, I see three figures. One of them is Dominic Miller, which I realize with a stomach-roil probably means that's *his* room now. His dad, Madoc, is standing next to him, and he seems to be laughing at something. I suck in a breath. He has no right to be *standing* there, *laughing*.

But the figure beside him is the real kicker: It's Ford.

What the *hell* is my best friend doing in there with the people who've stolen my life?

I want to march right in and ask him. I'm *going* to—screw the Millers.

But I can't do that. If I'm caught here, the Millers will raise hell—they'll probably think I've come to smash their windows or something petty like that. They might even call the cops.

At the same moment that I resolve *not* to act like a righteous ass, Madoc leaves the room. Dominic leans out through the open window, and points something out to Ford.

No, not something. Some*one*.

Me.

Shit.

I pull up the hood of my coat—a pretty pointless gesture seeing as my hair is really dark anyway—and turn away from the manor. Then I run.

Cold air burns my lungs with each hard breath. I don't slow down. I'm at the bridge before I look back, but somehow Dominic is already at the front door of the manor, just stepping out and peering at the shadowy treeline where I was standing a moment ago. He hasn't tracked me to the bridge yet, but it's only a matter of glancing in my direction.

Just then Ford bounds through the door behind him, yelling something I can't make out, and Dominic turns to answer him.

This is my shot.

There isn't enough time to make it back to the wall surrounding the property. Not without being clearly visible, anyway. And Dominic's probably a much faster runner than I am. It'd be just like him to carry a pocket Taser.

I don't feel like getting zapped tonight.

I reach the end of the bridge and duck down underneath it, letting the roar of the water swallow the sound of my ragged breathing. The scars on my hands sting with cold.

Maybe ten seconds later, I hear voices overhead—Dominic and Ford, I guess, unless Madoc has decided to join the search party.

They must be yelling for me to be able to hear them at all, but I can't make out the words. Their voices fade as they cross the bridge and head in the direction of the boundary wall—the same way I need to go to get out of here. *Typical.* But then they cross over the river again and go back toward the house.

I wait another few minutes in the dark beneath the bridge like a literal troll, icy vapor misting my skin, just to be sure Dominic doesn't come back with reinforcements. But then it occurs to me that he might be checking the manor's security footage, or worse—calling the cops to report an intruder.

I don't think the cameras would get a clear image of me at night and from so far away, but it's definitely not a good idea to still be here if the cops do show up. I slide out from my hiding place and sprint back to the boundary wall. In one swift move, I climb up and over, jump down the other side, and head back to my new home.

It's only as I'm walking back along the river past Copper Bell Dam that I remember: I still haven't covered up the goddamn mural.

FIVE

Uncle Ty has already left for an early faculty meeting when I set out for school in the morning. I turn the key in the ignition, half expecting Bessie to roll her eyes at me, but for once the car seems oblivious to the cold and starts up like a kitten.

Daphne and Carla aren't waiting at the bank of lockers, though that's hardly a surprise. Corinne—their usual ride to school—doesn't believe in *living her life by some asshole's schedule*, so Daphne and Carla tend to storm in right before the tardy bell.

This means I have to hang around at the lockers, waiting for them. That's not usually a problem because I'm locker-neighbors with Ford. But today I'm rightfully pissed at him.

His back is to me as I approach, and his shoulders tense the second he hears my footsteps. He turns, beaming his ridiculous full-toothed smile.

"What the hell was that yesterday?" I demand. "Ditching me for the *Miller twins*?"

Ford winces. He's a good-looking guy, though not my type. The way toothpaste tastes fine, but you wouldn't want to eat it. With his curly brown hair, pale skin that freckles the moment it sees the sun, and the tiny mole above his lip, there's something a little too angelic about Ford. His nose ring goes some way to downplaying the effect, but not far enough.

"I'm sorry," he says, voice pitched low like he's trying to soothe his way past an angry tiger. "I completely lost track of time—did you know Nic Miller has the most amazing collection of—"

"*Nic?* You call him *Nic* now?" I actually gag.

Ford changes tack and looks sheepishly at me. "I know, I'm the worst friend ever. But I did get you a little something to make up for it."

I bite off whatever I was about to snap at him. "You got me a gift? But it's not my birthday for a couple weeks yet."

I can tell he knows he's got my interest by the smug way he points to my locker.

"It's in there?" Suspicious now, I input the combination and open my locker a crack. Nothing leaps—or dribbles—out, and there's no obvious bad smell. So far so good.

I don't see anything unusual at first, but then my eyes land on a scrap of paper. When I pick it up, four photos of Ford stare back at me.

The photos are on one of those hokey picture-booth strips. In them, Ford gazes at the camera as he unbuttons his shirt—one button lower in each frame—until the fourth shot, where he's trying unsuccessfully to lick his own nipple.

I look up at him, biting the inside of my cheek so I won't laugh. Ford winks at me.

"A little something for your wank bank, milady."

The combination of the Mary Poppins–ish accent and his absurd cockiness is too much for me. I try to maintain my glare, but it's useless. A snort slips out, and I'm done for.

"Those'll be worth a fortune when I'm a famous Hollywood actor," he adds as my laughter dies down.

"I still don't forgive you for yesterday," I grumble, but even I can admit it's a lie. Ford and I have danced this dance too many times to count over the course of our friendship. There was the time he told me he was too sick to go skating for my tenth birthday, and I later found out he just couldn't tear himself away from his new gaming console. Or the time he borrowed my bike in middle school and it *somehow* ended up in the river. Or last month, when he asked me to pick him up after an audition in the city, then forgot to tell me it'd been canceled.

"You're right as always, my queen," he says. "That was unforgivable."

"And I'll need a full report on all the gross decor choices the Millers have made."

"Naturally."

I sigh. "Then I accept your weird and creepy peace offering."

Every time, he goofs his way around me. And like a sucker, I let him. But that's just what you do with friends, right? Put up with their crap?

Ford put up with plenty from me after my parents died. He kept inviting me to do stuff—go to parties or to watch a movie, even when I kept saying no. He'd skip whatever it was to come hang with me instead, the two of us sitting side by side in my room, playing *Rocket League* in silence. And he always picked up the phone when I needed to talk, even if it was three a.m. on a school night.

He'll never change, for better or worse. I just have to deal with that, and accept his weird apology gifts.

I go to put it in my bag, but Ford snatches it from me and sticks it to the inside of my locker with the gum from his mouth.

"That's disgusting."

He nods. "Like your face."

I punch him in the arm, nowhere near hard enough to hurt. Still, I expect Ford to make a big show of rubbing it like he normally would. Instead he reaches up and runs his thumb down my cheek. I lean away.

"Uh . . ."

"Mascara goop," he explains. "Anyway, what were you doing in the orchard last night?"

Damn. "You knew it was me?"

"Of course I knew it was you. Who else would be sneaking around out there without a flashlight?"

"Does Dominic know too?"

"No," Ford says with a look of extreme pride. "I ran interference for you, told him it must've been the manor's resident spook he saw. You're welcome, by the way."

"Thanks." I offer Ford a sincerely grateful smile. Having the Millers on my back for "trespassing" is the very last thing I need.

"You haven't answered my question, little snake. Why were you there?"

"Spying," I tell him. "I was insanely jealous about you hanging out with the Miller twins."

There's a grain of truth to this, but I still load it with enough sarcasm to send Ford's eyes rolling. I don't want to tell Ford why I was really there, though. He doesn't know about the mural I painted in the pavilion—first, because I was embarrassed about it essentially being homework from my therapist, Dr. Ehrenfeld. Second, because the whole thing was just too personal. I know I can talk to Ford if something's bugging me, but at the same time . . . I don't always *want* to. I don't want to be the friend who always leans on other people. The one who always brings their problems to the table, and nothing else.

"I just . . ." I scrabble around for a plausible excuse for being there last night. But Ford can tell when I'm bullshitting.

"Move it, serfs!"

I look up and see Carla baring her teeth at some unfortunate sophomores as she and Daphne march toward me. Carla has her hair twisted into a dozen little cones today, and her shadow stretches out ahead of her, hard and spiky as a weaselbat.

"That's my cue to . . ." Ford turns to face his open locker, totally missing my Very Not Pleased face. I hate the way he avoids Carla and Daphne.

"Did you study for the test?" Carla asks, not bothering with hello.

"Of course," I say, but we both know I haven't studied nearly enough. Math just doesn't make sense to me. Also it's boring. Except to Carla, apparently, who likes it enough to join the mathletes.

"We're only a few months away from graduation," she reminds me.

"I'm aware of that."

"And are you actually planning on graduating?"

"Are you actually planning on kissing my ass?" I counter. But she does kind of have a point. The school guidance counselor, Mr. Hamish, has been making distressing comments about the prospect of summer school or repeating the year. Apparently, there's a one-year time limit on grieving for your dead parents, and losing your lifelong home and family business doesn't even count as far as cutting me some academic slack. But I just can't seem to focus on my studies beyond art class.

"Ava." Ford tugs on my arm. "Have you heard this?"

It's only when I turn fully that I notice several other students in the hallway are gathered around Mateo Medel, one of the Miller twins' little shit-crew.

Mateo is captain of the football team. He's Latino, with naturally deep copper skin, a smile you can see around corners, and zero coordination when he's off the football field. (His truck has more dings in it than Bessie, and she's lived a long and eventful life.)

I used to think he was okay—for a jock, at least—but he morphed into a Miller-twins-wannabe the moment he started hanging out with them last year. Now he seems to be announcing something to his gathered fans, making big arm gestures to go with it.

Casper, final member of the Miller twins' ensemble, stands quietly next to Mateo as always. They're a couple, I think, but I don't know if that's fact or just hallway speculation. I've never really spoken to Casper, so I only know him as a set piece in their ghost-hunter videos who supposedly "senses things" in whatever location they're filming. He's thin and grungily pretty, with messy blond hair and hazel eyes—picture a bleached-blond Timothée Chalamet—and I'd always thought he was shy before he became one of the *Haunted Heartland* crew.

". . . she was, like, facedown at first, just floating there in the shallow water, but then he flipped her over and he knew right away she was dead . . ."

"What's he talking about?" I whisper to Ford. He answers without tearing his eyes away from Mateo.

"His dad found a girl's body at the bottom of the waterfall when he was walking his dog this morning."

"A *body*? Who?"

At the front of the crowd, Mateo continues spinning the story for his captive audience. "Her hair was all tangled around her face, so he had to kinda peel it away, and that's when he really freaked out because the girl had no eyes! Like, they were completely gone. Just two empty eye sockets staring up at him."

I shudder, imagining a cold breath brushing my nape. There's no way that's true about the girl's eyes. Mateo must be making it up. Nevertheless, a whisper of *Dead-Eyed Sadie* runs through the crowd.

Dead-Eyed Sadie is the name people in Burden Falls have given to the ghost that supposedly haunts Thorn Manor — especially the waterfall. She's a teenage girl who wanders the grounds, looking for her missing eyes. Rumor says she was murdered near the waterfall, her eyes gouged out in some grotesque ritual that left her spirit tied to the manor. I feel a kind of proprietary protectiveness toward her, same as I do toward the manor itself. But she isn't real, no matter what people around here believe.

No matter what Mom believed.

"Mateo sent me a pic his dad took at the scene," Ford says. "Some white girl with long blond hair. I don't recognize her. Wanna see?"

"Ew! Hard no, Ford. Why is Mateo sending you pics anyway?" They aren't friends as far as I know. Ford shrugs, like it's totally normal.

"I bet it was the impact of being washed over the waterfall that made the corpse's eyes pop out—if that's even true," Carla cuts in next to me, logical as ever. "Mateo's probably just making it up to win Sadie points."

"Still . . ." Daphne murmurs, and our eyes lock. I shake my head.

"Sadie's just a story," I say.

"Or it could have been caused by an animal," Carla continues as though we haven't spoken. "Remember what happened to Mr. Hayes's lambs?"

I do remember, and it was gross. It was lambing season, and Mr. Hayes—the nearest sheep farmer—had already had a dozen or so new lambs. But one morning he went down to check on the flock and found that all the lambs had had their eyes pecked out. Crows had attacked every single one of them. The old farmer was so shocked to find them that way, he had a heart attack and keeled over, and died right there in the middle of his field.

"Everyone in town started whispering Sadie's name then too," Carla ends pointedly.

"I know," I say, even though there's a part of me that isn't so sure this situation is the same. It's the part that remembers Mom spinning a story about some Thorn ancestor who saw Sadie in the moments before they died, and Dad shaking his head at the newspaper he was not reading. Then Mom would look from him to me and say, "*We'll see.*" Just that. And I don't know if the *we* meant her and Dad, or her and me, or both.

"Don't you think it's a huge coincidence that a body just washed up near Thorn Manor with no eyes? I mean, it's right next to where Sadie's supposed to . . . well, not *live*, but . . . hang out," Daphne says.

"Come *on*." I can see Carla's patience is at zero bars. "When you die, your eyes are always the first things to go—either eaten by pests, or they rot away. Or, in this case, get knocked out of your skull by a sixty-foot drop into a rocky pool of water."

"Gross," Daphne says, and she's not wrong. My stomach's churning quite unpleasantly by this point.

"*And*," Carla adds, "if Dead-Eyed Sadie was really out there murdering people and stealing their eyes, why didn't she come after *you* in all those years you lived at the manor? You were *right there* and, let's face it, you're not the fastest runner."

"Good point, Car. I'd've been easy pickings for a killer ghost," I deadpan. But I still jump when a sophomore brushes up against me as they edge past to get nearer to Mateo, who's still taking questions at the center of the crowd.

"Who do you think the girl is, though? Or *was*?" Daphne asks.

I'm about to tell her what Ford said about not recognizing her when Carla says, "Claire Palmer, of course."

It takes me a second to place the name. But then I remember her photograph on the local news—a smiling girl with long blond hair and braces on her teeth.

"The one who went missing last week in Kinnerton?"

Claire Palmer had been all over the news for a minute there, but then a local senator got caught having an affair and suddenly nobody was talking about her anymore.

"She didn't just go missing." Carla's tone is perfectly matter-of-fact. "Claire Palmer went to walk her dog along the river and never came home. Must've fallen in and been swept downstream. I think there was even a witness who saw her trying to get her dog's ball from the water."

"But that was over a week ago," I say. "For sure she'd have washed up before now?"

Carla shrugs. "Could've been spinning around the basin of the waterfall since then for all we know. But the time lag backs up my point about why her eyes are gone, *if* that's true."

Daphne clears her throat, and I look up to see the Miller twins have joined the edge of the circle around Mateo and Casper. Freya stands out as she pushes her way through the crowd toward him, her long flame-red hair swishing behind her.

Freya ignores me like she always does unless she's decided to be shitty.

She links arms with Mateo, leaning in to whisper something. I wonder if he's the one she was talking to on the phone last night? I mean, I thought he was gay, but maybe he's bi?

Either way, not my business.

I'm turning back to Ford when my gaze snags on Dominic Miller looming at the back of the crowd—a flash of pale, serious face and black, serious hair. The collar of Dominic's tailored wool coat is pulled up in a way that might be because of the cold, but it also just so happens to show off his razor-blade jawline. If I ran my finger along that jaw, I bet my hand would come away bloody. A lot of kids at school would say it was worth it to touch Dominic Miller, but not me. The Miller twins might look pretty, but that's true of many poisonous creatures.

When they first arrived in Burden Falls and I locked eyes

with Dominic, I will admit to having the *teensiest* pang of absolute thirst. But then I saw him and his sister looking at a painting hanging outside the art studio later that day, and Miss Shannon told them it was mine.

"Typical Thorn, stomping all over my turf," Freya muttered once the teacher had drifted away. "Do you think her artwork's better than mine?"

Dominic smirked at her. "As if."

Any totally superficial appreciation I might've had for Dominic Miller died a cold, hard death right then.

Ever since, Freya has taken every opportunity to needle me — away from the adoring gaze of everyone else, of course — and it only seemed to get worse after the crash that killed my parents. Dominic mostly just ignores me, like the self-important asshole he is. I decided that if they wanted to keep the feud going between our families, that was fine by me.

The Millers have been trying to screw my family over for generations. Dad told me that every few years they try to move in on our business or our land, and when they get nowhere they stir up trouble. Dominic's grandfather campaigned to shut down the Thorn distillery back in the seventies, and I'm sure Madoc Miller tried to get Dad kicked off the town council years ago over some bullshit to do with permits. I never saw any of it firsthand because Madoc and Lucille Miller moved away from Burden Falls before I was born, but I've heard all the stories about them, and now I get the joy that is the Miller twins in my face every day. They're spreading through every part of my life like a fungus.

My fingers curl painfully against my scarred palms. How

long have Dominic and Freya known they were moving into the manor? Days? Weeks?

How long have they been laughing behind my back?

I glare at him, like the heat of it might draw out the answer.

Dominic must feel my eyes on him, because his gaze cuts to mine. He rakes back the dark hair falling so artfully forward to give me his fiercest glower. It only lasts a split second before he turns and walks away, apparently bored by Mateo's increasingly gory descriptions of the poor girl's body.

What was that look about? Did he see me at the manor last night?

No. If he knew it was me, he'd have called the cops for sure.

Maybe Dominic was just grossed out by Mateo's showboating. I know I was. Though I doubt Dominic is easily grossed out, considering he makes videos about dead people all the time.

Shit.

With a dead body washing up just outside the property, there's no way he *won't* use it for an episode of *Haunted Heartland*. There's also no way he'll miss the chance to do an exposé on Dead-Eyed Sadie—and the manor she haunts.

SIX

One failed algebra test later, I'm in the art studio, working on a sketch for my final project, when I look up to find Freya Miller hovering over me.

"Hey, Morticia," she says. Freya has one of those voices that grates no matter what she's saying.

"What?" I say, instantly on guard.

"Just wondering what exactly this is meant to be. Is it a rocket ship? A cigar? Some other phallic object? It's hard to tell."

"A tower," I tell her flatly. It's actually the very first panel of a webcomic I'm supposed to be almost done with by now, but I can't seem to get past this first image. It shows a girl—only a silhouette, really—looking out from the top of a stone tower on a hill, with rows of gravestones circling it like sharks' teeth. Gnarled hands reach up from the graves like fleshy, rotting flowers.

I've already posted the digital version of this image to my online portfolio under the title *Mostly Deadish.* As far as Uncle Ty and Miss Shannon, the head of the art department, know, I'm now working on the rest of the panels that'll make up my final project. But the story stubbornly refuses to come. Whatever sketches I try to freestyle, they don't gel with this one.

I'm screwed, in other words. Not that I'm about to tell Freya Miller that. So instead I tell her "Fuck off."

She makes a show of looking *aghast,* checking to see if any of her adoring fans have overheard, but nobody's listening. Her friends are all huddled at the far side of the art room, probably still speculating about the girl who washed up in the river. I wonder if it really was Claire Palmer.

And if her eyes really were gone . . .

Uncle Ty is sitting at his desk up front, gaze fixed on his laptop screen, "grading assignments," which probably means checking the latest racing results online. Freya picks up my sketchbook before I can stop her. She holds it at arm's length and squints at it.

"I was only asking what you're working on. It's a little . . . basic, don't you think?"

"Don't be an asshole, Freya," I sigh. "Give it back."

But she holds it out of my reach, acting like she didn't even hear me. "You know, I heard they're choosing the student to put forward for the summer art program soon."

I lean in, despite myself. Madame Bisset's summer art program in Indianapolis only allows one student from each state high school to be nominated for their full-scholarship art program each year. There's always fierce competition among the arty seniors to get chosen for the spot. But the fact that Madame Bisset is a graphic-novel artist like I want to be . . . well, I'm hoping that'll win me a few points. This art program is the one good thing I've been focused on all year, and I'm *so close* to getting it.

Miss Shannon decides who's nominated from Burden Falls High. Freya and I are at the top of the list, although I'm sure the only reason Freya even put herself forward for consideration was to screw me over. There's no way Freya would actually give up whatever modeling and acting jobs she's booked for this summer.

"Where did you hear that?" I ask her. Because Uncle Ty hasn't said a word to me about it—not that he's allowed to play any part in selecting the candidate, of course. Choosing between me, his one and only niece, and Freya Miller, asshole daughter of the man who killed his brother and sister-in-law . . . ? Yeah, it wouldn't really fly.

Freya smiles, catlike. "A little bird."

With that, she drops my sketchbook on the floor and marches back to her desk at the back of the studio. I lean over to pick it up, then sigh when I see it. She deliberately stepped on it, so now there's a dirty shoeprint right across the sketch.

"Asshole," I mutter.

"*Ava.*" Uncle Ty gives me stern eyes over his laptop. I must've dragged him away from his game of *Minecraft* or whatever.

"Sorry, Mr. Thorn."

I go back to my spot, still staring at my ruined sketch as I sink down into the seat.

And feel something wet seep through the back of my jeans.

"What the hell?"

I jump up. There's a red smear — paint, I hope — across my chair. And now across the butt of my gray jeans. I whirl around, and immediately lock eyes with Freya. She's standing with Mateo and Casper, all the way across the room, watching me in absolute delight. One of the two boys must've put paint on my chair while she distracted me with that sketchpad bullshit.

"You're such a bitch, Freya," I hiss at her. The previously buzzing room falls silent, but I don't care. A collective *ooooooh* goes up around the studio, and I know instantly the crowd is not on my side. "Oh, for fuck's sake." I roll my eyes.

Uncle Ty jumps to his feet. "What's going on? Ava?"

I hold up a hand, smeared red where I've tried unsuccessfully to wipe the paint off my ass. For a second, I'm right back in the wreckage of the car, blood pouring from the wounds in my hands, my whole world broken.

Drip, drip, drip . . .

"Oh . . . uh . . . do you need to go to the nurse's office?" Uncle Ty asks, snapping me out of it.

"Nurse's office?"

"If it's your . . . ah . . . time of the month?"

A snicker rolls around the room.

"It's paint," I snap. "So *no,* I don't need to go to the nurse's office."

Uncle Ty's nostrils flare. "Tone it down."

"But she did this!" I insist, pointing at Freya—who could not look more innocent if she sprouted wings and a halo. And now I'm very aware of the fact that everyone's staring at me.

"Actually . . ."

I turn and find Yara, a girl who sometimes sits beside me in art, holding up a squashed tube of acrylic paint. "I think I might've leaned on this and . . . you know"—she points with her chin—"got your seat. Sorry."

"It was *you*?" Yara shrugs apologetically. "But . . ." I was *certain* Freya had engineered this.

Uncle Ty glances from me to Yara and back again, then shakes his head. "Ava, go get cleaned up."

"Aren't you going to make her apologize to me, Mr. Thorn?"

It only takes that one sentence delivered in Freya's obnoxious voice to bring the rage flooding back.

Uncle Ty sighs. "Ava?"

I blink at him. I mean, he can't be serious. Apologize to a

Miller? Uncle Ty might not be as open about it at school as I am (he is a teacher here, after all), but he hates the Millers as much as I do. He can't expect me to apologize to the spiteful little brat. Even if she didn't orchestrate the paint, she still ruined the sketch I was working on.

"Here's your apology," I snap, and hold up my middle finger.

"That's enough!" Uncle Ty bellows, making me blanch. I've never been shouted at by Uncle Ty before. Especially not in public. "Go get cleaned up, then head *straight* to the principal's office."

"But—"

"Now!"

This earns me another round of *oooohs* from the class.

"Quiet, all of you!" Uncle Ty cuts in. "Unless you want to go see the principal too? Didn't think so. And Mateo Medel—you're not even in this class. Get out of here, or you'll join Ava."

Unfortunately, Mateo does join me as I'm stomping out. I try to hold my bag so it'll cover the red mess on my jeans, but I don't think it's working.

Mateo leans in just as we leave the art studio. "I guess I see why they call you the *Bloody* Thorns now."

I step away from the pig, but he's already bouncing away down the hallway. I have to ball my hands to keep from running after him and smacking him. Except it's not really Mateo I want to hit.

It's Freya.

I chew on that feeling all the way to the principal's office, through the rest of the day's lessons, and to the end of detention.

SEVEN

Daphne: The body has officially been IDed as Claire Palmer. So sad, they found her dog waiting for her at the riverbank in Kinnerton. Looks like accidental drowning.

I let out a relieved breath. What with Mateo spinning his stories at school and everyone whispering Sadie's name, there was some tiny part of me that started to . . . well, not *believe*, but wonder.

Stupid.

Now that I know who the dead girl is, and that she died miles away from here — walking her poor little dog too — it makes it all very real. Very *not* ghostly.

I'm glad Daphne always makes a point of getting the inside scoop from her dad.

Carolyn's the only one home when I get back to the cottage after school. She sits at the kitchen table, a neat stack of papers in front of her, and she's tapping away at a calculator. Her blond hair is as perfectly groomed as always, her simple jeans and sweater on the cuter side of preppy, but she looks tired.

"Hey," I say as I ditch my coat on the back of a dining chair. "Whatcha doing?"

"Working on the budget."

She's been doing this every week since my parents died, trying her best to figure out a way to keep us from starving. Carolyn works at a pharmacy in town, and the pay isn't great. Even with Uncle Ty's teaching salary, they struggle to keep up with all the bills. I throw in half of what I make at the Pump'N'Go, but that probably doesn't even cover my coffee bill.

A year ago, I never used to think about money. It was there if I needed anything, no worries. Looking back, that was pretty gross. But God, I hate how money is *everything* when you haven't got it — how it grips your insides with stiff fingers until it's all you can think about.

Carolyn smiles. She looks much older than twenty-three tonight. "Just checking we're on track."

I grab a chilled coffee from the fridge, trying not to pull a face when I see it's decaf. Carolyn has been threatening to wean me off my beloved caffeine for a while now. Looks like she wasn't kidding.

"Did you hear about the girl who washed up in the river this morning?" I ask before taking a wary sip.

"Yeah, terrible," Carolyn says. I can tell she's still half focused on her paperwork, but then her gaze snaps up to mine. "Sorry, Ava. Was she anyone you knew?"

I shake my head. "It was that girl on the local news — Claire Palmer. The one who fell in the river and got swept downstream last week. Mateo Medel's dad found her. It was super weird about her eyes, wasn't it?"

"What about them?"

"I heard they were missing," I say.

Carolyn's brow furrows. "That *is* strange. Pretty gruesome."

"Doesn't it remind you . . ." I trail off, hoping Carolyn will see what I'm getting at without my having to pour the crazy right out there.

"Of . . . your dad?" she asks.

That wasn't where I was going, and the unexpected mention of what happened to Dad hits me right in the gut. I put down my coffee, gripping the edge of the kitchen counter so I won't just keel over.

Damn it.

I thought I was getting better at this — at holding it together. Or appearing to, anyway.

"I . . . no, I meant did it make you think of Dead-Eyed Sadie?" I force the words out. Force air back into my lungs. Force my fingers to unclench.

"Sadie?" Carolyn blinks, surprised. "Oh . . . yes, I suppose so. And it does seem like odd timing, doesn't it? As soon as we move out, someone dies in a way that *could* be interpreted as being the work of our resident spook. Maybe she's angry there are no more Thorns at Thorn Manor," she adds with a thin smile.

"But why would Sadie be pissed about that? She wasn't supposed to be one of us, was she?"

I've never heard anyone say she was a Thorn, though I'll admit I wondered about it as a kid. But Grandpa had a framed family tree on the wall of his study, and I checked it a bunch of times to see whether there was a Sadie on it. There wasn't. The closest I could find was a Sarah Thorn who died in 1882. Grandpa, usually a walking Wikipedia when it came to Thorn Manor and its history, gave me a tight-lipped look when I asked him if Sadie had been a relation of ours, and told me to "go on and play." Even at six years old, I knew that was Grandpa's way of telling me I was getting on his last nerve.

"I honestly have no idea," Carolyn says, but she has this thoughtful look on her face that tells me she's still considering the possibility. I look down at the papers in front of her, feeling a pang of guilt.

"I've distracted you from your budgeting. I'll go make a start on my homework," I say.

"Wait—I almost forgot. Ty called earlier and told me about what happened in school today. It sounded pretty rough. Are you okay?"

I pause halfway through the door to the garage. "Oh, the thing in art class? What did he say?"

"That another student accidentally spilled paint on you, so you swore at her and he had to send you to the principal." She grimaces at my outraged look. "Is that not what happened?"

My mouth opens, ready to spill the entire episode, but as the words form in my head I realize it sounds just as pathetic as Uncle Ty's version. I allowed Freya to get under my skin, then humiliated myself in front of the entire art class. I also had to walk around all day with a borrowed sweater tied around my waist so people wouldn't see the washed-out red smear on my butt.

"Uncle Ty could've taken my side, though," I grumble. Carolyn lifts her eyebrows questioningly, but says nothing. "Fine, he couldn't. But it still sucked getting yelled at by him in front of the whole class."

She nods. "Yeah, I guess he could've handled that better. But I think maybe you both need to cut each other a little slack right now. It's a tough time for you two, isn't it? With the anniversary in two days."

My grip tightens around the plastic coffee cup, so I set it down before it can split open. I think I've splattered my clothes enough for one day.

"Does it feel like it's been a whole year to you?" I ask quietly. "I know it's different for you—you'd only just moved into the manor when they died, and you hadn't really had a chance to get to know Mom and Dad. But doesn't it feel like it just happened yesterday?"

Carolyn reaches out and squeezes my hand, reminding me of Mom for a split second. Then I realize she's just stopping me absently rubbing at the scars on my palms. "Is that how it feels to you?"

Hot tears burn my eyes, but I force out a steady breath through my nose. "It feels like someone stole my life, and I don't know who I am anymore."

"Sure you do." Carolyn leans back and smiles, arms folded. "You're a Bloody Thorn, aren't you?"

I remember the first time I heard someone refer to my family as the "Bloody Thorns." It was at my grandfather's funeral, when I was eight. My dad mentioned it in his eulogy, like it was a well-known thing—almost a joke. I sat in the front pew, watching Dad talk about Grandpa in that surreal, squeaky-clean way people do at funerals. "*Always a kind word for a stranger . . . gave to underserved communities . . . never dropped a fart in his life . . .*" Leaving out all the real parts, trying to make him sound Better Than Jesus. And then Dad just threw it out there: "As all of you know, he was a Bloody Thorn through and through, and would've been tapping his watch at me right about now for talking too long."

"What does Bloody Thorn mean?" I whispered to Mom. She squeezed my hand in that *hush, honey* way of hers, but answered anyway.

"It means you know your own mind, and don't let anyone stand in your way." She eyed me sidelong, which was especially effective with her sharply winged eyeliner. "You should remember that, Ava."

Know your own mind, and don't let anyone stand in your way. That did sound like Grandpa. And Dad. And Mom.

Dad arrived back at the pew, and Uncle Ty took his place at the lectern. This was the first time I'd ever seen Uncle Ty in a suit. It looked strange and too big on his seventeen-year-old body, even though it had been tailored to fit him.

Somehow, I could tell even before Uncle Ty spoke that he was about to do something wrong. Maybe it was the way he loosened the tie at his throat, just a fraction. Or the faintest curve at the corners of his mouth.

"Dad always called me his 'dreamer.' The son who wanted to be an artist. Who wasn't going to follow in his big brother's footsteps and become a great businessman. Who wasn't much of a *Bloody Thorn,* I guess. But he always said it with a smile, and never told me not to pursue art. He wouldn't *pay* for me to go to art college, but he didn't tell me I *couldn't* go, either. I guess that's the fun part of being the spare son — you're not really worth investing in."

Uncle Ty paused, as though he expected people to laugh, but there was only awkward silence. "My dad was quite the dreamer himself, though, wasn't he? I'm sure plenty of you here heard his stories over the last few months — about how the orchard feeds on Thorn blood? Or how he kept seeing Dead-Eyed Sadie right before he — "

"Ty," Dad said, his deep voice carrying easily across the short distance to the lectern. "Wrap it up now."

Uncle Ty gave him a tight smile. "Of course, big brother. Whatever you say." He turned back to face his audience again. "I loved my father very much. And I look forward to getting along with him much better now."

"Ty!" Dad snapped, but Uncle Ty was already stepping down from the lectern. He didn't come back to sit with us. Instead, he yanked off his tie and dropped it in the collection plate by the church door on his way out.

When the service was over and I was home again with Mom and Dad, the manor still ringing with the silence of Grandpa leaving, I asked them what Uncle Ty had meant. "Why was he talking about Grandpa seeing Dead-Eyed Sadie?"

I'd heard of Sadie by then, of course. But this was my first time hearing of anyone I knew actually *seeing* her.

Mom's voice remained low and calm, but I noticed her fingertips whitening against her wineglass. "There's a Thorn family superstition that each of us sees Dead-Eyed Sadie before we die."

Dad said nothing, peering out through the lounge window toward the orchard as though he wasn't listening, but his eyes flickered to me when I went on.

"Like she *kills* us?" My voice rose, and Mom came to sit next to me, squeezing me to her side with a gentle laugh.

"Nothing like that," she said airily. "Her appearance is a

warning that danger's on the way. But she's harmless enough. She's just a girl who had something bad happen to her. That doesn't make *her* bad, does it?"

Then Dad turned away from the window and gave me a tight Thorn smile. "Your uncle just said all that because he's angry at Grandpa for leaving before they could work things out."

"But it's not like Grandpa had a choice about dying, is it?" I pressed.

"No," he said faintly. "He didn't."

EIGHT

I lie in bed, bundled in quilts and blankets, listening to the wind whistling through the gaps around the little round window of my room. If the barn owl is hiding out in the attic above me, it's keeping quiet. But, as the wind shifts direction, something up there starts to bang out a loud, jarring rhythm.

"What have you got against sleep?" I mutter to no one in particular.

I drag myself out of bed and, remembering the owl pellet from Saturday night, I put on my boots. The weasel skull I found that night has since been cleaned and polished, and now grins at me weaselishly from my windowsill. Carolyn said it added "character" to the room. I tend to agree, although it kind of makes me miss having a pet of my own. One with the fur *on,* I mean.

The junk area of the mill is dark and musty-smelling. I edge around the stacks of boxes to reach the ladder up to the loft, and stub my toe on one of Uncle Ty's never-used weights. I'm starting to think this mill might be haunted by a ghost who doesn't like me very much. Or I *might* just be a klutz.

Using the flashlight on my phone, I avoid stepping in any more owl grossness. The little round window — a twin to the one in my bedroom below — stands open. The window itself swings back and forth on its hinges, clattering against the frame on the backswing. I hurry over, hoping the glass hasn't already completely shattered. The mill's drafty enough without having a permanently open window in the side of it.

Hailstones pelt my arm like bullets as I reach out to grab the window latch. I pull, fighting against the wind. Just as I manage to fasten the latch, the glass panes — intact, by some miracle — flare with a burst of lightning outside. In the glare, I see evil eyes carved into the stone edging of the window. Seven of them, circling all the way around it.

A deep chill settles in my gut. I don't think I've ever seen so many in one place. I know they're just an old superstition, meant to protect against evil or whatever; lots of people here have them carved above their front door. In a town where most of the buildings are centuries old, you expect to find weird things like that. But seeing so many eyes together like this is damn creepy.

Especially after that dead girl washing up with none.

Back in my room, the lingering unsettled feeling from finding those eyes carries me over to the window. I lean across my desk to check the windowsill, looking for the same markings that are on the one in the attic. At first, I don't see them. But there, under a thick layer of masonry paint, are seven faintly indented evil eyes. I trace my finger over one of them, jumping as lightning flashes again outside. As my vision dances with light spots, I imagine for a moment I see someone standing on the bridge in the far distance, a dark speck against the ink-scratch crossing over the top of the waterfall.

But, as my vision clears, there is no dark figure. Only Burden Bridge, standing as it always has.

* * *

Getting summoned to see Mr. Hamish first thing in the morning is never a *great* sign, but part of me's hoping it might be good news about the summer art program.

It's not.

Mr. Hamish is in his mid-thirties, and is the kind of guidance counselor who wears tight-fitting khakis, and has beanbag chairs in one corner of his office that nobody but him ever uses. The kind who shaves a center part into his mustache, and rests his finger there while he listens.

When I knock on his door, he smiles and holds his arms out wide like he means to hug me, then gestures to the beanbags when I don't move from the doorway.

I go and sit down next to his desk, in an actual chair. He frowns, disappointed, and plops down on the opposite side.

"Ava, how are you doing?" he asks, then goes on without waiting for an answer. "I heard you had a little trouble yesterday, got yourself a detention. I thought we were past all that."

It isn't a question, but he tilts his head like it is.

"Just a misunderstanding," I say, forcing my jaw not to clench as I deliver the line Uncle Ty advised me to use. I say "advised," but it was not really advice so much as an order. "It won't happen again."

"*Mmhmm. Mmhmm.*" Mr. Hamish nods enthusiastically, pointer finger taking up position in the center part, but only for a second. "I did wonder if it was perhaps something to do with that unfortunate young woman who washed up yesterday . . . That must have brought up some painful memories for you, I'm sure."

I frown. "If you mean my parents, Mr. Hamish, then not really. They didn't drown—they died in a car wreck." He knows this perfectly well. All the faculty, as well as every kid in this school, knows what happened to my parents. The basic facts, at least.

"Of course, of course. I'm glad to hear yesterday's tragedy didn't dredge that up for you. Though I have to admit, some of your teachers have been saying lately that they're concerned about your grades. Very concerned, actually. It seems as though you're failing algebra 2 and chemistry, and are really behind in your final art project."

"I . . ." My mouth kind of hangs open while I process all this. Because it's a *lot*. "*Failing* failing?"

"Oh yes," Mr. Hamish confirms breezily. "But that's not a shock to you, surely? I really wish you'd followed my advice and hired a tutor before winter break."

It *is* a shock, though. Going from *your grades are slipping* to *you are failing* hadn't really crossed my mind, and now it's like a Klaxon going off in my head.

Mr. Hamish's suggestion had actually been to hire *him* as a tutor, and to be honest, even if we'd had the money to spare for it then, I wouldn't have chosen him. There's something distinctly . . . unacademic about Mr. Hamish. And is it even ethical for a guidance counselor to pimp himself out to students?

In any case, the idea of failing now, when graduation is literally just a few months away, changes things. I don't have a ton of money saved up from working at the Pump'N'Go, what with Bessie's gas needs, but there's enough to cover a few hours with a tutor.

"I'll catch up," I tell him. He gives me this real pitying look, like I've just claimed to be able to fly or something.

"I appreciate this has been a difficult year for you, but this is your *senior year.* There really isn't a lot of leeway left, Ava."

Leeway. Because that's what you get when your parents die in front of you.

"I'll work something out, I promise," I tell him. I'm already wondering how hard I'll need to grovel for Carla to agree to tutor me. She has absolutely zero patience for explaining shit, and I'm going to need a *lot* of shit explained to me . . . Yeah, I'm pretty sure she's going to ghost me until after graduation. Maybe I could get Daphne to ask her for me?

Mr. Hamish shrugs. "You still have options, Ava. I mean, you could always repeat the year. Or take makeup classes this summer."

"But the art program is this summer . . ."

"Ah, yes. I wouldn't pin *all* my hopes on that."

I feel an awful, yawning void open up beneath my chair. My fingers whiten on the armrests as Mr. Hamish goes on cheerfully nudging me into the vacuum.

"Miss Shannon is liaising with me about which candidate to put forward for the program. Only one student can go, so it's an important decision." He says this like it's *his* important decision. "It's only because we see such talent and potential in your past work that we're even considering you for the spot. But I have to say, with your academic record being what it is, you really shouldn't get your hopes up. And you need to be thinking longer term, in any case. The program is only six weeks. What then?"

I ignore that question because I have no idea how to answer it. "If I raise my grades, though, I still have a shot, right?"

Mr. Hamish leans back and goes to steeple his fingers in

front of him, but his arms are too short, so he ends up resting his hands on his stomach. "Sure, that'll be a start. And you're a smart girl. Creative. I think once you figure out how badly you want to graduate with your friends, you'll know what to do."

"Does that not strike you as a bit . . . extortion-y?" Daphne asks me at lunch, after I've relayed the conversation to her while we wait for Carla to arrive. I was hoping she'd dive in with an offer to broker some tutoring for me from Carla. Daphne is the only one who's able to tap into Carla's *extremely* well-hidden kinder nature.

But this response confuses the hell out of me.

"What do you mean, 'extortion-y'?"

Daphne blinks at me. "*How badly do you want it, Ava? A girl like you knows how to get creative, right?*" she says, dropping her voice so it's low and sleazy.

"He didn't say it like *that*."

"Are you sure? Because that's how I heard it, and you know you have some kind of . . . processing glitch when it comes to people being into you."

"I do not," I say. "Do I?"

"Does Ava what?" Carla slides into the seat next to me, and I catch an unwelcome waft of her mac 'n' cheese.

"Doesn't she completely miss the signals when someone's into her?" Daphne answers, and Carla nods without hesitation.

"Every time. Remember when Yara Almasi tried to get her phone number at the pre-holiday party in December?"

"Wait, what?" I cut in, despite the fact they seem happy to continue this conversation about me without my input. "Paint-my-ass Yara was into me?" Daphne and Carla *mmhmm* in unison. "I can't believe I totally missed that."

"Of course you did. Your instincts are terrible, and you rely on them way too much. Who's hitting on Ava now, though?" Carla asks.

"Mr. Hamish." Daphne's face sours.

"For real?" Carla side-eyes me. "Even *you* can do better than Hamish."

"I hate you so much," I tell her, meaning it in that moment.

Carla's gaze tracks to the far side of the cafeteria, where Freya Miller is laughing about something with her friends. For a second, I feel absolutely certain they're laughing at me, but I'm probably just being paranoid. Of their group, only Dominic is turned vaguely in our direction, his perma-scowl in full force. I feel like he wears that thing instead of developing an actual personality.

Then Mateo feigns like he's going to thumb-gouge Casper's eyes and shrieks, "*Sadie's coming for you!*" loudly enough that everyone stops and looks at him before returning to their food. It reminds me that the Miller twins' shit squad really are planning to shoot a Dead-Eyed Sadie special at the manor.

Why did I have to paint that damn mural?

And why didn't I make sure I covered it up before we left?

No matter what, I can't get sidetracked—I need to paint over it tonight. I may not be able to stop them from turning my old house into a horror show, but they don't get to use my painting to do it.

"I saw Freya coming out of Hamish's office on my way here," Carla says. "She looked kind of pissed, actually. Though I'm pretty sure Freya would break his face if he ever tried anything with her."

Despite my loathing of Freya Miller, I have to admit Carla's probably right about that. But this whole conversation is based on my highly suspect relaying skills, and I need to clear this up before it becomes something it's not.

"Look, Mr. Hamish *wasn't* hitting on me, okay? I probably just made what he said sound skeevy without meaning to."

Carla points a forkful of mac at Daphne. "She has a point. Ava is not good with words."

"Fuck you."

"Fuck *yourself,*" she counters. I feel like I just got schooled, though I'm not sure how, exactly.

Speaking of schooling . . . "*Heeeeyyy,* Carla, how would you feel about tutoring your favorite about-to-fail-out-of-school buddy? Algebra and chem? I can pay you . . ."

"No." She doesn't even drop a beat, just keeps eating her disgusting lunch. "Do you know how much homework we get in AP classes? I barely have time to do my own studying, especially with Corey and his new goddamned *theremin* of all things. It sounds like someone's trying to strangle the theme to *Star Trek* in his room. Anyway, I'd just end up wanting to kill you. You should ask Carolyn."

"Carolyn?"

That's actually a great idea. Carolyn was a chemistry major in college. I tend to forget how overqualified she is for her job at the local pharmacy, but there really aren't a lot of sciencey jobs in Burden Falls.

Truth is, if I hadn't been trying so damn hard to hide my

bad grades from her and Uncle Ty (really not easy when he's a teacher), she probably would've offered to help me already.

"Yeah, I'll do that," I say. "Thanks." I pick up my empty lunch tray. "I'm gonna work on my art project before next period. Catch you both later."

I'm just typing out a message to Carolyn at the tray-ditching station when I notice Dominic Miller approaching. He's probably decided to finally chew me out for being at the manor the other night, despite Ford promising me he'd covered my tracks.

"Thorn, wait a—"

"Kiss my ass." I'm pretty sure that's grammatically correct, thank you, Carla.

I hurry out of the cafeteria, feeling Dominic Miller's glower hitting me right between the shoulder blades.

NINE

I pull in at the public library on the way home. It's an old red-and-white brick building with a rounded turret at one end — think low-budget *Rapunzel*.

I go inside and head straight for the local-history section. It's in a small room off by itself where I can sit and use the Wi-Fi without anyone giving me eyes. I take out my sketchbook and a few pens for window dressing (though I really *should* be working on my final art project), pull out my phone, and click to download the movie Ford chose for us to watch later. He doesn't have Wi-Fi at home, either, so I'm forced to sneakily download here.

While I wait, I check out the local news stories about Claire Palmer. There isn't a lot of fresh information. No mention of her eyes. A crawling sense of unease comes over me as I picture the girl churning over and over in the basin of the waterfall, her eyes gone . . .

Like Sadie.

I close the browser and instead flick through the sketches for my art project, but my mind is elsewhere.

What was Freya talking to Hamish about earlier, when Carla saw her coming out of his office? Why did he speak to her *after* me? If she was pissed, like Carla said, then he can't have been telling her she was the top candidate for the art program . . . right? And I'm completely disregarding Daphne's reading of the whole thing as a creeper situation — I think even *I* would pick up on that.

But Freya's almost on a par with Carla grades-wise, so why else would she be getting called in to see the guidance counselor?

I jump as an alert pops up on my phone saying there's a new *Haunted Heartland* upload. Before I can talk myself out of it, I click on the post, praying to all that's dark and unholy that I'm not too late, and they haven't put my mural out there for the world to see.

"*Hey, Hauntlanders!*" Freya's voice comes out loud as a bullhorn, and I frantically lower the volume on my phone. It's only her in the frame, red hair blazing and lips to match, like a Disneyfied version of the devil. "*Just here to give you all a heads-up: The next episode we upload is going to be our most EPIC one yet! You will NOT want to miss it. Coming in just a few days, so keep those eyes peeled. Love ya!*" She winks one bright green eye, then the video ends.

Well, I don't need three guesses to figure out what the subject of their next upload will be. I had an awful feeling they'd zero in on Dead-Eyed Sadie the second they moved into the manor, and Claire Palmer washing up right next to the waterfall gives them a perfect lead-in.

I drop my phone, letting my head fall into my waiting hands. Why did *they* have to buy the manor? Why did I have to paint that damn mural? And why did I have to put Sadie in it?

I lift my head at the sound of someone else in the local-history section. I almost curse when I see who it is.

Dominic Miller.

He's not looking my way—instead craning back through the archway leading into the main area of the library like he's looking for someone. Then he strides across the room and stops next to a door marked *private*. It's set back among the bookshelves, and I've never paid much attention to it. But now Dominic tries the handle, finds it unlocked, then pauses to take one last look around. That's when he sees me.

We lock eyes, the moment stretching until it becomes super weird. Then I swear he actually smirks before turning back to the door he's obviously not meant to be going through, and slips inside.

I sit in my corner, staring at the door. It's still open a crack, almost like he's daring me to go in after him. But of course he isn't. No, it's just a sign of his goddamn arrogance, leaving the door open like that, showing he doesn't care if he's caught.

What's he even doing in there, anyway?

It's almost painful how slowly the pieces come together in my head.

Their new *Haunted Heartland* video. He's probably in there riffling through old town archives. I know they keep some stuff about local families back there, away from the prying eyes of neighborhood gossips. I bet Dominic's looking for dirt on Sadie, and the manor, and the Thorns to use in their stupid show.

I slide out of my seat and cross to the door he just went through.

"Hey, Ava!" I whirl, wide-eyed, to find Liam peering in at me through the archway. "Thought I saw you back here."

"I . . . uh . . . I was just working on my art project. It's going to be a graphic novel." I wave back at the table where I laid out my sketchbook. "Just stretching my legs while I think about the next panel. What are you up to?"

This is, admittedly, the most I have ever said to Liam. So

maybe I shouldn't be surprised when he leans against the nearest bookshelf like he's settling in for a long chat.

"Mostly trying to keep out of Mr. Maitland's way. I've had a *raging* hangover all day, and that seems to be his cue to give me a ton of work around here." I smell stale beer on his breath as he speaks, so I guess he's not kidding about the hangover. He seems excessively proud of it, actually. After living with Uncle Ty and *his* hangovers for a year now, I should let Liam know it's *not* a cute look. But I don't get a chance.

"So you're a comic nerd, huh? Wouldn't have called that one. What kind of stuff are you into?"

"Mostly horror," I say, expecting that to end the conversation, but he grins.

"Yeah, I can see that. It works with the whole goth-chick thing you have going on. It's a good look."

Okay, bad instincts or not, it's time for me to nope out.

"Hey, I think Mr. Maitland's coming over . . ." I grimace dramatically as I peer over his shoulder.

"Where?" Liam frowns, taking in the notably empty library.

"Oh . . . He was there a second ago. Anyway, I'd better get back to work on my project."

I don't wait for an answer, just retreat back to my corner and stare intently at my sketchbook until I'm sure Liam's gone. Then I hear footsteps approaching, and look up — way up — at Dominic Miller. He really is unnecessarily tall.

He tucks his phone into the pocket of his gray coat.

"Thanks for running interference with the asshole," he says, tossing a sharp look toward where Liam is now quite clearly hiding behind a shelf of romance novels. "I owe you one."

"I—"

But Dominic doesn't wait for my searing comeback, which was absolutely on the tip of my tongue, for sure. He just strides away, probably glowering.

After dinner, I walk north to Ford's along the riverbank. It's a clear night, and I don't want my parked car to be a potential give-away when I sneak onto the manor grounds later. There's also some morbidly curious part of me that wants to pass by the basin of the waterfall, where Mateo's dad found Claire Palmer's body, just to find out if it feels different from when I walked past it a couple nights ago. For all I know, she might have been only a few feet away from the path then, submerged under the thawing ice.

It's not long before I hear the bells chiming faintly at Copper Bell Dam. The footpath is frozen, crunchy with dead leaves.

There's a stillness to the air tonight. Nothing stirs—or screeches—in the branches above my head. Even the river barely murmurs as it glides past. I take a deep breath, hoping that stillness will seep in through my lungs. Calm my blood.

Out of habit, I let my fingers graze over the evil eye carved into the tree that marks the point where the river widens at Copper Bell Dam. It reminds me of the carved eyes I found last night around the two windows in the mill. Both look out onto the river. Facing the direction I'm heading: toward Burden Bridge and the manor.

Instinctively, I turn to look up at the bridge, but it's invisible from here—too many trees crowding in. I hurry on, suddenly frightened by the stillness. Rather than walk past the basin of the waterfall, I veer off and take River Road north until it branches onto Red Road, and toward Ford's house.

It's cold enough that my labored breathing mists the air around me after the uphill climb to reach the lane. I've only taken a few steps along it when something catches my eye. To my left, over the manor's boundary wall, a light flickers. It seems like it might be coming from the bridge, though there are too many trees in the way to say for sure. I stop and watch the light for a moment. I should ignore it and continue to Ford's as planned. It's probably just one of the Millers out walking around the property—maybe Freya making one of her sneaky phone calls again. She might even be trying to sex-talk Hamish into giving her my spot on the summer art program.

I try to shudder that nasty little thought right out of my mind. But some messed-up impulse sends me clambering over the wall, just to see if it *is* Freya on the phone.

I land quietly on the other side and stealth my way forward until I can make out where the light is coming from. There's someone standing on the bridge. Not Freya. I can't tell what's casting the light, but the figure standing silhouetted by it has black hair, not fire-engine red.

Dominic.

He leans against the guardrail of the bridge, gazing out over the waterfall. There's no way he's making a call, I realize, because the sound of the water thundering into the basin below would make conversation impossible without shouting.

I'm about to turn back, no longer interested in what Dominic's doing there, when I see something move in the shadows between me and the bridge. Another figure stands at the very edge of the trees lining the path on this side. I can't see that well from my hiding spot, but whoever it is seems to be watching Dominic too.

My skin creeps like I've just brushed against something dead and feathery.

The figure steps out of the shadows. In the moonlight, I can make out some type of cloak or long coat. It billows slightly as the person walks toward the bridge — not quickly, but with the assurance of someone who knows they haven't been spotted. That, and the fact that Dominic still seems to be unaware of anyone approaching him, sets my nerves on edge.

But he must be expecting whoever it is, right? That's probably why he's here — to meet up with someone. Except who wears a cloak the wrong side of Halloween? I don't, and I'm a poster girl for goth chic.

No, the only people who casually wear cloaks are weirdos. And if it were me I wouldn't want a weirdo creeping up on me as I leaned out over a sixty-foot drop.

What if it's not just some rando, though? What if it's actually . . . ?

I'm not even aware I'm moving toward the bridge until a twig snaps under my boot. There's an answering screech up in the branches overhead. Heart pounding, I look to see if the cloaked figure heard me, but they're probably too near the waterfall now to hear anything above the water's roar. I know that must be all Dominic can hear because he still hasn't turned around. And there's something about the way the person in the cloak is moving that I don't like.

I inch closer. I'm at the edge of the treeline now. If I run, I can probably reach Dominic before the figure touches him. Miller or not, I have to do something.

The figure raises its arms, sleeves falling back to expose long, slender fingers. That creeping feeling intensifies as my mind paints the face I can't see beyond the cloak—one with a gaping mouth and black holes for eyes.

It's as though everything slows—my heart, my breath, even the waterfall itself. It all distorts, getting sucked in by those twin black voids.

Her fingers curl into claws, reaching for Dominic from behind. He still doesn't sense her. How can he not? Every nerve in my body is shrieking in panic.

I have no choice.

"Dominic! Run!"

TEN

I scream the words as I rush from the shadows, hoping he'll hear me. Hoping I'm not too late.

Dominic answers with a yell of his own as her clawed fingers dig into his eyes. He bucks, trying to shake her off, but in doing so leans back too far against the guardrail. I shove Sadie aside as I reach out to pull him away from the edge.

I'm too late.

My fingers close on nothing but vapor. Dominic falls, vanishing into the bellowing void.

"What the hell are you doing? You completely ruined the shot!"

I'm turned roughly, but the girl facing me isn't the one I'm expecting.

Of course it isn't.

Freya Miller glares at me, strands of fake-looking black hair sticking to her face where the water has misted it. Her eyes, usually a vibrant green, are now black lid to lid. Thick dark makeup fills in the surrounding sockets. She's wearing contacts, I realize numbly. It's a costume. She's dressed up to look like Dead-Eyed Sadie—a prank-store version of her.

As I'm taking all this in, Freya's lips curve upward.

"Oh my God, Thorn—I thought you were just screwing around, but you actually believed I was a ghost, didn't you?" She laughs, her voice loud enough that I hear her clearly above the waterfall's roar. "You're so weird."

"But . . . your brother . . ."

I'm vaguely aware of more people joining us: Mateo Medel carrying the set light from where he must've been crouched with it on the far side of the bridge; Casper Jones holding up his phone, probably still recording my reaction. And behind them is Ford, his hands tangled in his hair like he's seconds away from tearing it all out. Of the four of them, Ford is the only one not smirking at me.

I feel something moving at my back, and turn in time to see Dominic dragging his lanky frame back over the guardrail. He stands up, looming over me. But it's only now that I notice the cord hanging from his waist — a tether that's connected to the rail.

Oh God. How can I be so damn slow putting the pieces together? They're filming for their Sadie special. I mean, I *knew* it was in the cards. It's the whole reason I'm here: to cover over the painting I left in the pavilion.

My cheeks blaze, despite the chill. I can't believe I actually thought Dominic Miller was in danger from a ghost. I can't believe I *cared*.

"Ava?" Dominic yells. "What are you doing here?"

My gaze darts toward the orchard on the far side of the bridge, and the pavilion that's all but hidden by it. But then Ford steps into my line of sight.

"She's here looking for me," he says. "I lost track of time — we were supposed to meet at my house to watch a movie."

Next to me, Freya pulls an odd face, and I think she might be rolling her eyes, though it's impossible to tell behind the black contacts. The sight of her is freaking me out, though, so I turn my focus to Ford.

"Why are *you* here?" *With them?* I'm pretty sure he hears those last two words and the accusation in them, even though I don't say them aloud.

Ford takes my elbow and ushers me back over the bridge, toward the boundary wall. When we're far enough away to speak at a normal level, he leans in and says, "I'll explain everything later, but it's not how it seems. I need to stick around here for a little while, but if you wait at my place I'll meet you there, okay? And I won't let Casper use that footage he recorded just now, I swear. Trust me. Just fifteen minutes, I promise."

"You also *promised* you'd never ditch me for the Millers again," I hiss back.

Ford has the nerve to look stung. He really just expects me to go wait for him like a meek little sheep.

When I glance back toward the bridge, Freya, Casper, and Mateo are laughing and jostling each other, Freya making dramatic clawing motions while Casper seemingly wards her off with the flash of his camera.

But Dominic is looking right at me—watching me with this intent frown, as if he's trying to figure something out. That look bothers me more than Freya and the others acting like dicks.

"They're just goofing around," Ford says. "Maybe if you tried—"

"Ford, shut up." I cut him off before he can make me completely lose my shit. "I don't want to hear it."

I turn away from him and stomp back to the boundary wall. I manage to climb it without falling on my ass, thank the Dark

Lord and all his little minions—no doubt Casper's phone is still tracking my every move, hoping for some extra little nugget of hilarity at my expense.

Just as I'm about to jump down the other side, I feel a touch on my arm. I jerk away from it, thinking it's Ford come to grovel, or at least explain himself, but it's Dominic. He has the sleeve of my coat in a firm grip, as though he's about to make a citizen's arrest.

"Why are you really here?" he asks brusquely.

I huff out an exasperated—and sure, embarrassed—breath. "Look, I covered for you at the library earlier, right?" Technically not *really* true, but he doesn't argue. "And you said you owe me one. If you meant that, don't drag my family on your show, okay?"

He frowns, letting my sleeve slip through his fingers, but says nothing. I should've known there was no point trying to appeal to Dominic's better nature. He obviously hasn't got one—he's a Miller.

I half jump, half tumble from the wall, and leave without looking back.

Not only is my best friend a back-stabbing snake, but I've failed to cover up the damn mural—*again*. I'm still seething about it all when my phone rings later that night. It's Ford, of course. I don't answer. The ringing stops when my voicemail kicks in, then starts again a second later. I send him straight to voicemail this time.

My text alert pings.

Ford: If you don't answer your phone, Ava, I'll just come over there.
Ava: I don't want to talk to you. Stop calling.

My phone is silent for a couple minutes, and I think he's actually got the message. But then it pings again. And, when I open the text, it's a whole goddamn essay.

Ford: Stop being stubborn and let me explain! I've been hanging out with the Millers to make sure they don't put anything shitty about you in their videos, but then Freya asked me to join the crew, and I couldn't really say no—they get all kinds of job offers and promo ops out of it. Did you know Freya even has a small part in a movie? It's gonna be on Netflix next year. Imagine if I got offered something like that! You get why I said yes, right? And I'm sorry I was late for our movie night. I really did just lose track of time. I need a watch, OK? Please stop being mad at me. I'm not cute when I grovel. I'm an ugly groveler. Forgive me?

I sigh when I've read it. Because I *do* get why Ford had to say yes to being in the Miller twins' stupid videos. He wants to be an actor, but there aren't many opportunities for that kind of thing around here. And there's no way Ford could pay for drama school—especially not one of the big arty ones in New York. But he still could've said something *before* I made a total ass of myself. I mean, I may not have actually been there looking for Ford, but he doesn't know that.

I'll let him stew for a little while before I tell him he's forgiven.

My eyes wander to a framed photo on my desk—one I unpacked earlier. It's of me and my parents at my sweet sixteen at the manor. I'm not a fan of big parties, so we kept mine fairly low-key: mocktails and cocktail dresses. My parents dressed up too, even though they only hung around long enough to get a photo with me, then graciously got the hell out of there.

I'm wearing a blood-red dress in the photo, and the beautiful ruby apple pendant my mom had given me that morning.

"Your father gave me this the day you were born. Now it's yours, my gorgeous girl."

And there I am, wearing it, beaming between my snappy-morning-suited dad and my peacock-blue-frocked mom. I had no idea then that it'd be the last birthday I celebrated with them. They died just a few days before my seventeenth; my eighteenth is next week. And tomorrow marks a year exactly since the car crash.

Jesus, how can it feel like just yesterday when we were cheesing for that picture? I was so clueless then. I had no idea what it felt like to lose everything.

Almost everything.

I pick up my phone, swallowing down hard on the hot lump in my throat.

Ava: It's fine, dickhead. We're cool.

ELEVEN

Then

The car ride was already tense. Mom was pissed at having to drive after Dad said he was feeling woozy.

"Maybe you wouldn't be *feeling woozy* if you hadn't had that cocktail with your brother," Mom muttered crisply. Dad pretended not to hear. "You know I hate driving in snow."

"I can drive," I offered from the back, and it was Mom's turn to act like she didn't hear me. About the only thing she disliked more than driving in snow was the prospect of *me* driving in snow. It was one of her excuses for putting off buying me my own car, even though she'd been promising me all year.

"*We decided it'd be better if you saved up for a car yourself,*" Dad had added as they handed me the small jewelry box for my sweet sixteen the year before.

Don't get me wrong: I loved the apple pendant. But Dad went on about how I needed to "*learn the value of owning something you've worked for*"—like the paper route he'd had as a kid was some big life-changing experience. He wanted me to get a part-time job, in other words. But when would I even have time to enjoy owning my hard-earned car if I had to spend my weekends waiting tables or choking on exhaust fumes working at the local gas station like Daphne did? His logic was highly flawed.

Besides, I knew if I kept working on him Dad would cave about the car thing eventually.

"I wish Ty would slow down a little," Mom said now, her voice tense. Her knuckles stood out bone-white where she gripped the steering wheel.

We were heading out for a fancy dinner to celebrate Uncle Ty moving into the manor with his new wife, Carolyn. It was still weird thinking of Uncle Ty being married. The newlyweds were in Uncle Ty's slinky sports car up ahead, the taillights growing smaller as he drove a little too fast for the weather. Probably having much more fun than we were in our car, I thought. I should've gone with them.

As if catching the stray thought, Mom turned her attention to me, though I didn't notice right away because I was busy thumbing my phone.

"I told you to leave that at home." Mom's eyes were sharp in the rearview mirror, just like her tone. "Pass it to your father. Now."

"I'm in the middle of a conversation," I said, not unreasonably, I thought. My friendship with Daphne and Carla was still new, still tentative. I didn't want to risk looking like a flake just because Mom was in a bad mood.

"Blake, take her phone."

"Seriously? I'm not a little kid, Mom," I complained, but Dad didn't turn his gaze from the snowy stretch of woodland outside anyway. We were just passing the northern edge of our property. Because the snow was thick, and the night was clear, the reflected starlight was bright enough to see the manor flashing between the trees butting up against the embankment. They were all bare of leaves and reaching skyward—like ink scratches on a blank page. I wished I was out there, leaving stomping big footprints in the snow, instead of being trapped in a car with my parents.

That was the very last time I'd ever wish for that, though I didn't know it yet.

"Why does everything have to turn into an arg—" Mom was saying when Dad cut in.

"I see her," he said.

"What?" Mom sounded exasperated. I knew it was just because she was on edge, but it was still annoying. "See who?"

"In the woods . . . It's her."

I peered through the window. There *was* someone out there—a pale figure outlined against the black shapes of the trees.

"She keeps moving like—" Dad's voice stopped abruptly, though I could still see his mouth opening and closing in his reflection in the window.

"Dad? Are you okay?"

He didn't answer.

"Jesus!" Mom hissed.

I turned to face her just in time to see an owl swooping in the headlights. It screeched as it winged up over the roof of the car.

Dad shuddered, tugging at his seat belt. Something was wrong.

I wasn't worried about some owl or about upsetting Daphne and Carla now. I knew something big was happening—something bad. My seat belt dug in as I leaned forward to grip Mom's shoulder a little too hard.

"Mom, pull over. I think Dad's having a seizure."

"A seizure?" Mom frowned in the rearview. *He hasn't had*

a seizure in years. I could almost hear her thinking it. "Blake? Honey? Are you—"

A horn blared. Light filled the car, too bright to see anything else.

Tires squealed and skidded over the icy road.

My mouth opened and closed, just as silently as Dad's.

The impact happened so fast, but it was drawn with laser-sharp precision.

Mom screamed as the Hummer rammed into us. Our car shot off the road, barrel-rolling five, six times—it was hard to tell. Glass flew everywhere. I felt the sting of it slicing my skin, and the brutal snap as my collarbone broke against the pull of the seat belt.

I blacked out.

When I opened my eyes again, everything was so dark. The car sat silent. I couldn't tell that yet, though, because my ears were ringing. Then there *was* a sound—a strange *drip, drip, drip.*

"Dad?" I felt the shape of the word, but it sounded like it was being spoken by someone else far away. "Mom?"

I searched the dark for them, shadows shifting as my eyes adjusted. Blood rushed behind my ears. The seat belt held me in place, a white-hot brand against my broken collarbone. I was upside down, I realized hazily.

Finally, I saw Mom looking back at me from the driver's seat. The roof over (under now) the front of the car had caved in much worse than in the back, so her head pressed against it at an awkward angle. She stared at me, wide-eyed.

"Mom?" I tried again. Then my seat belt shot free, dumping me out onto a carpet of broken glass. I *screamed.* When I held up my hands, they were covered in deep cuts. A slant of silvery light glinted on a long sliver of glass still sticking out of my left palm. Blood oozed out around it, making the glass hard to grip as I pulled it free, whimpering.

Mom still hadn't moved. She had to be in shock or something, I thought. She just watched me silently over her shoulder. I reached for her, leaving a smear of blood on her cheek.

That was when I noticed the way her neck was twisted right around. My mouth opened, a scream crushed deep in my throat.

"I saw her . . ." Dad's voice came foggy and weak from the front passenger seat. "I saw her . . ."

Slowly, no longer really processing what was happening, I turned to face Dad. Then I *did* scream.

Dad's face was a mask of blood, cuts from the shattered window scoring his cheeks. And his eyes . . .

Drip, drip, drip . . .

I couldn't even see where his eyes were supposed to be. There was so much blood.

"I saw her," he said.

I shook my head, even though he couldn't see me. I couldn't think past the blood. God, the blood. It was all I could see. All I could hear.

Something moved behind me, and I startled. Turned too quickly, broken bones grinding together. My torn skin gaped.

Uncle Ty peered in through the broken rear window, face white with shock. "Oh God . . . oh God . . . Shit. *Shit.* What do I do? What do I . . ."

I'd never heard the sound I made then—this awful tortured keening, like a wounded animal. It seemed to snap Uncle Ty out of his daze, but then he saw Mom.

"Oh Jesus . . ." He reached in and grasped my hand in his. It hurt, but I barely noticed. "Come on, Ava. Just keep looking at me, okay? Where's your dad? Blake! Blake, *help me!*"

I couldn't move. Literally couldn't. If I didn't move, then this couldn't be happening. Couldn't be real.

Uncle Ty used his sleeve to sweep the worst of the glass out of the way, then crawled inside the car to get me. But he froze when he saw Dad's face.

"Oh fuck . . . his *eyes!*"

Uncle Ty moved so that his body blocked my view. But I'd already seen. I already *knew*.

A horrible creaking sound came from outside. Outside but close by.

Carolyn called out, "Ty? Are they all right? I think you need to hurry . . ."

He tilted his head, as though that would help him see through the mangled body of the car to whatever was making that creaking sound. It came again, followed by a sharp crack.

"Crawl out through the window, Ava," he said tightly. "Go on."

"But—"

"I'll get your dad. We'll be right behind you. But we need to move."

"I . . ."

"We all have to crawl." Dad spoke so softly, I barely heard him. But I did what he said. I started to crawl, each movement a searing jolt to my broken collarbone, but Dad's words still rang through my head.

We all have to crawl we all have to crawl WE ALL HAVE TO CRAWL!

But it wasn't just in my head—Dad was chanting it, bellowing it now, over and over and over.

I scrambled for the nearest window, hair snagging on twisted metal, and broken shards attacking me from below. Sharp odors hit the back of my throat—blood and gasoline. They smelled so wrong, so awful. The wreck groaned and tightened around me, not wanting to let me go.

"WE ALL HAVE TO CRAWL."

I dragged myself out onto churned-up snow and, God help me, I was glad I couldn't hear Dad's horrible chant now. I clawed my way up the embankment and was immediately swept into Carolyn's embrace. I stood there, stiff and unyielding. Carolyn was still a stranger then, and I was confused—*Why is this person hugging me?* I just wanted to see what was happening with Uncle Ty and my dad.

When I squirmed away, she looked down in horror at where my hands had left bloody prints on her pretty yellow tea dress. Past her shoulder, I saw the front end of the wrecked car crumpled around a tree.

I searched the shadowy woods where I'd glimpsed the figure before . . . Had I really seen that? Or was it just a reflection playing on the inside of the car window?

There was nobody there now.

Across the road, another car sat sideways across both lanes. Steam poured from under the hood. Through it, I saw someone emerging, waving away the steam like nuisance flies.

Madoc Miller.

I recognized him right away, though I'd only seen him a couple times since he and his family moved to Burden Falls. The Millers were *bad news*, Dad had always said. "*Our family and theirs . . . there's history.*"

A loud screech made me and Carolyn whirl to face our car. The tree tilted farther forward over the wreck.

"Uncle Ty!" I screamed.

I slid down the embankment. When I reached the bottom, Uncle Ty was already pulling himself free of the wreckage. He staggered with me up the blood-smeared path I'd carved through the snow, back to where Carolyn stood, my ugly handprints on her dress lit up as she called 911.

I looked back down the embankment, waiting for Dad to emerge.

"Where is he?" My voice sounded broken. Uncle Ty put an arm around my shoulders, still breathing hard, but I shrugged him off. "*Where is he?*"

"It's too late, Ava."

Carolyn was talking to someone on the phone, her words coming out fast as her gaze turned to the other car across the road.

"We have to get Dad out of there," I said. "The tree —"

"He's already gone. They're both gone." Uncle Ty's statement was punctuated by an awful metallic crunch.

The tree fell almost in slow motion. When it landed, it was the sound of the world ending.

"*Dad!*"

I tried to run back to the car, to get him out, to save him — but Uncle Ty held me tight, even though he was shaking too.

"I saw exactly how it happened. It was the other driver's fault." Carolyn's voice was adamant as she spoke with whoever was on the line.

Footsteps crunched toward us, and I held my breath, thinking for one insane moment that Mom or Dad had made it out after all.

"Goddamn, these icy roads are a pain in my ass. Everyone all right over here?"

I looked up into the face of Madoc Miller. His steely gray eyes surveyed me, Uncle Ty, Carolyn. They narrowed as he took in the wreck of the car below us.

"Guess not," he said.

TWELVE

I wake up breathless. The nightmare is fresh on my tongue, trying to slither its way down my throat to wrap around my heart. Sadie among the trees; the screeching tires mingling with the shriek of the owl. The explosive *crack* of the world ending; the car rolling over and over and over . . .

I have this dream a lot. It came every night at first, while I was lying in the hospital with my hands in bandages. Sometimes I'd relive it while I was awake. I'd be sitting in class, the slow tick of the clock lulling me into that headspace where it would come blazing back to life, and I'd live through it over and over again. Feel the air torn out of me every time because Mom and Dad were gone.

They've been gone an entire year today.

Dr. Ehrenfeld—my grief counselor—said the nightmares would fade eventually. They have, kind of. I don't get them *every* night now. She also told me it might help if I wrote a journal, like a confession or something. Just get it *out*. But I've never been great with words. So I used my art, as soon as my hands had healed enough to hold a paintbrush. I re-created the scene over and over again, every detail. That's what's inside the pavilion. That's what Dominic and Freya Miller are probably going to home in on for their stupid show. Because I painted Dead-Eyed Sadie too. Just the way I saw her that night, standing among the trees.

Of course I know she wasn't really there. She isn't real.

I know . . .

I scrub a hand over my face, as if I can rub away the images. The feelings.

This is it. I have lived a year without my parents.

I get dressed in my usual all-black, add my funeral coat, and head through to the kitchen. Carolyn is there, and she wraps me in a massive hug as soon as she sees me.

"Is Uncle Ty ready to go to the cemetery?"

I didn't see him or Carolyn last night when I got in after that shitshow with Ford at the manor, but this was always the plan for the anniversary: We'd all go to the cemetery together, lay fresh flowers, maybe go for a walk before school.

Carolyn sighs, finally pulling away. "Sorry, Ava. He's in bed—"

"Hungover?" I snap. "*Today?*"

"Not hungover," Carolyn says. "He's running a fever. Ty was up and down all night, poor guy." Judging by the dark circles under her eyes, he wasn't the only one whose sleep was disturbed. I immediately feel like a turd for assuming the worst. "I'm going to take the day off work to stay home and take care of him. He looks awful."

"Oh. Okay."

"I think it might be better if we go to the cemetery when you get home this afternoon. Hopefully, Ty will be feeling much better by then. What do you say?"

It's not ideal. I wanted to go before school so I wouldn't spend the whole day dreading it. But it's not like I'm going to stomp my foot and demand she goes and drags Uncle Ty out of bed.

"Of course, that's fine," I tell her, and Carolyn smiles gratefully. "Oh—I wanted to wear Mom's apple necklace today, but I couldn't find it in my jewelry box. Did it get packed away in the safe?"

"No, I don't think so . . . unless you put it in there?"

"No," I say, a sick feeling taking hold of my stomach. "Could you . . . would you mind checking for me?"

The safe is in their room, so it's not like I can go in there and see for myself.

Carolyn heads upstairs and returns a minute later with a worried look on her face. "It's not in the safe, and Ty hasn't seen it. Do you think you might've packed it somewhere else for the move?"

I shake my head, mouth gone dry. I've only ever kept it in my jewelry box, but I didn't even think to check it before we moved. I only wear it on important occasions. I haven't actually seen Mom's necklace in weeks. It feels wrong not to wear it today.

"I can help you look for it?" Carolyn offers.

"No, it's okay. I'll do it when I get home."

As I pull up to the junction next to the Pump'N'Go on my way to school, I spot Dominic Miller's flashy-ass Porsche in the front lot.

It's just started snowing—fat, slow flakes too lazy to keep up with gravity. It's forecast to leave us with a few inches, but not get too wild, thank God. I'm so glad we're heading into spring (I know, I know, I should have my goth-girl badge revoked). But soon I won't have to think about icy roads or snow boots or chapped lips.

I linger near the gas station, mulling over that look Dominic gave me as I left the manor last night—like I'd insulted him by asking him to keep the Thorns out of the Dead-Eyed Sadie special. Is he so self-involved that he can't imagine how it would feel to have your family's history dragged on social media?

Well, maybe I should explain it to him.

Just as I slam on the turn signal to pull in behind his car, Freya Miller strides out of the Pump'N'Go and across the lot. She climbs into the driver's seat without even glancing in my direction, and screeches away like she has somewhere to be.

But the Porsche isn't in the lot when I arrive at school. It is hellishly early, so maybe she and Dominic had somewhere else to be first.

The art studio's still locked, the hallways weird and echoey at this time of the morning. I find a quiet corner in the school library where I can spend the next hour trying to work on the comic.

I know the next panel of *Mostly Deadish* needs to explain what the girl is doing in the tower, but I'm still struggling to come up with a storyline that fits. Is she trapped there? Is she some kind of cemetery guard? The only thing that seems solid about it is that first image: her looking out from the tower window, surrounded by all those graves.

I doodle a close-up of the girl in the tower window, except I can't seem to finish her face — the nose and mouth are almost there, but I can't settle on what eyes to give her. For the moment, I leave a blank space where her eyes should be.

"I thought I saw you huddled over here in the corner."

I look up to find Dominic Miller glowering down at me. He looks as impossibly perfect as always, with his finger-tousled hair and chiseled jawline just *slightly* shadowed with stubble. He's close enough that I'm forced to breathe him in. Dominic smells like expensive cologne—just faintly, as if to entice unwary victims to lean in. Someone should tell him eighteen-year-old guys are supposed to smell like Axe-nuked sweat and Pop-Tarts.

His deep green eyes, a little darker than Freya's, appear to be fixed on my sketchbook. I lay my pencil down on it with a snap and an arched eyebrow.

"So, what? Does your family own the school library now as well?"

Dominic closes his eyes briefly, like he's praying for strength.

"I wanted to speak with you . . . about what you said last night. I realize you might've misunderstood what we were doing."

"So you weren't recording an episode about Dead-Eyed Sadie?"

"Well, yes—"

"And you haven't been researching the history of the manor—which my family built—to use in your show?" He purses his lips. "Then no, I don't think I misunderstood at all."

"Look, Ava, I really don't see what the problem is. Yeah, I want to talk about the history of the manor in the show, but we don't have to mention your family by name. And I have absolutely no intention of *dragging* anyone. I'm really only interested in the place because that's where Sadie is usually sighted—near the waterfall."

I chew on that for a second. Still don't like how it tastes. "Why do you have to make a show about Sadie at all? Aren't there other ghosts you can run an exposé on?"

"I've kind of been wanting to feature Dead-Eyed Sadie for a while now," he says, leaning in like he's sharing a secret. "With the stories about her haunting the waterfall and the missing eyes and all that, she's a really interesting figure . . . Besides, we've already filmed a couple of scenes for the episode. Well, you saw one of them last night."

I bristle. "Where else did you film?"

"Only in the orchard." A look of understanding dawns on his face. "If you're worried about us shooting your—graffiti?—in that little stone shack thing in the orchard, you can relax. I've already painted over it."

"Pavilion," I correct him quietly. "Wait—you have?"

"Of course." He waves a hand like he's wafting away a fly, but goes on when he notices my doubtful expression. "I saw you sneaking around out there the night after we moved in, found the can of paint you left inside, and put two and two together. I would've done it anyway, though—you think I'd want to show my dad looking the way you painted him? Surveying the wreck of your parents' car and laughing?"

Dominic shakes his head, as if that image is absurd. But Dominic wasn't there when it happened. Maybe he doesn't want to think about what an evil asshole his father is, but I know. I saw him quite clearly not giving a shit about anything except the scratches on his Hummer.

The crash was officially ruled an accident, contributed to by my mom being distracted by Dad's suspected seizure. But that wasn't why it happened. It was Madoc Miller, driving like an asshole, not caring who he smashed into with his ridiculous tank of a car. But people in this town prefer to whisper about the Thorns being cursed than do anything about a criminal strutting around town. They think the Millers are *glamorous*.

Assholes, all of them.

Although, if Dominic really covered my mural so nobody else would see it, maybe he's not as much of an asshole as I thought. Just, like, ninety-nine percent asshole.

"So that was what I wanted to tell you," Dominic says, wrapping up his little speech. "Or ask you, actually. Why don't you help me with my research, then you can veto anything you'd rather I didn't use for *Haunted Heartland*? Within reason, of course. And maybe you can fill in some of the details I'm missing from Sadie's story."

I'm only half paying attention to this last part because he keeps looking at my sketchbook in the most distracting way, like he's planning on snatching it. "I don't think that's such a great idea."

Dominic continues studying my drawing. I slide it across the table, out of his reach. I still remember the day I saw him and Freya sneering at one of my paintings, shortly after they started at Burden Falls High.

"Was there something else?"

"I've seen that somewhere online," he says.

"Seen what?"

"The girl in the tower."

I purse my lips while I debate how to answer him. Because while it's possible he's seen *Mostly Deadish* online—my portfolio site is set to "public"—it's not exactly something he'd stumble across. Maybe Freya showed it to him, probably with some comment about how "basic" it is.

"These are sketches for my final art project," I say blandly. "I'm drawing a comic."

"So it *was* yours? The digital version I saw?" Dominic leans in, his hands resting on the edge of the desk. He looks weirdly . . . eager? "Incredible."

"Well, I haven't stolen it, if that's what you're implying."

"I'm not." He shakes his head dismissively. "It's based on Sadie, right?"

"Uh, no."

Dominic glances at me dubiously. "But she has no eyes."

"No eyes *yet*," I correct him.

He gets this *huh* look that I've never seen on him before — like genuine interest or something. "You know, I actually had a dream after seeing that one panel. The girl in the tower was there to guard all the zombies in the cemetery, making sure they didn't rise from their graves. But of course they did, so she pulled this lever marked *emergency only*."

He pauses, apparently waiting for a reaction, and I realize I've leaned in while he was speaking like some member of his thirst mob. I sit back, arms folded.

"What happened when she pulled the lever?"

"The tower started to corkscrew down into the ground, like some spinning elevator to the underworld. And, as it descended, all the zombies crawled in through the open windows, and the girl had to fight them off until the tower reached its destination, and she could open the trapdoor in the cellar to let them out."

As he talks, his words morph into images inside my head. I can see it all so clearly — I want to draw it. Now.

"Let them out *where*?"

Dominic shrugs. "The underworld? Hell, maybe? That's when I woke up."

I picture it, but it's not hell my mind goes to.

There's a trapdoor in the cellar at the manor—it leads down to what we used to call "the pit," which was probably used for cold storage back in the day before refrigerators were a thing. It was the one place in the manor I actually found spooky. But now it changes into something more in my brain—into a portal to Dominic's underworld. I could use it as a base . . .

Damn it. Why can't *I* have dreams about my comic? I can't use what Dominic just told me. If whatever storyline I come up with is even vaguely similar to Dominic's, I could get called out for plagiarism.

"So, what really happens?" Dominic asks, sliding into the seat opposite mine. I'm now just sitting in the empty library, having a chat with Dominic Miller, apparently.

"I don't know."

Again, that annoying frown. "Isn't it due in soon?"

"In two weeks," I agree stiffly. "I've been having trouble coming up with the right storyline."

Dominic's quiet for a long moment, and I find myself spinning my pencil between my fingers, mimicking the tower corkscrewing down into the earth. Finally, he says, "Use my idea, if you like it." I say nothing. "*Do* you like it?"

"I can't use your idea for my project. It's against the rules to have outside help."

"Only with the artwork, though, right? Not the story itself?"

I guess he's right about that. I mean, nobody else has to come up with a storyline for their projects. I'm not even going to be graded on that part of it.

"Help me with my Sadie research, and I'll even help you come up with an ending for the comic," Dominic says. The corners of his mouth tick up. If I didn't know better, I'd say he looks excited.

And that's what kicks me back to reality. Because a Miller never does anything nice for a Thorn. And I am *not* helping him dig around in my family history.

"Yeah, that's a no," I tell him. "I'll come up with my own storyline."

I start putting away my art supplies, intending to just get the hell out of the library.

"Come on, Thorn," he coaxes. "I've seen your artwork. I think we could create a brilliant comic together."

"Are you telling me you actually think my artwork is *good*?" I snap, waiting for him to say *as if*, just like he did that day with Freya, looking at my painting outside the art studio. But he doesn't.

"I wouldn't suggest we work together if I didn't think it was good."

I get to my feet, flushed with annoyance. "Why would you want to work with me anyway, *Miller*?"

Dominic isn't fazed by my abrupt tone. The smile still simmers at the corners of his lips. *Why am I looking at his lips?*

"I've always wanted to write a graphic novel," he says. "I just don't have the artistic skills for that side of it, and haven't come across the right partner yet."

I slow-blink. "Why don't you write one with Freya, then?"

For the briefest moment, the smile falters. "It's not Freya's kind of thing."

I'm amazed it's Dominic's kind of thing, honestly. Still . . . "It's not a good idea."

"Why not?"

Seriously? "Because we hate each other."

"*You* might hate *me*," he counters. "I don't have any particular feelings about you either way."

"Freya sure does."

"So? From what I've seen, you dish it out just as hard as she does."

"Look, you . . . you just don't get to own every part of my life, okay?"

"I wasn't the one who bought your house," Dominic says, sounding bored. He gets up from his seat and throws his bag onto his shoulder. "Think about it. I'll be here again after school if you decide you don't want to flunk your art project." With that, he strides out of the library.

The asshole couldn't even let me be the one to walk away first.

THIRTEEN

My annoyance at Dominic's impatient, overconfident tone serves as a pretty good distraction throughout the day. I'm grateful for anything that takes my mind off my parents, even if that thing is Dominic Miller.

Daphne stands with her paintbrush poised above the self-portrait she's working on during last period while I lay out the entire encounter for her. In the portrait, Daphne's disembodied head floats over a sea of blue glass marbles, and there's a ginger cat sleeping in a recess above her left temple. Daphne calls it *Peace of My Mind.* With the warm mix of colors — the browns in her skin, her eyes, her hair, the sun-flare-orange cat, and the tropical-ocean blues and turquoises in the marbles — there really is something oddly peaceful about the painting, despite her decapitation.

"So, what do you think I should do?" I ask her.

"You know why you're asking for my opinion now, don't you?" Daphne says.

"Because it'll save me having to explain it all over text later?"

Daphne shakes her head. "He offered to work with you on your comic this morning. You probably spent all day trying to come up with reasons why it's a bad idea to let him help you when you already *like* his story suggestions. Now that you've exhausted all the flimsy reasons you could come up with, you want me to give you an excuse to say no. But you're already making new panels, right? Just after one conversation with him."

Miss Shannon is covering today's lesson, and she seemed so happy when she saw me making actual progress with my project. Hopefully, she'll take that into account when deciding who gets the spot on the summer art program.

"And if you help him write the Sadie episode of *Haunted Heartland,*" Daphne continues, "you'll get a say in what goes into it, so at least there'll be no nasty surprises."

I frown down at the new panels resentfully. "My reasons for not wanting to work with him aren't 'flimsy.' His dad killed my parents. It's hard to move past that."

"I know." Daphne smiles sympathetically. "But Dominic isn't his dad. And if he can help you . . ."

She doesn't need to slam the point home. I know she's right. If I have any hope of graduating, not to mention winning the place on the summer art program, I'm going to have to get cozy with Dominic Miller.

Dominic isn't in the school library when I get there after the final bell. I was just stopping by to tell him I wouldn't be able to work on the comic today, but it looks like he's already gone off the idea anyway.

Damn it. I'm such an idiot to trust a Miller—even for a second.

My car is almost the last one in the lot when I wheelspin out of there, forgetting in my bad mood about the fresh layer of snow. Within a minute, all the windows fog and I signal to pull onto the side of the road while I wait for them to clear. As Bessie rumbles to a stop, my headlights land on someone sitting on a tree stump up ahead. There are tall fir trees all along this section of road, and it's already that fuzzy gray twilight time of day. Whoever's out there is risking hypothermia.

Probably an ax murderer, I tell myself as I open my car door, *waiting to lure some well-meaning dipshit to a gory death.*

RIP me, I guess.

When I get out of the car, I see the person is hunched over, their face in their hands.

"Uh, hi . . . are you okay?"

The hardening top layer of snow crunches beneath my boots as I walk toward the figure. Whoever it is mutters something, too low for me to make out.

"What?"

"LIGHTS OUT."

The bellow startles me, and I almost run back to the car. But then I recognize the voice. "Dominic? What the hell are you doing out here?"

He doesn't answer, but I gather from the way he's covering his eyes that the headlights are bothering him. I hurry to turn them off. Dominic slowly raises his head. He looks gray, and his eyes are weird. Kind of spaced out.

"What's wrong with you? And why are you sitting out here?"

"Migraine," is all he says. His teeth chatter, and his voice is raspier than I've ever heard it. Serves him right for yelling at me.

"Get in the car," I tell him. "I'll give you a ride home."

The windows have defogged by the time we get in. With shaking hands, he puts his seat belt on. I turn up the heater as high as it'll go.

"How long were you out there?" I ask as I pull back onto the road. Whenever a car approaches in the other lane, Dominic shuts his eyes like the oncoming headlights cause him physical pain.

"Not sure," he says after a beat. I grimace, but say nothing. It's literally freezing outside. He could've died.

"Why didn't you call someone to come get you?"

"Couldn't see my phone."

"Didn't you tell anyone you were leaving school? Why didn't you —"

"Quiet," he says, and it's almost a groan. "*Please.*"

The only reason I do as he asks is because he does genuinely seem to be in pain. I should find it delightful to see a Miller in this state, but apparently I'm not nearly as bloody-minded as my ancestors would've liked.

By the time we reach the manor gate, the sky above is a heavy slate gray, loaded for an even heavier snowfall tonight. *Lying weather forecast.*

"Okay, so . . ."

I wait for Dominic to get out of the car, but instead he pulls the gate remote from his bag and the manor gates swing open. They still bear my family's name. I guess Madoc hasn't had time to have new ones made yet. Ugh, will he actually rename it Miller Manor?

When Dominic still doesn't move, I realize I'm going to have to break the silence again.

"I don't think it's a good idea to drive you all the way in," I say. "Your parents will freak, right?"

"They're out of town," he says, and I think his voice sounds a little stronger now. His skin is still a nasty shade of gray, though. "Freya too. There's no one home."

I guess that explains why none of them came looking for him.

Slowly, I turn into the driveway. My tires crunch hesitantly up the gravel path.

The urge to turn the car around and floor it hits me like a brick. I don't belong here anymore. It's like finding a favorite sweater at the back of the closet, only to discover it no longer fits.

It doesn't help that the Millers have painted the manor what I can only describe as a muted pistachio.

"Seriously?" I mutter.

"What?"

"Nothing. Hey, how come you didn't have your car at school?" I ask, more to distract myself than because I really want to know.

"Freya borrowed it. She's got a catalog modeling job in . . ." Dominic's voice trails off. At first, I think the vile green of the manor has caused his migraine to flare up again, but he's frowning at something up ahead. Then I see it too—Dominic's shiny black Porsche, sitting in front of the manor like it belongs there. "I guess she made other travel plans."

Maybe with the secret boyfriend you don't know about, I think. Wasn't it for today she arranged her sketchy hookup with whoever was on the other end of that call?

But that's none of my business, and I don't want to explain how I know about it.

I eye the manor warily, half expecting to see Freya's nasty face scowling down at me from one of the windows, but the house is dark. It doesn't look like anyone's home.

"Are you gonna be okay?"

Dominic nods briskly and opens the door. A blast of freezing air rushes in.

"The worst is over. I just need to sleep it off. Thanks, Thorn." Dominic gets out, but doesn't close the door. "And I'm sorry I didn't tell you I couldn't meet you at the library after school. I meant to text, then realized I don't have your number. That might be useful if we're going to be working on this graphic novel together. And on my Sadie research, of course."

"I never said yes to any of that," I point out, but he just smirks.

"When I was at the library the other day, I found a bunch of articles about Sadie, and I guess two of your ancestors . . . Would you like to see?"

I sigh. "Yes."

"Here. Put your number in." He passes me his phone. For the briefest second, I wonder if it holds the video of me acting like a turd last night on the bridge — I'm tempted to check, see if he's shared it with anyone else. But I don't. I just input my number and hand it to him. He snorts. "Hello, Pomona."

"It's my middle name. *Avalon Pomona*." Both names basically mean "apple." My parents agreed on wanting an "apple" name because of the whole Thorn's Blood Apple Sour thing, but couldn't choose between the two. So I got both. (Cue my dad making "*fruit of my loins*" jokes for the next almost-seventeen years.) "I figured you wouldn't want anyone to see my name flashing up on your screen."

"My folks might find it a little weird, but they'd hardly be mad about it." He frowns, seeing my highly dubious expression. "After everything that's happened, they just want to move on. Freya, though . . ." Dominic snorts, and I don't need him to finish that thought.

But I'm pretty sure he's wrong about his parents' reaction —

after all, if Madoc wanted to bury the hatchet, he's had a whole goddamn year to reach out to me and Uncle Ty.

Dominic WhatsApps me a bunch of images of what look like old newspaper articles. "Now you have my number too. I don't have a middle name, though. What will you save mine as?"

"I'm sure I can come up with something suitable."

I wait while Dominic heads inside the manor. My windows are fogged again, so I have to hang around while they slowly—*soooo* slowly—clear.

My eyes wander in the direction of the orchard. The vague, blurry shapes of the trees stand out darkly against the snow-heavy sky.

Dominic said he painted over the mural, and I guess I believe him. But it wouldn't hurt to just check, would it?

I'm striding along the gravel path before I can talk myself out of it.

Even though the blood-apple trees are dead, and would normally barely be in bud now anyway, it seems as though the bare branches have laced together like twisted fingers, braced to keep me out of the orchard now that I have no claim on it. Jaw set, I force my way through them toward the pavilion. There are faint red stains on the earth in some spots—lingering traces from where old windfalls have bled to death. I smell them, like rotting corpses.

I check the time on my phone, then pocket it. I'll be home late, but only a little. As long as I go straight back to the cottage after this, Uncle Ty and Carolyn won't ask any questions, and we can all just head out to the cemetery as planned.

Something skitters in the branches above me, setting my

heart racing. I scan the trees, searching for a bird, or maybe a squirrel. I don't see one.

I can feel something, though. It's like there's someone standing just behind the next tree, watching from the shadows. That presence I sometimes used to imagine feeling at the manor but magnified, as if it — *she* — knows I'm an outsider now.

No. I'm being ridiculous.

I'm still a Bloody Thorn. And there's no goddamn ghost watching me.

I move slowly, as quietly as I can, checking in all directions in spite of myself. I don't see anyone. There's nobody here but me. I keep telling myself that, hoping it'll start to feel true.

As I get within reach of the pavilion, a bird lets out a shrill sound, and I trip on a tree root and land hard on all fours in the open doorway. My gloved right hand is buried in a pile of leaves that must've blown in. As I shake them off, I see my phone lying on the stone floor, a web of cracks across the screen.

"Stupid fucking bird!" I yell up at it, though I have a feeling it's probably gone by now.

I have no idea what a new screen will cost. However much it is, I can't afford it. I shove the phone angrily in my coat pocket and get up, dusting dirt off my knees. Then I glance across the pavilion.

Sitting on the stone bench against the black-painted wall facing me is Freya, wearing her freaky Dead-Eyed Sadie contacts again. I scream, clutching at my chest like some damsel from a black-and-white movie. "Jesus, Freya! What is *wrong* with you?"

She doesn't answer. Doesn't move. Just sits there, staring at me with her dead eyes, her pale hands in her lap like she's waiting for something.

Her dead . . .

"Freya?" I croak. Because she isn't moving *at all*. As my vision adjusts to the dimness of the pavilion, I notice her eyes don't actually look like contacts.

Her eyes don't look like eyes.

They're gaping holes.

I scream.

FOURTEEN

There are moments when you lose the ability to process time. It happened during the crash that killed my parents, so I know what I'm talking about. It's happening again now.

I mean, I see her. Sitting there on the stone bench, with bloody gouges where her eyes ought to be. Hands tucked in her lap. Body slumped slightly to one side against the wall of the pavilion. The wall Dominic painted black for me. It makes Freya's red hair all the more dazzling, though there are bloody tangles in it.

I reach out slowly, hand shaking as it nears her face. She doesn't look like herself anymore. The inhumanity of what's been done to her plants explanations in my back-brain—it's probably just a mannequin, a prop from one of their shows. She's playing another trick on me, hahahahahaha.

As my hand hovers next to her, I notice red marks on the bench. Smears on the rough stone. Handprints, I think. Some are big, but if I hold my hand *just so,* it pretty much covers one of them exactly. I slide off my glove. Yes, an almost perfect match.

I brush my fingertips across her blood-soaked cheek. I've never felt anything so cold.

"Ava? Are you all right? I heard screaming—"

Time snaps back, capturing Dominic in its wicked recoil. He looks past me. Rushes to his sister. I can only watch as he searches for a pulse, finds none. Talks to her, sharp and frantic. Starts CPR. I want to tell him to stop because I can see it's too late. I don't, though. He wouldn't want to hear it, and I don't want to be the one to shatter that hope.

"Dominic," I murmur. I don't think he's heard me until he lifts his head. His face is smeared with blood now too. He thrusts his phone at me.

"Get an ambulance!"

I nod, but he's already gone back to work on his sister's corpse.

"Miss Thorn? Ava?"

I blink up at the cops sitting across the table from me. The one asking the questions — Detective Holden, I think he said — is a wiry white guy in his mid-fifties. He's wearing a wrinkled gray suit with his tie hanging loose. I guess this was supposed to be the end of his workday. The other cop, Officer Cordell, is a younger Black woman in uniform. She hasn't said much, but she nods at me whenever she catches me looking her way. I'm not sure if it's meant to be reassuring, or just letting me know she's watching me.

"Sorry, what was the question?"

I've been here a while now . . . an hour? Two? It's a square, windowless room painted a shade of gray that acts like a sponge to both light and a person's will to live.

They took my fingerprints when I got here. Swabbed under my nails. Removed my shoes and put them in plastic bags "just to rule them out." So I'm sitting in an old pair of Uncle Ty's sneakers he had in his trunk, hugging myself, because I can't seem to stop shaking, even though it's warm in the police station.

I'm surprised he didn't just ask Carolyn to step in, but maybe he felt like he needed to come. Either way, I'm so glad he's here.

Uncle Ty sits beside me, looking washed out and sweaty from his fever. He was still in bed when the cops called him to come meet me at the station.

"I'm sorry to keep having to go over this," Holden says. "We just need to make sure we get all the details while they're fresh in your mind, you understand. So, can you tell me why you went to the pavilion?"

I glance at Uncle Ty, but he's staring at the far wall like a zombie. In the harsh lighting, he actually looks a little green.

"When I lived at the manor, I painted the inside of the pavilion — they were like comic panels, but they told our family history. It was supposed to be a kind of memorial after my parents died. I meant to paint over it before we moved, but I didn't get the chance."

Detective Holden nods. "So that's why you went there?"

"Um, no. Not exactly." I throw another glance at Uncle Ty. "Dominic told me he'd already done it, and I . . . just wanted to make sure."

"So, after you found Miss Miller's body, what happened then? Did you move her? Touch anything else inside the pavilion?"

I frown, trying to think. But the images come spiraling back on their own anyway. Me screaming for what felt like eons. Freya's empty eye sockets seeming to scream back at me. Then Dominic . . . I remember him appearing in the doorway, asking what was wrong. Looking past me.

His sister sitting against the cold black wall.

"I . . . no. I touched her face because I wasn't sure . . ." That's a lie. I knew she was dead, but it didn't seem possible. "Dominic came in then."

"So, between the time you arrived at the house with Dominic and when you found the body, how long would you say that was?"

I shrug. "Not long. Less than five minutes, I think."

Officer Cordell makes a note, but I can't see what it says. Maybe to check whether I was actually out there on my own long enough to murder Freya and carve out her eyes.

"What happened then?" Detective Holden says gently.

"Dominic tried to resuscitate her, but I could tell she was gone."

The detective taps the end of his pen against his chin. "How could you tell?"

She was too cold, I want to tell him. *Too pale, her lips grayish blue beneath the streaks of red.*

"I was with my parents when they died," I say instead. "I know what dead looks like."

A hand grips my arm. Uncle Ty's still facing the detective. It probably looks like a comforting gesture, but there's a tightness around his mouth I instinctively know means I should shut up.

"Are Mr. and Mrs. Miller back in town yet?" I ask. I don't care that they're the Millers right now; I just hate the idea that Dominic is alone. If Uncle Ty and Carolyn hadn't been there for me last year, I know I'd have fallen apart completely. I don't want that for Dominic. Or anyone.

"Should be arriving any time now," Detective Holden says with a nod. "You know them — Mr. and Mrs. Miller?"

I don't need a grip on my arm to tell me to tread carefully here. "Not well," I say. "But, you know, they bought the manor . . ." I shrug, like that explains the entirety of our family's connection with theirs.

"But you knew Freya from school, right?"

"We're in art class together."

"Not friends, though?" the detective presses.

"It's getting late," Uncle Ty says, his voice gruff. "I think it's time I got my niece home."

But Holden says, "Just one last question, if you don't mind, Ava." He continues without waiting for Uncle Ty's go-ahead, or mine. "Can you think of anyone who might've wanted to hurt Freya?"

A hard, cold lump forms in my chest.

Apart from me?

"I don't think so," I say.

"How about anyone she fell out with recently? A friend, boy-friend, girlfriend . . . ?" Holden splays his hands, inviting me to fill them with leads.

I'm about to say I can't think of anyone, but then I remember the night after we moved out of the manor—unintentionally eavesdropping on her call.

"She had a . . . well, a boyfriend, I think. I heard her talking to him on the phone Sunday night. I have no idea if they fell out or anything, but I don't think it's common knowledge that Freya is . . . *was* . . . even seeing anyone."

In my peripheral vision, I see Officer Cordell write something else in her notebook, but it's Holden who asks, "Where were you when you overheard her?"

"At the manor. Or around the property, anyway. I'd gone to . . . look for my friend, Ford."

He pauses, then says, "Can you remember what time this call was?"

"Around eight thirty?" I can't actually remember, but I left the cottage right after dinner, so this seems like it's in the right ballpark. "I think she was arranging to meet him today."

"Did you catch a name?"

"I'm sure Ava would've mentioned that, Detective," Uncle Ty says wearily. "And that was a lot more than just one question."

Holden smiles, but it's a put-upon smile. "Of course. But we may have some follow-up questions for Ava as our investigation progresses. You aren't planning any trips out of town in the next few weeks, are you, Mr. Thorn?"

"No, Detective," Uncle Ty says. "We're not going anywhere."

It's late by the time we get back from the police station. The cottage windows are all dark.

Like dead eyes . . .

Uncle Ty's about to get out of the car when I stop him.

"Do you think Freya's death has something to do with that girl who washed up the other day?" I ask.

"I dunno. I guess the cops'll figure out if it was connected, right?"

"But that girl drowned—it was an accident. What happened to Freya was no accident. So they can't really be connected, can they?"

He exhales slowly through his nose before answering. "It kinda makes you wonder, though . . ."

"What?"

"If maybe there's something to those stories about Dead-Eyed Sadie. Maybe she wants her eyes back."

"Are you kidding?"

I expect him to break into a grin, despite the fact that now is *not* the time for joking around. But he just stares back at me for a long moment, then shrugs and turns away.

It's not that I've somehow missed the connection up until now — gouged eyes are hard to miss. But Uncle Ty doesn't believe in Sadie. I think back to when I was little and he used to tease me with stories about the ghost-witch who was out to get me — it was obvious then that he didn't think she was real.

Wasn't it?

I mean, unless all his dicking around was to hide the fact that he was scared . . .

But, even if some tiny part of it's true, the stories my mom told me growing up painted Sadie as nothing but a warning: Take care, something bad's coming. *She* was never the "something bad." At least, I didn't think so.

"Are you okay, kiddo?" Uncle Ty says.

I nod slowly. "Are you? You look awful. Sorry for having to drag you out when you're so sick — "

"That doesn't matter. I mean are you *okay* okay? I know the whole dead body situation isn't exactly new to you, but that's a reason in itself for you to be feeling even more . . . I dunno . . . screwed up over it."

I take a deep breath, and let it out slowly, just like Dr. Ehrenfeld used to tell me to do. "I'm as okay as I can reasonably expect to be, Uncle Ty. If that changes, I'll let you know."

"Okay then." He nods. "So, why were you really at the manor? Is there something going on between you and the Miller boy?"

I can tell he's trying not to put any emotion at all behind the question, but I still hear the hard edge to it. Thorns do not *hang out* with Millers.

"Of course not. It's like I told the cops—I saw him sitting at the side of the road. I couldn't just leave him there to freeze to death, could I?"

Uncle Ty exhales slowly through his nose. "No. Of course you couldn't."

When I check my phone, there are a ton of messages and missed calls. But that's not what catches me by surprise. It's that the screen is perfectly intact—no cracks at all, except a tiny one in the corner that's been there for ages. I was sure it was smashed to hell when I picked it up in the pavilion, right before I saw . . . yeah.

It must've just been a trick of the light. Maybe a shadow from the spindly branches of the apple trees.

Most of the messages are from Daphne and Carla, of course. Daphne's dad was the first cop to arrive at the manor earlier, so it's no surprise she and Carla already know about Freya.

I reply to the latest message.

Ava: Just got home.

Daphne: You OK?

Carla: What the hell happened?! This is crazy!!!

I type and delete a response at least ten times before I give up. I just don't know what to say about it all.

Ava: Really tired. Going to bed. Talk to you both tomorrow.

I toss my phone on the nightstand, then head for the shower. No way can I sleep without showering. Even though there's no reason for it—I mean, I barely touched Freya's face with my fingertips—it feels like there's a layer of something coating my skin. Not dirt or sweat, but *death*. I know I probably can't wash it away, but I still have to try.

Once I'm wearing my coziest pj's, I head back to my room, not bothering to turn on the light. But, as I go to draw the curtains, lightning illuminates the river outside. In that white flash, I see Freya sitting propped against the black wall of the pavilion, two dark hollows in her pale face where her eyes should be.

Just like Sadie.

I blink away the image, trying to scrub the thought from my brain, and my phone buzzes suddenly.

"Damn it, Ford!" I say as his name pops up.

Ford: Still awake?

Instead of texting, I call him. He picks up after four rings.

"You doing okay? I heard about Freya."

I brace to say I'm fine, paint on a smile, but I just can't. "No. Not really . . . Are you?"

I hate that I'm reluctant to ask him a simple thing like *Are you okay?* because now is not the time to be petty. So what if Ford spent time with the Miller twins over the last few days? It's not like that's a crime or anything. And finding out Freya's dead has to be weird for him too.

"Freaking out, to be honest. What the hell happened?"

"I . . . Can we not talk about this tonight? I already spent hours with the cops, and I'm really tired, so — "

"Have the cops arrested anyone yet? Does Daphne know? She always tells you this stuff right away, doesn't she?"

I sigh. "I don't think they've arrested anyone yet. It's only been a few hours."

There's a pause while he loads up another question. "Who do you think killed her?"

"I have no idea."

"None at all?"

I sit on my bed, letting my head fall against the wall. Then I think about how Freya looked, and sit up straight. "Who do *you* think it was?"

"Dunno. If you'd asked me yesterday who wanted Freya dead most in the world, I'd have said you."

"That's not funny."

"Sorry. But it's true." I can picture him shrugging, like he just said the most obvious thing in the world. Is that what everyone at school will think too? That I'm a *suspect*?

Is that what the cops will think once they find out about all the history between my family and the Millers? And about the fact that Freya and I *hated* each other?

Because I've seen enough cop shows to know they'll dig around to see who Freya's enemies were, and Ford's right: I'm at the top of that list.

FIFTEEN

A twig snaps beneath my foot, but the white-faced owl I can clearly see sitting up in the branches of the apple tree doesn't move. Doesn't make a sound. I keep moving forward, into the orchard. It just sits there, watching.

I have to get to the pavilion. It's important that I get there. Something bad will happen if I don't . . .

The branches part ahead of me, the path clearing. I step through. The pavilion is mere feet away now, but the open doorway is impenetrably dark.

For the first time, I hesitate. Will something bad happen . . . or has it already happened?

I don't have time to shake the answer loose. I'm drawn forward as though the darkness has grown arms and is reaching for me.

Just as I cross the threshold, my foot catches on something and I fall forward into . . . my parents' car?

I look around me, my head filled with that ringing silence that says something has just gone terribly wrong.

"Mom? Dad?"

They don't answer. Then I see why. My parents aren't strapped upside down in their seats. They aren't here at all.

But someone is.

Her red hair cascading down to the upturned roof of the car, Freya gapes at me with hollowed-out eyes. She's so pale. So still. And then she moves.

Her mouth yawns wider, then snaps shut. Open, closed. Open . . .

Now I'm the one who's still. I can't move. I can only watch her jaw hinge wide open, then closed. It's like I'm hypnotized.

Something trickles from Freya's eye socket, cutting a thin line down her forehead. Blood, I think. Except it isn't blood, not really. A thick black liquid drips from her eye sockets and into the lengths of her hair.

Drip, drip, drip.

A stream at first, but then more. A river. A waterfall of darkness covering her hair, turning it black.

And the ringing in my head gets louder, takes form. A voice. Her voice, except it isn't Freya's voice. Because she isn't Freya anymore.

She's Sadie. And she's calling to me, with a long-dead, rasping voice.

"*We all have to crawl we all have to crawl we all have to crawl we all have to crawl we all have to crawl we all have to crawl we all have to crawl we all have to crawl WE ALL HAVE TO CRAWL . . .*"

Sadie drags herself free of the belt holding her, clawing a path toward me through the carpet of broken glass. She's coming for me. Reaching for me.

An owl's shriek cuts through her mantra, unfreezing my limbs.

I jolt awake, breath coming hard and fast in the dark. I look around, lost for a second, but then my room in the mill takes shape. The little round window. My desk. My bed.

Lighting up my phone, I see it's a little after one a.m.

Gradually, my heart stops thundering quite so hard against my rib cage—even when another owl screech echoes from the loft above me.

I hear the whispers from the moment I walk into school. Everyone's talking about the same thing.

". . . murdered . . ."

". . . eyes *gouged* . . ."

". . . Sadie . . . ?"

". . . *Sadie* . . . ?"

". . . *SADIE* . . . ?"

There's even a shrine at Freya's locker. Someone's set a couple of framed photos of her next to a silver skull ornament, with a few of those fake, flickery tea light candles dotted around. At the back is a vase of deep purple calla lilies, and above it, across the locker itself, someone's written *R.I.P. FREYA* in what's supposed to look like blood, but I'm guessing is actually red nail polish.

Principal Gower calls a special assembly to tell the whole school about Freya. She shouldn't have bothered. Everyone already knows.

I lean back in my seat, trying to steady my breathing. I feel like I'm going to cry or throw up, but I can't. Not here. Especially not after Uncle Ty's stern words over breakfast when I tried to wheedle a day off school.

"You have to face them head-on, Ava. That's what a Thorn does."

It feels weird hearing Uncle Ty give me the same lecture my dad used to give him. I guess that's one thing we can still hand down in our family.

Principal Gower stays vague on the details of Freya's death.

"Gone . . . so unexpected . . . a tragic loss . . ."

She offers sympathetic frowns and counseling to any students who are finding it hard to deal with the news. A lot of the faces around me are red-eyed and puffy by now. I don't think half of them even knew Freya personally, except from her stupid *Haunted Heartland* videos. And that raises another question: When are the media going to show up? Because, much as I've always rolled my eyes about it, Freya was kind of a celebrity. Her death must at least be regional-newsworthy, if not national.

I swallow a mouthful of sour spit. I hated Freya, and I won't lie about that just because she's dead. But I still think it's gross that her death is going to become some kind of circus.

"My thoughts and prayers go out to Freya's family," the principal continues, "especially her brother, Dominic — as I'm sure all of yours do too."

Dominic. I wonder how he's handling it all. Okay, I have a rough idea of how he's handling it — this isn't entirely alien territory for me. Maybe that's why I feel like I should . . . I don't know . . . reach out or something? Would that be weird?

I doodle distractedly in my notebook, letting the principal's words become a sound-blur. It's only when Carla nudges me with her elbow, sending a line of ink scratching across the page, that I see what I've been drawing: a face with no eyes, stretched into an inhuman scream.

A face that looks a lot like Freya.

Or like Sadie?

I close the notebook.

✳ ✳ ✳

After we file out of the assembly hall, it seems like everyone around me moves at double speed, eyes sparkling. Enjoying the gossip. I mean, of course they are. This is Burden Falls High. They'd roll around and make snow angels out of it if they could.

And everyone's making the same connection Uncle Ty did to Sadie. Two dead girls, both with missing eyes.

Daphne and Carla walk on either side of me along the hallway, keeping a prickly barrier between me and all the assholes who suddenly want to make not-so-idle conversation with me. Because it somehow got out that I was the one who found Freya's body. I know it wasn't Carla or Daphne who let that slither out among the gen pop, which really means it can only have been Ford. But I haven't asked him; I don't really have the energy to be mad right now.

Daphne sighs as we clear the throng and head for the lockers. "Locusts."

"Daph, did your dad tell you if they've figured out what happened? I mean . . . who did it?"

I catch Daphne twisting her necklace. It's her favorite—a long chain with a mosaic pendant she made using pieces of smashed pottery. The way she's worrying at it, I'm amazed it doesn't snap. But it reminds me that I still haven't found Mom's necklace. I wasn't exactly in a state to look for it last night.

Guilt floods through me: I didn't visit my parents at the cemetery. I let the anniversary of their deaths go completely unmarked.

"He hasn't said anything," Daphne says. "It's too early in the investigation. But I really don't think it's connected to Claire Palmer." She leans in secretively. "Apparently, she hadn't lost her eyes at all—that was just Mateo spinning BS. They'd only gone milky with her being in the water so long, but they were totally intact, not like Freya's. Still, it's super weird to have two girls turn up dead, isn't it? Even if Claire *wasn't* connected to Freya, *Freya's* death had to be connected with *Sadie,* right? I mean, the missing eyes . . ."

I shudder, picturing Freya in spite of myself. Starkly pale against the black wall with her bright red hair, and two dark voids where her eyes ought to have been.

"Do you really think . . ." I let the question hang unspoken. Because it's not possible that a ghost is really out murdering people, is it? Even if it feels like there's *something* not quite right — not quite natural — about this whole thing.

But if Sadie *is* real . . .

Maybe it's weird, especially now, but I feel oddly protective of Sadie. She was *our* ghost, handed down through the Thorn family like another wing of the manor. I remember what Mom told me after Grandpa's funeral:

"Her appearance is a warning that danger's on the way. But she's harmless enough . . ."

Carla gives an amused huff, dragging me back to the present. "Last year Jenna Calloway ran into school with her eyes all streaming and bloodshot, saying Sadie attacked her in the woods near Copper Bell Dam, and what did that turn out to be?" She pauses for effect. "Allergies."

"I don't think allergies killed Freya," I reply faintly.

"My point is: Neither did a ghost," Carla counters. "Besides, Claire Palmer definitely drowned. And I'm betting Freya didn't, seeing as she was in a fucking orchard. Until we find out *how* she died, there's really no point speculating."

She has a point. I know Freya probably didn't *die* from having her eyes torn out — as shudderingly gross as that is — but I didn't see any other obvious injuries on her. She was just . . . dead.

From unnatural causes?

Carla looks around at the mostly empty hallway and gives a frustrated sigh. "I'd better get to class. Catch you both later, okay?"

She goes over to where her AP chem friends are waiting. They swarm around her like nerdy little vampires, no doubt trying to leech the gory details out of her. When I turn back to Daphne, she's twisting the chain of her necklace again. "Dad told me he wants to ask you a few more questions, when you're up to it."

"More questions? Why? I already gave the cops a statement." I don't know anything else. But then I remember what Ford said about me being top of the list of people who hated Freya, and I wonder if Detective Holden has been building up a profile of me as some eye-gouging killer. I have a sudden sweat-summoning vision of him striding into class and dragging me out while everyone whispers.

As if reading my thoughts, Daphne shakes her head. "They've probably just narrowed down the time of death," she says, like her dad investigating a murder is something that happens all the time. Or ever. "They'll have to start gathering alibis, and they always begin with whoever found the body."

Because whoever found the body is usually the prime suspect. Even *I* know that.

We reach my locker to find a bunch of people kind of milling around it. I know immediately there's something going on even before I see it: an evil eye, scratched deep into the paint of my locker door. Just like the one at Copper Bell Dam; the ones around my window in the cottage; the ones in a hundred other places in this town.

"Do you think Sadie's coming for her next?" someone whispers behind me. I whip around. The idling gawkers shuffle a little, but don't scatter.

Jaw tight, I stare right back. "What?"

Some of them squirm and start to edge away. But others stay put—like Mateo Medel and Casper Jones.

Mateo looks like crap. His eyes are bloodshot, and he looks like he slept in his clothes. Next to him, Casper is checking his phone.

Or maybe not just checking it. "Are you recording me, Casper?"

"What?" He looks up, frowning, and I can immediately tell I was wrong.

I point to my locker. "Who did this?"

"How the hell would we know?" Mateo answers instead, voice hoarse. He pushes past a couple sophomores to get right in my face. "But it looks like someone's got their eye on you, Thorn. Can't say I blame them. Pretty convenient, wasn't it, that you happened to go look in the pavilion?"

I don't budge an inch, despite the fact that my mouth is bone dry and I'm finding it very hard to breathe evenly. Not so much because Mateo's looming over me, but because I can still see her. Still see the blood. Still taste the metallic, appley tang on the air.

"I didn't kill Freya." I'm surprised by how steady my voice is. Maybe there's some Thorn in me after all.

Mateo makes a skeptical sound in his throat and steps back enough for me to see that Casper's still frowning at me.

"Mateo, let's go," he says. "The cops'll figure out who did it soon enough."

SIXTEEN

Bloody Thorn or not, I've had enough of all the whispering by lunchtime. It's become a constant hiss around me: *Sadie, Sadie, SSSSSadie!*

My mind keeps wandering back to finding Freya yesterday, how she seemed to be staring at me through her empty eye sockets.

Dead-eyed . . .

Daphne and Carla are both waiting at my locker when I get there. One of them (definitely Daphne) has covered the evil eye with a colorful mandala sticker.

"Where have you been? Have you checked your phone?"

I frown at Carla's stressy tone, entirely not in the mood for it. Then I notice that even Daphne looks on edge. "Why?"

"Have you seen Ford today?" Daphne asks.

I haven't seen him at all, which is weird. His locker is right next to mine, after all.

Daphne and Carla watch me with matching grim expressions, and my heart plunges through the soles of my boots.

"Oh God, no . . . Has something happened to him?"

"No," Carla cuts in. "But I'm pretty sure something'll happen to him when you find out what he's done."

"Will one of you just tell me what this is about?"

Instead of answering, Daphne thrusts her phone at me. "Watch this."

I see a video thumbnail showing a glimpse of blood-red hair. "Is that Freya?"

Carla makes an affirmative sound, and Daphne adds, "It was her last Insta Story. Someone screencapped it, and now it's being shared everywhere."

Although the last thing I want to look at is a video of the girl whose body I found just twenty-four hours ago, I hit play.

"*Hey, friends.*" For a second, I think I might throw up. Hearing her voice, which yesterday would've seemed so normal, now feels like I'm trespassing somewhere I have no right to be. "*Just giving you all a heads-up that you're gonna want to watch the next episode of* Haunted Heartland *reeeeeal close because there's a huge shock coming your way . . . Also, not entirely unconnected, I want to intro my new buddy Ford, who's gonna be making an appearance in the new episode! Okay, so technically Ford is in the bathroom right now, but I'm here hanging out in his room, so what better way to get to know him than by poking through his stuff, am I right?*"

This must've been posted the night before she died. Onscreen, Freya is busy rifling through Ford's underwear drawer, which I could honestly live without seeing, even knocking the bottoms of the drawers in case they have hidden compartments. Then she moves on to his closet. Freya pulls a phone out of her pocket and holds it to her ear.

"*Uh, hi, is that the police?*" she says. "*Yeah, I need to report a fashion crime . . .*"

"Why are you showing me this?" I ask. Daphne shakes her head.

"Just keep watching," Carla says, her mouth drawn in a straight line.

Next Freya moves on to check under Ford's bed. A vintage 1980s skin mag appears (surprising choice, honestly) and then Freya utters an "*AHA!*" as she pulls out a small black box.

A box I recognize immediately.

"What . . ." My question is left hanging as Freya opens the box and pulls out a necklace. One with a distinctive red apple pendant.

My grip tightens on Daphne's phone, fingertips bloodless.

"*Oooh, look! I think I just found a late birthday present. What do you think, friends? Isn't it pretty?*"

Freya holds the pendant up to her throat.

My mother's necklace. The one my dad gave her. And the last gift either of them gave to me. What the hell was it doing under Ford's bed?

Freya preens for the camera, making kissy faces as she models my necklace, then dangles it above her open mouth as though she might swallow it. If I could reach through the screen, I'm not sure whether I'd snatch it back or throttle her with it. And I don't care how messed up that is right now.

"Ava?" Daphne's voice cuts through the white noise in my head.

I tear my eyes from the video, where Freya is now giggling as she shoves the jewelry box back under Ford's bed at the sound of his approaching footsteps.

"What?"

Then I look past Daphne along the hallway. Ford is coming toward us, laughing with a couple of his drama-club friends.

"You've got this weird, scary look on your face," Carla says. "Are you . . . oh." Her gaze follows the same path as mine.

Ford must feel something burning his skin. His smile drops, and his eyes meet mine.

"Tell me," I say, voice low and seething, "why Freya Miller found my mom's necklace under your bed."

I turn the video to face him, but Ford barely glances at it. His face has gone sickly pale. He knows exactly what I'm talking about. It's no mistake or misunderstanding.

My best friend in the world stole my dead mom's necklace from me. For all I know, he really was planning on giving it to Freya.

I can't breathe.

"Let me explain," Ford says.

I turn on my heel and slam back through the door to the parking lot.

If Ford's mom is home, I can just take back my necklace. That's the plan, such as it is.

I have to crawl along the road to Ford's house, thanks to the snow and the millions of cop cars dotted around town.

A girl was murdered here yesterday—of course the cops are patrolling.

I'm only surprised the media haven't rushed in yet. Hot on the heels of that thought, I spot a news van coming toward me, heading in the direction of the school.

There's no answer when I call at Ford's house, and his mom's car is gone. What now? I mean, I'll make Ford give back the necklace, obviously. But there's no way I'm going back to school, and I can't go home to the cottage because Carolyn has the afternoon off and will ask me questions I don't want to answer.

There's really only one thing I want to do right now. I head to the cemetery to see my parents. A really harsh part of me wants to blame my no-show yesterday on the Millers, like I usually would. But Dominic couldn't help getting a migraine. Freya couldn't help being dead. And Uncle Ty was still too sick to go to school today, so I guess I should just do this solo.

I park in the cemetery lot. Crooked iron gates mark the way in, and they creak as I open them. It's a squawk so birdlike, I look up at the surrounding trees, expecting to find an owl peering back at me.

All day I've had that sense of being watched, and it's followed me here. Or it was waiting for me, maybe. I head down the path toward the mausoleum. My feet crunch on frosty gravel. The sound makes me feel even more exposed somehow.

I'm just jittery. Who wouldn't be after finding a dead body, right?

Our family mausoleum is one of only a handful in the cemetery, set way back in the oldest section. Ancient, gnarled yew trees lean down over it like enormous spidery guardians.

My gaze lands on one of the more recent gravestones as I pass. The engraved lettering is relatively fresh, still painted gold: EDNA MILLER, AGED 88 YEARS. Madoc Miller's mother. Dominic and Freya's grandmother. I remember Mrs. Miller. She lived in one of the cottages not far from where I live now. She was a tall, wiry woman who always seemed to be in a hurry, and her gaze never failed to turn ice-cold whenever she saw me or my parents. Or anyone with the last name Thorn, I guess.

She was a math teacher years ago. The bane of Uncle Ty's middle-school existence, according to him, and more than happy to continue the bad blood between the Millers and the Thorns by trying to flunk him out of her class. Of course, that was around the time Dad, chair of the town conservation society, persuaded local officials to refuse Madoc and Lucille the filming permits they wanted to set up their business, more or less forcing them to move to Evansville.

I don't actually think I ever spoke to her. She got diagnosed with cancer right before the Millers moved back—I guess that's why they came—but she died not long after my parents.

And now Freya's gone as well.

There are too many people on both sides buried here—Thorns *and* Millers.

The angel on Edna Miller's tombstone smiles sadly, like she's agreeing with me. So much bad blood . . . but it all ends up here, doesn't it? Soaking into the dirt.

The graves grow older as I walk deeper into the cemetery. Many of them date back centuries, their weathered stone faces practically worn smooth, the grave owner's history obliterated. Does anyone still remember who they were? Or is it inevitable that we're all forgotten? Entire families erased.

Before I'm really ready, I reach the Thorn mausoleum. There's a wreath resting against the locked front gate. It's made up of red and white carnations, and reminds me of blood spattered in snow.

Who left it? One of Mom and Dad's friends from town, maybe?

But then I see the card written in Carolyn's neat handwriting. I guess she must've come here while Uncle Ty and I were at the police station. It's the kind of thoughtful thing she does. I unlock the gate and go inside.

It doesn't smell of anything in the narrow space between the individual marble chambers where my ancestors' ashes and bones are stored. It should smell of Mom and Dad—their perfume and shampoo or something. Or maybe of dust and long-dead spiders. Just . . . something. The fact it smells so nothingy makes me feel their absence like it's a part of me, a hollowness in my bones.

Each member of my family who's interred here has their own plaque in front of their burial space. And they're not buried, really. The chambers are like the morgue lockers you see on crime dramas—barely big enough to crawl into, if you were inclined to try. But I guess we Thorns all end up inside one of these meat lockers sometime.

We all have to crawl.

I don't stay long. Just whisper a few words to Mom and Dad (I skip over finding Freya's body—don't really want them to know about that), then cry some. Less than I would've done last year. I think they'd be happy about that part. But I still miss them horribly.

Each day when I wake up and remember they're gone, it's like being punched in the heart. It's not something you get used to, exactly, but over time it at least stops being a surprise. Maybe that was what Dr. Ehrenfeld meant by moving on.

As I trudge back down the path, I pass Edna Miller's grave again. Freya will no doubt be buried somewhere nearby in a week or so.

That's a screwed-up thought. People my age aren't supposed to have graves. And, although there was definitely no love between me and Freya, I can't deny she was a *force.* Like she filled a room, you know? I can't imagine all that Freya-ness being relegated to dirt.

A sound drags my attention away from Edna's grave. There's someone sitting on a bench set against the nearest wall of the cemetery. He's hunched over, elbows resting on his knees, face in his hands as he lets out these deep, rib-breaking sobs.

I never imagined seeing Dominic Miller cry. And now I have, twice.

My chest aches looking at him.

Why is he here, though? Where are his parents? I stand frozen, not sure whether to leave and pretend I haven't seen him, or go over. I'm saved from making the decision when his phone rings. Without even glancing my way, Dominic roughly wipes a palm across his face. Then he takes a deep breath, and answers.

"Hey, Mom . . . No, I'm fine. I just needed to get out of the house for a while . . . No . . . I'm sorry, I didn't mean to worry you . . . Dad was asleep and I . . . Yeah, I'll be right back . . ."

I don't hear any more as I'm making my way briskly back to my car. And the worst thing is I'm *relieved* I didn't have to talk to Dominic. The guy just lost his sister, and is feeling the kind of pain I understand like few other people our age do. And maybe he wouldn't have wanted to talk to me, or even see me. Maybe I couldn't have said anything to make him feel better. But I didn't even try.

There's still a couple hours before I can safely go home, and the cemetery is right across the street from the public library, so I head in there to work on *Mostly Deadish.* I walk up the stone steps to the grand arched doorway of the library where the outer wooden doors stand open. It's only as I pass through them that I notice something I must've walked past a thousand times in my life: Within the ornate carvings covering the wood—swirling vines and birds, lizards and flowers—there are eyes. There's one hidden in the center of a rose. Another in the curling tail of a lizard. And another on the wing of an eagle.

They really are *everywhere* in this town.

Mr. Maitland, the head librarian, looks up as I walk in.

"If you're looking for young Mr. Walsh, I'm afraid he hasn't come in today," Mr. Maitland tells me, a little sharply. Before I can correct him that I definitely *wasn't* looking for Liam, he smiles briefly, as though to show that the sharpness wasn't aimed at me. "It seems he was rather distressed by the death of his friend."

"His friend?" I ask, surprised.

"The young Miller girl."

"Oh . . . I didn't realize they knew each other," I say, but Mr. Maitland's already striding away, presumably to whatever corner of the library where people are not. That's weird, though, about Liam knowing Freya. I can't remember ever seeing them together, even on social.

I go to my usual spot in the local-history section, really meaning to work on my art project this time, but as I pass by the door marked *private* I remember about the documents Dominic found in there. He sent them to me yesterday, but I didn't look at any of it, what with finding a dead body and all.

I take out my phone and scroll through. It's all pics of old documents, newspaper clippings, photographs, that kind of thing. But the first one I zoom in on is a diagram showing my family tree, more or less, with dates and abbreviated notes next to some of the names.

Next is a faded architect's blueprint titled *Thorn House, 1856.* The outline of the building is a lot smaller than it is today, without the east and west wings or the orangery, which I know were added a few decades after the original house was built. That's probably when they started calling it a "manor" instead of a "house." Not that my ancestors were pretentious, of course.

The Thorns are an apple-seed family—my great-great-whoever Thorn planted the orchard so it circled the land where the manor now sits, and got to claim it once the trees were established and bearing fruit. I wonder grimly if the death of the orchard is why we lost it, as though some cosmic force thought we were no longer worthy.

I study the faded lines on the drawing. It shows the three floors of the house—two rectangles for the first and second stories, divided into miniature cube rooms (my bedroom didn't exist back then, meh), and an additional square showing the wine cellar. Although I guess it was just a regular cellar back then. I still get a shiver looking at it.

In one corner of the cellar, there's a circle with a line extending from it past the outline of the house, like someone meant to add a label but forgot. The circle's too small to be noteworthy, really, except that I know what it is.

The pit.

My breath comes out a little shaky, and I tell myself not to be such a tool. The pit is a round stone hole beneath the cellar, which you can only get to by a trapdoor and a ladder. When I was six years old, and Uncle Ty was still an asshole teenager, he took me to the cellar and told me that a witch lived down there in the dark. Then he opened the trapdoor and acted like he was going to shove me in, only pulling me back at the last second.

I absolutely lost. My. Shit.

Grandpa came running downstairs, summoned by my screams, and managed to calm me down. He made Uncle Ty go down into the pit to show me it was perfectly safe. Then, when Uncle Ty climbed out, Grandpa slapped him right on the back of the neck, leaving a bright red handprint.

"You ever scare her like that again, I'll send you down there and lock the door," he told Uncle Ty, low enough that I knew to act like I hadn't heard.

Once Grandpa went back upstairs, Uncle Ty said he was sorry for freaking me out.

"Did you see the witch down there?" I asked. But he just shook his head and said there was no witch. I didn't believe him, though . . . not entirely. The idea had grown in me like a seed. He was just lying so I wouldn't see the witch coming for me.

It took a long time for me to shake off the idea that Sadie was real. And it took Uncle Ty a lot of turns on his Xbox to get me to trust him again.

I skip to the next image, and see other news articles and pictures Dominic's included. They're an odd mix of topics, but all connected to the manor, our family, or Burden Falls.

Tragedy strikes at Thorn Manor. This article is decades old; about how my great-grandmother died when she slipped on the riverbank and got swept over the waterfall.

Bumper harvest yields windfall for ailing distillery—from ten years ago, right after Dad started running the family business.

I can't read the most recent article. A glance at the grainy photo of our mangled car surrounded by emergency responders is enough to tell me what it's about.

I put away my phone. Still, I eye the *private* door. What else might be back there?

I sidle over to it and test the handle. Locked. Of course it is. I'm not lucky enough to just find it lying open. Although maybe they started locking it after realizing someone had been sneaking in there . . .

When I step outside the library, a shot of frigid air hits me right at the back of the throat. I cough my way across the road to where my car still waits in the cemetery lot. I almost get in and just drive away, but I know I can't. I need to see if Dominic's still there and check that he's okay.

Before I can chicken out again, I push open the cemetery gate and follow the path back to the bench where I saw him.

It's empty now.

I'm halfway home before I realize that Dominic probably saw Bessie parked in the cemetery lot. Probably guessed I'd seen him and said nothing. No matter how he feels about me or my family, that can't have felt good.

SEVENTEEN

When I arrive at the cottage, Carolyn presents me with a color-coded study plan.

"One hour, every day after school, and I know we can get your grades back up where they need to be in no time," she says cheerily. I'm really not in the mood for her trademark optimism, and have to remind myself that she's doing this to help me. But there's no denying Carolyn when she sets her mind to a task. So I drink one of the chilled coffees and knuckle down.

A little while later, Carolyn glances at my phone as it lights up for about the millionth time. Ford keeps trying to call me. Message me. But he can't dipshit his way out of this one. There's no cute pic that'll make me forget he *stole* something really important from me.

Daphne and Carla are mostly staying quiet about it, but I can tell they agree with me that Ford has gone *way* over the line this time. Carla thinks Ford treats me like, and I quote, "*a girlfriend he really enjoys cheating on*," and, although I am definitely *not* Ford's girlfriend, I think I'm starting to see what she means.

"Are you going to answer that?" Carolyn says, eyeing my phone. I haven't told her what's going on with Ford, but I'm sure she's guessed something's up.

"Nope." I turn it over so the screen's facedown on the kitchen table. "I'm completely focused on"—I check the notes in front of me—"algebra."

Carolyn snorts. "*Mmhmm.*"

It's almost a half hour later when Uncle Ty appears. I'm about to ask if he's feeling better (even though he doesn't look it) when Detective Holden and Daphne's dad follow him in.

It's suddenly very crowded and airless in the tiny cottage kitchen.

I completely forgot what Daphne said about her dad wanting to ask me more questions. After everything at school with my locker and then Ford, I totally spaced.

Carolyn stands slowly. "Were we expecting — ?"

"The detective and *Officer Chavez* have a couple more questions for Ava," Ty cuts in. I can tell he's not happy about them being here. I think it's the first time I've ever heard him call Daphne's dad anything other than Dave. It must be weird having his poker buddy turn up and suddenly have to be all *yes, sir* with him. I mean, I guess it's similar to when I see Uncle Ty at school, but more . . . possible jail time-y.

"Why don't you take a seat, officers, and I'll make some tea?" Carolyn says, stepping back from the kitchen table to make room for the cops to sit. I wait for Uncle Ty to take the seat next to me, but he just stands in the doorway, face grim.

The two cops look like polar opposites, aside from the fact they're both men. Officer Chavez is Black, a little stocky for his uniform, with a round baby face and a smooth, bald head. Detective Holden is wearing what looks like the same rumpled suit he had on last time we met, and has so many lines on his face, it makes me think of a prisoner marking time on the wall of a prison cell.

Daphne's dad smiles at me across the table. Detective Holden doesn't.

"Just a few routine questions," the detective says. "Do you mind if we record this?"

"I think we'd need to consult a lawyer before agreeing to that," Uncle Ty says flatly, and Officer Chavez pauses halfway through laying the recorder on the table.

Detective Holden takes it in his stride, though. "Of course. We can always go over this again at the station if we need to."

Uncle Ty shrugs. I'm starting to get annoyed by the whole dick-measuring vibe between the two of them. I clear my throat.

"What did you want to ask me, Detective?"

"Let's start with your whereabouts yesterday, before you discovered the body. Can you go through your day for us?"

"Uh . . . sure." I give a basic rundown of what happened, which is pretty much the same as what I told them at the station yesterday. At least I think it is; last night I felt like my head was full of ice chips, so I guess I could've said anything.

"You didn't leave school at all during the day yesterday?" Holden leans in.

"No." *Unlike today.*

"You didn't see Freya at any time yesterday?"

"No. Well, not until I . . . you know, found her. Dead."

"Of course. But how about on your way to school yesterday morning—you didn't see Freya Miller then?"

I open my mouth to say no, then stop. I *did* see Freya yesterday morning, at the Pump'N'Go.

"I didn't talk to her, but I saw her putting gas in her car. Well, her brother's car."

"Did you intend to speak with her?"

I frown. "No."

"So you didn't follow her when she left the gas station?"

My mouth is suddenly a sandbox. I focus on the scars on my hands and try to keep my voice steady. "I didn't *follow* her. We were just headed the same way—north, along River Road. But at the junction Freya must've turned left, in the direction of the manor. I went right, toward school. Her car definitely wasn't in the lot when I got there."

"I see." Detective Holden nods. "There are a few things I wanted to go over with you about the crime scene. Can you go through your steps with me again? From when you and Dominic Miller parted ways at your car."

I nod, if only to give myself time to prep. Then I run through the whole thing again, step by step, until the point where Officer Chavez arrived.

"And when did you move the body?"

"I didn't," I say, frowning. "You've already asked me this like a hundred times. Dominic moved Freya while he was doing CPR."

What's the big deal about moving her, anyway? There must be some reason for the question, but I can't see if it's to try and catch me out somehow, or make me point a finger at Dominic. Do they suspect *him*?

"Sunday night, when you say you overheard a phone call between Freya and her mysterious boyfriend, what exactly were you doing at the manor?"

I swallow hard, not missing the definite note of suspicion in Holden's tone now.

"I'd gone to cover over the mural I told you about, but I didn't get a chance." If I'd done it then, I'd have had no reason to go looking in the pavilion yesterday. I wouldn't have found Freya's body. Wouldn't be staring at two cops now.

"How would you describe your relationship with Freya Miller?" The detective's question takes me a moment to decipher.

"Relationship? We didn't really—"

My voice chokes off as I look up into Detective Holden's eyes. Or what should be his eyes.

In their place are two dark, empty holes.

For a moment, all I can do is gape—it's as though all the air, all the sound, has been sucked into that blackness. Like it's trying to draw me in too.

There's a loud screech as my chair scrapes back across the kitchen floor. I back away until I'm pressed against the wall. He tilts his head to one side, and for a moment I'm back in the pavilion, finding Freya slumped against the stone wall.

"Ava?" Uncle Ty steps toward me. I drag my gaze from Detective Holden to him and immediately stifle a shriek. Uncle Ty's eyes are gone too.

So are Officer Chavez's.

My breath seizes in my chest, making each thunderclap of my heart even louder. *Boom, boom, BOOM.* I look from one face to the next. As I do, those horrific gouged eyes begin to bleed. Thin rivulets at first, gliding down Officer Chavez's cheeks and trickling from his chin, *drip, drip, drip* . . .

Then the blood starts to gush from the mangled sockets, pumping out in the same pounding rhythm as my heartbeat, sluicing down onto the kitchen floor like a cascade. A waterfall. Pooling on the floor. Spreading toward me like a tide . . .

The kettle shrieks on the stove, a shrill note that builds until I think my skull will burst.

"Wow, what a racket!" Carolyn deftly silences the kettle by taking it off the burner. "Sorry, Ava—did it startle you?"

"It wasn't . . ." I begin, but fall silent. Because Carolyn's eyes are perfectly normal. I turn back to Uncle Ty and the cops, and see theirs are exactly where they're supposed to be too. No gory, empty sockets. No red tide sweeping across the floor toward me.

Normal. Fine.

I put a hand out to steady myself, and the wall feels unnaturally cold against my sweaty palm.

What the hell just happened?

"I'm sorry, I'm not feeling well. Can we talk some other time?" I say quietly, not waiting for an answer before I dart through the door from the kitchen, through the garage, then into my little room in the mill.

I pace the floor, lungs still heaving and a clammy line running all the way down my back.

There must be some rational reason for what just happened. I try to channel Carla, come up with some sciencey explanation for it. Have I caught Uncle Ty's fever? If he's been dealing with shit like this, he sure kept it quiet. God, I've never experienced anything like that before, not even after the crash. Awful Technicolor nightmares, sure, but not this. It had to be a daydream or whatever, right? After finding Freya like that yesterday . . .

I'm sitting at my desk, sketching, when Carolyn knocks on my door a few minutes later. She leans in the doorway, worry lines cutting across her forehead.

"You okay?" she asks.

"Yeah, sorry. I just got a little weirded out for a second. Are they gone now?"

"Ty's just showing them out. I think they wanted to talk with him alone."

"Why?"

Carolyn offers me a reassuring smile, but I don't miss the way she grips the door frame, her fingertips turning bloodless. "Ty was Freya's teacher. Maybe they wanted to ask him who her friends were, something like that."

Somehow, I doubt that's what they needed to talk to him alone for. They're probably checking to see if I'm on any kind of medication. Or whether I should be.

I don't have to wonder about it long. Uncle Ty pops his head around the door, resting his chin on Carolyn's shoulder.

"What did they say?" Carolyn asks before I get a chance.

"Holden wanted to know what happened in the art studio Monday," Uncle Ty says slowly. It takes me a moment to work out what he means.

"The paint thing?"

"Yes." He straightens, shoving his hands into his pockets and exhaling hard through his nose. "But, more specifically, the fact that the two of you argued — *in public* — and two days later Freya turned up dead."

EIGHTEEN

I lie on my bed for a while after the cops leave. I'm still sweating—maybe this really is the start of a fever.

There's a crack in my ceiling that I don't think was there when we moved in. It's only a fine hairline, but I don't like that it's right above my bed. The longer I stare at it, the more convinced I become that I can actually see it spreading.

Then stop looking at it, dipshit.

I pick up my phone and type out a message.

Ava: Saw you at the cemetery earlier. Wasn't sure if you wanted to be alone. Maybe I'm the last person you want to hear from right now, but if you want to talk, I'm here. I know how badly you're hurting.

Jesus. There's no way I can send that to *Dominic Miller*. I delete the entire message. Start again.

Ava: Hey, how's it going? I just wanted to

Delete.

Ava: I'm sorry about Freya

Delete. I mean, I *am* sorry she's dead, the same way I'd be sorry *anyone* is dead, but it'd sound insincere as hell when Dominic knows exactly how I felt about her.

Sighing like a hurricane, I type out one word and hit send before I can doubt myself.

Ava: Hey.

Nooooo! Why the hell did I just send that? And why isn't there a claw-back function on a goddamn text message?

I almost swallow my tongue when the ellipses start dancing right away, letting me know Dominic (or "Monica" as he's known in my contacts list) is currently typing out a reply. I have a moment of cold dread, imagining it'll be something along the lines of *leave me the hell alone.* After all, why would he want to hear from someone who openly hated his sister? Especially *now,* right after she's been murdered?

I put the phone down, deciding I'd rather not see his response. Then pick it up again.

Monica: I'll meet you at the public library tomorrow after school. Bring your comic.

I stare at the message, certain I must be reading it wrong. Because there's no way Dominic *wants* to work on my art project right now, and I'm actually kind of pissed he thinks that's why I messaged him. Although I guess my "Hey" might've been a little vague.

Ava: Just wanted to see how you're doing.

Again, the ellipses start up right away.

Monica: Do you want to work on it or not?

I hiss out an irritated breath. Literally everything Dominic Miller does seems designed to piss me off. And this time I can't even tell him to go *fuck thyself,* or whatever Carla said. Not only because his sister just died, either; I actually do need to work on the comic. Somehow, Dominic has become a key part of that.

I've sketched out several new panels to add to the one I did on my own, but they're still rough. I hoped Dominic would help me figure out the captions and dialogue to make it all work.

Ava: See you tomorrow then.

As soon as I hit send, my phone starts to ring, startling me so badly, I almost drop the damn thing.

It's Ford. His stupid face fills the screen.

I flip him the bird—as though he can actually see me—and turn off my phone.

Bang! Bang! BANG!

I wake with a shout, knuckles grazing my bedroom wall as I flail upright. I'm in bed, at the cottage. I was having the dream again—the crash. I think Freya might've been there too. Or was it Sadie?

The banging continues.

What the hell?

The wind roars outside, whistling through a gap somewhere.

Bang!

I know that sound. It's the window in the loft. Must've blown open again.

Letting out a shaky breath, I drag myself out of bed to go close it.

I can't get back to sleep after that. Every nerve feels raw, like I'm hooked up to a car battery. But it's the middle of the night, I have nowhere to go, and there's no way I'll be able to focus on TV right now. I take out my sketchpad and start to draw. I begin with some experimental panels for *Mostly Deadish*, redoing and refining them by the light of my desk lamp. But at some point my focus shifts, and I start drawing all the things I can't seem to push out of my head.

I don't even notice the hours passing until the alarm on my phone goes off, making me jump. I yelp at an angry twinge in my neck. When I look around me, my floor is covered in sheets and sheets of drawings. There's the girl from the river, eyes milky and faded the way I imagine they looked. There's Freya, of course. Sitting in the pavilion, slumped a little to one side, with her hands in her lap and dark pencil marks showing the mess where her eyes used to be. There are drawings of Sadie too. So many pictures of her.

And eyes. Dozens of them. Hundreds.

A sea of eyes, all watching me.

NINETEEN

Later that morning, my head is so foggy, I don't even remember the drive to school. If I weren't too tired to care, it would be worrying. But I don't seem to be running a fever, so that's something.

One thing my head has cleared enough to know: If I'm ever going to sleep well again, I need to stop thinking about ghosts, and start focusing on what's real.

Someone killed Freya Miller.

Some*one* or some*thing*? No. Much as I hate to agree with Carla on anything, I think she has a point—it's kind of hard to picture a ghost going after Freya with a melon-baller.

Doesn't stop every dickhead at school muttering *Sadie* as I walk past. Or maybe it just feels that way.

"Hey."

My head jerks up so fast, I catch the edge of my locker door right above my eye.

"Jesus!"

"God, Ava, are you okay?" Ford says. "Such a klutz . . ."

I'm too busy rubbing the point of impact to answer him. Then his hand lands on my arm, and I jerk away.

"Where's my necklace?" I snap.

"It's at home. And I'm not giving it back until you let me explain—"

I hold up my free hand, stopping him. "I don't want to hear it,

Ford. Just give me the damn necklace, and then leave me alone."

"Ava, don't be like that . . ."

I push past him and through the crowd of students waiting to go to homeroom. There's only one place I can go where he can't follow without looking like a creep, so I head to the bathroom.

The mirror above the sink shows an angry red stripe running vertically above my right eyebrow. I wet some tissue with cold water and press it to the mark. Just then I spot Daphne in the mirror, coming out of the stall behind me. She's wearing an A-line houndstooth dress over orange wool stockings and black patent-leather boots, her hair elaborately pinned up, looking very Vintage Witch.

"Oh my God!" she says. "Your head!"

"Before you ask," I say, "I did not get into a fight. Well, only with my locker."

Daphne winces, then starts poking tentatively at my forehead. "You should pick a locker your own size next time. You look kinda washed out too. Are you having the dreams again?"

She and Carla have always known about them. Sometimes we'd be having a sleepover and I'd wake up screaming, my hands bleeding again where I'd ripped the stitches trying to scramble out of the car in my nightmare. I am a fun friend.

"These dreams are . . . different," I say, hoping she'll leave it at that. For once, she does.

"Are you worried about the investigation into Freya's murder?"

"Not really," I lie. "I mean, it's not like I killed her."

Daphne looks around to see who might be within earshot, but

the bathroom is empty except for the two of us. "I overheard Dad talking to that detective they brought in from the city—"

"Detective Holden," I supply.

"Yeah, him. He called my dad to go deal with some press who were camped outside the manor gates last night. Anyway, he *also* said something about the time of death being around twelve p.m. Wednesday."

"I was in school then," I say.

"So you have an alibi?"

"Why are you making that sound like a question?"

"I'm not." Daphne shakes her head, wide-eyed. "I just wondered because you weren't with me and Carla at lunchtime."

I think about that for a moment, tracking back to Wednesday. Where the hell was I at midday? "I was in the art studio?" I say, but now I'm the one making it sound like a question.

"Anyway," Daphne continues, "I heard her eyes weren't actually *removed*—they were smashed *in*. Like with an ice pick or something."

Acid burns the back of my throat, and I have only two seconds to dive into a stall before I'm heaving my guts up.

I feel Daphne's hands in my hair, holding it back for me. "Sorry," she says, sounding it. "I didn't think."

"Not your fault," I croak. "I think this is just a delayed reaction, honestly. Or maybe a fun new side to the bug I caught off Uncle Ty. Did you overhear anything about them catching the killer?" I ask hopefully, taking the bottle of water Daphne offers me.

"Well . . . I mean, not really. It turns out Freya had surprisingly few people who hated her apart from you, and the next people the cops look at are the ones who found the body—also you—or whoever the victim was dating. But Freya wasn't—"

"She was dating someone," I cut in. "Sexting someone, anyway."

"Really? Who?"

"I'm not sure. I just overheard her talking on the phone about some nudes, and arranging to meet up. I told the cops, though, so they're probably checking that out."

"Wow. I had no idea Freya was seeing someone. That could seriously be the person who killed her."

"Do they know *how* she died yet?" I ask, then grimace. "Or was it the ice pick?"

Again, Daphne checks all around us before she answers, as though someone might've snuck in unnoticed. "I'm not a hundred percent sure, but I did hear Dad say something about strangulation. And I guess that's something else in your favor."

"*In my favor*? What does that mean?"

"Well . . . you don't *want* to be on the suspects list, do you?" She doesn't give me a chance to answer that. "And they'll have to rule you out because of your hands, right?"

I look down at the jagged pink lines on my palms. "You think I couldn't strangle someone?"

Daphne's eyeing me curiously when I glance up at her. "I dunno. Could you?"

TWENTY

I step past the carved wooden doors into the public library after school, feeling its eyes following me in. Eyes everywhere. For a second, I experience a surge of panic, remembering how it seemed as though Uncle Ty's and the cops' eyes were missing when they came to question me yesterday. I take in a deep breath, let it out slowly. Try to think about kittens.

Dominic's already inside. I expected him to look haggard and unkempt, the way Mateo and Casper have every time I've seen them the past couple days. But Dominic looks the same as usual in a dark sweater that probably cost more than my car, his wavy black hair falling forward in that accidentally-on-purpose way of his as he reads a comic book on the table in front of him. It's *Uzumaki* by Junji Ito—a horror classic, and one of my all-time favorites. I feel weirdly resentful that he's reading it.

I clear my throat. Dominic looks up a moment later, dragging his focus out of the book.

"Hi, Ava. How are you?"

His voice is smooth and even. The only giveaway that his sister just died are the dark circles under his eyes. I'd never know he was the same guy I saw yesterday, sobbing in the cemetery.

"Hey," I begin, taking the seat opposite. "I'm sorry—"

"Can we not do that?" Dominic cuts me off. "The whole *I'm sorry for your loss* thing? I'd rather just concentrate on the comic."

"Not researching Sadie?"

He hesitates, and I think for a blistering second that I've said the wrong thing. I mean, *duh,* that was for *Haunted Heartland.* Of course he's not bothered about that anymore. And yet he doesn't say no.

All the idiots at school are whispering about Sadie being behind Freya's murder, but there's no way Dominic believes that . . . is there?

Or is it easier for him to believe in a murdering ghost than to think about someone hating Freya enough to want her dead? No, not just *want* her dead, but to actually kill her and destroy her eyes? I try and imagine how much hate that would take. The closest I can compare it to is how I feel about Madoc Miller causing the crash that killed my parents, and even I can admit it's not apples to apples. I hate Madoc for being careless, and for acting like an unfeeling jerk after it happened. I hate him for taking my parents from me and ruining my life. But someone hurt Freya on purpose. That's another kind of evil, and I'm not sure I wouldn't be reaching for a supernatural explanation if I were in Dominic's shoes.

"Let's work on the comic first," he says at last. "Then maybe we can go through the Sadie stuff I sent you."

"Fine by me."

Dominic relaxes back into his chair. I take that as my cue to dig out the sketches I've been working on.

"I've laid out the panels from the point the girl first looks out from the tower and sees the zombies starting to uproot themselves, up to where she opens the trapdoor in the basement of the tower and releases all the zombies into the hell dimension. See?"

I trace over the panels with their empty captions and speech bubbles, watching Dominic's face for his reaction. I'm ready to snatch the sketches away if he so much as sneers. But he studies each panel carefully before opening a notebook in front of him. "I assume you want my input for the captions and dialogue, seeing as you've left them blank?"

"Yeah."

"Good. I've also written a rough outline of what I thought could come after the trapdoor chapter, but of course you might have a completely different direction in mind. Here, read this while I make some notes."

Dominic hands me a neatly typed sheaf of papers. He's laid out bullet-pointed scenes detailing how Sadie (because of course that's what he's called the girl, despite me telling him this isn't about Dead-Eyed Sadie) finds she needs a key in order to switch directions in the elevator tower so it'll take her back up to the hilltop. And that key, as a demon gatekeeper tells her, is in the possession of the last keeper of the tower—who now resides in the far reaches of hell. So Sadie has to set out to find the keeper, fighting her way past zombies, demons, and the unhappy souls of the damned.

Even in bullet points, I can tell from the way Dominic has phrased it that it won't just be scary—it'll be funny too. It gives me serious *Hellboy* vibes, which is probably the highest compliment I could pay him, not that I have any intention of paying said compliment. I can't deny the surge of excitement in my gut at just the *prospect* of this comic coming together the way it *feels* like it will. My fingers itch to get sketching.

I love this.

And how fucked up is that, to be enjoying myself like this when Dominic's going through hell?

I crane my neck, trying to read what he's writing in his little notebook. Of course, he looks up and catches me.

"What do you think?"

I nod quickly. "I think I can work with it. But we're not calling her Sadie."

There's a faint upticking at the corners of his mouth.

"All right," he says. "What should we call her?"

I turn over possible names in my head, testing out how they sound. Nothing seems right.

"I'll think about it and get back to you." Dominic huffs in amusement. "It's not going to be Sadie, though. And wouldn't it be weird to call her Sadie after what happened to—"

I hadn't realized how warm Dominic's expression had been until my words shut it down like an ice bath.

"Sorry," I say. And I mean it. He shakes his head.

"I knew we couldn't avoid the subject forever. I just wanted to not think about it for a while."

"Yeah. Again, sorry."

Dominic closes his notebook. "I guess you've spoken to the cops."

"Twice. Pretty sure I'm on their suspects list." I figure it's better to just get it out there. I assume Dominic doesn't think I killed Freya, or there's no way he'd be spending his free time here with me. I'm still not entirely sure why he is, to be honest. Maybe it's some elaborate ruse to . . .

Okay, so I can't think what Dominic's ruse would be here.

But accepting a Miller's intentions at face value just feels weird.

"I can't see how you'd be a viable suspect," Dominic says evenly. "You were at school when she died." He's heard about the time of death, then. "You know, it's actually very lucky you found her. I mean, we would've noticed Freya was missing pretty soon, but it might've taken a long time to figure out where she was if you hadn't found her like you did."

"Yeah," I say, "*lucky*."

He leans forward. "No, it *was*. The weather's so cold right now that the police forensics people would've had a much harder time figuring out her time of death if she'd been left outside overnight. That would've made it a lot harder to find alibis for everyone who wasn't guilty — or rather, made it a lot easier for the killer to hide in a crowd."

"I see." I still don't feel lucky about finding Freya's butchered body, but I take his point. "I've been wondering, though," I lie, because this is literally the first time it's occurred to me. "Didn't the security cameras pick up anything? They should've caught anyone sneaking onto the property, right?"

Dominic slumps back in his seat, deflated. "No, unfortunately. Some of the cameras needed to be taken down when my parents had the house painters in, so the system wasn't working. Aside from the gate cameras, the only one recording anything was the static I left hooked up near the bridge after our *Haunted Heartland* filming session. That one was pointed away from the house, so it caught nothing."

"Not nothing," I point out. "It tells you whoever did it didn't come from the direction of the bridge." If I was going to sneak onto the property to commit a murder, that's the way I'd go. But

I don't say that out loud, obviously. "Do you know who else the cops are looking at?"

Dominic shrugs. "Everyone, I suppose. They're interviewing all the kids at school who knew her or saw her earlier this week."

"What about . . ." I let my question trail off until Dominic squints at me quizzically. "I mean, didn't Freya have a boyfriend? Because that's who cops usually look at first, isn't it?"

I could tell Dominic what I overheard that night in the orchard. He knows I was there. But do I really want to tell him that his very recently deceased sister seemed to be arranging a secret hookup? Not really. And I've already told the cops.

"I wouldn't know," Dominic says. "It wasn't the kind of thing we talked about. I'm—*I was*—her older brother, not her *bestie*." I almost laugh at the way his lip curls around the word *bestie*, as though it's entirely alien to him. "Besides, having somewhat overbearing parents teaches you to be discreet. It's annoying when they constantly pry into your business."

"I wouldn't know," I parrot back, regretting it as soon as I do. "Sorry. That wasn't really aimed at you."

And it isn't. Somehow, Dominic has become separated from my feelings toward the Millers. I wouldn't go so far as to say I actually like him, but I don't actively hate his guts, either.

He nods, thawing a little. "The cops have her cell phone and her laptop. I suppose if there's anything or anyone suspicious to find on either of them, they will."

Dominic sighs, and with that one shaky breath I see it. He's been hiding it so well until now, but it's there: that stark look in his eyes. I know that look. It shows the horrible dawning surprise that you can be hurt by something so much—*so damn much*—and somehow be expected to just . . . carry on. That's exactly how I felt after my parents died.

And it feels fucked up that looking at Dominic Miller—the son of the guy who destroyed my life—is like looking in a mirror. Yet somehow I still want to reach out to him. Because I know how it feels. I *know.*

"I should go," I murmur.

Dominic blinks, apparently lost in his own thoughts. "Do you have enough to work with over the weekend?"

"Plenty." I nod. "Thanks."

"You have my number if you want to run through anything."

I pack away my sketches and Dominic's notes, shrugging on my coat. He doesn't make a move to do the same.

"Are you sticking around here for a while?" I ask.

He pauses before answering, and I wonder if I've said the wrong thing again. "My parents are meeting with the funeral director at the house, and there are still one or two reporters hanging around outside. I'd rather keep out of the way."

And now I feel like an ass for saying I had to leave when really I'm in no particular rush. I don't love that I'm kind of depending on a Miller to help me finish my final art project—and hopefully graduate—but he *is* helping me, despite this being literally the worst time in his life.

"My shift at the gas station doesn't actually start until seven, so I can totally work on the comic some more," I tell him. "I just didn't want to take up your whole Friday afternoon with it."

Dominic arches one eyebrow. "Go home, Thorn. I don't need a babysitter."

As if to prove my company isn't needed, he picks up *Uzumaki* again and flips back to the page where he left off when I arrived. It's only as I turn to leave that he says, "But don't worry, I haven't forgotten. We can go through my Sadie research next time."

I pretend not to hear, but Dominic must notice the tightening in my shoulders as I cross toward the library door. His low chuckle follows me out into the cold.

TWENTY-ONE

It's quiet in the Pump'N'Go, as per always. But tonight I'm on my own at the counter while my boss does a stock check out back, so I don't feel too shady using the gas station Wi-Fi to watch videos on my phone. I suck down the dregs of the coffee I picked up from the cottage, eyes glued to the little screen. Because these aren't just videos. They're research.

I keep thinking about the guy Freya was talking to on the phone the night I overheard her at the manor. It'd have to be someone I know, right? Or at least someone her family would know? And someone she really shouldn't have been hooking up with, judging by how sneaky she was being with that call.

Considering the guy ought to be at the top of the cops' suspects list, it seems like I'm the only one who gives a rat's ass about finding him. If I can figure out who he is, maybe that'll mean finding the real killer — and the cops will stop looking at me like they're sizing me up for an orange onesie.

Who is he, though? I immediately leap to Mateo and Casper. I mean, they all seem super clingy with each other. But I thought Mateo and Casper were together. I could be wrong, though. Or what if they *are* together, but one of them was also seeing Freya in secret?

I honestly don't know any of them well enough to make anything but the biggest of leaps, and the theory just doesn't sit right in my gut. But, as Carla and Daphne have often pointed out, I trust my gut a little too much sometimes, and should give my brain a try. (Okay, that last part was all Carla.)

This is why I'm going through recent episodes of *Haunted Heartland,* studying the interactions between Mateo and Freya and Casper. Body language, eye contact. Little things that might mean they were something other than friends.

I click on a video from two weeks ago. Freya appears in close-up, and I almost shut it down again. I see her—not as she is on-screen, but the way she was in the pavilion. Her face, impossibly pale. Those two hollow pits.

Dead-eyed.

Blink.

Alive.

Blink.

Dead . . .

Blink, blink, blink.

But then the camera pans out, and I see Casper and Dominic next to her, all three of them in thick winter gear. They're stand-ing on a jetty, its rickety old boards stretching out beyond them over a dark lake. I can't tell which one it is—there are so many in Indiana, and I've only been to a couple—but fine wisps of mist float across the surface of the still, glassy water. It's around sun-set, the light exactly right to pick out the blood-red undertones of Freya's hair, amping up the whole Sansa Stark vibe she has going on.

I can see why anyone—including a good portion of the internet—would find her attractive. She was beautiful.

The camera lingers on her.

"Good evening, Hauntlanders! Tonight we're gonna be in

deep water—literally—as we investigate a tiny island at the center of this lake where Hacksaw Henry, the nineties serial killer who managed to evade the police, is rumored to have spent his last days."

The video jumps forward to the four of them in a boat, Mateo holding the camera out on a selfie stick to capture everyone in one shot as they chug across the lake. He's leaning back . . . Is his hand on Freya's leg? No, just a weird angle.

Another cut, and they're scrambling up the shore on what is presumably Hacksaw Henry's island.

"*I see his shack up ahead!*" Casper says, as if he just spotted Santa's sleigh. It looks like Dominic is holding the camera now, and is it me or does it *not* linger on Freya the same way it did in Mateo's hands?

The camera zooms in to where Casper's pointing, but it isn't a shack at all. Standing at the island's peak is a narrow building, its stone sides forming an octagon, covered in faded, peeling paint. It stretches up maybe fifteen feet, and has dozens of tiny windows peeking out over the lake.

For a moment, I think they've posted a video of the pavilion after all. The building is almost identical, except for those odd little windows.

But I know what this is. It's not a pavilion, it's a dovecote. I remember Grandpa telling me there used to be one at the manor—a twin to the pavilion—but it was removed when they built the distillery at the northern edge of our land.

"Seriously, where do they come up with this garbage?" I mutter, but then my smirk drops as I realize there won't be any more *Haunted Heartland* episodes. Not unless Dominic and the others decide to keep making it without Freya, and I just can't see that, even if Dominic does want to continue researching Sadie. Despite my feelings about the Millers' crew generally, the four of them always seem so tight. *Seemed.*

"*We're gonna have to turn on the flashlights as we go in because it's dark and really creepy in there.*" Freya has dropped the fake smile in favor of wide-eyed pensiveness.

The camera follows Freya, Mateo, and Casper as they wander around the inside of the dovecote. Streaks of bird crap paint the walls. Mateo crouches and beckons the camera closer.

"*Did you find something?*" Freya asks breathlessly.

"*I found . . . this.*" He whirls around and suddenly a terrifying, howling face fills the screen. The camera jumps as Dominic steps away, and I see that Mateo is holding a fat toad in his hands.

"Dick," I mutter, my heart still pounding.

Mateo laughs his ass off as he squeezes the creature again, and it lets out another shrill howl.

"*Put that poor thing back where you found it,*" Freya says, but she's laughing too. Dominic pans over to his sister.

"*Cas,*" Freya whispers, "*do you feel anything yet?*"

"*It's getting cooler . . . There's definitely a presence here.*"

"*Hacksaw Henry murdered six women and girls between 1988 and 1992,*" Freya's voice whispers through my phone speakers. I find myself leaning in, in spite of myself. "*He dismembered their bodies, dumping the pieces in trash cans throughout multiple neighborhoods of southern Indiana. Henry left the final body in Heron Gate park with the hacksaw he'd used on all his victims — a message, many say, that he was done killing.*"

The camera is following Freya as she walks another circuit

when a shadow flits past one of the windows. There and gone, only a brief flash.

Neither Freya nor any of the guys seems to notice. The camera moves on, tracking Freya's tour of the perimeter. I guess it was just a bird.

Then it happens again. A shadow crosses the window behind her, a little slower this time, so I can just make out the blurry shape of a face before it disappears from view.

What the hell?

My pulse quickens, even though I know it's probably just someone the Miller twins strong-armed into making the video with them. I'd probably recognize the person from school if I looked closely enough.

I pause the video and take it back to a few seconds before the first shadow passed behind Freya. When I play it this time, I don't see it. I let it run at quarter speed up to the point where I got the clearer view of the face at the window. There's nobody there. I play it again twice more, just to be sure. I pause the video and lean in to study it.

There's no sign of the shape I saw at the window. But, as I stare at it, the shadows begin to move at Freya's back. Just a deepening darkness at first, like a void folding inward. But it's growing. Stretching.

It towers over Freya now. It's a person, definitely. Or the shape of a person . . .

Freya just stands there, smiling out from the screen.

First you see her, then you—

Someone clears their throat in front of me, and I drop my phone with a squeak. Madoc Miller stands at the counter in his winter overcoat and leather gloves. He scowls from beneath his heavy eyebrows.

"What are you doing here?" I snap. Usually, if he catches sight of me at the counter, Madoc keeps on driving. He doesn't want to see me any more than I want to see him. The arrangement suits us both. And now the fucker has broken it.

"Fifty on number four," he says gruffly. His voice is nothing like Dominic's, I realize. Dominic's is deep and smooth — quite a nice voice, if you like that kind of thing. But Madoc sounds like he's smoked forty a day since kindergarten and gargled broken glass in between. I think this is actually the first time he's spoken to me directly since the day he drove his Hummer into my parents' car.

And now his daughter's dead.

"Ava?"

"What?"

"Fifty bucks. Pump four." Madoc Miller pushes cash across the counter to underline the statement.

Wordlessly, I ring up the gas sale. He pockets the receipt and I wait for him to leave, but he just stands there. "Was there something else?"

Madoc purses his lips before speaking, as though choosing his words with great care.

"You were the one who found my daughter."

Not a question. A statement.

Did he actually come here to accuse me of something?

"That's right, I was."

"I'm sorry for that," he says, then turns abruptly and leaves.

✳ ✳ ✳

It's pretty late when I get home, and I don't expect to find anyone still up, but Carolyn is leaning against the kitchen counter, holding a mug of tea.

"Hey, sweetie. Ford came by earlier. I told him you were working—did he call in at the gas station?"

I grit my teeth. "No. Did he . . . leave anything for me?"

I can tell by Carolyn's confused look that he didn't. Why hasn't he given my mom's necklace back yet?

An ugly thought creeps into my head: What if he *can't* give it back? What if he actually gave it to Freya, and just doesn't have the guts to tell me?

Damn it. Damn *him*. Tomorrow's Saturday—I'll go over to Ford's before work and get it back myself.

"Busy shift?" Carolyn asks, probably thinking that's the reason behind my suddenly sour mood.

"Nah. Weird one, though. Madoc Miller came in." I take a sip from my coffee, trying to appear nonchalant, but Carolyn stiffens.

"What did he say? Was he rude to you? If he said anything—"

"No, it was fine. I mean, *odd,* but fine. He just said he was sorry I was the one who found Freya."

Carolyn relaxes a little, but she's still frowning. "That's hardly the thing he should be apologizing for."

"Yeah."

He never apologized for killing my parents—not at the inquest, or in private. Not that any "sorry" would've made a damn bit of difference. Mom and Dad would still be dead. I'd still hate him.

"There was something else, though . . ."

Carolyn puts down her tea, listening.

"I was watching a *Haunted Heartland* video on my phone, and I thought I saw something in the background, but when I played it back, it wasn't there. Weird, right?" I force a laugh.

"What kind of 'something' did you think you saw?" Carolyn asks.

"Like a person, maybe? Just someone in the background."

"So, something they staged to creep people out?"

I shake my head. "I don't think this was someone who was supposed to be there."

"I see." Carolyn nods slowly. "Are you thinking it might've been something else? Something like Sadie?"

"No, I . . ." But isn't that who my instincts told me it was? That video was recorded a couple weeks ago.

First you see her, then you die.

Like my dad did.

My pulse thuds loudly in my head, making it hard to think. Or maybe I just don't want to.

Was it actually true, what Dad said right before he died? That he *did* see Sadie in the woods—and it wasn't just a symptom of his seizure? He always told me Sadie was a myth. Always laughed whenever Mom warned him not to talk that way *or Sadie might come early just to set you straight*. But he believed in the end, didn't he? Even though I've been denying it ever since, I think a part of me started to believe then too.

But why would she appear in Freya's video? As a warning that Freya was about to die?

But Freya didn't actually see Sadie in the video. I did.

"Ava, I'm going to shoot straight here, okay?" Carolyn says, cutting through my dawning horror. "You found a girl's body with the eyes mutilated, and on the anniversary of your parents' deaths. Naturally, you haven't been sleeping too well." She smooths a hand over my cheek and looks me dead in the eyes. "We're going to have to commit you, sweetie."

I laugh in surprise. "What?"

She nods faux-sadly. "Yup. Ty's filing the papers right now."

"Shut up," I say, still laughing.

Finally, she cracks a grin, but it soon softens. "Ava, after all you've been through, I'd be shocked if you weren't a little strung out. Don't give yourself such a hard time, okay? Maybe it was too soon for you to stop seeing Dr. Ehrenfeld . . ."

"No, it was time," I say quickly. It's not that I thought the sessions weren't helping me, but I felt guilty asking Carolyn and Uncle Ty to keep paying for therapy when I knew money was so tight.

"As long as you're sure." She taps a fingernail on my coffee lid. "But maybe stick to decaf with these, yeah? I got some more for you."

"Okay. Thanks."

Carolyn gives my arm a squeeze and disappears into the living room. I switch out my empty coffee for a glass of water and head to my room. As I'm crossing to the desk, I look at the round window above it and see a pale face staring in at me.

I drop the glass of water. It shatters at my feet, shards spraying everywhere.

But the face is just my reflection. Just me.

There's nobody out there.

TWENTY-TWO

I t's early, and still dark out, but when I try to start Bessie, I find she's having one of her temperamental days. I'm wide-awake now, though, so I put on my boots and decide to brave the walk to Ford's instead. There's only a couple of inches of snow.

Grabbing a coffee and an apple for breakfast, I head out.

The path to the river stretches away crisp and white, unspoiled yet by either humans or animals. It feels wrong to stomp through it in my boots, but also kind of satisfying.

The river itself is a swirling white sheet with darker patches where the thaw is trying to break through. We're inching into spring now. Like my mom used to say, this is the last snap of winter's fingers.

Frost gives way to frozen dirt on the path as the trees press in close to the river. The sun must be coming up by now, but the clouds overhead are so thick, it could almost still be night. I hear the bells murmuring from upriver. It isn't familiar and comforting like it usually is. Now it's eerie, playing on my nerves like a current in the air.

By the time I see the scarred tree marking Copper Bell Dam, my feet are two blocks of ice. Still, I pause to run my fingers over the evil eye carved into the tree. It's a tradition. But it stirs something uneasy in me, remembering the one etched into my locker door. It might've been some rando at school who did it after hearing I was the one who found Freya, but it felt personal. Now all the evil eyes seem like they're turned toward me. Watching.

As soon as I catch sight of the dam, something feels off. My head spins like I've just stepped off a carousel. I lean back against the scarred tree and close my eyes, waiting for the weird head rush to pass.

Carolyn's right—I really should switch to decaf.

Cautiously, I open my eyes. Everything has stopped swimming. I'm actually relieved for a second before I realize everything hasn't just stopped *swimming*—it's stopped altogether.

The bells are silent. My breath comes heavy, but doesn't mist the air in front of me. Even the river's murmur beneath the ice has died.

I rub my eyes, then my temples, hoping I can somehow massage reality back into its proper place. Trying to breathe evenly, I push away from the tree. But across the feathered white of the river I see someone standing on the far bank. Her head is bowed, as though she's looking for something in the river. Lank black hair hangs forward to hide her face.

Oh God. Oh Jesus.

It's her.

"Sadie." I don't mean to say it out loud, but the whisper breaks whatever spell is holding time prisoner. A bird squawks and swoops low over the path before winging up toward the slate-gray sky. The bells chime as though they've been struck.

"First you see her, then you die."

I run, the whisper coiling itself deep in my ear. The shapes of the trees against the sky look razor-sharp and vicious, no longer a shaded path but a possible trap. Every footstep, every crunch of frozen ground, seems magnified. *Multiplied,* because they aren't just my footsteps. Not just my breaths. She's tracking me, I know it, but I can't bear to look back across the river. Can't turn and stare into those empty, hungry eye sockets, and see my own death there.

I duck to avoid a low branch, but it still captures a strand of my hair. It's as though she's using it all to reach for me—the river, the path, the trees—bearing down to pin me to the riverbank.

Something claws at my cheek, and I scream.

Just a twig. Only a damn twig.

I keep going. Breathing hard, I keep sprinting on until the path veers away from the water toward River Road. I only stop once I'm in sight of the pavement, with its passing cars and thrum of life. A kid on a bike curses and swerves at my sudden appearance, and I've never been happier to get cussed out by a middle-schooler.

With shaking hands, I pull out my phone and call the one person I can count on to be real with me, no matter what.

Carla answers on the second ring. "Don't tell me—you've found another corpse?"

"Carla, stop being an asshole for a second and tell me I'm not losing my mind."

"Okay," she says slowly. "I'm going to need some context before I commit to that."

"I just saw Dead-Eyed Sadie at Copper Bell Dam."

There's a beat of silence. "More information, please."

"I was walking and my head started spinning, so I closed my eyes. When I opened them, she was standing right across the river from me."

"Okay. She was across the river—that's what, fifty feet? Are you sure it wasn't just someone out walking their dog?"

"There was no dog!" I snap.

"Well, what was she wearing?"

"I . . ." I try to think, to picture it. "Something dark? I couldn't really make it out with the trees behind her."

"But you saw her face?"

"Not exactly. She was sort of leaning forward, looking down at the river."

There's a longer silence now, and I hear someone in the background asking who's on the phone. Probably Daphne. Carla's dads are really cool about the two of them—more so than Daphne's parents, who aren't openly assholey about Daphne being gay, but it's taking them a minute to get used to the idea.

"Okay," Carla says, "assuming you haven't been smoking something or huffing aerosols, this is my official verdict: You just saw some rando out for an early walk, and freaked out. I'm putting that down to recent events, not inconsiderable stress, and the fact it's *fucking early*. You're fine."

Just hearing Carla say that in her no-shit, confident tone actually makes me believe her. Almost.

"All right?" When I don't answer, she says it again. "*All right?*"

"Just to make absolutely sure: Despite the fact that anyone in the Thorn family who sees Sadie is supposed to die, *I'm* not going to die, right?"

"Of course you are," she says matter-of-factly. "But probably not for a really long time, and definitely not because you had a ghostly visitation, Ebenezer."

"What?"

"Ebenezer Scrooge from *A Christmas Carol* . . . Oh, never mind. My point is, you're fine. There's nothing you need to worry about, okay?"

I exhale deeply. "Yes. Thank you, Dr. Carla. Sorry for waking you."

"Whatever." Carla mutters something like *try reading a fucking book sometime,* then hangs up.

I knock at Ford's door, forgetting for a moment that his mom might've been on a late shift at the care home. But she's bright-eyed and dressed when she opens the door, ushering me inside as always.

"Are you okay, sweetie? You look a little under the weather."

Truthfully, I'm a sweaty mess. My legs are shaky from running most of the way here, and my skin is doing this weird tingling thing that makes me want to turn it inside out. But I just smile weakly and tell her, "I'm fine. Thanks, Ms. Sutter. Is Ford home?"

"He's still in bed." She rolls her eyes. "You know what he's like in the mornings. But I'll go wake him and we can have some coffee while he de-zombifies himself, if you like?"

I try to muster a genuine smile for Ms. Sutter. No matter how pissed I am with Ford, she's always been so kind to me—especially right after my parents died. I spent so much time here then, it was almost like she adopted me.

Now things have gone sour between me and Ford, and I might never set foot inside this house again. Man, I'm so pissed at him right now, I want to shake him.

"Actually, Ms. Sutter, would it be okay if I just go up?"

"If you can handle the smell of feet and morning breath, you go ahead." She chuckles to herself on her way to the kitchen. I head upstairs.

Ford's room is the biggest of the three bedrooms—typical of his mom to let him take the best room—and it looks out directly over the east gate of the manor.

His door is closed. I listen for a moment for any signs of movement. It's all quiet inside. I consider just going in there, retrieving my necklace, and leaving, but I can't simply bust into his room without warning. Even assholes deserve boundaries.

I knock, loud enough that I know it'll startle him awake.

"Mom? What is it?" he calls through the door.

"It's me," I say. "I'm coming in."

"*Ava?*"

I wait another beat before opening the door, just in case he needs to cover up. Not that I haven't seen, like, ninety-nine percent of Ford before, thanks to his habit of stripping off at any given opportunity. The guy doesn't even know what tan lines are. Still, he can keep his one percent to himself, thank you.

I go in. Ford's sitting up in bed, his curly hair sticking out all over like he just got Tasered, and a hand-shaped mark down one side of his face. There is a cat sleeping on either side of him, and he glares at them like they're strangers before focusing back on me. Jaffa—the orange cat—jumps down and immediately coils around my ankles. I reach down to pet him on autopilot.

"Ava, I'm so glad you're here—"

"I only came for my necklace," I tell him.

"Will you just listen to why I took it?"

I consider marching over and snatching it out from under his bed—if it's even still hidden there. But I can be the bigger, more dignified person here.

"Fine."

"Okay." Ford sits up straighter, and I have a horrible feeling he's been rehearsing whatever he's about to say. "You remember right before the manor went up for sale, and Ty was still trying to pay off the debts from the distillery?"

I nod. "Trying to save the house."

"Right." Ford widens his eyes briefly, as if that's somehow untrue. "But the thing is, I saw him in town outside the pawnbroker—you know the one next to that seedy little law office? Anyway, I went over to say hey, but when I reached the pawnshop I saw him laying out a bunch of your parents' stuff on the counter. I mean, things I know for certain they would've wanted you to have—like your dad's Rolex, their wedding rings, stuff like that."

I open my mouth, then close it again. Because Ford's wrong: I gave Uncle Ty the Rolex to keep after the accident, and my parents were buried with their rings.

"I knew he'd get around to taking your mom's necklace, and I also knew how important it is to you. So I hid it—*for you*. You get that, right? I was just looking out for you. I meant to tell you I had it, but then I kinda forgot until . . . Well, you saw it on the video Freya posted."

And there it is—the reminder I needed to stoke my anger back up to boiling point.

"You're trying to tell me you stole it so *Uncle Ty wouldn't steal it*? Do you know how ridiculous that sounds? Uncle Ty would never steal from me. He's my *family*. And the necklace isn't even worth that much."

Ford huffs. "Enough to bet on a couple horses, though."

My fists clench at my sides. "He wouldn't do that!"

"Wouldn't he?"

"No! Besides, if you really believed that, you should've told me."

Ford leans back against his headboard, arms folded behind his head. "Whatever. Ty's a saint. It doesn't change the fact that I was only looking out for you."

He watches me expectantly.

"What? Am I supposed to thank you now? I felt sick thinking I'd lost it in the move! I wanted to wear it on the anniversary . . . Oh, what does it even matter to you?" I hold out my hand. "Give me back my necklace, Ford."

He holds my glare for a long moment, and I actually think he might refuse. Or maybe he actually did give it to Freya, and all this bullshit is just to throw me off . . . But then he leans over the side of his bed and pulls the little black jewelry case out from under it. How long has it been there? How many times have I been curled on that bed playing *Rocket League* with him, not knowing my stolen necklace was inches away?

Ford tosses it at me. "Fine. Just don't come crying to me when Ty sells it."

I gape at him. "As if."

But a little niggling voice in the back of my head reminds me that Uncle Ty sold the manor, didn't he? To the Millers, of all people. Would he really see anything wrong in selling the necklace?

I look inside the box, just to make absolutely sure it's there.

The chain's a little tangled after being thrown across the room, but not damaged.

When I look up, Ford has rolled out of bed and is leaning against his windowsill, looking out toward the manor.

"You could cut me some slack, you know," he mutters. "I know you hated her, but my friend just died."

My fingers tighten around the jewelry box, and it closes with a snap. Is he actually trying to use Freya's death as an excuse for the necklace thing? I open my mouth, fully intending to tell him to go screw himself, when I catch sight of his reflection in the window. I've known Ford a long time, and I can tell when he's acting and when he's genuinely upset. Right now, it's the latter. It catches me by surprise. I guess it never occurred to me he was hanging out with Freya because he *liked* her.

Could it have been more than *like*?

Could Ford have been the one on the phone with her that night?

Wait, no, that's not possible. Ford was inside the manor with Dominic then—I saw them both through my old bedroom window. There's no way he was arranging a hookup with her right in front of her brother. Still, that doesn't mean Ford didn't have a crush on Freya. He wouldn't be the only person to have their feelings stomped on by a Miller.

Anyway, I'm not going to bust his chops any more right now. I've said all I needed to. But I guess Ford hasn't.

"Aren't you freaked out by it?" he says. "Some psycho wandering around just a few feet away . . . You lived at the manor until last week, and now a girl's been murdered right *there*." Ford jabs the window with his finger.

"I'm aware of that," I say acidly. "I found her, remember?"

"Of course I remember." He turns to face me, lip curled. "I couldn't forget how it was all about *you,* could I?"

"I'm not saying it's all about me —"

"Aren't you? Because that's exactly what you've been doing for the past year."

"You mean since my parents *died*?" I throw up my hands, but Ford just glares at me. We're done here anyway. *Done* done.

"Would you both like some pancakes?" Ms. Sutter says from the doorway behind me, and I cringe all the way up my spine. "I thought we could have some for breakfast . . ."

"No thank you, Ms. Sutter," I say, gaze still locked on her asshole of a son. "I have to head home."

"Oh, sweetie, are you sure?"

"Positive. Thanks."

I turn and leave with my mom's necklace, and not a single word to Ford.

TWENTY-THREE

'm scheduled to work at the Pump'N'Go later that morning, but I'm in such a foul mood, I seriously consider calling in sick. But I can't ditch Daphne to work a double shift on her own.

Every customer who comes in heads straight for the news-stand, where Freya Miller smiles on the cover of every local news-paper. It's really freaking me out, actually. Like she's watching me. Except the moment I turn my head, even a little, her picture changes in my peripheral vision — eyes becoming bloody voids, her mouth hanging open, all the color drained from her skin. In the end, I grab every paper with her face on it and turn them around in the stand. Mia, my boss, will be pissed. But less pissed than if I walk out.

Still, everyone wants to talk about Freya at the counter. Every-one has a theory. A suspect in mind. Most believe it's connected to Claire Palmer, despite the fact that her death was definitely an accident. (Daphne's adamant, and I trust her.) But all the gossips — all of them — say, "But it makes you wonder, doesn't it, if there's something to all that Dead-Eyed Sadie business . . . ?"

I leave Daphne to deal with them.

The cops are buzzing around town way more than usual too. Somehow, I don't think they're going to find the killer just wan-dering down the road carrying a sign saying *I DID IT.*

I wonder if they'll even find the killer at all.

In school on Monday, it seems like everyone's been interviewed by the cops now. A freshman who talked to the media and claimed to be BFFs with Freya is now strutting around like he's her goddamn Mini-Me.

Some of the faces around me are more worried. Despite the fact that Claire Palmer *did* still have her eyes (though "gone milky," per Daphne's account) and her death has been ruled accidental, I keep hearing whispers about Sadie going on some kind of killing spree. Everyone's wondering who'll be next, and the way they're speculating, it's not entirely like they're scared. I wish I could say the same.

The shrine at Freya's locker has grown, spilling across half the hallway. Photographs, candles, stuffed toys (and I really can't see Freya as a teddy bear kind of girl, to be honest). Someone's even framed a newspaper article: a "so shooketh" piece about *a glittering life full of promise, cut tragically short.* And now everyone seems to have a story to tell the media lingering around town, some reason to traipse in and out of Hamish's office with red eyes.

Don't get me wrong, I agree Freya's death is tragic — I'm not a monster. What's bugging me is that people aren't upset, not exactly. There's this hunger in the air, like two dead bodies in just over a week isn't enough for them now, and they want something worse — some twist to make the horror fresh again.

It's not just kids at school, either. Last night I caught the local news, and Liam from the library was being interviewed. He talked about how he used to play lacrosse with Dominic at their old school, St. David's, and Freya would show up to watch the games.

"I know she kinda had this image as a firecracker ghost-hunter or whatever," he said, "but to me she was always just a sweet, moony-eyed kid." My stomach full-on lurched when he got a faraway look in his eyes. "That's how I'll always remember her."

The news anchor asked what he thought about rumors of Dead-Eyed Sadie and, with a wry smile, he answered, "I wouldn't be surprised by much in this town."

When I reach my locker, I half expect to see more evil-eye graffiti on it, but it hasn't been tampered with again. At least that's something.

I'm so distracted by the grisly vibe filling the school hallways that I don't notice Ford until our eyes accidentally meet next to the locker bank. My hand goes automatically to the necklace at my throat. I've decided to wear it every day now. Not because of anything Ford said about Uncle Ty—it just feels right to keep it close. Safer.

Ford glances down at my hand and then away, slamming his locker. He stalks off in the direction of his homeroom.

"That wasn't awkward at all," Carla mutters next to me.

The Freya buzz flares even louder when Dominic shows up at school Tuesday. I'm selfishly glad to see him, even though I'm surprised he's back so soon. After my art marathon over the weekend, I've pretty much run out of panels to draw for the comic. And watching him stride the hallways of Burden Falls High just like always is weirdly comforting.

Mateo and Casper stick to him like glue, and I don't want to sidle into the middle of that, so I wait until I see him alone at the end of the day before I talk to him.

"How's today been?" I ask. For a second, Dominic seems surprised, like he thought I'd act differently at school than when we're alone in a library or wherever.

"Today has been . . . well, it's cleared something up for me."

We fall into step as we head out to the parking lot.

"Cleared what up?"

"I'm leaving school," he says, no hint of doubt in his voice. "I'll finish the year online. It's something I've been thinking about for a while now, since before . . . well, you know. But as soon as the investigation is wrapped up and they catch the bastard who did it, I'm getting out of here."

"Really?"

"I never wanted to stay in Burden Falls after Grandma died. I only stuck around because that's what my parents and Freya wanted to do. Now Freya's gone, and my parents are already throwing themselves back into work, which means they'll be out of town a lot. Staying here just feels like I'm being . . ."

"Left behind," I finish. Dominic nods. "Where will you go?"

"For a couple of years now, I've been making a list of places with their own strange urban legends. Slender Man, Mothman, Big Foot — that type of thing, but even more weird and obscure. Small towns, out-of-the-way places . . . I want to go on a road trip to see them all and just *explore*." He gets this almost gleeful look on his face that I've only ever seen when we're working on the comic together. I guess Dominic has been planning this a long time.

"Wait, is this list how *Haunted Heartland* got started?"

"Kind of," he says, and his smile falters. "Freya was so interested when I told her about some of the places on my list.

But she wanted to go the whole staged-haunting route with it."

"It's STAGED?" I say, fake-outraged.

"I never wanted to be a . . ." He trails off, pursing his lips.

"Were you going to say 'celebrity'?" I tease. His cheeks flush, and I just can't help myself. "Oh my God, I can't believe I'm actually standing next to *the* Dominic Miller. Wow, do you get fans fawning all over you? Asking for your autograph? Sending you underwear in the mail?" Dominic doesn't answer, just turns a satisfying crimson. I put on my TV announcer voice. "Haunted Heartland *hearttthrob Dominic Miller joins cast of* Celebrity Love Island*!*"

He glances sharply at me. A couple weeks ago, I'd have called it a glower, but not now. It's just a *Dominic* look. "I actually got asked to do that a few weeks ago. Turned it down, of course. And did you just call me a 'hearttthrob'?"

I ignore that. "So, if not a celebrity, what *do* you want to be? Aside from a graphic-novel writer."

Dominic shrugs, a faint smile on his lips. "Isn't that enough? Maybe my road trip will spark some more story ideas. Of course, they won't be much good without my illustrator."

We work on the comic at the public library every day after school. Only for an hour—I haven't told Uncle Ty or Carolyn that I'm working on it with Dominic, and I don't want Carolyn to get suspicious if I'm continually late for our tutoring sessions. She and Uncle Ty wouldn't understand why I'd choose to spend time with a Miller.

Dominic and I fall into a comfortable safe zone of talking about movies we like (we both have a big thing for shark movies, which is possibly the weirdest thing I'd ever expect to have in common with him) and comics, of which he has a *huge* collection I'm sorely jealous of back at the manor.

But we don't talk about our families. We don't talk about the crash, or about Freya's murder. We don't mention what we've both lost. We just sketch and write and chat, all while doing cartwheels to avoid the rotting, festering elephant in the room.

It's Thursday afternoon, near the end of our allotted hour, when I finally break that unspoken agreement.

"Mateo again?" I say, gesturing to Dominic's phone. Mateo has been blowing it up ever since we got to the library, and I can't help wondering if he knows Dominic and I are hanging out—and why.

Dominic looks up from the pages he's reading over. "Mateo's . . . we had a disagreement earlier."

"About . . . ?" When he doesn't immediately elaborate, I reach for the nearest possibility. "Something to do with *Haunted Heartland*?" I guess. Dominic raises an eyebrow.

"Actually, no. I was already out of the show, as far as the others were concerned. It's up to the guys if they want to pick it back up."

"You were out of it?"

"Don't you remember? I fell to my death from Burden Bridge after Dead-Eyed Sadie gouged out my eyes—though your attempt to save me was really something."

"Oh, that." I cringe, despite everything that's happened since.

"Your friend Ford was supposed to be my replacement."

I ignore the spike of anger I feel at just the mention of his name. "What did you and Mateo *disagree* about, then?"

Dominic turns to look across the library floor, and I track his gaze to where Liam is stacking books in a far corner.

"I found out Mateo has been keeping something from me." Dominic sounds tired. He always does lately, not that I blame him. I just hope these comic sessions are a good distraction for him, not *adding* to the shit pile he has to deal with. "I'll start at the beginning: There was an incident, back in our old school. An older boy was harassing Freya, being totally out of line. My parents found out—saw some messages he'd sent on her phone— and got involved right away. They went to the school and dealt with it."

There's something so definite about the way he says *dealt with it,* I can almost picture the boy limping away with his nuts in a takeout carton. "But it turns out the same boy has been in touch with Freya again recently. Mateo knew about it, and of course he told the cops in case it had anything to do with what happened to her, but I was pissed he didn't tell *me* when it was happening."

"What would you have done about it if you'd known?" I ask, genuinely curious.

"I would have dealt with it." He cuts me a look so sharp, I actually stop breathing for a second.

"So, *did* this boy have something to do with Freya's murder?" I hate the eager note in my voice, but this is the first time anyone's mentioned an actual suspect to me. I hadn't quite realized how much I needed to hear that there was someone very much alive behind the murder.

"The cops looked into it. I have to assume they didn't find a reason to arrest him, seeing as he's right over there."

I follow his gaze to where Liam is still restocking shelves.

"It was *Liam*?"

Dominic doesn't answer, but his gaze remains fixed on the other guy, and this is definitely a glower.

"I had no idea . . ." But my voice trails off as I'm about to say I had no idea they knew each other, because that's exactly what Liam said on the news: He used to play lacrosse with Freya's brother. Of course, he failed to mention that he'd acted like a creep with her.

Although . . . what if it wasn't as one-sided as Dominic and his parents assumed? He said his mom and dad found the messages, *not* that Freya told them about it. Liam must be a couple years older than us, so that might've been a big deal to the Millers — enough reason for Freya to keep it secret? As in making secret phone calls from outside the manor . . . ?

"She was fourteen," Dominic says.

I blink at him. "Who was?"

"Freya. When Liam was bothering her back at St. David's."

"Oh. So it was, like, *years* ago?"

Dominic frowns. "More like eighteen months. You know Freya just turned sixteen, right? Her birthday was New Year's Eve."

Well . . . shit. I did not know that. But then I remember the New Year's party she livestreamed; that must've been her sweet sixteen. Most of the seniors at Burden Falls High are already eighteen, or about to be. Damn, how did I not realize she was that much younger than us? I mean, I knew she'd been moved up a grade, but not *two*. And maybe the whole "Miller twins" thing got stuck in my head because I always thought of Freya as being the same age as me.

She was so young. And now she's dead.

I breathe carefully, trying not to vomit over my sketches.

Suspects. Focus on suspects.

At sixteen—or fifteen, if it started before New Year's—it'd be fucked up for pretty much *any* guy to be swapping nudes with her.

Like Liam.

Or Ford?

I shove that thought right out of my head. I'm pissed at him, but he wouldn't swap nudes with an underage girl. And he definitely wouldn't murder one. I'm sure about that.

Right?

TWENTY-FOUR

My Thursday night shift at the Pump'N'Go is as thrilling as a flat tire, so maybe that's why my mind goes into overdrive.

The more I think about it, the more convinced I am there must be some way I can figure out who killed Freya. After all, I overheard her sex convo; I know the manor like the back of my hand; I found her body . . .

And all these things must be pretty damning in the eyes of the cops. How hard are they looking at me right now? I mean, if they don't find the real killer, am I the next best thing? I picture myself being dragged from the gas station in handcuffs.

Focus.

Was there something important I missed in that phone conversation? Did she say a name, and I just dismissed it at the time? I try to remember, but nothing miraculously springs to mind. What about when I found her body, then?

I've spent the last days trying my hardest *not* to think about the murder scene, but I force myself to go over it again now. I close my eyes, picture myself walking through the orchard. Stumbling at the doorway, then looking up and seeing her there. Her eyes — of course, her eyes were the first thing I saw. Or didn't see. How she sat slumped against the pavilion wall. How her hands lay in her lap. How her blood was on her face, her neck . . .

I summon that same smell — sour apples and something

metallic . . . Blood, I realize. That metallic smell was her blood.

My phone rings beneath the counter, scaring the crap out of me. The lone customer glances over at my yelp, and I smile apologetically as I silence the ringer.

It's Ford. Of course it is.

I reject the call and put my phone on silent. But a message comes through before I've even set it down.

Ford: Don't hang up. Please, I need to talk to you about something.

For God's sake. Ford and I haven't spoken since he was such a massive asshole in his room. I've calmed down a *micro*-bit since then, but I still have nothing to say to the guy. He hasn't seemed too keen to talk to me, either, until now. Every time I've seen him, he's looked drawn and pale. I guess Freya's death freaked him out even more than I realized.

I think that's what makes me pick up my phone again. Checking the customer isn't looking, I fire off a quick reply.

Ava: Talk about what?

As soon as I hit send, he's calling again. I put him through to voicemail, then type another message.

Ava: I'm at work! What do you want?

This was a bad idea. But the three dots tell me he's already writing a reply.

Ford: I saw something in Freya's video. It might be important. Need to show it to you in person, don't want anyone else to see.

Damn him. It's like he knows exactly how to lure me in. Which, of course he does. He's been worming his way on and off my shitlist for years.

Ava: Working at the Pump'N'Go until 12.

Ford: I'll be there in 20.

Ava: No, I'll call you when I'm done here.

But he doesn't answer, and the dots don't reappear. I jab the screen to write another message, but accidentally click onto my thread with Dominic. There isn't much to it, just arranging to meet and work on the comic, mostly.

I never did finish going through those images he sent me. And Dominic and I never talked about what he found out about Sadie to use on *Haunted Heartland*—after that day, it seemed like a moot point to me, and Dominic only mentioned it that one time.

I open the thread now, picking up where I left off.

WITCHCRAFT MURDER TRIAL CONCLUDES

The article he's photographed is from a newspaper dated 1866, called the *Evansville Beacon*. I didn't even know there were printed newspapers back then, but I'm not exactly a history nerd. (Carla definitely would've known.) I'm even more surprised to see a headline about witchcraft—I thought that shit ended with Salem.

THE TRIAL OF NOTED APPLE FARMER MISTER EPHRAIM THORN SENIOR ENDED TODAY UPON NEWS OF THE DEFENDANT'S DEATH IN CUSTODY, THE CAUSE OF WHICH IS BELIEVED TO BE NATURAL. CHARGES PENDING AGAINST HIS WIDOW, SUSANNAH, WILL NO LONGER BE PURSUED.

UPON HEARING THE NEWS, A MIGHTY UPROAR ERUPTED OUTSIDE THE COURTROOM, WHERE A NUMBER OF WOMEN, FORMERLY UNDER THE THORNS' EMPLOY, WERE HEARD BY THIS REPORTER TO CALL FOR "JUSTICE FOR OUR SADIE!"

SADIE BURNETT, THE YOUNG WOMAN MISTER AND MRS. THORN STOOD ACCUSED OF MURDERING AND CONSPIRING TO MURDER, RESPECTIVELY, WAS LAST SEEN BY OTHER MEMBERS OF THE THORN HOUSEHOLD ON THE NIGHT OF JUNE 18TH, AND HEARD LATER THAT

SAME NIGHT, WHEN SHE REPORTEDLY CRIED OUT FOR HELP. THIS
REPORTER SPOKE WITH ONE OF THE WOMEN OUTSIDE THE COURT-
ROOM, A MISS REBECCA OAKLEY, WHO CLAIMS SHE HEARD MISS
BURNETT EXCLAIMING, "PLEASE, NOT MY EYES!"—THE SAME FOL-
LOWED BY A TERRIBLE SCREAM.

THROUGHOUT THE TRIAL THUS FAR, MISTER THORN SENIOR
PROCLAIMED HIS INNOCENCE AND THAT OF HIS WIFE ON ACCOUNT OF
MISS BURNETT BEING WELL-KNOWN AS A PRACTITIONER OF WITCH-
CRAFT, AND INSISTED THAT THEY DID NOT END MISS BURNETT'S
LIFE, NOR "COMMIT VIOLENCE UPON HER BEYOND THAT WHICH GOD
WOULD CONDONE." IN HER TESTIMONY, MRS. THORN—A PIOUS
WOMAN, BY ALL ACCOUNTS—STATED THAT SHE "PUT OUT THE EYES
THAT SO BEWITCHED [HER] HUSBAND, THEREBY SEVERING THE DEV-
IL'S HOLD ON HIM." THE PAIR CLAIM TO HAVE THEN LOCKED MISS
BURNETT IN A DISUSED PART OF THE CELLAR, THAT HER SCREAMS
SHOULD NOT DISTURB THE REST OF THE HOUSEHOLD. WHEN A SER-
VANT WENT DOWN TO RELEASE HER COME MORNING, MISS BURNETT
HAD BY ALL APPEARANCE VANISHED WITHOUT TRACE. MRS. THORN
CLAIMED THIS AS EVIDENCE OF THE DEVIL'S SORCERY AT WORK.

THE LADY WAS RELEASED INTO THE CARE OF HER SON, MISTER
EPHRAIM THORN JUNIOR.

WARY OF SIMILAR INSTANCES ARISING DUE TO FEARMONGER-
ING AMONGST THE LOCAL TOWNSPEOPLE, THE JUDGE PROPOSED A
BY-LAW ATTACHING A FINE OF ONE YEAR'S SALARY TO ANY PER-
SON FOUND TO BE PRACTICING OR MAKING PUBLIC REFERENCES
TO WITCHCRAFT. THE PROPOSAL WAS AGREED AND INSTATED AS A
TOWN BY-LAW BY OFFICIALS OF BURDEN FALLS.

I swipe to the next page, hoping to find more of this bizarre
news article, but there's nothing—it jumps ahead to a report of

a storm causing a fire that burned down part of the manor in 1902.

But the trial article . . . Sadie Burnett . . . she *has* to be Dead-Eyed Sadie, right? She was a real person, not just some made-up phantom from a ghost story. And it seems like two of my ancestors killed her. It's right here, in black and white.

Did my great-great-whatever-grandparents actually murder a girl because they thought she was a witch?

I flip back to reread the article and realize I missed an image in between. This one is an article dated two years after the Sadie trial, and at first I think it's another unrelated event: some laborer being prosecuted for vandalizing private property. But I only have to read a couple of lines before I find the name Thorn. Ours was the vandalized property—specifically a barn that was being used to process apples. The laborer, a John B. Miller—no, the last name is not lost on me—was fired from his job at Thorn's orchard after getting his hand mangled in an apple press, and was caught a few days later:

CARVING WHAT IN LOW PARLANCE IS OFTEN REFERRED TO AS THE EVIL EYE ONTO THE WOOD SIDING OF THE AFOREMENTIONED BARN.

THE MAN DID NOT APPEAR IN THE LEAST CONTRITE, IN FACT GOING ON TO SAY THAT: "THE THORNS DESERVED ALL THEY GOT, AND A LOT MORE BESIDES. THEY MAY THINK WE FORGOT WHAT THEY DID, THAT THEY CAN KEEP DOING WRONG BY OTHERS WITHOUT FEAR OF CONSEQUENCE, BUT THE TOWNSFOLK OF BURDEN FALLS REMEMBER. WE SEE. ALL THE THORNS' WRONGDOINGS WILL COME BACK AROUND, MARK MY WORDS."

JOHN BURNETT MILLER WAS SENTENCED TO THIRTY DAYS IN THE COUNTY JAIL. MISTER EPHRAIM THORN JUNIOR APPEARED

I can't quite catch my breath by the time I finish the article. Did Dominic read this before he sent it to me? Was this John *Burnett Miller* actually his ancestor, and somehow related to Sadie Burnett? Was this where the bad blood between our families really started, with murder and revenge?

If it's true—and I have no reason to think it isn't—I really do come from a long line of bastards. And the Millers have far more claim on Sadie than I've ever had.

So why was Freya the one to die like that? Why wasn't it me?

And was the incident in this news story where all the evil eyes came from—where it all started? Were they some underground signal among people who hated my family? A reminder of what we'd done to Sadie Burnett—what we were capable of? Or are they all curses aimed at Thorn Manor?

"Hey."

I jump like I've been Tasered. Ford stands on the opposite side of the counter, snow dusting his hair and shoulders. His eyes look bloodshot, like he's been awake for days.

"What are you doing here?" My voice is tight and a little shrill. "I said I'd call you."

"I need to show you something," he says, looking back over his shoulder as though expecting someone else to stride in through the door. "Can you take a break?"

"I have a customer," I hiss. The customer, who's taking so long, I feel fairly certain she's working up the courage to shoplift something, cuts a quick glance our way. Obviously listening. "Hang on," I sigh. "I'll see if Mia can cover the counter."

Mia's fine with it, and waves me off.

I catch Ford's sleeve and tug him outside and beyond the gas pumps to the bench that serves as a bus stop at the side of the road. The bench is covered in ice-crusted snow, so it's useless to sit on. We kind of hover next to it — me just waiting, Ford pacing, his breath fogging the air around his head. At least it's stopped snowing for now.

"Ford, I don't have long . . ."

He comes to a sudden stop. "You're still pissed at me, aren't you?"

I let my glare answer for me.

"Come on, Ava. I hate it when we fight."

"Then maybe you shouldn't act like such a jerk all the time. Look, just say whatever you came to say, okay?"

I'm not sure he's listening, because he starts pacing again. Then stops just as abruptly. "I've been going over everything in my head, trying to figure out what the hell happened and who the killer could be, and I spotted something important in Freya's video . . ."

Now that he's facing me, I catch a whiff of something smoky on his breath. "Ford, are you *high* right now?"

"No!" He throws his hands up, but that only wafts it my way again. "Fine, I had a smoke, but I've had this weird feeling all week like someone's watching me, and I needed to calm down."

"Seems like it worked real well," I say drily.

I fold my arms, majorly unimpressed. I mean, I'm not the fun police, but I did not sign up for this. It's also damn cold standing out here.

"You don't understand—I just keep looking out my window and thinking about it, what it must've felt like, how scared she must've been . . ."

A bus rolls along the road toward us, slowing as though to stop, but I wave it on.

"You dragged me out of work because you're high and paranoid and think you've had some huge stoner epiphany that I need to hear right now? Go home, Ford. You're pissing me off."

"Jesus, will you just *listen*—"

There's a rumble in the road behind me. Ford's face is lit up starkly in the headlights for a second, harsh and irritated. Then his eyes go wide. For one crystalline moment, I can just tell something awful is about to happen. It's like I'm back in my parents' car, watching Dad's mouth open and close in his reflection in the window.

Ford launches himself away from the road, knocking me off-balance, and I stumble backward, toward the lights.

TWENTY-FIVE

My scream hangs in my throat, ready to be punched out of me on impact. I fall and land hard on my knees. My hands burn as they scrape against the sidewalk.

Tires screech at my back as the car skids on the ice. I wait for the crushing pain.

And wait.

It never comes.

When I look up, the car is idling at an angle in the road. Its front fender stands inches away from where I'm crouched. Chest heaving, too stunned to move, that aborted scream comes out as a whimper.

"Shit, Ava, I didn't mean to do that. I just . . ." Ford trails off—maybe because it's hard to come up with an excuse for not even bothering to warn me that a car was about to plow right into me. No, Ford just shoved me aside like always.

The window rolls down next to me, and Mr. Hamish's head appears. He looks almost as shook up as me.

"Ava Thorn? Is that you? Are you all right?"

I can't answer. My mind is numb, caught on the fact that I almost just died, thanks to my best friend.

No. Ford's not my best friend. He's not any kind of friend.

I get up, brushing away the snow that's fast turning to wet patches on my knees. My hands shake, and my mouth's too dry to get a word out.

"Ava?" Mr. Hamish calls uncertainly.

"Yes, I . . ." I turn around to reassure him that I'm not hurt—not physically—then stop. "*Freya?*"

I gasp when I see the girl sitting in the seat next to the guidance counselor. Even in the dim interior, I see the blood-red color of her hair.

"What did she just call me?" she asks Mr. Hamish, and then I know I'm mistaken. Whoever she is, her voice is too high and girlish to be Freya.

And *of course* it isn't her. I saw her dead body just a few days ago. I've seen it a hundred times since then, in the dark.

Ford's staring at me, one hand clapped over his mouth. I'm not sure if it's because he made the same mistake I did, or if he can't believe what just happened.

"My break's over," I say tersely.

"Ava, wait . . ." Ford follows me as I stride toward the Pump'N'Go. But I don't slow down.

"Fuck off, Ford. We're done," I say, and I keep walking.

Ford hangs around outside until Mia spots him on the security monitor in her office and tells him to go home. I watch him walk away from the gas station, but then my phone starts to ping, of course. His messages veer from telling me I was overreacting to baiting me.

> Ford: I'm so sorry. I didn't mean to push you, I was just trying to get out of the way of the car and I judged it wrong. Fucked it up, like always. You know I'd never hurt you on purpose.

Thoughtless ass!

Maybe Ford didn't shove me on purpose, but he also didn't

give a shit whether I got out of the way in time. Just looking out for himself, as usual.

When he doesn't get a response, his texts get weirder.

Ford: Don't ignore me, Ava.

Ford: I never showed you what I saw in the video Freya took in my room. It might help figure out who killed her.

He knows exactly how to get me to engage, but I refuse this time. Still, I watch the video back under the gas-station counter, just in case. But I can't see any big clue.

He's just talking crap. Trying to lure me back into his bullshit the way he always does.

And how can I even think about being friends with someone who doesn't think twice about shoving me into danger if it'll save his own ass?

I can't. And I'm honestly pretty tired of forgiving Ford for the inconsiderate shit he does. I actually think Carla's right — Ford doesn't see me as a friend. I was just a convenient place-filler for him until he could weasel his way in with the Millers. More *useful* friends.

It's after midnight when I get home, but I'm still wired after my near-death experience. At least Ford has given up trying to worm his way around me now.

I sit at my desk, sipping the last of my decaf coffee, and am about to turn off my phone when I get a message from Daphne.

Daphne: Heads-up: Mateo and Casper are arranging a danse tomorrow at Copper Bell Dam in memory of Freya.

I pretty much knew this was coming. I'm actually surprised it's taken this long. But I won't be going to this *danse,* obviously. It'd be too weird, considering I hated Freya.

Ava: Are you going?

Daphne: Everyone's going. I think you should too.

Ava: I'd rather avoid seeing Ford right now.

Daphne: What did he do this time?

I consider trying to explain over text, but I know Daphne will be all shades of pissed on my behalf, and I don't really want to get into it right now. Last time Ford and I had a big bust-up, she went all philosophical on me, explaining what she calls her Dimple Theory.

Basically, it revolves around the fact that Carla has this one particular smile that brings out her dimples. They're cute as hell. But they only ever seem to come out when Daphne's around. Of course, Daphne noticed this. And it spawned her Dimple Theory: that when you're in a relationship with someone, you bring out something no one else can. Sometimes that can be good—like with Carla's magnificent dimples. "And sometimes," Daphne added pointedly, "two people bring out the worst in each other."

What I gathered from this theory is that she thinks Ford and I are kind of shitty when we're around each other. I hate to admit it, but she's probably right.

Damn it. I'm so done agonizing over Ford Sutter.

Searching for a distraction, I skim over those old news articles Dominic sent me. If Uncle Ty had been up when I got home, I'd have asked him if he knew about the possible murder in our family's past, and how the evil eyes are maybe connected.

Daphne: Ava? Are you OK?

Damn. I forgot to reply.

Ava: I'm fine, just got distracted for a sec. Ford thing was nothing major. I'll tell you about it tomorrow.

Daphne: OK, if you're sure. But don't let him stop you going to the danse. You need to be there.

Ava: Why?

Daphne: Because EVERYONE'S going. It'll look like you're hiding if you don't.

She has a point. I'm sure half the kids at school think I had *some* part in Freya's death. Everyone knows I hated her.

I trace the indentation of one of the eyes carved around my window, wondering if it'll shoot pain into my fingertip, like a demon walking into a church and getting struck by lightning. There's no shooting pain, but I do knock over the little weasel skull. It lies on its side. For a weird moment, its empty eye socket seems to blink.

My phone leaps in my hand — another message. I force a half-laugh, telling myself I'm definitely too sleep-deprived if I'm seeing long-dead rodents winking at me.

Daphne: Dominic will be there.

I frown at my phone.

Ava: So?

It takes Daphne a while to respond this time. I can just picture her twirling the chain of her necklace while she comes up with the right way to put whatever she's about to say — which I'm pretty sure I'm not going to like.

Daphne: So we should all be there to show moral support, no matter how we felt about Freya.

There it is: the perfect mix of guilt and goading.

"Whatever," I murmur, and turn off my phone.

I wake up with my face pressed against something hard, and a savage crick in my neck.

I must've fallen asleep sketching at my desk again. My lamp is on, and it's still dark outside my window. The windowpane is opaque, frost built up into a solid layer on the outside.

I carefully lift my head, stretching out my fingers over the page of the comic I was working on. Except the page isn't one from my project. It's just a piece of scrap with doodles all over it. I blink, trying to wake up my brain.

Eyes?

The paper has been torn from my drafting sketchbook. One where I was trying to figure out the right eyes to give the girl from my comic. The entire page is covered in them — nothing but eyes, all staring back up at me.

I find the sketchbook and tuck the page back inside, my skin feeling prickly. I don't remember working on that. I'm sure I was working on a panel from the comic where the girl is leaning over the open trapdoor in the cellar, peering down into it.

No, that page is set neatly to one side at the corner of my desk. I must've switched to working on her eyes again, but I don't remember it. I turn off the lamp, waiting for a moment while my vision adjusts to the dark. But as it clears, and the round window in front of me becomes a frosted silvery disc, I see the hazy outline of someone standing outside it.

TWENTY-SIX

*R*_{*ight*} outside.

My chair tips backward as I leap to my feet, jerking again when it clatters loudly against the stone floor. Outside the window, the figure doesn't move except to tilt its head slightly, as though responding to the sound.

"Who's out there?" I shout, voice high and thin. The voice of a victim, not a Thorn.

The figure doesn't react. Stays perfectly still, in fact, and I wonder if they're listening for the sound of my heartbeat. I'm pretty sure they'll hear it, it's pounding so loudly.

It's probably just Ford come to bug me in person.

Steeling myself, I pull my sleeve over my fist and wipe it across the window.

A face gapes in at me, no more than an inch away from the glass. Pale, surrounded by black, stringy hair, and with twin black holes where her eyes should be. Definitely not Ford.

I scream.

Turning, I trip over the fallen chair and land hard on my bedroom floor, but I don't stop to cry about it. I dive for the door and sprint through the garage, still yelling at full volume. I slam through the door to the kitchen, skidding to a stop when I see Carolyn at the sink.

"What's wrong? What happened?"

"Sadie! Outside my window! She's outside!"

Carolyn's eyes widen in surprise, but she doesn't hesitate. "Wait here," she says, nodding firmly, then strides out the way I just came in.

"Carolyn, no! Wait!" I go after her because I can't not, even though my legs are telling me to turn and run the other way. The light is on when I follow her into my bedroom, the chair still lying on its side next to my desk. Carolyn leans over it to peer through the window.

"Can't see anyone. I'll go take a look outside."

She returns quickly, shaking her head. "Nope. And there's actually nothing for anyone to stand on out there — the river runs right under your window. Are you sure you saw someone out there?"

But I'm looking around the room, at all the sketches of eyeless girls and corpses crawling through graveyards, and I'm not sure about anything anymore.

"It's okay," I say quietly. "I think it was just the tail end of a nightmare." One that followed me into the waking world.

Carolyn wraps me in a hug, and I breathe in the fresh smell of her shampoo. "Sorry, I bet I woke you with all my yelling," I say. She pulls away, smiling.

"Don't be silly, I just came down for some water. And listen, anyone would be having nightmares in your situation. You have nothing to apologize for."

When she leaves, I lie in bed, staring at the crack in my ceiling until my eyes finally close, and I sleep.

Uncle Ty looks up from the crossword puzzle he's working on when I walk through the kitchen the next morning. I notice he's had to scribble over a few of his answers in the grid. Carolyn will probably correct them again later.

"Hey, cupcake. How did you sleep? Carolyn told me you had another nightmare."

I shrug. I'm not sure what I saw last night, but I'm sleeping with my curtains shut from now on.

I printed out the article Dominic sent me—the one about Sadie, specifically. I lay it in front of Uncle Ty. "Can I ask you about some old Thorn family stuff?"

He laughs. "Okay. Did you hire a PI or something?"

"No, just looked through some old records." It's not like I can tell him Dominic gave me the article.

Uncle Ty reads the article. When he nears the end, I'm surprised to see his eyes light up.

"There really was a witch in the pit!" He smacks a hand on the table, like he just won a bet.

"What?"

"Don't you remember, when you were little? I told you there was a witch living in the pit beneath the cellar."

I do remember. It was one of the scariest moments of my young life. "So you already knew about Sadie Burnett—Dead-Eyed Sadie?"

"Not exactly. That story about the witch was one your dad told me when I was little." He grins crookedly. "It's like a rite of passage for young Thorns to go down there and prove you're not scared of the witch. I figured it might have something to do with the Dead-Eyed Sadie thing, but I never knew it was based on anything *real*. It was always just kids' stories, you know? But maybe I should've waited until you were a little older before taking you down there, huh? Boy, did you *scream*."

I force a laugh. I still remember how terrifying it felt at the time, but I know Uncle Ty didn't really mean to scare me so much. And I never did make it down into the pit.

"So you didn't know about Sadie being related to the Millers?"

"She was?" Uncle Ty leans back in his seat, brows raised. "I guess I shouldn't be surprised the Millers are descended from witches," he adds wryly.

"Do you believe that everyone in our family sees Sadie right before they die? Like Dad did?" Uncle Ty stares back at me, the humor gone from his face now. "You don't believe it was just a symptom of his seizure, do you?"

"I . . . Well. I don't think I ever told you this," Uncle Ty says, "but my dad said he saw Sadie a couple times in the days before his accident too."

Accident. The word we always use when we talk about Grandpa's death, even though he probably wasn't just cleaning his pistol when it went off.

"I remember you said something about it at his funeral."

Uncle Ty sucks his teeth. "Yeah, not my finest moment. But the truth is, I don't know if anyone's really seen Sadie. Probably never will . . . until it's my turn, anyway."

"Not funny," I say, looking down at the scars on my hands.

I'm not at all sure whether to confess to Uncle Ty the thing that's burning at the back of my mind — that's been smoldering there for over a year now. But keeping it to myself hasn't done me any good so far, and maybe sharing it will.

"I think I saw her too," I say. I see Uncle Ty lean forward in my peripheral vision.

"You did? When?"

"The day of the crash. And again at the river a few days ago. Then last night, outside my window. And I don't know if it's real, or just something in my head. I mean, when I found Freya, she looked so much like her . . ."

He's frowning when I look up, but not like he thinks I've totally lost my mind. Just concerned. And a little uncomfortable. This is heavier stuff than Uncle Ty and I usually talk about. But I've made it this far.

"Do you think I should go see a therapist again? Dr. Ehrenfeld, maybe?" I say.

There's no mistaking his grimace, and I know he's thinking about the money. Still, he says, "Okay, if you think you *need* to. I'm sure we can make it work somehow . . . I'll look into it." At my raised eyebrow, he smiles. "All right, I'll ask Carolyn to look into it."

But, now that it's out there, I'm not so sure anymore. I mean, I'm pretty sure Dr. Ehrenfeld would tell me this is all part of my "healing process." And I've probably been making it worse for myself, always looking for Sadie around every corner, hiding in every shadow. I just need to chill out, hang with my friends. Stop looking for ghosts.

"Actually, can you not?" I say. "I kinda feel better just talking to you about it."

Uncle Ty smiles, clearly relieved. "You let me know if you change your mind, okay?" He taps his finger on the article before handing it back. "But maybe give the digging a rest, yeah? Every family has shitty parts to their history, and ours is no different. Maybe it's better to let the dead rest, and try to get on with living."

"Sure." And speaking of . . . "By the way, there's a party tonight at Copper Bell Dam. A bunch of kids from school will be there. Is it all right if I go?"

His eyebrows shoot up. "Of course. You know you don't need my permission. Is it one of those *danse* things?" I nod. "You need me to pick anything up for you on my way home? Booze, condoms . . . ?"

I laugh. "Nah, I'm all set."

I'm moving on autopilot when I pull into the school parking lot a few minutes later. My focus quickly snaps back when I see a squad car in the far corner, lights flashing.

Shit. Did something else happen?

Or are they here to arrest someone?

Are they here to arrest *me*?

But Daphne's dad—fully in Officer Chavez mode—gets out and opens the back door of the squad car. A very pissed-looking Mateo climbs out, snaps something at Officer Chavez, then stomps off toward the main entrance. Daphne's dad gets back in his car and drives away, tipping me a quick wave on the way past.

Huh. I wonder what all that was about.

I head inside, and I'm pleased to find Daphne and Carla have arrived first for a change.

"What's going on with Mateo?" I ask as soon as I'm close enough to whisper. Mateo's farther along the hallway, acting very pissy with the contents of his locker. Daphne and Carla both stare at me like I've grown horns. "I just saw him getting out of your dad's squad car . . . ?" I prompt.

"You did?" Daphne's indignant frown tells me all I need to know.

"He didn't say anything to you?"

"No! Let me go text him . . ."

Carla and I exchange a knowing look while Daphne moves three feet away for some reason, then returns moments later.

"He says he can't tell me about it," she huffs.

My digging thwarted, I have to wait until lunchtime to go look for Dominic and see if I can get any info from him. But I can't find him, and some careful questioning of our few mutuals tells me he's taken the day off.

I wait until I have a free period, then head out to the lot to call him from my car.

He picks up after one ring. It's almost like he was expecting me to call. *Hoping* I would?

"How come you're not in school?" I ask, rather than wasting time on hello. (I think Carla might be a bad influence on me.)

"I had another migraine last night, so decided to take the day. What's up?"

Okay, not just waiting around for me to call. "Two things, really. First up, why the hell did Mateo get dropped at school by a squad car?"

Dominic makes a sound that's half sigh, half snicker. "I heard he had to go make a statement about a scuffle he got into with your pal Liam Walsh."

"A scuffle? And Liam isn't my *pal*, pal."

"Good," he says. Is he . . . relieved? But then I guess he would be — the guy used to creep on his little sister. "And, from what Mat told me, he overheard Liam with some journalist talking crap about Freya. So he hit him."

"You sound proud," I tell him.

"Not really. I'm just relieved Mateo didn't get into serious trouble over it. Besides, put a football in his hand and Mateo is a machine, but the guy throws a weak punch." There's a pause before Dominic adds, "Please don't tell him I said that. He could literally kill me." Another pause. "By which I mean figuratively, of course."

"You sound like Carla. So fancy with your words," I tease without thinking, and he laughs openly this time. He has a loud bark of a laugh, completely unrestrained. It's not at all the kind of laugh I'd expect him to have. I . . . don't hate it?

"What was the other thing you wanted to talk to me about?" he asks.

I grimace, glad he can't actually see me. Because there's no way to say this without sounding weird. So I just come right out with it.

"In those articles you sent me, it says Sadie's last name was Burnett. But there's also a John Burnett *Miller*, who I'm guessing was some relation to her . . . He's your ancestor, right? Why didn't you tell me sooner that you're related to Sadie?"

There's a silence on the line. I close my eyes to listen, hoping for some clue as to what he's thinking. But all I hear is the steady sound of his breathing. I keep my eyes closed for a moment.

"John Burnett was Sadie's older brother," he says at last. "He and the rest of his family added Miller as their last name after she died — probably to try to distance themselves from Ephraim and

Susannah Thorn's claim that Sadie was a witch. Eventually my ancestors dropped the Burnett altogether."

I take a beat to process all this. "Why didn't you tell me, though? Why make me piece it together from those old articles?"

"I . . . I guess I didn't want it to seem like I was trying to take something else away from you," he says.

"Sadie isn't *mine*."

"Isn't she? It's always seemed like she means something to you — something more than just a ghost story."

Now it's my turn to go quiet. It doesn't last long, though. "Do you believe in curses?"

"Do you mean like hexes, or more general bad luck?"

"The first one, I guess."

"Where's this coming from, Thorn?"

"Well, the articles you sent me, mostly. But not just that . . . I dunno. Do you think my family is actually cursed because of all the bad shit my ancestors did? I assume you read it, right? Was that why you really sent it to me . . . you think I'm cursed?"

"Ava, no. Of course not. I honestly hadn't thought about it that way. I mean, yeah, there's good and bad if you look through your family tree — it's the same for everyone, me included. But with that connection between our two families going back over a century, and how we still have — well, let's just call it bad blood — I thought it was interesting. Figured you might too. I never meant to upset you with any of it. I'm sorry if I did."

"So you don't think my cursed family might've caught your family up in some witchy backlash now?"

The line goes quiet for a moment, and I'd swear I hear him murmuring *witchy backlash* to himself on the other end of the line.

"Thorn, you had nothing to do with Freya's murder. Besides, you could just as easily say this *town* is as cursed as your family. Or the land the manor's built on. Or the orchard. Or any of the arbitrary things I've heard people say are cursed in the year I've lived here."

"My mom used to say the waterfall was cursed," I admit. "The story goes that the water's supposed to carry away your burdens, right? But she told me if you try to solve your problems that way, they only come back to bite your ass harder."

Dominic laughs again. "I suspect your mom was just trying to teach you that you can't solve your problems by pretending they don't exist."

"Yeah, maybe. That does sound like her."

We hang up a little while later, but I don't get out of my car for a moment.

As I'm looking around the lot outside—the parked cars, the line of trees running parallel to the school building—I can't help noticing all the eyes.

They're everywhere.

There's one on the back of the school welcome sign. Another one etched into a gatepost. And another spray-painted onto that dumpster.

Did people really start leaving these marks as a reminder of what my family did to Sadie? A warning that you shouldn't trust a Thorn, or they might butcher you and get away with it? Wasn't that pretty much what happened to John Burnett Miller as well—maimed while working for my family, then cast out with nothing? Maybe people *should* be warned about us.

Stay away.

Maybe anyone who gets close to us gets hurt.

TWENTY-SEVEN

Carolyn spots me through the open kitchen door just as I'm leaving later that night. She comes over and fixes my mask so it's on straight.

"You look amazing," she says, stepping back to take in the entire outfit.

I shrug. "This old thing?"

I'm wearing deep plum lipstick and heavy eyeliner (which you can barely see under the lace eye mask, but still), and a pair of curved black horns on my head. The rest of my clothes are fairly par for the course for me—black skinny jeans with knee-high boots, a plum silk shirt with a black furry vest over it, and my black wool gloves. And my coat, of course—the temperature has taken a (hopefully) final plunge today, so we're going to freeze our asses off tonight. Thank the Dark Lord for booze warmth.

"Have fun," Carolyn says, laughing, then nudges me toward the door.

I text Daphne and Carla to let them know I'm on my way and set off along the river to Copper Bell Dam. I see the lights swaying from the trees long before I reach them, strings of tiny lanterns flickering like fireflies in glass cages. And there's the music, of course. All I hear to begin with is the deep, gritty bass, but then I catch the eerie, compelling vocal—it's "Carrion Flowers" by Chelsea Wolfe. My stomach tightens a little as I remember the last time I was here—when I had that weird dizzy spell and thought I saw Dead-Eyed Sadie standing on the far riverbank. I hunch a little tighter into my coat.

At last, I hear people's voices among the trees. I'm soon faced with an array of dark creatures—someone in a tuxedo wearing the head of a warthog; a gray-skinned elf with completely black eyes; and a hijabi knight with a metal breastplate and gauntlets decorated with swirling red symbols who I don't recognize until she turns slightly, and I realize I'm looking at Yara from my art class.

Moving past them, I look around for Daphne and Carla. I know from our texts earlier that Carla will be dressed as a zombie, and Daphne as a clockwork spider, whatever that is. I move through the little clusters of teenagers swaying to the music along the riverbank path. There are a lot of people here, but not nearly as many as there'd normally be at a *danse*. I guess some parents are worried about letting kids go out at night after what happened to Freya. Or maybe it's just the cold keeping them indoors.

The river itself is frozen, faint patterns on its surface like some giant hand has swirled white paint onto it. Without meaning to, I twist those patterns into the shape of an eye.

I weave between a macabre group of skeletal cats I recognize as part of the cheerleading squad, then find myself face-to-face with Slender Man. Seeing his black suit with tentacles protruding from the back, and a blank white mask covering his entire head, it's easy to lie to myself that I can't tell who's beneath it.

I wonder how he's feeling. I mean, does having a *danse* for his dead sister feel wrong to Dominic? Or like a necessary passage—a way for us to mark the loss of someone our age the way a funeral or a memorial never seems to. This is how we do things here. And, no matter my feelings about her, Freya was one of us.

This will probably be Dominic's last *danse* in Burden Falls.

He shakes his head, palms up.

"Oh," I say, realizing he's wondering what I'm dressed as. "Non-specific dark fae. I worked with what I had available. I like your costume, though." Silently, Slender Man holds out his white-gloved hand. "Are you . . . asking me to dance?"

He nods. And somehow, with our masks in place, it doesn't feel weird to step into his arms. We move together, swaying to the slow, pulsing music. The tiny lanterns hanging from the trees sway with us.

The sound of people talking, dancing, laughing is like a veil around us. I don't want to speak. Don't want to do anything that will break this moment and make it impossible to stay here, like this. Because a Thorn doesn't dance with a Miller. That's what I've always believed. But do I still? Do those centuries of bad blood still run between us?

I lean into him when he wraps his arms around my waist. There's that faint scent of expensive cologne. My fingers wander from his shoulder, and I slide off my glove to trace the sharp edge of his jaw through the thin material of his mask. I smile when I take my hand away.

Not bloody.

I look up into his face. But there's only that blank mask, faint hollows where his eyes should be. And it doesn't feel like I'm looking at a mask. It feels like a memory — or a premonition.

I slid off my glove to touch Freya's cold, eyeless face . . .

"No!"

I stumble backward, hands up as though I can ward it off.

Dominic rolls away the mask. "Thorn? What's wrong?"

"I—"

My reply is cut off as a scream echoes across the river. Dominic and I stare at each other for a moment before we run in that direction. All around us, the music keeps playing. There's a crowd gathered on the bank, yelling and pointing out at the frozen river. I spot Daphne and Carla among them.

Daphne's wearing a headdress decorated with eight gears of varying sizes to make up a clockwork spider's eyes, and her black leotard has been decorated with chunky brass-colored hinges at every joint. Next to her, Carla has her fingers laced with Daphne's.

Carla's zombie makeup is on point, as expected. There are gaping wounds on her cheeks and neck, her eyes look yellowed and bloodshot, and her hair hangs in crusty-looking rats' tails around her shoulders. Her clothes are about as Standard Carla as mine are Standard Ava, but she has dirtied them up a little with some fake blood.

"Hey," I call to them as I hurry over. "What's going on?"

"I think someone's fallen through the ice!" Daphne points to the river beyond the thickest cluster of onlookers. As her arm extends, it fans out four extra attached limbs.

"Did you just get here?" Carla asks.

"Yeah." I can't help shooting a glance to where Dominic was standing a second ago, but he's not there now.

The shouting at the river's edge seems to swell, but I'm too short to see what's happening. I push my way through until I'm standing right on the riverbank. Then I see it—or *him,* in fact—bursting up through a break in the ice.

"Help me!" Mateo screams, hands clawing at the cracked ice around where he fell through. "There's someone in the water—"

He sputters as he sinks down and water rushes into his mouth. Damn, I can't even imagine how cold that must be. We have to get him out of there *now*.

Then Dominic appears, edging out across the ice, Slender Man tentacles fanning out around him. He drops to his fore-arms and shins, spreading his weight, and starts to crawl toward Mateo. But it won't do either of them any good if Dominic falls through as well. The ice is obviously too thin in places—dark patches showing where the river has only frozen a sliver.

"We need to make a chain," I say, more to myself than anyone else, but my words are echoed through the crowd and suddenly we're moving forward. Casper follows Dominic, then Carla, and I end up between her and Daphne, grabbing onto Carla's ankle as I feel Daphne gripping my boot behind me. I scoot down onto all fours and shuffle forward. The chill bleeds through my clothes like a warning.

"Help!" Mateo cries up ahead, then sinks again. He's not flailing around anymore, probably too numb with cold to do more than tread water. If we don't hurry, he'll sink down below the ice and get carried away by the current. There'll be no way to save him then.

The ice creaks as we scramble across it. Looking up, I see Dominic is almost close enough to grab Mateo if he just reaches up out of the water, but I see no sign of Mateo in the ice break now. Dominic inches forward again. There's a crack loud enough that I hear it four people back in the chain, but the ice holds under him—for now.

Dominic plunges one arm into the water with a wordless yell. That water must be painfully cold. Still, he keeps reaching forward, feeling around for Mateo under the water. Then he yells again. "Pull!"

Gritting my teeth, I start to edge back, gripping Carla's ankle. I feel a tug from behind, and I slide backward on the ice. I look back to find the whole crowd now pulling from the riverbank. Carla comes next, and we both get lifted back up onto solid ground as Casper and Dominic are dragged back to shore. I see Casper now back on the riverbank, Dominic about to follow, and Mateo still being hauled from the ice—and someone else behind him.

Mateo hits the edge of the river. People jostle around me. As they part to make room for Mateo to come back up, I see who's behind him. Mateo's hand is tangled in a head of dark, sodden curls. He's pulling someone along by the hair, but they don't seem to care. They aren't fighting.

"Oh my God, it's a body! There was a body in the water!" someone screams.

Now *I* scream. But I can't do anything else as the figure with the curly hair is rolled onto its back, head lolling to face me on the frozen river.

Ford gapes up at me, lips blue and stretched in a soundless scream.

And he has no eyes.

TWENTY-EIGHT

There's an itchy blanket wrapped around my shoulders, but it doesn't do much to stop me shivering. I lean against the trunk of Officer Chavez's patrol car on the far side of the trees, watching the first responders move purposefully around with clipboards and medical bags. The trees aren't twinkling with lanterns now, but flashing red and blue.

"I assume my daughter was never here," Officer Chavez says, with some not very subtle side-eye. I shake my head. Pretty much everyone who was at the *danse* is gone. They disappeared as soon as word spread that the cops were on their way. Even Daphne and Carla. They offered to stay with me, but I sent them away. No point in them getting caught at a party where kids were drinking underage, even if the three of us hadn't actually had time to drink anything yet. Carla has her place at NYU to consider, and Daphne would be grounded for the rest of her life if her dad caught her here.

Mateo was taken away in an ambulance, yelling for them to hurry as he was stretchered in, and how he'd sue everyone if he lost a nut to frostbite.

Dominic is talking to some other cops on the far side of the clearing. He keeps squinting and rubbing the side of his head, and I wonder if he got hurt hauling Mateo and Ford from the river, or if the whole thing has brought on another migraine. But he still looks a lot more held-together than I feel.

And Ford . . . Jesus.

Ford.

I saw him, but it still doesn't seem real. I want to call him, ask if he's heard about the guy from our class who got pulled from the river . . . Ford can't be dead, not really.

His eyes, though . . .

My stomach rolls, and this time there's no stopping it. Officer Chavez quickly steps aside as I bend over and throw up on the grass right next to his rear fender. I heave until there's nothing left, then sleeve-wipe my mouth, grimacing. When I look up, Officer Chavez is holding out a bottle of water.

"Thanks."

"Ava?" I jump, sloshing water over my hand as Detective Holden appears next to us. He's wearing a navy suit this evening. I wonder if he ever takes a night off. "How are you doing?"

I glance down at the pile of vomit, which is now giving off curls of steam in the squad car's taillights. "Not great, Detective."

"Think you can handle answering a few questions for me?"

I remember Uncle Ty's warning not to speak to the cops without him there, and right now I can't even think about anything beyond crawling into bed and shutting my eyes tight against the world. "I really just want to go home."

He nods. "Of course, of course. Except for just one thing, if you don't mind?" He leans against the car next to me, carefully avoiding the puke puddle. "A couple of the kids I've spoken to said you and Ford Sutter were pretty close. Is that right?"

I swallow hard, my throat still burning. "We were best friends for years," I croak. "Detective, my clothes are soaked. I'm exhausted and freezing. Please can I go home?"

Detective Holden feigns surprise, like he hadn't noticed. I don't think there's much he doesn't notice, though.

"Of course, Ava. But I hope you won't mind if I call to see you tomorrow morning to get a full statement."

I push away from Officer Chavez's car, leaving without another word.

For the first time in ages, I sleep, if not exactly peacefully. There are dreams—I sense their after-images like hand marks on my skin—but I don't remember what they were.

All I know is that Ford is dead.

My best friend since forever—gone.

I haven't forgotten that he stole from me, or that he almost let me get hit by a car. Maybe I never would've spoken to him again. But now that's not even a possibility. And I *hate* that the last words we said to each other were angry.

Beyond this sad, numb, guilt-riddled mood I seem to be in when I wake up, I'm angry. Someone did that to Ford. They killed him, turned his eyes into raw gouges, and dumped him in the river. And that's the lingering image I'll have of him. The one his mom will probably be imagining right now too.

A sob wracks through me thinking of Ford's mom. She'll be absolutely broken by this.

I drag myself out of bed. Somehow, I end up showered and dressed, though I couldn't tell you how. I go through to the kitchen, intending to head straight over to see Ms. Sutter, but there are cops sitting at the dining table. Detective Holden and Officer Cordell—the same policewoman who was there when I gave my statement about Freya.

227

Detective Holden smiles when he sees me. "Looks like she's awake after all," he announces, and I realize Uncle Ty must've been trying to get rid of him when I walked in. Why couldn't I have waited just a few more minutes?

Uncle Ty scowls across the table at him. Carolyn leans against the counter, arms folded across her chest.

Both she and Uncle Ty were shocked to hell when I stumbled in last night and told them Ford had been pulled from the river. They both knew him, *liked* him, Uncle Ty especially. Judging by the dark circles under their eyes, I don't think either of them slept too well.

"Feeling ready to talk to us, Ava?"

It doesn't really look like I have a choice. I slide into the seat next to Uncle Ty.

"What would you like to know, Detective?" My voice sounds a lot steadier than I feel. Holden leans forward, eager to catch every word that falls out of me.

"First of all," he begins, "I'm really sorry we have to do this right now—I know you and Ford were close, and with this happening right after Freya Miller's murder, well . . . we all need to do whatever we can to help catch the person who did it, don't we?"

"Of course," I say flatly. Why is he talking to me like I'm five years old?

"So, from what we can tell, Ford died sometime late Thursday night. I believe you might have been the last one to see him alive."

"You mean aside from whoever killed him," Uncle Ty snaps, but my mind is already trying to rewind to Thursday. It's Saturday now somehow. So it shouldn't be hard to remember what I was doing a couple nights ago, but it's like time has taken on this weird elastic quality, where everything only just happened but was also a long, long time ago.

"Thursday night?" I say.

Holden nods. "According to Ford's mother, he came to see you after she'd gone to bed. She found a note from him in the morning as she was going to work, and didn't realize Ford was even missing until last night, shortly before she got the unfortunate news of his death."

"Oh. Right, yes. I was working at the Pump'N'Go on Thursday. Ford wanted to talk to me about something he'd noticed in the last video Freya posted."

"What was it?"

"I don't know. He never told me."

"What time did you see him at the gas station?" Holden asks.

"I think it was around eleven thirty. My boss was there, so she might be able to tell you. Oh, and there are cameras at the Pump'N'Go—you'd get the exact time from the video." I notice Officer Cordell scribbling this in her little notepad. "I guess you might want to talk to Mr. Hamish as well. He saw us talking outside. Actually, he almost ran into me with his car."

Uncle Ty makes a surprised sound, so I clarify. "I . . . slipped on the sidewalk. No harm done."

"After that," Holden continues, "did Ford say where he was going? If he was on his way to meet anyone?"

"No. I assumed he was headed home. I thought—" My voice lodges in my throat.

"Are you all right, Miss Thorn?" Officer Cordell asks, frowning.

I shake my head and force out the words that are trying to

choke me. "Ford wouldn't even have been out that night if I'd answered the phone . . . It's my fault he was there."

I flinch when someone squeezes my shoulder, but it's just Uncle Ty. "No, Ava. It was his choice to come see you at the gas station."

"And when he left," Detective Holden says, "was Ford driving, or on foot?"

"He can't—couldn't—drive. But I didn't actually see him leave. I just know he left a few minutes after I went back inside."

"A few minutes after?" Holden's eyes bore into me across the table as I study my scarred palms.

"We argued. Ford . . . well, he kinda shoved me as he was getting out of the way, and I fell into the road. That's why Mr. Hamish almost ran me over."

"*What?*" Uncle Ty gapes, and there's even a look of surprise on Holden's face.

"You're saying Ford pushed you toward the car?" Officer Cordell asks.

"Not on purpose," I say. "I think he was just startled."

And didn't give a shit whether I was okay.

"What were you arguing about?" Holden says.

I open my mouth, but immediately close it again. I mean, we were *kind of* arguing about who killed Freya, but beyond that it was all pretty weird and confusing.

I already regret saying this much to the cops because I'm sure it'll get back to Ford's mom, and I don't want her to hear anything bad about Ford. Or about me, if I'm totally honest.

So I don't mention Ford taking my necklace. There's no point; it's not like that had anything to do with him dying. And I can't bear the idea of Ms. Sutter hearing Ford was a thief. Especially not that it came from me.

"Nothing, really," I say softly. "Just a bunch of little things."

"Seems like bad things happen to people who argue with you, Ava," Detective Holden says.

"Now wait a minute—" Uncle Ty says, but Holden raises his hands.

"Just an observation. But tell me, Ava, how did Ford seem when you parted ways? Was he still angry? Upset?"

"I . . . upset, I guess. He was really freaked out when the car almost hit me."

What would've happened if I'd stayed and talked to Ford? Would it have changed anything that came after? I swallow, mouth suddenly dry.

"And what about this . . . Mr. Hamish? He's the same Mr. Hamish who works at Burden Falls High School?" I nod. "Was he still there with Ford when you went back inside the gas station?"

I frown down at my hands, trying to remember. "Yes, I think so. And he had someone in the car with him. A woman. I didn't recognize her."

True, sort of. I thought she was Freya Miller for that split second when I first caught sight of her. But I keep that little tidbit to myself.

"And you finished working at the gas station at what time?"

"Midnight," I say, certain of that, at least.

"Where did you go after that?"

"Back here. I had school the next morning."

"*Straight* back here? You're sure?"

"I heard her come in," Carolyn says from behind me. I'd

almost forgotten she was in the room. "I was getting into bed. It was just after midnight, like Ava said. The Pump'N'Go is only a short walk from here."

A hawkish look flickers over Detective Holden's face. "And where in the house is your room, exactly?" he asks Carolyn.

"Um, at the back of the house. Above the living room."

He turns back to me. "Did you come in through the main door to the house?"

I try to hide a wince. "No, through the garage door on the side." I point out through the kitchen door, but lower my arm at the *gotcha* look Holden gives me.

"Did you slam the door? Call out?" he asks.

"I . . . don't think so." In fact, I know I didn't. The whole point of coming in through the garage was so I wouldn't wake Carolyn or Uncle Ty. I didn't know it was going to be my god-damn alibi.

I catch Holden exchanging a look with Officer Cordell, who's just finished writing in her notebook again.

"Okay. And after that—you didn't leave to go back out again? Didn't feel like maybe you should clear the air with Ford, anything like that?"

"No," I say, expecting another quick-fire question, but Holden just watches me, like he's waiting for some elaboration. "What?"

"So that was the very last communication you had with Ford Sutter?"

The way he phrases it knocks the wind out of me. Because yeah, that was the last conversation I will ever have with Ford. And it was awful, and I kind of hated him that night.

And now he's dead.

I lean forward, elbows braced on the table, and try to breathe.

"Ava?" Holden prompts.

But Uncle Ty snaps at him, "Give her a damn minute, will you? Her best friend just died!"

And that tips me over the edge. Before I can even try to hold it in, I'm sobbing in this loud, painful way, tears and spit and just this awful sense of *never*. I'll never see him alive again. Never lose to him at *Rocket League*. Never laugh at one of his awful jokes, or argue with him about which of the *Alien* movies is the best.

Someone slides a box of Kleenex in front of me, and I wipe the worst of the mess away before looking up to find Carolyn hovering next to me.

"You don't have to do this now," she says softly—but firm enough that I know she'll go to bat against Holden if he keeps pushing.

But the truth is I want to get this over with. Having another of these conversations in my future will just hang over me like an anxiety cloud.

"I had a bunch of texts from him right after we spoke," I say hoarsely.

"What did these texts say?" Holden asks.

I take out my phone, pull up the thread and hand it over to him. He scrolls through, brow furrowed as he reads. Then he looks up.

"This video he mentions in the last message—do you know which video he meant?"

"Freya's last Story post. Someone screencapped it and it's been going around school." He looks like I just said a lot of words in an alien language. "The one where Freya was poking around Ford's bedroom?"

Holden's frown vanishes. "Oh yes. That one. Thank you."

"Detective, did you ever find out who the guy was she was talking to on the phone that night? Her boyfriend or whatever?"

"Actually," Holden says, leaning back in his chair, "we found no record of Freya making or receiving a call around that time. In fact, there were no calls at all the entire evening."

"*What?* That's impossible. I heard her talking on the phone!"

Holden frowns. "Was this the same night you went there looking for Ford?"

I space for a second, but then I remember: This was the lie I told him when he interviewed me after finding Freya. "Uh, yeah. That's right." The lie feels no more convincing this time around, but if I change it now, it'll look ten times more suspicious.

"Are you absolutely certain it was the Sunday, not some other night?" Holden asks.

"I'm positive," I say, but my mind is racing now. Could Freya have been faking the phone call for some reason? No, that wouldn't make sense — not unless she knew I was close enough to overhear. And I can't think why she'd want me to hear her talking about her sex life. "Could she have been using someone else's phone? The house phone, maybe?"

Detective Holden shakes his head. "We have the records for the entire household. Every call has been accounted for."

"Have you asked Madoc Miller about Ford Sutter yet?" Uncle Ty asks. "Because I'm sure you realize that the river Ford washed up in runs through a fair piece of his land, not to mention the fact that the Millers and Sutters are neighbors. Three kids turning up dead right on his doorstep seems a little fishy, don't you think? Or," Uncle Ty adds, "have you considered the possibility that Ford was the one who murdered Freya, and someone killed him in retaliation?" I gasp, but he just glances at me with a barely apologetic shrug. "Just a thought."

The detective waits a moment before answering, his eyes moving between me and Uncle Ty. "We're following a number of lines of inquiry, Mr. Thorn," he says finally. "I'm actually rather curious to know why neither of you mentioned the unfortunate connection between your family and the Millers."

Panicked, my pulse quickens, but Uncle Ty sits back and sighs. "The accident that killed my brother and sister-in-law had no bearing on anything, Detective. We've moved on."

I'm amazed at how convincingly he lies, but then I wonder — *is* he lying? He taught Freya for over a year without any issues. Sold Madoc Miller our house. As far as I know, Uncle Ty didn't even visit Mom and Dad at the cemetery last week.

Am *I* the only one who still holds a grudge?

Maybe there's a reason I'm at the top of the cops' suspects list.

"Right," Holden says, getting up. "Just to remind you, we're now asking all kids to stay indoors after dark, and not to go any-where secluded alone during the day. Two doesn't necessarily make a pattern, but it's better to be safe."

Uncle Ty and I watch the cop car rolling slowly down the lane.

"Two?" I say. "Not three? They still don't think the first girl is connected to Freya and Ford?"

Uncle Ty shrugs. "Maybe she wasn't. Coincidences do hap-pen."

"It's a pretty huge coincidence."

Still, I can't think what connection there could be between Claire Palmer and Ford and Freya. Ford would've said if he knew her. And, aside from being pulled from the river like Ford, her death wasn't at all similar. She drowned, and still had her eyes.

Either way, Ford's and Freya's murders must be connected.

Their eyeless faces flash through my mind, making me feel nauseated.

Do the cops know about Dead-Eyed Sadie? Someone in this town must've mentioned the legend while they were being questioned. But the cops won't think a ghost could be involved in these deaths. They haven't seen her like I have.

Or think I have.

For a moment, I feel someone behind me, standing in the open doorway of the cottage. The floor creaks, and a breath whispers at my nape. My skin crawls at the sensation. I whirl around, but she's not there. It's just an empty hallway.

But somehow I still feel like I'm being watched.

TWENTY-NINE

t isn't Ford's mom who answers the door, but a strange woman who looks like a younger version of her. She's wearing a lilac one-piece snowsuit as if she just swished off a ski slope.

". . . Aunt Lisa?" I say, before realizing how weird it is to be calling her that when she probably has no idea who I am. The last time I saw Ms. Sutter's younger sister was years ago, right after Trump got elected. She took off backpacking around the world, saying she'd be back *"when that damned disgrace leaves the White House."* Aunt Lisa's kind of a legend.

Her eyes are red and puffy, but she still musters a smile.

"Ava, right? Damn, you grew up too, huh?"

We stare at each other for a moment, the significance of what she just said hitting us at the same instant. Because now Ford doesn't get to grow up anymore.

Seventeen and done.

We're both blinking back tears as she ushers me into the living room. The heating is on full blast, which it never is. Ms. Sutter sits in her armchair, staring at the spot on the couch that was always Ford's preferred place to sit. She's dressed in a smart blouse and sweatpants, like she just grabbed the first things out of her closet. I feel like a dick standing here in my long funeral coat. But my school coat was soaked after crawling over the frozen river in it last night, so it was this or hypothermia.

Ford's mom takes one look at me and bursts into tears.

"I'd better put the kettle on," Aunt Lisa says.

I stay for a little while, listening to Ms. Sutter's grief and her questions about who could ever possibly want to hurt her son. I have no answers. But she seems a little calmer by the time I leave, so I guess that's something.

"Thank you for coming over," Aunt Lisa says as she walks me out. "It know it means a lot to Gloria."

"Are you staying in town long?" I ask hopefully.

"A few weeks," she says. "I'll see how it goes." Aunt Lisa doesn't exactly sound thrilled, and I get the impression it's not just because of the circumstances she's come back home to. "I hear you moved out of the manor."

"Yep," I say, glancing in that direction as we linger at the front door. It's mid-morning, so I guess Dominic is probably up, though it's impossible to tell whether he's at home. "A couple weeks ago now."

"Does that mean you'll be taking off after graduation?"

"I don't think I'll be going to college," I tell her, but she shakes her head.

"I didn't mean college. I thought you might want to get out of this town now that you're not tied here."

Not tied here?

I mean, I guess that's true. Daphne and Carla will be in college, but I always assumed that after I (fingers crossed) do the summer art program in Indianapolis, I'd come back here and . . . Well, working with Mom and Dad at the distillery was the original plan. But that's not even a thing anymore.

So I'll . . . what? Find a job in Burden Falls? See if Mia will take me on full-time at the Pump'N'Go?

No thank you, Satan.

Or.

I could go anywhere. Not that I can afford to just take off on some epic vacation, but I know Aunt Lisa wasn't exactly rolling in it when she set off around the world. She worked wherever she went. Bars, cafes, that kind of thing. Maybe I could do something like that.

I have a momentary glimpse of myself sketching portraits of tourists on the streets of Paris, or Milan, or some other beautiful place. Uncle Ty did that the summer after he graduated.

It would certainly beat the shit out of starting my adult life behind bars. Now that the seed is planted, the idea of just getting the hell out of here blooms. I could get away from the cops, and the deaths, and the memories.

And Sadie.

"I guess I have some thinking to do," I tell Aunt Lisa.

I'm barely through the front gate when my phone rings. I answer without checking who it is, assuming it's Uncle Ty or Carolyn. But it's not.

"I thought that was you I saw across the lane," Dominic says without greeting. "Can you come over to the house?"

"Uh, no."

"My parents aren't here, if that's what you're worried about."

I mean, it was, mostly. "Aren't they back yet?"

"Not until tomorrow," he says.

"Why aren't they coming home *now*? Another kid died."

Dominic is silent for a moment. "I didn't tell them about Ford," he says at last.

"You didn't? Why not?"

"Because they'd worry, and they needed this break away from everything. And the whole town, my parents included, were under the impression my sister's murder was a freak occurrence. Now that Ford has turned up dead with his eyes missing too, I think people will panic."

"Don't you think they *should* panic?"

"Look, can you come over so we're not having this conversation like two six-year-olds holding tin cans and a string?" he snaps.

I hang up without saying anything. By the time I reach the manor gates, they're already swinging open.

Dominic hasn't slept. Or showered, I'm guessing, from the fact he's still wearing most of his Slender Man costume. Not the mask, obviously, and he's detached the tentacles. So basically he's wearing a funeral suit. I guess his outfit pairs well with my long black coat.

"Come in," he says, stepping back from the door. My breath catches once I'm in the foyer.

I knew the manor would look different, of course. The repulsive green coating they've given the outside gave me a heads-up on that. But I guess I never really pictured the innards changing.

The thick plum carpet and William Morris print wallpaper in the foyer—the same kind they hang in some castles in the UK— are gone. Instead, the floorboards are bare, no doubt waiting for some soulless grey tiles to be installed. The walls have been painted stark white, with chrome-framed photographs hastily thrown up where we had classic landscapes and portraits painted in oils. Looking closer, the pictures aren't even of the Millers and their kids, which I guess would be understandable. From the handful on the wall nearest to me, I think they're all movie people Madoc and Lucille Miller have worked with. There's even one of them drinking cocktails with some horror director who I'm pretty sure got arrested for killing his wife.

I step back, repulsed.

"Come up to my room," Dominic says, and strides up the stairs before I can even utter a *what the hell.*

And, damn him, I follow. I mean, I'm pretty sure he didn't demand I come over so he could lure me into his bedroom, but here we are.

Dominic disappears ahead of me down the east-wing corridor, but I know exactly where I'm going, of course. To my old room.

I brace myself as I reach the door, and step inside. It looks . . . exactly how it used to.

Different furniture, of course, but it's all laid out just how I had it. The bed in the same place; the desk over by the window. Walls the same stormy deep-water blue; same marbled gray carpet. He even has a full-length mirror hanging in the same spot I used to hang mine.

"Weird," I murmur, and Dominic looks up from where he's now hunched over his laptop on the bed.

"Being here again?"

The Millers must've arranged for contractors to start work

here the very same day they moved in. There's no way it could look this different otherwise. It's like they couldn't bear to live with my family's decor for even a week.

"Kinda. I thought . . . I just thought this room would look different, like the rest of the house. But it doesn't."

"Oh. I like the colors you chose. It's like being at the bottom of the waterfall." I never noticed before, but he's right. If you stand in the center of the room and let your eyes blur, you can imagine the water crashing down around you, the rocks beneath your feet. "Besides, I don't see the point in redecorating when I'm not planning on sticking around."

Something shifts painfully inside me, and for the first time I realize I kind of hate the idea of Dominic leaving.

Maybe he'll be safer if he does.

"When will you go?"

He shrugs. "A few weeks. I need to be here until the cops finish investigating. But don't worry, I'll make sure we have time to finish the comic—at least enough for you to submit for your final project."

I nod, not wanting to tell him that I already have more than enough. That it's almost finished and will be ready to upload first thing Monday, just to make sure Miss Shannon or Hamish or whoever is making the choice about the summer art program doesn't disqualify me for being late. And I'm really happy with the pages Dominic and I worked on together. I love the direction it's taking in the next chapter we started. But we might not get a chance to finish that now.

"What did you want to show me?" I ask, my voice a little strangled.

"This." He waves me over. I go and perch on the edge of the bed next to him. Any tension I feel — or imagine — vanishes as soon as I read what's on his laptop screen.

It's a list of what look like social-media handles, followed by some of the most disgusting, nasty comments I've ever seen. Calling Freya gross names, making sexual comments and threats.

"What the hell is this?"

"These are all the comments made under the *Haunted Heartland* videos from the last six months — the vile ones, at least."

Dominic scrolls through the list as he says this, and I see there are pages and pages of them.

"This is from just *six months*?" I feel sick looking at them. God knows how Freya must've felt.

"Actually, these are just the ones I could localize to this state." He casts me a sideways look. "Not that I should've been able to do that, but I have some software . . . It's not strictly legal."

Like I care if it's legal. The assholes who left these comments should be tracked down and arrested. "Have you given this information to the cops?"

"Of course," Dominic says impatiently. "They've had it since the day after Freya died. Not that they've gotten very far in their investigation. But they have ruled out Liam Walsh, I guess. He was in a meeting with his college professor in Evansville when Freya was killed. Anyway, ruling him out doesn't help much. That's why I'm going over everything myself — the video footage from the bridge camera, Freya's emails and social media, this . . . trash." He jabs a finger at the screen, and I understand what's frustrating him.

"You haven't found anything, have you?"

"No," he admits. "But I'm hoping you might. Will you read through it, see if anything stands out? Usernames, any words or phrases you might recognize—maybe from one of the kids at school?"

I'm about to ask why he thinks I'd have any more luck at identifying any of the trolls when I remember that Dominic has only been in Burden Falls for a year. Somehow, it seems like the Miller twins have always been here.

I read every comment, even though I want to physically recoil from a lot of them. Dominic waits patiently while I study the handles, the type of insults, looking for something to leap out and say, "Aha! I'm the killer!" But nothing does. They're all just random, gross people saying random, gross things about a sixteen-year-old girl, and none of them mention Ford.

"I'm sorry," I tell him at last. "But do you really think it was some internet rando who did it? I can see how someone *might've* tracked down Freya, but she literally just announced Ford was joining the show. How would a stalker have had time to find him? And *why*?"

Dominic sighs, closing his eyes. "I know. I just want to feel like I'm doing something useful, but every lead I come up with goes nowhere."

I put my hand on his arm, and he looks over at me. His green eyes are heavy with misery.

"There is something else Ford said that might be useful."

I tell Dominic about the last text Ford sent me—the one where he claimed to have seen something critical in the video Freya posted where she snooped around his room. Dominic pulls up the video on his laptop without a word, and we both watch it play out. Or rather *he* watches it. I can't look. Seeing Freya on-screen is just too much right now, especially after reading all those awful comments.

Instead, I watch Dominic's face while the video plays. His lips press together when Freya appears, like he's holding back tears.

"*Heeey!*" The sound of Ford's playful scolding is like a hand clamped around my windpipe. I'd forgotten he appears briefly at the end of the video, right before Freya winks to the camera and ends the stream.

Both Ford and Freya are dead now.

Wait, Ford saw something in that video—and now he's dead.

Ice-cold fear seizes my insides.

First you see her, then you die . . .

Dominic's still studying the video. "Do you see anything?" I ask, my voice barely a whisper. But he shakes his head.

"Play it again," I say, forcing my eyes to move to the screen. If Sadie's there in the video, I need to know.

Just as Dominic's about to hit replay, a volley of barking sounds from somewhere downstairs.

"Pilot," he explains. "I'll just go let him out."

I nod, not reaching for the laptop he leaves on the bed. I know I should. I have to. But I don't think I can watch it solo if she's there.

Watching as he leaves my room—*his* room—I notice the door along the hallway is slightly open. That room used to be my parents' bedroom. I get a sudden flash of memory—lying on their bed with Dad when I was little, watching Mom put her makeup on in the mirror. Dad giving a whispered narration, like we were watching a wildlife show. Mom trying to keep a serious face, but I'd catch her locking eyes with Dad in the glass, see those little smile lines crease at the corners of her eyes. Then she'd turn suddenly and roar like a lion, and there'd be lipstick all over her teeth.

That was a lifetime ago.

With a heavy feeling, I step toward the door. Through the sliver of doorway, I see a four-poster bed with blood-red sheets.

That's got to be Freya's room now.

Before I even really decide to do it, I'm going in. Dominic's bounding footsteps continue downstairs, in the direction of the kitchen.

Freya's bedroom looks like she just stepped out. A dressing table near the window has her makeup scattered across it, the chair pushed out as though she left it in a rush.

I'm sure the cops must've taken a look around in here, gathered up anything that might lead them to a possible suspect. I wonder if any of the stuff she kept in here pointed them in my direction. A diary, maybe, saying how horrible Ava Thorn was to her. Because I was. At the time, it felt justified—Freya was such an asshole from the moment I met her.

I regret the things I said to her now, though. And isn't that the beauty of being the one left behind? I get to relive those nasty little remarks over and over, for the rest of my life.

"What are you doing in here?"

I jump, and turn to find Dominic in the doorway. He's holding a drink in each hand—a glass of water, and one of the cold coffees I always drink.

"Sorry. I should've asked. I haven't touched anything."

He holds out the coffee to me, still looking wary.

"Thanks. This is my favorite."

"I know," he says simply. "So why are you in here?"

I try not to look guilty because it was really just idle curiosity. But now that I'm in here, something does occur to me.

"I was just thinking: The way Freya was going through Ford's stuff in that video, like tapping on the bottom of his underwear drawer to see if there was a hidden compartment, checking inside his shoes in the closet, stuff like that . . . It seems like she was the type of person who might hide things in her own room. Things she might not want your mom and dad to see. Or is that completely off base?"

Dominic stares at me, neither agreeing nor disagreeing.

"So, maybe if she had a secret boyfriend she didn't want anyone to know about, there might be evidence somewhere in here . . . don't you think?"

"What kind of evidence?" he says.

"Notes? Photographs? Mementos from dates? I mean, the cops already have her phone, which is the obvious thing, but . . ." I shrug, then open the coffee Dominic gave me. "Shit, this tastes *amazing*." It's creamy and sweet, but without that bitter afternote I'm used to. I check the label, but it's the exact same brand I have at home. How's that even possible?

Oh God. I prefer the taste of Dominic Miller's coffee. I'm doomed.

"The police did go through everything—in here, and on her phone," he says, but I can tell he's uncertain.

"Could she have had another . . ."

My mouth hangs open. I suddenly know what Ford saw in that video. And it wasn't Sadie, or some secret compartment.

"She was recording herself on her phone, and pretending to use another one!"

Dominic's eyes widen. "Two phones." He looks around the room, already searching out possible hiding places the cops might've missed. "I'll start in the closet. Can you go through the drawers? I don't really want to deal with my sister's underwear."

Neither do I, particularly, but I take pity on the guy.

We set to work, checking every possible nook where a phone might fit but be overlooked by the police. I'm careful to put everything back exactly as it was before I move on from one drawer to the next, one part of her room to another. The whole time I'm doing it, I feel like Freya's standing over me, watching me poke through her stuff.

"Is everything okay?" Dominic asks, noticing my sudden lack of movement. "Did you find something?"

I'm about to answer when a phone rings across the hall in Dominic's room. I look at him, but he shakes his head.

"Not my ringtone."

I hurry over and grab my long coat from where I left it on his bed, searching through the folds to try to find the pocket where I left my phone. Finally, I lay my hand on it.

But, when I look to see who's calling, the screen is black. Not just black — cracked. I stare at it, baffled. The ringing continues somewhere nearby.

"It must be yours," I call out absently, still trying to figure out how the hell my screen got cracked.

Just like I thought it did the day I found Freya.

"I've got my phone in here," Dominic calls back.

The sound is still coming from my coat.

From the *other* pocket.

I reach in and take out my phone. Another one. And this one is perfectly intact (well, aside from a very small crack in the corner of the screen). Daphne's face cheeses up at me.

How the hell do I have two phones? At a glance, they look pretty similar, except for the damaged screen. But, now that I have them side by side, I see the damaged one is slightly smaller, the screen a little more rounded at the corners. And it's definitely not mine. I mean, I know whose it is. Whose it *must* be. But how the hell did it get in my coat pocket?

Then I remember: I was wearing this coat the day I found Freya's body. When I stumbled into the pavilion and picked up a cracked phone that I thought was mine.

This is the phone Dominic and I just spent thirty minutes searching for.

THIRTY

"How did you *not know* you had that in your pocket for almost two weeks?"

Dominic has this look of total exasperation on his face that makes his eyes look twice as big.

"I don't usually wear this coat." I cringe when my voice wobbles. But I know I'll have to explain all this again to the cops, and they'll probably think I hid the phone on purpose, or that I, I don't know, *stole it from Freya when I murdered her.* "Look, a phone that seemed to magically fix itself wasn't exactly at the top of my Weird Shit List that day, okay?"

Dominic pinches the bridge of his nose. I suspect I'm giving him a migraine. "Fine. I'm sorry for yelling."

He wasn't, really. But somehow his apology just makes me feel even worse. Before I can hold it in, I'm crying. Not just a melancholy stray tear, but kneeling on my old bedroom carpet, face in my hands, tears flooding out of me.

It's all too much. All of it.

Ford. Freya. The cops.

Sadie.

And for some reason I'm caught up in the middle of . . . *whatever* this is, and I don't know why.

An arm wraps around me, and I turn to lean into Dominic's shoulder. It's an awkward angle, both of us kneeling, and as he shifts I lose my balance and we end up tangled on the floor. And somehow — *somehow* — when I sleeve-wipe my face and look up at him, we're millimeters apart. My breath stalls. I can't hear him breathe, either.

Oh, screw it.

I kiss him. Pressed together on the floor like this, it's so easy, his lips warm and sure against mine. His fingers brush down the side of my face, my neck, mirroring the way I touched him when we danced last night. Was this how it felt to him? Did my touch make his skin tingle like this?

I roll off him onto the carpet and stare up at the ceiling, needing to catch my breath before I do something stupid right here on the floor of my old room. Damn it, he even kisses well.

After the longest silence in history, I say, "That was weird."

He rolls his head toward me and I'm pleased to see his breathing is pretty ragged too. "Bad weird?"

I shake my head. He grins.

"Dominic?"

"What?"

"I think I got snot on your Slender Man costume," I tell him.

He nods earnestly. "I know."

When I drive away from the manor a little while later, I take the burner phone. Dominic offered to tell the cops it was him who picked it up and forgot about it, but lying to them about something like this feels wrong — even if telling the truth hasn't been working out too well for me lately.

I really hope whatever's on that phone leads the cops to the real killer. If it doesn't, I'm all out of ideas. Or rather, there are too many ideas. Including one particularly unlikely one, but I can't deny my mind keeps wandering back to Sadie . . .

No. Focus on what's real.

Freya had her online haters, some of them kind of unhinged, judging by those comments I saw earlier. Pretty much anyone from school could have had some secret obsession with her.

Ford's another story, I guess. I literally can't think of a single person who might've wanted him dead. But the fact that both he and Freya were murdered makes me think it must have been someone who knew them both.

Someone who knew I had reason to hate them?

I shake that idea away. Only the police and the people closest to me knew about my argument with Ford, and none of them would've taken it on themselves to kill him as some kind of act of retribution. No, I don't think I'm the connection. But maybe *Haunted Heartland* was? I mean, Ford had just been announced as a new member of the Hauntlanders crew, so maybe that pissed someone off?

Like Mateo, maybe? Or Casper?

But I don't see Casper getting violent. From the way Dominic described Mateo's aborted fight with Liam, I can't picture him killing Freya and Ford either. It must take a special kind of sicko to mash a person's eyes with an ice pick or whatever.

Someone like my ancestors . . .

Yeah. Not dwelling on that right now.

I'm still churning this over in my mind as I leave the police station after handing in the phone. My pocket rings again just as I'm getting into my car. It's Daphne.

"Hey, Daph. What's up?"

"Oh, hey. I was worried when you didn't pick up earlier. Is everything okay?"

"Yeah . . . I mean, everything's shitty, but I'm okay. Why?"

She takes a deep breath and lets it out slowly. "Oh, you know. Just that kids keep dying."

Oh. Daphne was *worried* worried. "Sorry, I should've called you back. I was just in the middle of this whole thing with Dominic at the manor . . ." I explain what happened, and Daphne listens quietly while I lay it all out—up to the point where I found Freya's phone in my damn pocket. I think I'll wait to tell her about the whole kissing Dominic Miller thing until I've processed what the hell I want to do about it.

"But that's good, though, right?" Daphne says. "They'll figure out who Freya was seeing, and that's got to be who killed her. Except . . ."

"Except what?"

"Well, why would Freya's secret boyfriend want to kill Ford? Unless . . . maybe Ford and Freya had a side thing going on?" she suggests.

I frown. "I guess it's possible." But somehow, even though I considered this possibility myself, I just don't think that's it. "Can you really see Ford being okay with being a side thing, though?"

"Yeah, maybe not," Daphne says, and the silence stretches. "Sorry, I know now's not the time to talk about all this. Do you feel like coming over tonight to watch a movie or something? We can make it like a pre-birthday celebration."

"Birthday?"

Daphne laughs. "You know . . . your eighteenth? This Monday?"

Two days from now. Jesus, with everything that's going on, I forgot my own damn birthday. Who does that?

Someone whose best friend just died.

Or, like last year, someone whose parents just died.

"I don't really feel like celebrating," I say honestly.

"That's cool. Come over anyway—we can just hang."

I think about it, but the prospect of making polite small talk with Officer Chavez while we both pretend he isn't watching me like a hawk isn't exactly enticing.

"I'll take a rain check."

THIRTY-ONE

Having to go to school on my eighteenth birthday is the worst, but even more so when I'm running late. I spent half the night having screwed-up dreams again. Sadie watching me and my parents in the car wreck. Sadie standing next to me in the pavilion as I stumble on Freya's body. Sadie with her dead eyes fixed on the river as Ford's corpse is pulled through the ice.

Uncle Ty and Carolyn try to make a fuss with chocolate-chip pancakes and balloons all set up on the kitchen table, but I'm late, and it's so weird to even think about celebrating. I barely eat a mouthful on my way out, almost barreling right into some old guy in a suit at the front door.

"Miss Avalon Pomona Thorn?" he says stiffly, instantly putting me on guard.

"Are you a cop?" I ask dubiously.

"Lawyer, actually. Steele, Boothroyd, and Finch. I'm Mr. Steele." I thought Dominic gave good glower, but he could learn a thing or two from this guy. He shoves a letter at me.

"Am I being sued?"

"No," he sighs. I take the envelope from him, forefinger and thumb. "Good day."

The guy turns on his heel, heading back to his sleek gray car.

"Hey! What is this?"

The man pauses halfway into the driver's seat. "A happy birthday, I should say."

Then he drives away without saying anything else. I get in

my car and am about to tear open the envelope when I see the time on my dashboard clock.

"Damn it!"

I shove the letter in my bag to read once I'm not up against the tardy bell.

When I get to school, I immediately hear everyone whispering. It has that same dark tang as when Freya was murdered, only now I see some kids are starting to look scared.

I edge nearer to the main huddle of people, trying to listen in. I'm right next to the Freya shrine — only it's now a Freya & Ford shrine, with photographs and mementos of Ford hastily thrown in around the edges. Then my eyes fall on the item that's got everyone whispering.

It's the doodle I drew in the assembly when the principal announced Freya had died. The one of Freya with no eyes. As if that didn't look bad enough, someone's added to it. Written above the sketch now are five words in block caps:

SADIE MADE ME DO IT

Someone nudges me, and I look up to find Yara giving me an odd look. She points at the drawing tacked onto Freya's locker.

"Did you actually draw that?" Yara gapes at me. "That's so gross."

"I drew it," I snap, "but someone else fucked with it. I didn't write that, and I certainly didn't stick it on her locker."

I don't wait for Yara's response. Instead, I push my way through to Freya's locker and tear down the sketch. Mutters start up right away: "*It was hers! Do you think she did it? Must be some kinda psycho . . .*"

Screwing the damn picture into a tiny ball, I turn and head to homeroom, face blazing.

Daphne and Carla are lying in wait for me there. Daphne starts singing "Happy Birthday"—the superior Stevie Wonder version—while Carla pulls a party streamer right above my head. I force a smile for their benefit, hoping like hell none of the shrine-gawkers have followed me, but definitely not about to turn around and look.

"Thanks. It's gonna take ages to get all these little paper ribbons out of my hair."

"Look at that smile!" Daphne teases. "That joyful glow!"

"Welcome to adulthood, Thorn," Carla says, chucking me under the chin.

"You'll never guess what some asshole did just now," I say, about to pull the screwed-up sketch from my bag. But I stop when Mr. Hamish appears next to us.

"Ava, can I have a word?"

"Uh, sure."

Shit. Has someone gone to the guidance counselor about the sketch? Definitely not this fast. I wonder how the hell someone had even gotten a hold of it . . . although I guess I take my sketchpad out of my bag and my locker a hundred times a day, so maybe it fell out then. Some sicko probably just picked it up and thought it'd be funny to stick it on Freya's locker.

I mean, that's preferable to the alternative: that someone deliberately stole my sketch and put it there, knowing it'd make me look like a killer.

Daphne, Carla, and I exchange *see you later* raised eyebrows, and I follow Hamish to his office.

There's a stack of papers littering his desk, and my eye is drawn to a handwritten sheet on top with lots of words scribbled out and notes added in the margins. The name Freya is on it a bunch of times. And I notice there's a photograph on his desk that I'm sure wasn't there last time I was in here. It's of Hamish and the woman I guess is his girlfriend, set so it faces out into the room. He has an arm around her, and her small hand is placed on his chest to show off the engagement ring on her finger. Fiancée then, not girlfriend. I wonder if that's a recent thing.

The woman's hair is more auburn than Freya's vivid red, and her eyes are brown. But the overall shape of her features, her bone structure, is very similar. It's creepy.

"So here's the thing."

I look up from studying the photograph and find Hamish touching that weird parting in his mustache. It's exactly as wide as the space between his eyebrows.

"The deadline for nominating a student for the summer art program scholarship placement is this week."

I am instantly at attention. With everything that's happened, I haven't even thought about it in days.

"After we learned about the over-eighteen rule, which automatically disqualified Freya, you were obviously in a strong position."

I blanch at how matter-of-factly he can talk about Freya being disqualified. A few weeks ago, I would've been doing a victory dance at this news, but now it feels sour and hollow. This wasn't how I wanted to get my spot in the program. Not that I'm going to turn it down, of course. I'm not a martyr.

"Thank you, Mr. Hamish. I—"

"But I'm afraid, what with the police investigation, and their continued interest in you, we've decided to nominate another student this year. I'm sure you'll be happy for Yara."

"WHAT?" I think we're both startled by the volume of my voice, but seriously—WHAT? "That's not fair! Yara isn't even interested in the summer art program." I don't know that for a fact, but it could be true. "And the cops are investigating *everyone,* not just me. I'm not an actual *suspect.*"

"It's not just about that, Ava," Hamish says. I guess he's aiming for a soothing tone, but it's making me want to throat-punch him.

I'll go talk to Miss Shannon. She's head of the art department—if I can convince her to change her mind, I can't see Hamish being able to overrule her decision. Maybe I can even talk Uncle Ty into having a quiet word with her for me.

I'm not losing my place in the art program because of this mustache-toucher. I'm *not.*

"I was honestly a little concerned about how competitive you seemed to feel toward Freya," Hamish waffles on. "She was such a lovely girl . . . you're both so talented. Were. Are . . ."

"*Lovely?*" I repeat.

I bet I know some other parts of me you'll think are pretty lovely *too . . .* Wasn't that what Freya said that night on the phone?

Mr. Hamish is still talking across his desk at me, but I'm barely listening. Instead, I'm thinking about what Carla told me over lunch last week—that she saw Freya coming out of Hamish's office, looking upset. Was that when Hamish told Freya she was too young to be eligible for the summer art program? Or could that have been a lovers' spat? Some kind of botched hookup, maybe?

My eyes zero in on the woman in the photograph. She really does look the double of Freya. What does that mean? Does he have some kind of weird fetish for redheads?

Was it you?

I flinch when Hamish spreads his hands, but he's just making a helpless gesture.

"I'm afraid the decision has already been made. On a more positive note, I'm thrilled to see how your grades have been picking up . . ."

If he was having an affair with Freya, and it somehow turned sour, maybe he was worried it'd go public. With her being so young, and a student under his care, that'd be jail time for sure, right?

Bile burns the back of my throat.

I study his hands, still spread on the desk. Did he wrap them around her throat and squeeze until the life went out of her? Grab an ice pick and smash in her eyes?

What kind of sicko could do something like that?

Fuck. It could actually be him.

My pulse pounds, underscoring this new creeping sense of certainty.

But what about Ford? Why kill him?

Maybe Ford found out. He figured out the thing with the phones in the video — maybe he saw something else we all missed.

Ford was acting pretty paranoid before he died, and he said someone was watching him . . . What if Hamish *was* watching him? I put it down to Ford being high, but maybe I was wrong?

I stare at Hamish's smug head bobbing from side to side as he talks. I can't even remember what the conversation is about. Hamish's rambling is lost beneath the *whoosh-whoosh-whoosh* behind my ears.

I look down at my hands and try to focus on breathing. But the pink lines on my palms start to writhe in that same *whooshing* rhythm. Squirming, like there's something under my skin.

I think I'm going to throw up. But I can't tear my eyes from the scars. One of them looks like it's about to burst—

And then it does. The scar opens, edges parting to reveal a pocket in the flesh. Then another scar opens, and another. Until they've all unpeeled themselves, these holes in my hands. They almost look like . . .

Eye sockets.

The moment that thought occurs to me, they blink. I scream, hands held out in front of me as if I can somehow escape them.

"Ava? Ava! What's the matter?"

Hamish comes toward me. As he moves past the office window, his reflection changes into a dark-haired girl, her empty eye sockets fixed on me. I scramble backward, my chair falling over with a clatter.

"My hands," I gasp, holding them up, either to show him or to get him to back the fuck up, I'm not sure. But, when I catch sight of my left palm, the holes are gone. The lines aren't moving. They're just scars—thin pink lines that my doctors have told me will hardly be visible at all in a few years.

And there's no ghostly reflection peering at me from the window.

I stumble over to his office door and bolt.

THIRTY-TWO

I've been sitting in my car for around ten minutes, and I'm already starting to shake with cold. That or shock, I guess. I could turn on the engine for warmth, but Bessie takes ages to heat up. I should probably go back inside anyway. My initial plan — to flee school and possibly cut off my own evil hands — struck me as being slightly impractical once the cold air hit me. I mean, aside from the obvious downside to removing my own hands, I'm not sure someone who's clearly not seeing things as they really are should be driving.

All of which is to say I'm freaking out. First of all, about those holes in my hands. Some rational, Carla-esque voice in my brain reminds me that I'm under a lot of stress right now. Coupled with my high caffeine levels and lack of sleep, that *might* be making things a little . . . fuzzy. But I should really go see a doctor. If I'm losing it, I need help. Therapy. Meds. Whatever they can give me to stop freaky shit like what I just saw in Hamish's office.

I turn my palms over slowly, half expecting to see them blinking at me again. But everything is as it should be. Scarred but normal. When I check my rearview mirror, there's no sign of Sadie.

There's also a louder voice that says, *If the cops find out you're seeing things that aren't there, that's only going to make them think you're an even better prime suspect.*

I've tried ignoring that voice all my life. Never worked.

So, maybe I should just wait until the cops catch the killer, *then* go give Dr. Ehrenfeld a call?

Which leads to the other giant elephant I'm freaking out about: Hamish.

Hearing that one word — *lovely* — isn't a lot to go on, but the more I consider him as a possibility, the more things seem to fit. The fact that he's older and works in our high school would be a hell of a reason to keep a relationship secret. He's always fawned over Freya, so keen to put her forward for the summer art program. And there was that day when Carla saw Freya coming out of Hamish's office, looking upset. And something about that photograph appearing on his desk . . . like he has something to prove. *Look at me! I have a fiancée! I can't possibly be a creep who's murdered two teenagers!*

I reach down for my bag and fumble around for my water bottle, noticing as I do that the screwed-up drawing from Freya's locker is no longer there. I check my pockets, but no dice.

Shit. Did it fall out in Hamish's office? In the hallway?

My search becomes more frantic as I haul out the contents of my bag. Then my hand lands on the letter that weird lawyer guy gave me this morning.

I stop throwing my crap around and stare at it. Then I tear it open.

Dear Miss Thorn,

 Pursuant to the recent sale . . .
 on behalf of Mr. Madoc Miller . . .
 share of proceeds . . .
 advent of your eighteenth birthday . . .
 the sum of $250,000 . . .

What.

WHAT?

I must be seeing things again. Because there's no way this letter says what I think it says. I look in the envelope and, sure as hell, there's a check in there. An enormous check—with my name on it.

Signed by Madoc Miller.

There's a knock at my window. I jump so violently, I almost tear the check in half. The glass is fogged when I look up, and my heart pounds at the sight of a blurred figure outside. I don't move.

"Leave me alone!"

"Ava? Open the window."

I heave out a breath at the sound of Dominic's voice. The window button doesn't work, so I just open the door.

"Happy birthday," he says with a grin, holding out one of my favorite coffees.

"What the hell is this?" I say, waving the check at him. Dominic glances at it, gives the briefest raise of his eyebrows, then takes my free hand and pulls me out of the car. "Hey!"

"You're freezing," he says, tugging me along toward his Porsche, which I now see is parked just a couple spots down. "And *my* car is not an icebox on wheels. If we're going to fight, I'd rather do it where it's warm."

He opens the passenger-side door for me. I glare at him for a long moment, then get in. There's a paper bag with a prescription label on it sitting in the footwell. Maybe that's why he's late getting to school.

Dominic climbs in the driver's seat and turns on the heaters.

Immediately, a wave of warm air floods the car, and I notice my butt's getting warmer too.

"Heated seats," Dominic says, correctly reading my expression.

I give him a half-lidded stare. "Really? I thought I just peed myself." I thrust the check at him. "Tell me what this is supposed to be. *Please.* Because I'm about to lose my shit for the second time today."

"Well, we can come back to that last part in a second, but there should have been a letter with the check to explain it."

"There was. It was very . . . lawyer-y. But you knew about it?" I don't know why that stings so much, but it does.

"Yes. I mean, it wasn't a secret or anything—unlike my parents buying the manor, which they kept under wraps until *two days* before we moved in." Dominic catches my incredulous look. "They didn't want us—by which I mean Freya—making a big thing about it in front of you at school." He shrugs. "I want you to know I wasn't hiding it from you. Seeing as we're . . . whatever we are. I honestly had no idea you didn't know this money was coming. And I don't know all the details, but Dad told me that when he bought the manor, part of the deal he made with your uncle was that your share of the proceeds would be held in trust until you turned eighteen. Again, happy birthday."

I look doubtfully down at the check, trying not to dwell on that "*whatever we are.*" "So, this was Uncle Ty's idea?"

"Uh, no. My dad's. He wanted to make sure the money wouldn't get . . . swallowed up before you could use it."

My cheeks grow warm, and not just because of Dominic's

fancy heaters. "He thought Uncle Ty would spend the money."

It's not a question, but he nods. "I know how you feel about my dad. About my family. And I don't blame you, honestly. But Dad wanted to do something to try and make things . . . well, a little easier. You lost so much, so fast. I'm impressed at how well you've held it together all year."

I snort at that. I mean, I'm holding it together so well, I'm full-on seeing things that aren't real.

"Better than my dad has, anyway." Dominic's voice is quiet on that last part, and he looks out through the window at the falling snow.

"What do you mean?"

"Dad . . . he . . . started drinking more after the accident. He'd stay in his room, sometimes for days at a time. He was depressed. I know it's nothing like what you went through, but we were worried about him — Freya, especially. They've always been close. I think seeing him like that was part of the reason she wasn't your biggest fan. I know it wasn't fair of her to blame you, but there was no one else she *could* blame."

A few weeks ago, I might've taken some sick delight in hearing how Madoc Miller suffered. Freya too. But not now. I think a part of me will always hate Madoc for killing my parents, but I don't want anyone else to be hurt by it, even him. And certainly not Dominic. I can tell it's hard for him to talk about this.

"That's why Freya hated me so much? She blamed me for your dad's depression?"

He side-eyes me. "That was part of it. But you really were awful to her."

"I was not!" I say, but immediately backtrack. "Okay, maybe

I was, but she was *always* trying to just . . . get at me." I make an illustrative jabbing motion with my pointer finger.

"Our first day in this school, you told her that her artwork was 'not bad.'"

"So?"

"Come on, Thorn. You know she was better than 'not bad.'" And she'd just said yours was amazing. Freya wasn't nearly as confident as she liked to make out, and her art was really important to her."

"No, I . . ." I mean, I vaguely remember the conversation, but I wouldn't have said that, would I? Not before I knew her. Not before the crash. "Oh God. I definitely said it."

I think that was the day I later overheard the conversation between Freya and Dominic outside the art studio—the one where she asked if my artwork was better than hers. Now his *as if* takes on a different tone. The tone of an older brother trying to reassure his sister. Not an asshole, like I decided.

Dominic laughs as I curl up in a ball of shame.

"Don't worry about it. She would've hated you anyway, because of how bad things got with Dad. You two were alike that way. Very family-first."

"What happened with your dad?" I say, ignoring the *alike* part because it's blatantly untrue.

"He checked into rehab for a month at the end of last year, and I'm hoping he won't need to do that again, but we'll see. He goes to therapy every week now. It's helping him deal with losing Freya, I think."

"But . . ." I hesitate, the question almost out before I can think better of it. Dominic just waits, though, so in the end I spit it out. "If your dad was so cut up about the accident, how could he buy the manor? Why would he want you all to live there?"

Dominic purses his lips, considering. "I think buying the manor was the only way he could come up with to make amends to you. Stepping in before the banks foreclosed . . . Well, it got your uncle out of a lot of trouble, from what I heard. And Dad wanted to make sure you could have the future you *should've* had . . . at least part of it."

I turn the check over and over in my hands. The edges are already starting to look wrinkled.

This is A LOT of money. I could hire a lawyer. A top-notch therapist. *Pay* for a spot in the summer art program, maybe. Hell, I could even go to art college if I wanted to.

If I don't end up in jail first.

"Will you keep it?" Dominic asks.

I think about it hard before answering. "I'm not sure yet."

He nods, like that's a good enough answer. "So what was the other meltdown about?"

I look at my hands, which haven't suddenly developed those disgusting holes again, and decide to just tell him the part about Freya.

"Hamish said something earlier, and it reminded me of a conversation I overheard a few days before Freya died. It got me thinking . . . Could Freya have been involved with Hamish?"

I sit next to Dominic at the police station while he tells Detective Holden about a day around New Year's when he saw Freya talking to Hamish inside his car in the school parking lot.

"They looked . . . well, guilty, in hindsight. At the time, I just thought I'd startled them both." Dominic leans back in his seat. "Look, Detective, if Hamish or some other older guy was taking advantage of my sister, they need to at least be questioned."

Detective Holden bristles. I can tell he doesn't enjoy being told how to do his job by a couple of teenagers. I've already filled him in on my suspicions, though I can admit they sound a lot flimsier when I try to explain them to a cop. Dominic seems to think we're making our case well enough, though.

"I saw Hamish and his girlfriend . . . fiancée . . . the night Ford died," I blurt. "They were still with him when I went back inside the gas station. What if he was trying to run into Ford with his car? Or what if Ford said something to him about Freya after I left? Maybe Hamish followed him to the river?"

With his fiancée in the car?

Okay, that seems unlikely. Unless she's in on it?

No. That makes no sense. But none of this makes any sense.

"I'll look into it," Holden says, and stands. "Thank you both for coming in. But perhaps you should be getting back to school?"

"Did you find anything on the phone yet?" I ask before he can actually kick us out the door. "I'm sure if you check for Mr. Hamish's number—"

"It's in hand, Miss Thorn," Detective Holden says through clenched teeth.

"Come on, Ava," Dominic says. "Let's leave the detective to do his job."

And as we make our way out, walking past another interview room along the corridor, I spot a familiar face.

Sitting there, with a fading black eye and the hangdog expression of someone expecting a world of trouble, is Liam Walsh.

***

When I get home from school, Carolyn and Uncle Ty are still at work, so I don't have to decide whether or not to tell them about Madoc Miller's check. I mean, I assume Uncle Ty knows about it, at least. But the fact he didn't give me a heads-up is weird. Did he just want it to be a surprise? Or was a part of him ashamed for agreeing to take Madoc Miller's money?

Either way, I need to figure out what I'm going to do about the check before I talk to Carolyn and Uncle Ty about it.

Daphne and Carla arrive with pizzas and gifts a short while later. Even though I didn't want to celebrate this birthday, I'm glad I let them talk me into it.

"Hasn't your dad told you why Liam was at the police station?" I ask Daphne. We're sprawled on my bed like cats, my laptop propped against the headboard, but none of us are really paying attention to the movie that's playing.

Daphne pouts. "He's gotten very stingy with information lately. Says now that it's a murder investigation involving people I know, he can't share all the details like he usually would."

Dominic doesn't know, either. Apparently, the cops are even less forthcoming with his parents about who's at the top of their suspects list.

Carla idly picks up a birthday card from my nightstand, wincing as she reads it. "Ford's mom gave you a card?"

"Yeah. It was so sweet of her to remember."

"How's she doing?" Daphne asks.

I shrug. Ms. Sutter looked gaunt, her eyes vacant, as if all the spark that was usually there had just . . . gone out. For the first time, I wonder if Dominic's seeing the same thing with his parents. He puts on such a convincing show of being fine most of the time, I selfishly forget he's actually going through the worst time of his life right now. Of all people, I shouldn't be the one to forget that.

"I miss Ford like hell," I say, "and I hate that he's not here right now. But I'm also still really pissed at him, you know?"

Before my parents died, I'd have felt terrible for admitting I was still mad at Ford. But Dr. Ehrenfeld was the one who got me to see it was normal to have mixed-up feelings after someone dies. Like I was *so mad* at Madoc Miller, but sometimes that anger spilled over and I got angry with Mom for not seeing Madoc's car in time. Mad at Dad for having a seizure *right then,* which I know is completely irrational. I even got mad at the damn owl for swooping in front of our car and distracting Mom for that second when she might otherwise have been noticing the Hummer careening toward us.

The anger passed, mostly. So I know I won't always be pissed at Ford. Maybe my feelings about him, about our friendship, won't ever be clear-cut — good or bad — but I still get to miss him.

Carla nods. "I wasn't his biggest fan, but it sucks he's not here."

"Are you still having the dreams?" Daphne asks. I bite my lip, not sure how truthful to be. But I figure we're sharing, so I might as well get *all* my shit out in the open.

"Most nights, yeah. But it's not just dreams anymore. I mean, I think I might actually be seeing things that aren't really there."

"What kinds of things?" Daphne asks, but Carla cuts in before I can answer.

"Have you seen Sadie again?"

"Yeah. I saw her today in Hamish's office, and the other night at my window." Daphne and Carla both turn at once to look at the little round window. It'd be funny, if I weren't losing my damn mind. "But it's more than that. Sometimes when I look at people, I see them without any eyes. And this morning I had a weird episode where I thought the scars on my hands had opened up like empty eye sockets."

Carla and Daphne stare at me, horrified.

"Forget I said anything. Who wants cake?"

"Whoa there, birthday girl," Carla says, stopping me as I'm about to head to the kitchen in a cloud of embarrassment. "We're not just skimming over this one. You're really worried about this, aren't you?"

"It totally freaked me out."

"Then go see your old shrink," Carla says. "What was her name? Dr. Ehrenfeld?"

"It couldn't hurt," Daphne says, "although . . ."

"What?" I think she's about to point out the same problem I came up with earlier—about looking even more like a suspect to the cops. But she doesn't.

"It does feel like there's something weird behind what's been happening. Something supernatural . . . don't you think?"

I keep my mouth shut because I've had that same feeling. A lot.

"Obviously, I think that's crap—sorry, Daph," Carla says, taking a bite of pizza. "But maybe you should see a regular doctor, not a psychiatrist."

"Why?"

"Because there could be some other reason you're hallucinating."

"Like . . . ?" I press. Damn it, if there's an explanation for what I'm seeing that doesn't involve ghosts or me going mad, I'm pretty much open to anything.

"Well, people hallucinate for all kinds of reasons. Head trauma, oxygen deprivation, poison, drug abuse, gas leaks, brain tumors . . ."

"Jeez, Car." Daphne nudges her.

"What? I'm just saying Ava shouldn't assume she's losing her mind. That's a good thing," Carla says. "Now, what do you say we watch the rest of this shitty vampire movie?"

THIRTY-THREE

There's a joint memorial for Ford and Freya at school Thursday evening. I think it's so the funerals can be done privately.

It's just as awful as I expected it to be. The school assembly hall is packed. But whoever laid out the folding chairs seems to have anticipated a lower turnout, so there are people standing several rows deep around the edges, with some at the front opting to sit cross-legged on the floor. It looks more like a folk festival than a memorial.

With people crammed in like this, and everyone wrapped up in thick winter clothes because of the icy weather, it's getting pretty sweaty.

Ford's mom sits up front. Madoc is a couple seats along, with Dominic between them like a buffer. I don't see Dominic and Freya's mom anywhere.

Ms. Sutter is one of those people who has Big Energy, even when she's not doing anything. Always super busy, but like she enjoys being busy, you know? When she walks, it's almost like skipping. Her feet don't get time to touch down. If I drew her, she'd be in a glowing bubble, floating just a little off the ground. Always in motion. But today she looks exhausted. It's in her sunken cheeks, the dark circles under her eyes. Gravity and grief have caught up with her. She looks over her shoulder from her seat in the front row, peering out at the assembly. Her eyes move from one face to the next. Is she looking for someone? The person who murdered her son? Or just making a tally of who's here for Ford, and who for Freya?

She pauses when she sees me. For the briefest moment, Ms. Sutter smiles.

A sudden downpour of rain wails on the corrugated roof of the assembly hall, making me flinch. I can barely hear what Principal Gower is saying into the mic. I strain to pick out the words, then realize she's actually reading out Ford's latest report card.

"Jesus," I mutter. It's not even a great report card. I don't know whether to laugh or cry.

Carolyn squeezes my hand, despite the fact it probably feels sweaty through the glove. Uncle Ty just looks like the heat's getting to him, his cheeks all red and splotchy. I'm glad they're both here, even though I've kind of been avoiding them for the past couple days. I don't know how to bring up Madoc Miller's check. I still can't decide whether to keep it.

"Ford would've *hated* this," Carolyn whispers.

I imagine him sitting next to me, scanning the faces of the crowd and giving me a look like, *Can you believe these assholes actually showed up?*

Most of the people here are from school, but there are plenty of adults too. Friends of Ford's mom and Freya's parents, I guess. Or at least people who know them.

I sit between Carolyn and Daphne, with Daphne's dad on her other side, and Uncle Ty next to Carolyn. Officer Chavez isn't in uniform; only here to pay his respects, he said as we came in, not on official police business. But there are plenty of cops who *are*. They're dotted around the back of the gym, by the exits, up front near the stage. For a second, I think I see a girl with long dark hair hanging over her face standing between two cops in uniform, but when I blink, she's gone.

Detective Holden stands stiffly against the back wall. Even if I hadn't already met him, I'd sense the cop vibes he's giving off a mile away. He strides to the front of the gym, taking Principal Gower's spot at the podium, and taps on the mic. The sound booms across the room, followed by an ear-splitting surge of feedback.

"Excuse me," he says, like he doesn't already have everyone's attention. "My name is Detective Mike Holden, and I'm here working with your local police force to investigate the deaths of Ford Sutter and Freya Miller, whom you've all come here today to remember. I wanted to take a moment to let everyone know that we're doing everything we can to get to the bottom of what happened. I know a lot of you have already spoken with us, and we're very grateful for your help. I'd like to reassure you that we don't believe Ford's and Freya's deaths are the start of a pattern, though we do encourage everyone to avoid going out alone after dark. You'll also have noticed an increased police presence on your streets. Now, I won't take up any more time here tonight, but, if anyone has any information that might be pertinent to the murder investigations, I'll be leaving my contact information with Principal Gower, and she'll be happy to put you in touch with me."

He's about to leave the stage when someone in the audience calls out, "What about our kids? Are they safe?"

"Should our kids have a police escort to and from school?"

"Who's letting all these media people have access to students at the school gates?"

Another adds, "Are you really sure the first dead girl wasn't murdered too? Is this the work of a serial killer?"

"Why haven't you arrested anyone yet? It's been two weeks since Freya Miller was killed!"

Detective Holden raises his hand, and the shouting dies down. "There's no need to worry at this point. We strongly believe these two deaths are related, and that it's *highly unlikely* the perpetrator is targeting anyone else. And, to clarify, there doesn't seem to be any connection at all to the accidental drowning of Claire Palmer. Thank you." He doesn't hang around to see if there are more questions, just marches off briskly to resume his spot at the back.

"It really doesn't sound like they're getting anywhere," Carolyn murmurs next to me.

I tilt my head at her. "You think?"

She shrugs. "They haven't arrested anyone, have they?"

"What about Liam? I haven't seen him at the library in a while."

Carolyn leans in. "Mr. Maitland came into the pharmacy earlier. Apparently, Liam had nothing to do with the murders but, when the cops checked his phone to rule him out of the Freya Miller case, they found a lot of messages to underage girls on there. I'm not sure if the cops are pressing charges, but he definitely got canned from the library."

"Wow, really?" That's gross. I'm glad he got fired.

"I'd like to say a few words about my son."

Carolyn and I both turn back to face the stage at the sound of Ms. Sutter's voice coming through the PA system. She stands at the mic, dressed in a tight-fitting black shift dress and a baggy blazer that look like they were made for two different people.

Ford had the same curly hair as his mom, though hers is starting to turn gray. And he had her eyes, I think. Clear, steady blue eyes. I see those in the blown-up picture of Ford next to Ms. Sutter; the photo looks a little fuzzy, like it's been taken from one of his social media profiles. He squints at the camera, not cheesing, but not moody, either. Almost like he's listening to what's being said about him at his memorial.

At least he's not trying to lick his own nipple.

I almost smile, thinking about those photos he gave me at my locker, but then a hot lump forms in my throat. He'll never give me stupid photos again. Never try to make me laugh. God, I can't believe that was just a couple weeks ago. But then I remember the last time I saw him alive, outside the gas station. How freaked out he was, and how he knocked me into the path of Hamish's car. If Ford hadn't died, would I have ended up forgiving him—for that, and for all the other shitty things he did? The hurt in my chest says no, but the honest answer is: *I don't know.*

Ms. Sutter keeps reaching out to graze her fingertips along the edge of the picture frame, as though to remind herself that Ford is there . . . or that he isn't.

"I see some of you here who knew Ford. Friends of his . . ." She frowns as her gaze travels over everyone facing her, searching for someone to make that assertion true. Then she spots me again, and gives a relieved sigh. I feel a sharp pang of guilt. But I muster a smile for Ms. Sutter's benefit. "I know you knew Ford, but perhaps some of you didn't, so I'd like to tell you a little about him.

"Ford loved animals—cats, especially. We have four. You probably know our house isn't a four-cat kind of size. But Ford's the one who feeds them and makes sure they come in at night. If one goes wandering for too long, he'll be out walking the streets with his flashlight, calling it home."

Ford and his mom inherited those cats along with the house when old Mrs. Sutter moved into a retirement home. Don't get me wrong, Ford loved them, but he'd be turning all kinds of shades of embarrassed if he knew they were headlining at his memorial. But, as my mom always used to say, *"It's a mother's prerogative to embarrass the hell out of her kids."* I guess that's true, no matter what.

"And now I have to deal with four cats yowling night and day for him to come back, but he—" Ms. Sutter's voice cracks, and she takes a moment to steady herself before she goes on. "Every Mother's Day, he'd make me something he called his *Momzine,* with little articles and pictures and recipes in it he knew I'd like, and he'd write a funny story about the two of us having some big day out to celebrate because we could never afford to do that for real. He used to . . . used to . . ."

I remember Ford's *Momzines.* He used to make them when he was a little kid. Funny, I haven't thought about them in years, but I guess they meant a lot to Ms. Sutter.

There are tears running down her cheeks. Despite my determination *not* to cry at this thing, I feel tears welling in my own eyes.

Principal Gower starts heading across the platform toward her, but Ford's mom waves her away.

"Another thing most of you won't know is that he used to visit his grandmother every weekend in the old folks' home. Mom hasn't recognized anyone in over a year, not even her own family, but that never stopped Ford going to read to her."

I bite the inside of my cheek until it hurts. I get why Ms. Sutter is only talking about the good parts of him—everyone does it at a funeral . . . memorial . . . whatever. But it still feels like *her* Ford is only one side of the Ford I knew. This version sounds so . . . bland. Like a paper cutout of the guy I knew all my life. Maybe that's just the way memories work, though. If you're remembered by a hundred people, they'll remember a hundred different versions of you. You just have to hope at least one of them is good.

"He was going to be an actor. He wanted . . . He wanted . . ."

Ms. Sutter takes a deep breath, but seems to change her mind. She nods to herself, and says a terse "I think that's enough, thank you" before going back to her seat.

Madoc Miller strides up onto the stage next. His jaw is set firmly, and his eyes rake over the crowd. I see now where Dominic learned to glower.

"I'm Madoc Miller, Freya and Nic's father. And I'm not here to tell you about my daughter. I think she gave you enough of an inside view of her life while she was here. I've come here to say one thing, and one thing only. Whoever murdered my daughter is going to pay. I will do everything in my power to make sure that happens, and I will not rest until it's done. If that's you," he says, eyes sweeping like a laser over the crowd again, "I suggest you turn yourself in to the police."

There's an unspoken threat underlying every single word, and it makes a shiver run right through me. His eyes never land on me, though. Madoc must see me here, sitting with Uncle Ty and Carolyn, yet his gaze never pauses on us.

I'm still relieved when he steps down and Principal Gower

takes his spot. She clears her throat, then starts to wrap up the memorial. But then there's movement at the back of the gym, and Mr. Hamish hurries forward, head down, a sheaf of papers clutched in his hand. He walks right over to the stage, and Principal Gower steps aside with a frown.

Why is *he* here? Why haven't the cops arrested him? Or at least stopped him from barging into the damn memorial service?

Dominic stands up in the front row. I can't see his face, but I can just imagine his eyes blazing. His father puts a hand on his shoulder, leaning in to say something, and they both take their seats again.

"I'd like to say a few words," Hamish says, then clears his throat and begins reading from his notes. "As guidance counselor to both Freya and Ford, I saw great promise in them both. Ford with his acting, and Freya . . . honestly, Freya could have taken any number of amazing paths, and been a success."

He reads on, listing her academic achievements, talking about *Haunted Heartland,* her "great artistic talent"—only occasionally even mentioning Ford. It's the most stomach-turning thing I've ever seen, and I can't believe he's doing it while Ms. Sutter is sitting there in the front row. Doesn't he realize how screwed up it is to heap all this praise on Freya, and treat Ford like an afterthought?

Why is he doing this, anyway? It's almost like he's trying to prove something . . .

Hamish doesn't go on for long, thankfully. When everyone finally files out, I'm glad of the cold air outside. I let it sweep me away from the stifling atmosphere in the gym.

✳ ✳ ✳

I lie awake in bed, not wanting to go to sleep. I don't know what nightmares will be waiting for me.

On impulse, I grab my phone and call Dominic.

"Hey," he says, answering on the first ring.

"I guess you weren't sleeping, either."

"I'm just going through the video footage from our security system the night Ford died. I had a hunch that maybe he came here, to where Freya was found, looking for clues or something, or that maybe this was where he got thrown in the river."

"Find anything?"

"One pretty dramatic shot of an owl swooping at the camera near the bridge, but nothing useful."

"An owl . . . Wait, there's still a camera near the bridge?" I thought he'd have taken that down by now.

"It's the one we were using to film my death scene for *Haunted Heartland,* remember?"

He laughs softly. In spite of the spike of fear I still feel when I remember the moment I thought Sadie had just pushed him to his death, I get another kind of chill too. It feels so strange to be lying in bed with Dominic's voice in my ear. Weird, but not bad weird.

"I left it hooked up. There's a motion detector on it, so it starts to record if someone comes within range."

"Why?"

"I thought I might get some footage of Sadie."

"Are you being serious?" Because that's the last thing I expect to hear from glowering Dominic Miller. But maybe I'm not the only one who's seen her . . . Maybe I'm not losing my mind after all. "You actually believe she's real?"

He's silent for a second, and I picture him pursing his lips the way he does when he's considering his response. "I'm open to the possibility."

"The possibility of *ghosts*?"

"I think it would be extremely arrogant to assume that something isn't real when so many people claim to have seen it, simply because I haven't."

I'm . . . genuinely speechless. As the silence lengthens, Dominic continues.

"But maybe ghosts aren't quite what people think they are, not trapped spirits or anything like that. I see them more as . . . scars."

"Scars?"

"*Hmm* . . . like a mark left on a place by some traumatic event. And maybe they only become visible when that same kind of trauma-energy occurs in the same spot."

I think about that—about Sadie. How she's supposedly tied to the waterfall where she died. How she's meant to appear to Thorns right before they die. There's something comforting about the idea that she's just an echo, or a *scar* as Dominic says. I'd hate to think of her soul being trapped there forever.

"Could the mark be left on an entire family, do you think?"

"Maybe," he says. "A scar handed down from one generation to the next."

"Deep," I say, allowing a teasing note to creep in, because that's better than letting him hear the panic his idea strikes in me. If he's right, it means it isn't the manor that's haunted—*scarred*. It's my entire family.

"There's more to see in this world than what our eyes have already seen, Thorn."

"Was that a quote?"

"Yes. I believe it was first said by Dominic Adrien Miller, a proven genius."

"*Adrien?* You told me you didn't have a middle name!" I laugh, and some of my tension begins to unravel. It's so strange how easy it is to talk to Dominic now, about almost anything.

"That was before I knew the alternative was being called 'Monica.'"

"Oh my God—your initials are DAM? Like, *daaaayum*?"

I'm laughing for real now, trying to muffle the sound under my duvet, even though I know my voice won't carry to Carolyn and Uncle Ty upstairs in the main house.

"I'm glad you called me," Dominic says, laughing a little too. "I think I needed this after that shitshow at the memorial."

"Right? I can't believe Hamish actually got up and gave a speech. Haven't the police spoken to him yet?"

"Oh, they have," Dominic says, sighing. "Apparently, he *did* talk to Freya on the phone a couple of times, but not the night you overheard her. That was another number, and they haven't been able to trace it to anybody. It's probably a burner phone, like the one Freya had. If the guy's trying to cover his tracks, that phone's probably dust by now. Besides, they'd already ruled out Hamish as a murder suspect because he had an alibi for the times both Freya and Ford were killed."

"Oh." I let all that sink in. "So it's not him, then?"

"Well, I'm not so sure. From what I gather, his alibi for when Freya was killed is that he was in his office at lunchtime, watching a Netflix show. That seems shaky to me. I mean, the fact his laptop was playing a video at that time doesn't mean he was physically there, watching it. And, when Ford died, Hamish's girlfriend claims he was with her. But maybe she's covering for him."

"So you still think he did it?"

"I . . . maybe. I mean, he's definitely hiding something. He told the cops the reason Freya called him on his cell was to ask him to tutor her, but my sister didn't need a tutor. Her grades were even better than mine."

"Another proven genius, huh?" I say, not teasing, but with maybe just a hint of envy.

Dominic's quiet for a moment. "You should probably know that Hamish gave the police a drawing he claims is yours. He made a point of telling my parents about it."

My stomach sinks right through the stone floor of my room.

"Shit. I'm really sorry—the drawing wasn't actually supposed to be Freya. I was just doodling without thinking. I definitely *didn't* write those words on it, or pin it to your sister's locker, I swear—"

"Thorn, it's okay." But his flat tone tells me it's not. I've fucked up.

"Dominic, I'm sorry. I didn't mean for the drawing to turn out how it did."

"I'm not upset." He exhales deeply. "I know you use your drawings to . . . I don't know, work through things. And I came to terms with the fact you and Freya didn't like each other a long time ago. I mean, I know you'd have liked each other if you weren't both so damned quick to judge, but the fact you don't take any shit is one of the reasons I like you."

"You like me?" I can't keep the grin out of my voice.

"Don't let it go to your head. And can we please focus? There's still a murderer out there."

"So what are we going to do? It doesn't seem like the cops are getting anywhere, and I have a bad feeling that if no better suspect leaps out in front of them, waving a confession, they're gonna come back to me."

I'm hoping Dominic, self-certified genius that he is, will contradict that statement, but he doesn't. Instead, he says, "We'd better find out for sure what part Hamish played in all this."

"How? Are we going to toss his office? Beat a confession out of the guy? I mean, I doubt that'd do us much good, but I'm game if you are." I'm only half joking. The urge to throat-punch Hamish still lingers from earlier.

"Maybe we don't need to be *so* criminal about it? We could try to trick him into confessing."

I think about the greasy way Hamish tried to get me to hire him as a tutor before the holidays. Is that how he talked his way into Freya's life? And did Ford figure that out?

"I have an idea," I say at last.

THIRTY-FOUR

The alarm on my phone goes off at eight p.m. the following night, as if I weren't watching the time like an anxious
hawk. I turn it off and run through my checklist once again. I
have pepper spray (bought this afternoon in a completely legal
fashion with my own ID), an old thumb drive, my phone, super-
warm clothes I can run in, and my gloves, of course.

I slid a typed note under Hamish's office door at lunchtime,
after checking nobody was around to see. Assuming he read it,
he's either getting ready to come meet me in two hours, or—if he
really has nothing to hide—he's gone to the cops to tell them some
weirdo sent him a threatening note.

This is what it said:

*I know what you did to Freya Miller. I have the proof from
her phone. Meet me at Burden Bridge tonight at 10 p.m.
and I'll tell you how you can get it back. If not, I take it to
the cops. Your call.*

If this works, he'll show up, I'll claim to have removed the
videos from her gallery before I gave the burner phone to the
cops—including one where she talks about Hamish by name, and
how they were planning to meet the day she was killed—and I'll
offer to give him the thumb drive if he'll get me into the summer
art program.

I got the idea after thinking over what Carolyn told me about
Liam getting caught creeping on young girls because of evidence

from his phone. It *always* comes back to a phone. And Freya was forever recording herself. Why wouldn't she make a video as security? When I explained the plan to Dominic last night, he was skeptical, to say the least.

"Why would Freya record a video like that, though? He won't believe she was that careless."

"It doesn't matter if he doesn't fully believe it," I told him. "He just needs a sliver of doubt. It'll be enough. And it's not like I'm asking for money or anything it would actually hurt him to trade for it, so I don't see why he won't agree."

At least, that's what I'm hoping. Of course, if Hamish has murdered two people in cold blood, he might think it's safer just to get rid of me too. And that's what the pepper spray and running clothes are for.

"Look," I said to Dominic when he still wasn't convinced, "if it comes down to it and I have to run, there are a million hiding places I know around the manor where Hamish will never find me in the dark. All the security cameras are working now, and you'll be inside, watching everything on the screens in your mom's office. You can call the cops if it starts to look dicey."

"*Dicey*," he repeated. "I don't want to put your life at risk, Thorn."

I laughed. "Neither do I, *Adrien*."

Dominic sighed, but I could tell he wasn't going to argue anymore. He wants to see Hamish pay for what he's done as much as I do—maybe more.

"I think I preferred it when you called me Monica," he said.

"Really?"

"No, not really. But you could try calling me Nic, if you wanted to."

I waited until we were saying good night about an hour later before trying it out. It actually felt okay.

I make one last check that I've got everything, then head through the kitchen, planning on grabbing some necessary caffeine on my way out. I find Carolyn leaning into the fridge.

"Aren't you young folk on some kind of nighttime curfew?" she says, nodding to the dark square of the window.

"Yep. But I'm not walking anywhere. I'll take Bessie. And I won't be long."

"Where are you headed?"

I bite my lip, not sure whether to lie. Because I definitely can't tell her *why* I'm going to the manor. She'd never let me go. So I choose a half-truth instead.

"I think I can find out for sure who killed Freya," I say. "But I need to get something from the manor."

Carolyn frowns. "Get what? Aren't the Millers there?"

"They're in Haverford until late tonight. And this is kinda time-sensitive."

"Ava, what is this? You're freaking me out here."

Damn it. Carolyn really does look worried. I shouldn't have said anything.

I paste on a smile and lie harder. "Hey, it's nothing to freak out about. I'll be back in a couple hours, okay? And I have my phone with me." *And pepper spray.*

"Maybe we should check with Ty . . ."

"*No.*" It comes out louder than I intended. "Uncle Ty's always saying he's not my boss, and I'm eighteen now. An adult. So let's just talk about this when I get back, okay?"

Carolyn sighs. "How about I come with you, then?"

I laugh and shake my head. "No. Honestly. This isn't a big deal." I lean in and kiss her cheek. "Thank you, though."

Carolyn shrugs me off, but she's smiling again. "Just be careful, okay? And here." She leans back into the fridge and hands me a chilled coffee. "One for the road."

I take out my phone and light up the screen before waving at the camera as I cross Burden Bridge. If it works the way Dominic explained, it should be recording me now. I recite the alphabet as I go, keeping my voice pitched at the same volume I would if I was talking to someone on the far side. If Dominic's fancy background-noise-canceling camera mic isn't good enough to capture Hamish's confession clearly over the sound of the waterfall, then this is all going to be a waste of time.

The snow has stopped for now, but the clouds hang thick and heavy overhead, so I don't think it's done for tonight. My heart races in my chest, and I'm sweating despite the cold.

God, I hope this doesn't go horribly wrong. I really, really don't want to die.

I left Bessie out in the lane and came in over the wall. Maybe that's the way Hamish will go if he's avoiding the cameras around the property. And, if he actually is the murderer, then he knew enough to do that the last time he was here.

My footsteps crunch along the gravel path to the front door of the manor. The house stands completely dark except for one light above the door. Later, when I come back out to wait for Hamish, Dominic will turn out that light too, to make it seem as though the house is completely empty tonight.

Just as I start to wonder if Dominic's spy camera is even turned on, I spot someone at the edge of the orchard. I guess he's walking Pilot.

I bury my hands deeper in my pockets, trying to stomp some warmth into my limbs while I wait for Dominic to join me. But he doesn't come any closer. In fact, he's moving kind of oddly. It's like the shadows around him are shifting, swirling into him, as if he's drawing in fog.

Wait — *is* that Dominic?

The figure tilts its head, neck-snap quick, and I fall still.

That's definitely not Dominic.

It's Sadie.

As though she heard me thinking her name, her head jerks in my direction.

Heart thudding, I back away toward the manor.

"Ava? What are you looking at?"

Dominic stands in the open front doorway, the electric lantern above him shining down a circle of light. I glance back at the orchard, but there's nothing there now.

My breath comes in shallow gusts that fog the air around us.

"Do you have a camera aimed at the orchard there?" I point, showing Dominic where I saw the figure.

"Yes. I was just watching you on the feed. I didn't see anyone. Did you?"

"I . . . no. Probably not."

He ushers me into the darkness of the house. "Let's just check the video footage to make sure. We need to know if Hamish is already lurking out there."

I take one last look over the orchard. Nothing moves there now, but we both flinch when a barn owl screeches somewhere off in the distance. Dominic turns out the porch light, locks the door, then slides the chain across.

"And if you stand here"—Dominic indicates a spot on his laptop screen, next to the orchard side of the bridge—"and you stop him when he reaches here, that should be perfect for the camera to pick up."

Our little test run when I came over the bridge earlier proved that Dominic's camera set-up works brilliantly. When I pointed this out to him, he gave me an arch look and said, "This isn't my first rodeo."

Yes, I did laugh. Probably more than I should have, but I'm nervous as hell right now. I'm pretty sure Dominic can tell.

"We don't have to do this, you know," he says. "Or *I* can go out there and talk to him—it doesn't have to be you."

"Yes, it does," I tell him. "He'd never believe you'd keep evidence about your sister's murder from the cops. And he doesn't have anything you'd want to blackmail him for, like I have with the summer art program. *And* you don't know the layout of the grounds as well as I do, especially not in the dark. I need you in here, making sure we get this bastard on record, and calling the cops as soon as we have his confession."

Dominic studies me, lips pursed. "You'll pepper-spray and run at the first *hint* that he's dangerous? Doesn't matter if he's confessed to anything or not—you being safe is the top priority here."

I can't help smiling. "Your concern for my well-being is awfully sweet, you know. Are you some kind of nice guy, Nic Miller?"

The light from the laptop screen reflects in his eyes, making them look endless. "Not always," he says.

Well, *shit*.

I need to kiss this boy again.

Later, I promise myself. It's one more really great reason to make sure I survive this.

Something flickers on the laptop screen, and he turns to look at it, frowning. There's a grid showing the feeds from the different cameras around the property, including the gates and the one on Burden Bridge. But now they're all showing static.

Dominic makes an irritated sound. "Must be a glitch in the system, or maybe a blown fuse. Let me check." Barking comes from the kitchen, and he adds, "And let Pilot go do his business."

He leaves the study. Outside, the hallway lies in total darkness. It's probably just nerves, but something feels different. I see Dominic's silhouette crossing over to the kitchen.

I slide into the seat in front of the laptop, but in the process manage to knock over the cold coffee he gave me. "Shit!"

There wasn't a whole lot left, but still enough to leak a milky puddle on his mom's glass desktop. I look around me for a napkin, but of course there are none in the chrome office. I pick up the now empty coffee cup and use the edge of my hand to scrape the liquid off the edge of the desk and back into it. But that still leaves me with a hand covered in coffee. I make a face at it. But then seeing it shining wet in the light of the laptop slams two pieces together in my head.

Handprints at the murder scene.

I noticed it at the time—that one of the handprints on the stone bench where Freya was propped up was small, about the size of my own hand. The others all seemed bigger. And I didn't think much of it then, what with the shock and all, but I guess I kind of figured it might be Freya's handprint. Except her hands weren't bloody. She was already dead when whoever killed her smashed in her eyes, so she never got blood on them trying to defend herself.

There were two murderers.

Hamish and his fiancée? It crossed my mind before, but I dismissed it. But what if Hamish's fiancée found out he was screwing around with a student, and made him kill Freya as some kind of test? Making him choose her over Freya?

Did she stand over him while he did it? Or did she join in?

Maybe the cops know this—maybe that's why they haven't arrested me.

But then doubt creeps in. When they questioned me about moving Freya's body, they must've decided the smaller handprint was mine. After all, I had her blood on me from when I touched her face. And my hand was the right size for the print. Would they have been able to lift fingerprints from a rough stone bench? I have no idea.

But maybe they didn't even see it. Maybe the smaller print got messed up when Dominic moved Freya to try CPR.

"Nic!" I shout, but there's no answer, and I can't hear him in the kitchen. I creep over to the door, but there's no sign of him. Faintly, the sound of Pilot barking carries from outside. I guess Dominic is still out there.

I cross the dark hallway and head for the kitchen, trying to tread lightly so I'm not stomping over the newly tiled floor. When I reach the kitchen doorway, an icy breeze hits me. Poking my head inside, I see the French doors leading to the backyard are swinging open, a cold February wind drifting into the house. Moonlight turns the yard outside into a silvery scene.

"Nic?" I whisper. But there's no reply. I edge over to the open doors and peer out.

He's out there, lying facedown on the lawn. My hand flies to my mouth. Then I see the figure standing over him. I think it's Sadie at first.

I step closer. And closer.

No, it's not Sadie. It's a man holding what looks like a crowbar.

Hamish?

No.

"Uncle Ty?"

THIRTY-FIVE

"What are you doing here?" I ask him. "Did Carolyn tell you to come after me?"

Uncle Ty says nothing, just watches me with this odd frown on his face like he's trying to come up with the best way to break bad news.

"Uncle Ty? What happened to Dominic?" I start to go over and check that Dominic's okay, but something in Uncle Ty's posture stops me. "Why are you . . ."

And then the pieces start to slot together. An older guy. Someone from school. Someone who saw Freya almost every day.

He's holding a fucking crowbar.

A crowbar with an end that's awfully similar to an ice pick.

"It was you."

The guy on the phone. The guy Freya was sending naked pictures to.

"I think I'm gonna be sick. *How could you?* She was sixteen, for God's sake! And Ford? What did he ever do to you?"

Uncle Ty takes a step toward me. Behind him, I see Dominic's leg move. I stifle a sob of relief. He's not dead—but he must be hurt, and I can't tell how badly.

Please be okay . . .

"Ava, it's not what you think," Uncle Ty says, stepping closer again. It takes everything in me not to turn and run back into the house. "None of this was supposed to happen the way it did."

"You had an affair with a *child*!" I yell. Again, I think I see Dominic moving. I fight the urge to run over to him. I don't want Uncle Ty to notice he's conscious, or he might hurt him again. I need to keep his focus on me.

Uncle Ty holds up his hands. "Whoa, no." He has the nerve to look offended. "I would *never* cheat on Carolyn. Not ever. The only reason I got Freya to send me those pictures was so I could use them to get some more money out of that tight asshole Madoc. If he'd just given me a fair price to begin with—"

"Wait, wait—what are you saying? You wanted to use her photos as *blackmail*?"

He actually shrugs. "Well, that was the original plan. But then, when Hamish came and told me about Freya being ineligible for that damn summer program because she just turned sixteen, well . . . I realized I might've miscalculated."

Miscalculated??

"I never wanted to kill Freya. But she started sending me those photos right after Thanksgiving—she was fifteen then, but I didn't know that. I thought she was eighteen, like her brother. I mean, why the hell does everyone call them twins if they're not? But what I *did* know was that, no matter how I tried to end the relationship she *thought* we were having, it would all come out. Do you know what happens to guys who get arrested for child pornography? Do you, Ava?"

Much less than you deserve.

Uncle Ty moves closer, and I take a step back. Panic thrums through me, even as my mind screams that this is Uncle Ty—there's no reason to be afraid. But I know there is. I *know*.

"It was only ever about the money. The money I *should've*

inherited when Dad died, but he left it all to Blake. How was I supposed to feel about that, Ava? I wasn't even the second favorite—I was more like the goddamn family dog!"

"But I've got money now, Uncle Ty," I say quickly. "From the sale of the manor. You could've had it—you still can. All of it, if you want."

He gives me a considering look. "I really didn't want to hurt you, Ava. But I'm in this too deep now, and this is my only way out."

Hurt me?

Jesus. Okay. Okay, think.

I need to get him away from Dominic before he realizes he's conscious.

I need to call the cops.

I need to *run*.

How can this be happening?

"Why Ford, though? Did he find out what you were doing?" I ask. I think it's pretty obvious I'm trying to stall now, and I'm not surprised Uncle Ty doesn't answer. But my brain seems to have turned to a block of ice. *Just keep talking!* "That day, when Freya died, you were sick . . . or was that all fake?" My heart pounds in my chest, a warning drumbeat. "What's Carolyn going to say when she finds out what you did?"

And then I hear another voice to my right.

"Oh, don't worry about me, sweetie."

My head whips around, and Carolyn is standing right there in the snow. She's wearing a long, hooded coat. It casts a deep shadow over her eyes. For a moment, I'd swear she was Dead-Eyed Sadie.

The second handprint.

How did I not see it sooner?

"It was *you* I saw at the river, thinking it was Sadie," I say, voice almost a whisper. "*Why?*"

She sighs, sounding almost disappointed. "I needed to make it look right when they find you. All your friends will back me up, your teachers. 'She was seeing things,' they'll say. 'After that first girl washed up dead, she became totally obsessed with the ghost story about Dead-Eyed Sadie, and the idea that Sadie wanted her eyes back. She even started to believe Sadie was making her kill . . .'"

Carolyn gives me a twisted smile, and I remember the words scrawled across that sketch on Freya's locker: *SADIE MADE ME DO IT.* The sketch Uncle Ty could easily have taken from my bag and added to the shrine before anyone else was at school.

"That girl drowning was what gave me the idea. Ford was never meant to be a part of the plan, but when he came to the cottage that night, asking to see you after your little fight, he told me he'd figured out a clue from a video Freya posted . . . Well, we couldn't take any chances. Not when the rest of it was working out so beautifully."

I let out a sob. "Ford didn't even know anything! Not really. All he saw was that Freya had two phones—and I had the other phone the whole time. You murdered him for nothing!"

Carolyn shrugs. "Not nothing. It did help to paint a picture of a completely unhinged teenage girl."

She steps toward me, but I shrink back, closer to the kitchen door. "I followed him on his way home. Took that crowbar Ty just used on your boyfriend over there. And I hit him." Her face twists in a snarl. "As hard as I could. He went down hard too, right there on the riverbank. But it had to look the same as the other one, didn't it? So I took the crowbar and jabbed it"—she makes a punching motion toward my face, and I back up another step—"right in his eyes. But do you know what? He *still* wasn't dead!"

I feel a scream rising in me, threatening to erupt at any second.

"Are you picturing it, Ava? Can you see it playing out in front of you, almost like you were there? He crawled, pleading for help, right out onto the ice. Kept crawling until it gave way under him. We all have to crawl in the end, though, don't we, Ava? Isn't that what you always used to wake up screaming?" Carolyn's almost laughing now, she's enjoying herself so much.

"It's what Dad said, right before he died," I mutter, feeling like I'm in a chokehold.

"Funny that, isn't it?" She grins.

"Carolyn, that's enough," Uncle Ty warns. He's moved to stand next to her, and she shoots him a look I've never seen before—one that's pure resentment. Uncle Ty seems not to notice.

I stare at them. Uncle Ty and Carolyn. My guardians. The two people who I thought were my last family in the world— they're monsters.

Carolyn pouts. "But I gave her a much higher dose tonight. I want to see if it's working. Who knows? Maybe we can even get her to jump off the bridge herself."

What. The. Fuck. "A higher dose . . . ?"

But then I remember what Carla said on my birthday—the reasons someone sane might hallucinate.

"You've been *poisoning* me?"

Carolyn laughs, sounding delighted. "Well, drugging you, technically. Little teensy microdoses of PCP—until now. Tell me, how does it feel? Like you need to peel off your own skin?"

"Come on, Carolyn . . ." Uncle Ty says. He almost sounds embarrassed.

Guilty?

"Uncle Ty, you aren't really gonna let her hurt me, are you?" I try, an invisible hand squeezing my heart. I never, ever imagined saying anything like this to him. Or to Carolyn.

But he doesn't do anything. Doesn't stop her moving closer to me. Just lowers his gaze so it doesn't meet mine.

"I wonder if the PCP was what made your dad claw out his own eyes?" Carolyn muses, as if I haven't spoken.

I feel like I've just been sucker-punched. "You drugged them too? Mom and Dad?"

"Only your dad, actually. He was supposed to be driving. So the crash really was just a happy accident in the end."

I slap her. My hand connects so hard, it feels like my scars are tearing.

"You little—" Carolyn screams, and for a moment I have no clue what's going on. Then I hear the growling.

Pilot launches himself at Carolyn, his powerful jaws clamping around her calf. I take out the pepper spray from my coat pocket and blast Uncle Ty with it. He curses.

I don't wait to see what happens. I run back in the house, slamming the French doors behind me and locking them.

Call the cops.

My phone is on the desk in Lucille's study.

I hurry back through the kitchen, stubbing my toe on the

corner of the counter in the dark. But my eyes are adjusting, and I can see well enough by the time I'm in the hallway to move quickly now.

Then I stop at the sound of glass smashing. I plaster my back to the wall and try to peer around the dark silhouette of the gallery staircase. The frosted window next to the front door is gone, and there's an arm reaching through, opening the front-door locks.

"Hurry up, Ty. She probably has her phone in there."

"My goddamn face is on fire!" he snaps.

I shrink back under the curved staircase. If they come in and turn on the lights, they'll see me right away. I need to get out of here. Back out through the kitchen?

Before I can move, the front door opens.

"I'll start setting up down here. You go find her, then we can finish this," Carolyn hisses. Uncle Ty doesn't even argue, just heads straight for the staircase I'm hiding under.

But he doesn't turn on the lights. And then I realize why the camera feed glitched earlier—they've tampered with the power somehow, maybe flipped a breaker switch.

Uncle Ty climbs the stairs two at a time, thumping right over where I'm crouched in the dark. I hear Carolyn rattling around inside Lucille's office. What is she doing?

Making sure there's no security footage?

I can't wait around here to find out. I pad quietly back through the kitchen and unlock the door. But the moment I open it I'm shoved back against the kitchen counter, a hand at my throat.

It releases me immediately.

"God, Ava, I'm sorry," Dominic whispers. "Are you okay? I thought you were one of them—"

"I'm fine," I tell him. "But we need to get out of here. Did you hear them in the yard? It's Uncle Ty and Carolyn—they did all of *this,* just for money."

Dominic nods. "I heard most of it, I think."

"What did Ty do to you? Are you okay?"

"Hit me with something. I've got a lump on the back of my head, and a killer headache, but I think I'll live."

Suddenly light floods in from the hallway, silhouetting a figure just outside. I grab Dominic's arm and pull him down next to me, shimmying back until we're pressed into the recess next to the cellar door.

"Ty!" Carolyn's voice carries through from somewhere nearby. "What are you doing? We need to keep the lights off!"

"Well, how the hell am I supposed to find her in the dark? I can barely see as it is!" Uncle Ty steps farther into the kitchen. I jump when a gust of wind makes the French doors swing shut, barely stifling a gasp. He crosses over to them, peering out at the empty backyard. Probably checking there are no footprints leading away from the house. He must decide I'm still in here, because he locks them, pockets the key, then heads out into the hall.

What do we do? Run for it?

Hide?

I don't know.

Then I feel Dominic tugging at my sleeve. I turn to find him crawling silently through the open cellar door. I follow, and push the door shut. The cellar is totally black. There are no windows, and I barely avoid tumbling down the steep stairs in the dark.

Immediately, the scent of old apples hits me—the fermented fruit of Thorn's Blood Apple Sour. There are hundreds of bottles of it down here, though it's too dark to make out a thing. But I know they're there, just like I know the trapdoor leading to the pit is over in the far corner. In the pitch-blackness, it's easy to picture a witch's gnarled hand reaching up from it, trying to lure me closer with a curled finger . . .

I feel for Dominic's hand. We wait, listening to Uncle Ty moving around on the other side of the door. I hear his footsteps. Quick, sharp breaths. A strange tearing sound. It goes on for some time, and then he seems to move away. I'm about to inch open the door when I hear Ty and Carolyn speaking again. They sound much fainter with the cellar door between us.

"Look, if she called the cops, we'll just have to play the delusional card," Ty says. "She can't have gotten out — all the windows and doors are locked, and it's all set up down here."

"Just go check upstairs one more time," Carolyn orders, sounding more pissed than I've ever heard her. "We need to make sure she's actually in here before we leave."

They're leaving?

I let out a quiet breath. We just need to wait for them to go, and then we can get out of here and call the cops without worrying about flying crowbars.

Dominic squeezes my hand, and I squeeze back.

"Fine," Ty says. "I'll check again. Meet me out back, okay? And watch out for that damn dog. I only stunned it."

My heart is thumping so loudly, I'm surprised the sound doesn't carry through the door.

Uncle Ty hurries away again, then there's silence for a minute.

"Can you smell something?" Dominic whispers next to my ear. I'm about to shake my head when I catch it above the scent of sour apples—something strong and chemical. Before I can say anything, lighter footsteps pass by the cellar door. There are more clicking, scraping sounds, then an odd sort of *whoosh*.

Light flickers in through the cracks around the door, and in it I see Dominic staring at me, wide-eyed. *Fire,* he mouths.

I pull open the door, but immediately shut it again. A carpet of flames has consumed the entire kitchen floor.

"Shit! How are we gonna get out?" I say, my voice cracking in fear.

"Is there a window or something down here?"

"No," I say. "Only the trapdoor to the pit, and that doesn't help us."

"The pit?"

"An old cold-storage room below the cellar."

Smoke has started to pour in around the door now. By silent agreement, we retreat down the cellar steps. I snuck down these same stairs plenty of times over the last couple years to take one of the least-noticeable bottles from the racks of wine and liquor. I know every creaky board, every uneven stair.

It quickly becomes too dark to see again, so Dominic takes out his phone. In the light it gives, I see the cellar already filling with smoke.

"We'll die from smoke inhalation if we don't get out of here," I say, and immediately begin coughing. "We need to call for help."

"I called the cops while I was outside," Dominic says, coughing too. "They're coming, but the fresh snow on the roads will probably hold them up."

We drop down onto our hands and knees, trying to breathe

the clearer air under the smoke. I can already feel the effects of it making me sluggish.

In the light of Dominic's phone, I take in the familiar space around us. It looks exactly the same as the day I left—the tall racks housing hundreds and hundreds of vintage bottles standing in rows, filling almost the entire space. There's even one of Grandpa's reaching ladders sitting over in the corner, giving the cellar the appearance of a library. A library of liquor. I remember Uncle Ty saying the buyer had negotiated to include the liquor collection; he'd seemed gutted to be handing over all that booze. *Good,* I think now. Except I realize it's not good at all—it's pretty fucking terrible.

"When the fire gets through that door, this whole room will go up." I try not to imagine the feel of the flames swallowing us, the blistering agony of dying that way.

"If the pit was used for cold storage, it might give us some protection," Dominic says. I can tell he's trying hard not to sound scared. "At least for a while."

I nod, then lead the way, still keeping low, coughing into my elbow as my eyes stream. When I reach the far corner, I feel around on the floor for the outline of the trapdoor.

There—got it.

I pull the ring and heave it open. A cold, decayed breath rushes up from the pit. It takes every bit of my willpower not to cower away from it. Dominic shines his phone's flashlight down.

The light is weak against the darkness of the pit. Still, I make out the familiar circular stone walls, the ancient metal rungs leading down from the hatch, the damp earth lining the base. I do *not* want to go down there. My fingers dig into the edge of the hole, but then my hand slips, and I jerk forward, about to plunge headfirst into the pit.

Dominic grabs my shoulder, hauling me back.

"Thanks," I say, and in that moment I see the stark contrast between him—a boy I would've sworn a few weeks ago was my mortal enemy—and Uncle Ty, who's my sole remaining blood relative. In this exact same spot, one of them pushed me into danger, and the other pulled me back from it.

When Ford shoved me aside so I almost got hit by an out-of-control car, I knew then that when it came down to it, he just didn't care about me. Why didn't I realize the same thing about Uncle Ty? Why didn't I see him for who he is, not just for what I wanted him to be?

"Can you do this?" Dominic asks, probably watching me go through several shades of freaked out.

"We have to," I tell him. The pit is where my ancestors are said to have thrown Sadie. The room she disappeared from without a trace. Of course, I don't believe that—I know they must have murdered her and hidden her body somewhere.

A scar handed down from one generation to the next.

The thought passes through my mind like a shiver.

Maybe that's what it really means to be a Bloody Thorn.

The light catches the underside of the hatch, where a witch mark is carved deep into the wood. The only one I've ever seen inside the manor. It's another kind of scar: a mark to stop evil getting into the house. Or maybe from getting out.

I feel the pit yawning below me.

And I know we have no choice.

THIRTY-SIX

Dominic pulls the hatch closed above us just as a loud crack of splintering wood comes from the top of the cellar stairs. Either someone is trying to get in or, more likely, the door is about to give way. When it does, the fire will rush down into a cellar full of liquor.

I adjust my grip on the metal rungs, palms sweaty despite the cold.

Okay, okay. We just have to wait. Wait, and hope the cops and the fire department arrive in time to save us. Just wait, and stay alive.

The burning in my muscles from leaning on the ladder at such an awkward angle isn't helping. I take a deep breath and start to climb down. It's only ten feet or so, and maybe eight feet across the circular space. At the bottom, the floor is a crusted layer of mud that reaches up the stone walls to around head level.

I shudder, not from cold exactly, but a sense that I was never meant to be down here—that I've broken some unspoken rule simply by setting foot in this place. Dominic shines his flashlight up again. From here, I can barely make out the witch mark on the trapdoor. It's as though the pit swallows light.

Who carved that mark, though? Was it Sadie? Or someone else, making sure what was done to Sadie was never forgotten, that it would scar the manor forever?

Just how many servants did my ancestors throw down here?

Bile rises in my throat at the thought, but I try and force the thought from my head. If I let myself think about that now, I'll have a total meltdown.

Dominic climbs down the ladder, jumping the last few rungs to land next to me.

"The smoke has started to seep through the hatch," he says. "We don't have long. I'll call 911 again, let them know where we are and see how long they're going to be."

I nod, not trusting my voice right now. Hugging myself, I circle the pit while Dominic dials.

Something crumbles beneath my boot, and I trip backward, nailing the wall with my elbow.

"Are you all right?" I nod as Dominic comes over and helps me up. "I can't make a call from down here—no signal. But the cops must be on their way, so we just need to sit tight and . . ."

He notices I'm not listening. Because I've seen something in the wall where I just whacked my elbow—a hole.

"What is that?" Dominic shines his light on the spot. Where the caked-on mud has cracked away, it's left behind a dark, elbow-sized recess. I angle my head, trying to see what's inside.

Nothing. Just more blackness. It's as though there's only a dark void beyond the crusted layer of earth. Nothing for the light to snag on. I press against the edges of the hole, and it crumbles inward. Before long, the hole is the size of my head. After a few more seconds, I've revealed a circular hole in the wall of the pit, maybe two feet in diameter. It's lined with bricks, not stone, as if it's newer than the pit.

"What the hell . . . ?" My muttered words race away from us through the exposed tunnel. *Is* it a tunnel? Or some kind of *pipe*?

An image comes into my mind: the blueprint of the manor Dominic sent me. The drawing of the cellar, and that straight line running right through the exterior wall of the house. I thought it was for some kind of label, but I was wrong. I look around me again, at the shape of the pit, and the caked-on mud showing where there must at one time have been moisture. It's bone dry now, but might this once have been filled with water — channeled in from the river, maybe? Like a well inside the house? And if this pipe fed the well, and is now dry, then maybe . . .

The newspaper article strongly implied that the story about Sadie vanishing from the cellar was a lie to cover up my ancestors murdering her. But what if she *did* disappear?

It sparks an idea. Not a good idea, or one I particularly want to have. But an idea.

"I think this might be a way out," I say. Again, the sound rushes away into the darkness.

Dominic doesn't seem too happy about the idea, either, but he nods. "It's worth checking out, right?"

It looks big enough to crawl in on my hands and knees, so I can always back out again if I come face-to-face with any dead-eyed ghosts.

You just had to think about Sadie, didn't you?

Maybe I should focus on the much more likely possibility that I'm about to crawl into a confined space with a lot of rats, spiders, and snakes.

Better than choking to death, or waiting for the fire.

I stoop and pick up a chunk of the mud I elbowed loose, and throw it as far as I can down the pipe. It clatters along for a few feet, beyond the reach of Dominic's flashlight. Nothing stirs at the intrusion. Still, I hesitate.

"I can go first," he offers, "but I'm more likely to get wedged in than you are, and it's better if at least one of us makes it out."

"It's not like I'd leave you here to die."

He smirks. "I appreciate that. But you could go for help."

"Okay." I take a deep breath. "Let's do this."

My eyes blur as I look down the circular tunnel. It seems to be growing narrower and narrower. Of all the terrible, terrible ways I've considered I might die, being trapped in an underground water pipe has got to be right up there. The moment I think that, I imagine getting wedged into the tight space, not able to go forward or back, darkness all around me, and it suddenly starting to fill with water.

My breath comes quick and shallow. Yep, I'm full-on hyperventilating.

"Ava?"

I crouch down, tucking my head between my knees, and try to think calm thoughts. Logical thoughts. But they all seem to circle back to the fact that we're trapped in a creepy-ass underground pit while the manor above us burns, and our only potential way out is through that hell-pipe.

"Are you all right? I heard Carolyn say something about drugging you earlier."

I nod, because what else can I do? "Yeah, apparently she's been lacing my coffee with something called PCP."

Dominic hisses out a breath. "Jesus. That's a strong hallucinogenic."

"No shit. I've been seeing all kinds of weird things the last couple weeks, and I have no idea how much of it was real."

"But is it affecting you now?"

I straighten up, assess. "I don't think so. Carolyn said she put a megadose in my coffee tonight, but I only had a tiny sip. It tasted disgusting, so I thought it'd gone bad. I actually felt guilty for wasting it." I laugh, but it sounds strained. "Let's get on with this."

Before I can start to hyperventilate again, I climb into the water pipe.

THIRTY-SEVEN

Dominic passes me his phone to use as a flashlight, and I hold it between my teeth so I can keep my hands free. My breathing is loud in my own ears. It bounces along the brick tunnel ahead of me like it's dancing with the light from the phone.

So far, I haven't seen any rats. Or snakes. Or ghosts. One spider, but it was long dead. Its husk had gone glassy and dried up with age. I hope that doesn't happen to us.

I hope that didn't happen to Sadie, either.

Damn it. Why didn't it occur to me that maybe — just maybe — the reason Sadie disappeared was because she got *stuck in this goddamn pipe*? What if she died in here? Are we about to crawl across a hundred-year-old skeleton? Then I see it: There's something up ahead and it's moving. A spider, maybe, except it's too big. Still, it moves like one. Legs hinged back, it crawls along the roof of the tunnel. I take the phone from my mouth, angling the light toward it.

"Dominic," I whisper, not wanting to draw its attention, but my voice is lost in the rasp of my dry throat. Because the not-spider is huge. Like, person-sized. And it's still skittering in our direction, a vague black shape beyond the reach of my flashlight.

Dominic bumps me from behind, and I almost drop the phone. The light jitters around the inside of the pipe, filling the shadows that just a moment ago housed an enormous spider-thing.

"Are you okay?" Dominic asks, voice muffled by my own ass.

"I think . . ." I shake my head, trying to clear the fuzzy waves that have started to appear at the edge of my vision. "Yeah, I think that PCP might be having an effect on me after all."

"You're okay. I'm with you. Just keep going," Dominic says from behind me. No matter what else is freaking me out right now, I'm glad he's here with me. More for my benefit than his, of course, but I'm still glad.

"Keep going," I repeat. The pipe mutters back to me. But, in my head, the shuffling sound of our hands and knees in the old dirt dredges up another chant from my memory.

We all have to crawl . . .

We all have to crawl.

WE ALL HAVE TO CRAWL.

Something brushes against my cheek, and I scream. The phone clatters onto the dirt in front of me.

We're plunged into darkness.

No!

"What is it? What happened?" Dominic calls from behind me.

I scrabble around for the phone. As soon as I find it and pick it up, the light returns. It was lying with the light facing down, that's all. I let out a whimper of relief.

"Sorry," I say. "Something touched my face, but I think it was just my hair."

I dust off the phone before putting it back in my mouth, and we continue.

Then a snicker sounds up ahead. Although the flashlight doesn't reach far, I can't see anyone, or anything, rushing to meet us. I can't see much at all.

Oh God, what's up there?

I have no idea how far we've crawled, or whether we might still be close to the pit, or nearer to wherever the pipe leads. But we can't go back. There's no way to turn around, and we can't crawl back into a fire. So I keep moving forward. Faster, faster. Crusted dirt and brick scrape my hands and knees, but I don't care. I keep moving, ignoring the way my breaths echo back to me. Ignoring the snickers bouncing from up ahead of us. I don't want to know what I'm hurrying toward, not really. I just want to get out. We have to keep crawling. Have to crawl.

We all have to crawl . . .

"*Fuu-huu-huuuck*," I groan, phone still jammed between my teeth. I have spit and tears running down my chin, but there's not a lot I can do about it. I just have to keep going. I have to keep —

The pipe ends directly in front of me.

I'm facing a wall of earth.

There's no rhyme nor reason to it, it just . . . ends. I take the phone from my mouth.

"What's going on?" Dominic says behind me. "Are you stuck?"

"I'm not sure," I say, trying my best to sound calm, even though we both know that's a lie. I prod the wall in front of me, just to check I'm not hallucinating it. "Maybe the pipe collapsed. It might be what blocked off the flow of water to the pit."

The earth feels damp against my fingers, like clay. I press against it, and a lump falls onto the floor of the pipe in front of me.

"Maybe I can dig through it. It could lead to a way out."

Or it could unleash a torrent of water from the river, and we'll drown stuck in this pipe. I'm pretty sure the same thought occurs to Dominic, because he says nothing.

Damn it.

I'm just going to have to hope that whatever water channel was feeding this pipe has now dried up. Digging my fingers into the mud wall ahead of me, I begin to claw out goopy handfuls. I push deeper, testing to see how thick the wall is.

A trickle of water sluices out toward me.

"Keep going," Dominic says.

I dig. The floor of the pipe in front of me is filling with clay and water and I still can't dig it out fast enough. It's pouring in now, and I start using my forearms, dragging armfuls of wet mud toward us. Finally, a big lump of the blockage falls away from me, leaving a gaping black hole.

No more water rushes in. But I hear it—the roar of the river somewhere nearby. It vibrates along the pipe, a sound of unstoppable rage. I let it fill me as I shove, one hand, then the other, forcing more of the clay outward, making the hole bigger. I throw my weight into it. Too late, I have the awful thought that maybe it comes out somewhere on the sheer cliff face near the waterfall—out onto a deadly drop. But it's not loud enough for that, only a thrum, really. Anyway, we can't go back now.

Taking the phone from my mouth, I shine it around the dark space. The light bounces off a circle of water just below the pipe. Above it, the walls are circular and made from stone, just like the walls of the pit, only the space is narrower—maybe five feet across. It smells dank and old, like something that's gone beyond the point of rot.

"It's another well," I say out loud, my voice dulled by the dark water next to me. This must have been the original source of water for the house before the pipe was added to connect it to the pit. I trace the path of the pipe in my mind, try to guess where this well sits on the property.

The orchard?

No, not quite—*the pavilion.*

"This must've been under it the whole time," I mutter.

Did Sadie make it to this point, I wonder. Is she still here, hidden in that darkness?

Yes.

It might be the drug in my system, but I have the strongest sense that she's down there. Her bones sunk deep at the bottom, buried by decades of dirt in that silent blackness. How deep is it, I wonder. If something dragged you down into the water, would you drown before you hit the bottom?

"Are you able to climb out?" Dominic calls from behind me. His voice sounds odd. Worn out. It snaps me out of my weird daydream.

Shining the light upward, I find a boarded ceiling maybe six or seven feet above my head. Wood—not stone. I check the phone for a signal, but it's still a bust. Practically growling in frustration, I set it down so I can use my hands.

"How hard can it be to John Wick my way out of a well?"

Using gaps between the stones in the walls as handholds, I maneuver so I'm standing with my feet at the edge of the pipe. From here, I can reach up and touch the wooden ceiling, but only just. If I lose my balance, I'll plunge into the water in front of me.

My fingertips dig into the rough stone walls as my head swims. It feels like something down there is pulling me forward, willing me to slip. I close my eyes. Think John Wick thoughts.

Something reaches up from the water and wraps around my ankle.

"It's not real," I whisper. But I can feel it. Hear the water dripping from long-dead bones. Imagine the slime sluicing out of those vacant eye sockets.

I look down.

The dead water is still.

I take a deep, shuddering breath and look up again, feeling a little steadier. So I reach toward the ceiling, pressing against it with my fingertips. Unsurprisingly, it doesn't move.

"I think I'm gonna need to borrow your height advantage," I call down to Dominic, expecting to see him hauling his rangy frame from the pipe, but there's no sign of him. "Nic?"

Nothing.

It's a difficult maneuver to crouch down so I can peer back into the pipe, but I finally manage it.

"Nic!"

He's lying facedown in the dirt lining the water pipe, one hand reaching toward me. For a moment, it sends me back to the day I found Freya, her pale hands resting in her lap, but I blink the image away. Dominic isn't dead. He can't be.

"Nic!" I grab his wrist and shake him. He doesn't wake up, but his head rolls to one side. Dominic's lips are parted slightly, and as I wait, frozen, for him to move I see a puff of dust blowing up as he exhales.

Not dead, thank God.

Not doing great, though. That crowbar to the head might've done more damage than either of us realized.

I bite my lip to keep from crying while I figure out what to do. Beyond Dominic is total darkness, but I know where it leads, and I think I could crawl over him if I have to. But there's no way I could abandon him here alone in the dark, so I'd have to leave his phone with him.

If I made it back to the pit and somehow got out of the blazing house, would I have a chance to tell someone where Dominic is before Uncle Ty or Carolyn could catch me? Or would I be leaving Nic to die down here? Would his parents, his friends, be left wondering where he disappeared to?

Again I think of Sadie, how she must've died in this terrible darkness. If she did put a curse on my family, I honestly can't blame her. But that doesn't mean I'm just going to wait here for it to catch up with me.

You're trapped inside a well, probably with a witch's corpse somewhere close by, and the only way out leads to an inferno. It already caught you, dipshit.

As though to underline that thought, I hear a rumbling *whoosh* traveling down the water pipe toward us. And I don't need to see the flames to know what that sound means: The liquor in the cellar just went up. There's no way I can get out that way now.

Back to Plan A: Break through the wooden boards covering the well. But the pavilion floor is gravelly, so who knows if breaking through the wood will be the hardest part — what if there's concrete above it? And I can barely reach it.

I scramble out of the pipe and reach for the ceiling again, just in case I grew in the last five minutes. I did not.

The well is around five feet across, so too wide for me to be able to chimney-climb, though Dominic could probably do it. If he weren't unconscious, that is. And not that he'd need to, because he could reach the damn ceiling easily.

"*FUUUUUUCK!*" I scream up at it.

And it's only as my voice trails off that I realize it doesn't have that same deadened quality it had before. Like it's . . . escaping.

I reach down for Dominic's phone—which seems to have a beast of a battery, praise Satan—and hold the light up closer to the wooden boards for a better look. They seem pretty solid, but there are—

The phone buzzes in my hand, and I almost drop it. But, as the screen lights up, I see a ton of messages and missed calls coming through.

There's a goddamn *signal* down here!

It disappears when I bring the phone down nearer head level, but up in the corner, near those hateful wooden boards, there's a bar. I don't know Dominic's passcode, but I don't need it to call Emergency.

I'm just trying to do that one-handed while I still cling to the wall, when the phone buzzes again. Mateo's picture fills the screen. I thumb-swipe to answer, putting him on speaker so I can keep the phone raised.

"*Nic? Nic! Where the hell are you, man?*" His voice comes through a little patchy, but it's not hard to connect the dots. "*The fucking house is on fire and I've been trying to reach you, but it kept going to voicemail and I thought you were fucking dead—*"

"Mateo!" I yell as loud as I can, hoping he'll hear me and shut up. It seems to work.

"Who's that?"

"Ava! I'm with Dominic, but he's hurt and we're stuck in an old well!"

There's a beat of silence, then, *"You fucking what?"*

"There's a covered well inside the pavilion . . . where Freya's body was found," I say, trying to figure out the best way to direct him here quickly. There was footage of the outside of the pavilion on the local news, the place still crawling with cops at the time, but I'm guessing Mateo saw it. "We're inside and can't get out! My uncle and his wife are trying to kill us—they're the ones who murdered Freya and Ford and . . . Can you just come get us, please?"

I wait for him to answer, but there's just silence.

"Mateo?"

Then I hear the beep of the call disconnecting.

Shit. Did he get that?

I move the phone around, hoping the signal will dip back in and he'll call again, but nothing happens. Time to try Emergency.

But then a groan comes from behind me. "Nic?" I spin—or try to—but my foot slips from the edge of the pipe and suddenly I'm falling into inky-black water.

THIRTY-EIGHT

The water is ice cold. It forces all the air out of me as I thrash around, trying to claw my way out of it. My palms sing out in pain as my scars react to the sudden chill.

No!

Dominic's phone slides from my grip, and I watch in horror as the light spirals down, down, down . . .

It blinks out, either landing light-down at the bottom, or just too deep to see any longer.

It's only been a few seconds, but my chest is already beginning to burn for air, and in the pitch-blackness I feel as though I might be sinking down into the depths of the water, just like the phone.

Panic clutches at me. I scrabble to find purchase on the stone walls with ice-pick fingers. In a split second of clarity, I think this must've been how Sadie felt. Betrayed by the people she should've been able to trust. Facing death in the dark, alone.

Except I'm not alone, really, am I?

My hand finds the edge of the pipe opening. I cling to it and drag myself up out of the water until I'm curled up inside the pipe. I feel for Dominic, find his outstretched hand. He's cold, but I'm colder.

"Nic?" I whisper through chattering teeth.

He groans faintly, then squeezes my hand. I could weep with

relief. "Please tell me it's actually dark in here, and I haven't just had my eyes stolen by a ghost."

Well, that is one thing I can reassure him about. "It's dark, yeah. I think you passed out. How are you feeling?"

Dominic laughs drily. "Like I've been hit over the head with a crowbar. But otherwise great."

I can't see any humor in this, though. "I lost your phone. And we're still stuck in here." I sniff, catching a smell that instantly fills me with dread. "And I think the pipe is filling with smoke."

"I see." There's no panic in Dominic's tone, and I can't decide whether to be reassured by that or to wonder if that crowbar messed with his ability to assess our absolute fuckedness. "I take it you couldn't get the lid off the well?"

"It's too high. I can barely reach it with my fingertips. And now you can't even see enough to give it a try."

"Describe the space to me."

I do, explaining as well as I can how he'll need to perch at the opening of the pipe and use the wall to grip on to. Before he can squeeze past me, there's an enormous bang from somewhere above us.

"What the hell was that?" he hisses. The bang comes again, even louder this time.

But I'm grinning so widely, I'm surprised he can't see it glowing. "Hopefully, that's Mateo coming to dig us up."

"You spoke to him?"

"Yeah, but it was a bad signal, and I wasn't sure he heard enough to figure out where we are. Looks like I was wrong."

Dominic doesn't answer.

"What?"

"Not to be negative, but it's also possible your uncle figured out where we might be and doesn't want to take the chance of us finding a way to escape."

My smile dims. As far as I know, Uncle Ty has no idea this pipe even exists. But I also thought I knew Uncle Ty would never try to kill me for money, so there's that.

"I guess we'll find out soon enough."

The banging continues for a few minutes—though it's hard to gauge time while we're huddled together in the dark. Dominic does his best to crowd some warmth into me. I'm pretty sure I'm just making us both feel colder, though. And the smoke is definitely getting thicker. I can taste it on every inhalation, and my head is starting to swim.

Bits of wood and dirt rain down with each strike from above. I'm *almost* sure it's Mateo. I mean, it has to be. If not, we're about to come face-to-face with Uncle Ty and what sounds like a god-damn pickax.

"Nic, when he breaks through that cover, I want you to stay hidden," I whisper between strikes.

"Why would I do that?" I don't need to see him to know he's humoring me.

"Because if it *is* Ty, I can tell him you didn't make it out of the house. And, no offense, but I think he's more worried about me escaping than you."

"Or we could *both* hide until we know who it is."

"Oh. Yeah, I guess that could work."

The pieces tumbling from above grow larger, until finally a

shaft of light shines down into the well. It's not bright—starlight cutting in through the pavilion windows, I'm guessing—but after the dense blackness of the water pipe, it's like a floodlight.

The smoke surrounding us swirls, thick and hazy. I don't know much about smoke inhalation or when it becomes life-threatening, but I'm hoping we'll be out of here before I find out. Dominic and I huddle together inside the water pipe, out of view of whoever might look down.

The banging stops.

I hold my breath. As soon as I do, I have a fierce urge to cough. It burns inside me, like my lungs are actually on fire. I start hacking. I wrap my arms around my face, but there's no way whoever's up there hasn't heard me. I look pleadingly at Dominic, hoping he'll get the message and go farther into the pipe to hide like I originally suggested, but he's not looking at me. He's staring out into the well, jaw set.

The smoke begins to drift up through the hole in the wooden boards. It's easily large enough for us to climb out through. As the air clears around us, my breathing grows easier, but my heart still races. I expect a face to appear at any moment, and the fact there's nobody peering down at us only sets me more on edge.

Dominic and I lock eyes.

"Who's there?" I call out, voice raspy from the smoke.

No answer.

"Mateo?" Dominic tries, a definite note of doubt in his voice.

When there's still no response, I shout, "TYLER THORN!"

I brace for . . . well, something. But there's nothing, just the slow drift of smoke escaping through our makeshift chimney.

I glance at Dominic. He looks perfectly calm, as always, but I know him well enough now to notice the tightness in his jaw and the stiff set of his shoulders. He's just as freaked out as I am. But there's only one way out of here.

"Give me a boost up?"

THIRTY-NINE

ilthy and shivering, I drag myself to my feet. I hear a faint roar coming from outside — the waterfall, yes, but something else too. It takes me a moment to realize that sound is the manor burning. The smell of smoke and apples poisons the air, though it isn't nearly as choking now I'm out of that damned pipe. Through the windows, the accusing fingers of the blood-apple trees cut lines in the haze.

Dominic's head appears over the edge of the hole, and I help pull him up.

"Thank you," he says, but I'm too busy looking at the state of the pavilion to respond. The stone bench where I found Freya's body lies in pieces, the seat cast aside and one of the legs lying near the hole in the well cover. It looks like whoever broke through the concrete (inch-thick chunks of which litter the floor) and boards used the stone bench leg to do it.

"Where do you think he went?" I whisper because it feels necessary to stay quiet, even though my ears are still ringing from all the banging.

"I have no idea. But we need to get out of here." Dominic nods toward the arched pavilion doorway. Outside, through the trees, I see a flickering orange glow. I'm confused for a moment because I shouldn't be able to see the manor in that direction. Then I realize the orchard is burning too. All this dead wood — despite the snow, it's going up like a tinderbox.

I lead the way through the trees, heading away from the manor and the worst of the smoke. Soon the rushing sound of the waterfall grows louder than the fire, but that awful sour smell of burnt apples keeps hitting the back of my throat, making me gag.

Through some wordless communication, Dominic and I stay in physical contact—my fingers gripping his sleeve, his hand on the small of my back.

Then Dominic halts me with a touch on my shoulder, one finger held to his lips. His eyes scan the trees around us, looking for something. Now I hear it too. Twigs snapping, like someone walking toward us.

A figure steps out right in front of us.

"Cas!" Dominic yells, grinning. Casper looks at me, his eyes go wide, and he turns and starts running the other way. He only makes it a few steps, though, before Mateo is blocking his path. Mateo looks over at us, frowning, then he meets my eyes and crosses himself.

"She's not Dead-Eyed Sadie," Mateo tells Casper gruffly. "It's just Ava Thorn looking like shit."

I turn to Dominic. "What's he talking about?"

Dominic shrugs. "Your face and hair are streaked with some black oily stuff. You look like you just crawled straight out of a Japanese horror movie." He doesn't get a chance to say any more before Mateo smothers him with a hug. Casper is still eyeing me warily from behind them, but he gives Dominic a very bro-ish slap on the shoulder.

I feel a painful twinge watching them—how they obviously have each other's backs. Because I used to think I had that with Ford, but did we, really? If I'd called him and said someone was trying to kill me, would he have rushed over to try and save me? Would he have smashed through concrete to get me out of danger? I look at the cuts and grazes covering Mateo's hands, and I know the answer.

"Where did you go after busting open the well?" I ask Mateo once he and Dominic have disentangled themselves. He grimaces when he looks at me, but I get the impression it's because of my general appearance rather than the usual dickish attitude I'd put it down to. He answers as we push our way out of the orchard, the brittle branches clawing at us like they're desperate for us to stay. But the fire is still spreading. It will swallow the orchard within an hour, I'd guess.

"I couldn't see a damn thing with all the smoke pouring out of there, and I was coughing too much to call out," Mateo says, and his voice does sound hoarse. "I wasn't sure what to do, so I went to get Cas. He was standing watch in case your uncle and aunt heard all the banging."

"Where are they now?" Dominic asks. "And where are the cops?"

At that moment, sirens sound in the distance. "Looks like they're almost here," Casper says. "And, last I saw, Ava's aunt was watching the house burn from near the bridge."

"What about Uncle Ty?" I press.

Casper shrugs. "Haven't seen him since we arrived, and we did a full circle of the house trying to find you."

"I'm glad you didn't try to go inside," Dominic says.

"We did try," Mateo answers. "Place is a fucking inferno . . ."

I zone out of what they're saying, watching my family's home for generations burning, eyes hot with tears and smoke.

This was the place I thought I'd always live. Where I last saw my parents laughing. Where Grandpa taught me to play poker.

Where I grew up thinking Uncle Ty loved me like a little sister.

I turn away, my gaze drawn through the smoke and drifting snow to Burden Bridge. I know Carolyn is there, alone. And I know what I need to do.

I set off for the bridge, footsteps crackling over the frozen ground like I'm walking through fire.

Ash and snow swirl together against the dark sky. They drift into patterns that for moments at a time seem to peer back at me. Evil eyes blink, become empty sockets, become nothing but smoke. But in the distance, far from the orange glow of the manor, I see her standing near the bridge.

I don't think she notices me right away. The orchard at my back casts a strong silhouette, and I'm just one shadow walking among many. But then part of the east wing of the manor collapses, and I turn just in time to see the flames flare outward. When I look back at Carolyn, her hand is clasped over her mouth, and somehow I know she's seen me. Well, good.

I have no plan in mind beyond wanting her to know I'm alive, that she and Uncle Ty did all this for nothing. A tiny voice in my head says she could be armed, could still hurt me, but it doesn't slow my stride. Because I just escaped a burning house by crawling through a goddamn water pipe into a sealed well, and I don't think *anything* can hurt me right now. I'm still at least a hundred feet from her when I open my mouth to call out, but Carolyn backs away.

No you fucking don't.

I start to run—or as much as I can with legs aching from crawling for so long—and she staggers backward. It's like she wants to get away but can't tear her eyes off me. Carolyn reaches the bridge. I close the distance between us.

"Stop! I'm not one of them, not really! I'm not a Thorn!"

Say what now?

Confusion finally slows me down, but Carolyn doesn't stop. Her momentum carries her back toward the guardrail of the bridge. If she takes another couple steps, she could fall right over the edge. Instinct forces me to call out to her. "Stop!"

"Ava?"

I see the moment realization hits her, because it mirrors mine. I look like some creature pulled from a tar pit; she must've thought I was Dead-Eyed Sadie. But she sees her mistake too late. Her back hits the rail, and she loses her balance.

Teeters.

For a second, I think she's going to fall, but she finds her footing.

"The cops are coming!" I scream at her. "You're going to . . ."

I fall silent. Behind Carolyn, in the haze of water vapor, a figure takes shape. It looms up behind her, a girl made of shadows, with two deep gouges where her eyes ought to be.

Carolyn's eyes widen. Perhaps she hears some telltale sound above the water's roar. Or maybe it's Sadie's cold breath on the back of her neck. Whatever it is, Carolyn doesn't turn around. She stares at me, frozen, as two clawed hands reach from behind her and plunge deep into her eye sockets. Blood oozes down her face.

Carolyn screams. So do I.

The waterfall roars.

With Dead-Eyed Sadie still clinging to her, Carolyn flips backward over the rail and disappears into the rising mist. I rush forward, but by the time I lean over the guardrail, there's no sign of either of them.

FORTY

Patrol-car lights turn the snow into a kaleidoscope. It almost makes a pretty sight of the burning manor.

That's it—the final piece of my family history literally going up in smoke. No more Thorn Manor. No more Bloody Thorns. Weirdly, I think I feel okay about that. Our legacy isn't one I want to continue, frankly.

But I can't get the echo of Carolyn's scream out of my head. She definitely fell, I know that, but was what I saw real? Or a hallucination? The deep chill in my gut tells me I saw *something* otherworldly, but I can't trust my gut right now—if I ever could.

"Ava?"

I look up, startled. Daphne pulls me into the fiercest hug. A moment later, Carla does the same.

"Oh my God, when I heard Dad get a call to come in because the manor was on fire with people possibly trapped inside, I just had the *worst* feeling it was you," she says, the words pouring out almost too fast for me to follow. "I should've seen it coming—the cards are always so dark when I read for you. I should've known it had to be something like this. Dad told me not to come down here, but there was no way I could just wait at home to see if you were okay, especially when you didn't answer your phone, and I thought—" She puts a hand over her mouth, and I see she's crying.

"I'm okay," I say, even though I feel about thirty seconds away from collapsing. As for my phone, I'm guessing that's a puddle of melted plastic by now. "Carolyn . . . she—"

Daphne nods briskly. "We heard. It's horrible."

But they haven't heard—not all of it. I'm still trying to process seeing Sadie clawing Carolyn's eyes, dragging her back, tipping her over the edge . . . *Was it real?* Will I ever know for sure?

"What the hell happened?" Carla asks, in her usual blunt manner. "Carolyn called the cops and told them you'd freaked out and said Sadie told you to burn the manor so the Millers couldn't have it. That's not . . . I mean, none of that's true, right?"

"Not even remotely," Dominic says, and I'm relieved to feel the warmth of his hand in mine. Judging by the raised eyebrows I get from Daphne and Carla, they don't miss it, either.

"I've already told the cops what happened. From planning to murder my parents and me a year ago, to the fucked-up attempt to blackmail Madoc Miller, to murdering Freya and Ford and trying to pin the blame on me by drugging and gaslighting me," I spit. "I guess they'll just have to figure it out if they don't believe me."

Carla frowns. "You know *we* believe you, right?" Before I can answer, she and Daphne both have me caught up in another tangled hug. It eases something in me, knowing I have them on my side. We don't need blood between us to be family.

"Why did they even listen to Carolyn?" Dominic says. "I spoke with the police earlier and *told* them Carolyn and Ty were the ones who killed my sister and Ford."

Daphne grimaces. "They thought you might've been under duress when you made that call. I heard you sounded pretty out of it."

Dominic glowers. "I had just been hit over the head with a crowbar."

"We need to get someone to take a look at you," I say.

"The EMTs already tried to drag me away, but I'm not going anywhere until we get this cleared up with the cops," Dominic says. "The camera on the bridge would've kept running even with the power out, so it will have caught everything that just happened here. There won't be any question about you being to blame."

Wait — will it have captured Sadie too? Or will the video show something else? Either way, I feel like I need to see it.

I shiver, leaning into Dominic.

"Where did Uncle Ty go, though? We can't just let him walk away from this."

As though to punctuate that statement, there's a sound of glass breaking. What looks like a dining chair is hurled through a first-floor window of the manor and lands smoldering on the front lawn. Then a figure emerges after it.

Uncle Ty looks like something from a nightmare. His face is striped with blisters and soot, and part of his hair seems to have been singed away right to the scalp. A trail of smoke follows him as he staggers toward the mass of cops and firefighters who can only gape at him for a moment before launching into action. Several of them approach to try and help him, but he keeps limping straight ahead. For an awful moment, I think he's coming for me, but he veers instead toward the bridge.

"Carolyn!" he bellows, then starts hacking up a lung. "You left me to burn!" Uncle Ty sinks to his knees in the snow. "I did all of it, *all of it,* for you — and you left me to burn! *Carolyn!*"

Holden signals for his officers to move in, and a group of

them haul Uncle Ty to his feet and take him to where the squad cars are waiting. I guess he'll need treatment for his burns before they drag his ass to jail, but I'm having trouble caring too much about that right now.

I can't shake off what I saw, and not just Carolyn dying.

I saw Sadie. Like, really, truly *saw* her. At least, I think so. And I have to wonder:

Is she done with my family now?

FORTY-ONE

U ncle Ty claims Carolyn was the one who murdered both Freya and Ford. He says she threatened to kill me if he didn't go along with her plans. That he's acting like he has any concern at all for *my* well-being is almost funny. Or it would be if it didn't still hurt so damn much.

I always knew Uncle Ty had his weak spots, but deep down I believed he loved me. Carolyn too. We were family. But I guess that meant something more to me than it did to them. Underneath it all, they just wanted money.

Seems like Carolyn thought she was marrying Big Money when she met Uncle Ty, with his flashy sports car and the manor. And I guess the shine eventually wore off when she realized there was nothing to back up all of his bullshit. Maybe that's why she left him to burn.

How could Uncle Ty do that to Freya, though? And let Carolyn murder Ford? How could any amount of money be worth the deaths of two people? Four, if you count trying to kill my parents, which I very much *do*. So do the cops. And then trying to kill me and Dominic . . .

Uncle Ty is looking at some serious time.

The evidence is all coming together now that the cops know where to look. The security camera above the French doors where Uncle Ty and Carolyn admitted everything to me didn't record the audio, but it showed Uncle Ty hitting Dominic with the crowbar. They also found the phone he was using to text Freya, and have DNA evidence from the crowbar tying him and Carolyn to Ford *and* Freya. And there's the testimony from me and Dominic, so it should be enough to convict him.

After spending a long night at the police station while Dominic got treated for a concussion and I was interviewed for what felt like years, I finally see him the next morning in the police station lobby. He looks tired and smells of ash and sour apples, but I don't care. I'm still streaked with corpse water. I reach up and touch the side of his face, tracing his jaw with my fingers. He allows it for a second, then pulls me into his arms.

"How you doing, Thorn?" he says into my hair.

"Freaked out," I say honestly. "But I guess that's just something I have to live with until I figure out which parts of the wild shit I've seen over the last weeks are real, and what was thanks to the PCP." Dominic is quiet for a moment. "What?"

"I might be able to settle a little of that for you," he says quietly. "About what happened to Carolyn on the bridge."

I told him last night what I saw. Dominic listened without dismissing it or blaming it all on the drug.

"How?" But I realize the answer a moment later. "You have the footage from the bridge camera?"

He nods, pulling what looks like a second-hand phone from his pocket. "I downloaded it last night. Do you want to see?"

I think about it for a minute. Watching what happened will be horrifying, but it can't be any worse than living through it. And I need to know if what I saw was real.

"Show me," I tell him.

I watch on the tiny screen as the scene unravels. There's Carolyn, waiting. Watching the manor burn. I'm still out of frame when she sees me and starts backing toward the waterfall. At the moment where I remember Sadie appearing behind Carolyn, the footage shows an odd shadow gathering in the vapor swirling above the waterfall. It seems to wrap around her as she stumbles back, her hands flying up to her face in the moment before she tips over the guardrail and vanishes.

It's nothing as far as the police are concerned. But the shiver running through me as I watched it told me not to be so sure. Maybe it was the PCP conjuring up Sadie in my mind — or maybe it made me see things more clearly. Either way, it's over. I just have to try and move on.

We're quiet for a long moment after the video ends. Then Dominic says, "Did you hear about what happened to Hamish?"

I'd forgotten all about Hamish, to be honest. I pull back just enough to see Dominic's face. "No?"

"Apparently, your note scared him so badly, he turned himself in at the police station to make a full confession. It seems he took a bribe from my sister to secure her a spot in the summer art program, then refused to give back the money when it turned out she was too young to go. He'd already spent it on an engagement ring for his girlfriend."

"Wow." It isn't at all what I expected, but Hamish is still a giant asshole.

Dominic sighs. "I'm sorry Freya did that to you, though. It wasn't right."

"That doesn't matter now," I tell him. I can't muster the energy to be even slightly pissed off about it. How could I after what Uncle Ty and Carolyn did? What they took from Dominic and his family? "Nic, I can't even tell you how sorry I am for—"

"Don't," he says, quiet but firm. "You had no control over what they did. This is in no way your fault."

I sigh. "Freya deserved a lot better than what she got."

So did Ford.

Neither of them was perfect, but who the hell is? They should've been allowed the chance to grow up, be adults, build lives. *Live.*

"I have to go give a statement," Dominic says. "Where will you be later? My parents and I are checked in at a hotel in Haverford. Are you staying with someone?"

Both Daphne and Carla have offered to let me stay with them, but I need a little time on my own to process everything. "I'll be at the cottage whenever you're done."

A few days later, after the literal dust settles, I sit down and talk to Madoc and Lucille Miller. About a lot of things—the crash, the manor, the bad feeling between our families. And the money Madoc gave me.

I try to give the check back, but the Millers insist I keep it.

"It truly was your share of the sale price for the manor," Madoc says firmly. "I only wish I'd been able to predict what your uncle might do to get his hands on it. I'm so, so sorry, Ava."

"It's not your fault," I tell him, and for the first time I mean it. "I lived with him and Carolyn for a year, and had no idea what they were planning."

"What on earth could make a couple become so twisted?" Lucille wonders aloud. It makes me think of the article I read about Dead-Eyed Sadie, and the way Ephraim and Susannah Thorn murdered her.

"I guess in any relationship, each person brings out something unique in the other," I say, quoting Daphne's Dimple Theory. "Sometimes that's a really bad thing."

It's strange being alone in the cottage. But it has given me space to figure out what I want to do. By the time Carla and Daphne come over to watch a movie the following week, I've come to a decision.

"Nic has asked me to go on a road trip with him," I say, and can't help grinning when Daphne lets out a gasp. Even Carla pauses the film.

Before the fire, Dominic already had his shiny new RV for the "road trip of legends" as I'm calling it. (He does not approve.) It was parked in the garage, away from the house, so it's one of the very few items to survive the fire.

I feel sick for the Millers. Not only are they dealing with losing Freya, but now they've lost their home too. And maybe the house wasn't theirs for very long, but it *was* theirs.

The manor I loved is starting to feel distant now, like a dream that fades after waking. Maybe it's for the best that it's no longer there. It can't tie me to the horrors I've lived through—only my memories can do that. And hopefully they'll start to feel distant one day too.

Dominic says his parents are planning to move back to Evansville. I can't say I blame them.

"So when do you leave?" Daphne asks. She's acting excited for my benefit, but she doesn't hide her feelings well.

"I don't," I say. "At least, not until after graduation. Because I *do* want to graduate, and keep my options open for the future. Nic's coming back to pick me up as soon as school's over."

"He is?" Daphne cheeses so hard, I burst out laughing.

It's going to be hard not seeing Dominic for three months, but I'm determined to use the time well. Make sure I graduate. Keep going for checkups to make sure the PCP I got dosed with hasn't done any permanent damage. And, maybe most importantly, start seeing a therapist again. I don't want everything that's happened to get twisted inside me and turn me into anything remotely like Carolyn or Uncle Ty.

In the meantime, Dominic and I can always video chat. I happen to know he's pretty handy with a camera.

"Who knew Dominic Miller was such a romantic asshole?" Carla deadpans, but I can tell she sort of means it in a nice way. "But what about the summer art program? I thought that was like your One Thing in Life. Aren't you still going to fight for a spot?"

I wrinkle my nose. "Actually, what I really want is to keep working on *Mostly Deadish* with Nic. It feels like it might turn into something great, you know?"

"Uh-huh," Daphne teases.

"Shut up."

"So you're all in with the comics, then?" Carla asks skeptically. "No backup plan?"

"I have to give it my best shot, right?"

I'm going to try my hardest not to touch the money I got from the sale of the manor. It's not that I feel like it's blood money now — I would definitely have felt that way a few months ago, knowing it'd come from the Millers' pockets. But it feels important to try to make my own way, not just fall back on the money my family took for granted for so long. And maybe one day I'll figure out something worthwhile to do with Madoc's money — something positive that might tip the balance back a little.

For now, I have my savings from the Pump'N'Go, and I'll just have to see what else is out there for me when I leave Burden Falls.

Daphne and Carla have got college to look forward to. They both got into NYU, and will be living together for the first time when they go there. I'm excited for them. I'm excited for me too, for the first time in a *looong* while.

Dominic and I are going hunting for monsters to write amazing, exciting comics about, and I cannot. Fucking. Wait.

EPILOGUE

Three months later

I wave Daphne and Carla off, trying my best not to blubber again. I've already had to reapply my eyeliner twice, and I'm in danger of turning into the Crow. Dominic is due to arrive any minute, and *snotty mess* is not really the look I'm going for the first time he sees me in months.

The cottage is all packed up, the furniture sold, and the few bags I'm taking sit on the front step next to me. The only thing that really matters, though, is the necklace around my neck. This one piece of my parents is all I need to remind me what a Thorn *should* be.

Daphne, Carla, and I celebrated graduation in style last week. Mateo and Casper threw a huge party, and I was actually invited. We've come to a sort of uneasy okayness with each other over the past three months. I can't say I'll ever be besties with them, but I don't feel the urge to throat-punch either of them now, which is progress.

My heart races at the sound of an engine pulling into the lane. A few seconds later, I see him. Or rather *it*. The RV is an enormous beast, and I can't wait to take a turn driving it.

Dominic jumps down from the cab and I run over to meet him. He looks tan and ridiculously hot, and when he spins me around I breathe him in and thank the Dark Lord he doesn't smell like Axe-nuked sweat and Pop-Tarts.

"You got even hotter," I accuse.

"I know." I gape at him in outrage, but he just laughs and says, "Damn it, I've waited months to do this again."

Dominic Miller kisses me. *Damn,* does he kiss me.

And I kiss him right back.

We set off as soon as my bags are in the RV. As I'm about to pull away from the cottage, I notice Dominic peering up at it with an odd look on his face.

"What is it?"

He turns to me, a wicked glint in his eye. "Just checking there are no ghosts waving us off. Did I ever tell you my ancestors used to live here?"

"Really? *Ancestors* as in Sadie?"

"Maybe. I told you my family stopped using Burnett as our last name after Sadie died, and went by Miller after that. They must've been working at the mill for a while by then for the name to stick."

Of course — *miller.* I feel pretty dense for not connecting those dots before now.

"There are evil eyes carved into the frames of all the windows looking out toward the manor," I say, glancing in that direction, even though the manor isn't actually visible from where we're parked. I imagine some long-dead relative of Dominic's carving them there carefully, hoping they might send the Thorns the bad fortune they so very much deserved after getting away with Sadie's murder. "Do you want to go in and see?"

But Dominic shakes his head. "I'm ready for something new. Aren't you?"

I watch the WELCOME TO BURDEN FALLS sign come and go as we drive past. Sadie still stands with her back turned, gazing at the waterfall. Unchanging, and stuck there forever. Unlike me and Dominic. I'm not sure how to feel about that.

I know I'll never stop thinking about Sadie, wondering how much of what I saw was real or just the effects of the drug. But for now I'm focusing on what's in front of me. This is the start of something. I can feel it.

I look at Dominic, see the way his lips purse when he's concentrating, as he is now. He's pretty thorough when it comes to route-planning, apparently. I guess one of us has to be.

"So which place on The List are we visiting first?" I ask.

Dominic looks up, eyes shining. "How do you feel about cannibals?"

"Uh, not generally in favor."

He laughs that open, booming laugh, and I realize something: I've only ever heard him laugh that way with me.

"Oh my God, that's your dimple!"

His grin falters. "My what?"

But I just shake my head. "Doesn't matter. Just tell me which way to go."

Nic turns back to his map. "We more or less follow the river west all the way. I mean, it splits and reconnects at a few points, but it's actually weird how our river feeds the lake there."

"Maybe that's where all the bad stuff ends up," I say. Dominic glances at me, frowning. "You know—the *burdens*. They have to go somewhere, right? Maybe it all ends up there."

I reach up to adjust the rearview mirror, catching one last glimpse of the sign as I do so. I take a sharp breath.

346

"What is it? Did you forget something?" Dominic says.

On the roadside beneath the sign, a dark figure stands with her head bowed. She wasn't there a moment ago, I'm sure of it. I adjust the mirror back the other way, and she's gone.

"Ava?"

I shake my head and fix my eyes back on the road. Ignore the churning in my gut. Focus on what's in front of me.

"It was nothing," I say.

And I really hope that's the truth.

ACKNOWLEDGMENTS

Here it is: another book. The difference this time is that it was mostly written during a global pandemic, and so I've decided that if there are any errors—grammatical, factual, or general—it's the pandemic's fault. Sorry about that.

But even in a socially distanced world, I've been surrounded by the many wonderful people who helped bring this book to life. So here are my thanks:

To my editors, Emma Jones at Puffin, and Jessica Dandino Garrison at Dial; you are a joy to work with, and I thank you both for your immense insight and expertise. Huge thanks also to the teams at Penguin Random House UK and US for their work on this book, from designing the gorgeous covers to catching the strayest commas; for finding me new readers and so much more: Stephanie Barrett, Jane Tait, Simon Armstrong, Jasmin Kauldhar, Adam Webling, Jan Bielecki, Beth Fennell, Sabrina Chong, Susanne Evans and Alice Grigg in the UK, and Rosie Ahmed, Regina Castillo, Mina Chung, Elaine C. Damasco, Lizzie Goodell, Lauri Hornik and Nancy Mercado in the US.

To my agent, Molly Ker Hawn; you are my wisest, mightiest champion, and I'm so grateful for all that you do.

Thanks to my brilliant friends Jani Grey and Dawn Kurtagich, for always cheering me on, and as always to my husband, friends, and family, for all your encouragement and support.

And thank you to my readers; I hope you love this book. I made it extra creepy for you.